The Far Journey

A TIMESLIP NOVEL OF SURVIVAL ON THE OREGON TRAIL

Tom Reppert

ISBN: 0692424342
ISBN 13: 9780692424346
Library of Congress Control Number: 2015905358
Helen's Sons Publishing
120 W. Garfield Bay Road
Sagle, Idaho

Chapter 1

"We are the Rude Girls," I announce proudly.

My friends echo, "We are the Rude Girls."

The four of us hook middle fingers over the lunch table and snap back with a pop. Everyone in the school cafeteria glances at us enviously. We are the most exclusive crew around. Sixteen years old and wicked hot, licensed to kill. That's us. I'm the chief bad kitty. A pure dime, everyone says. Abercrombie fashion queen. Natural blond. Bod to die for. That's me. I have swag. Girls want to be me and boys desperately want to do me.

"Rude, rude, rude," Rachel adds with a nervous giggle, trying too hard.

We sip our cafeteria lattes and nibble our whole wheat sandwiches and talk about the three most important things in our lives: looking good, boys and social climbing. All around us sit a swirl of cliques with enough gossip and back stabbing to make a Borgia from that TV show blush. Typical lunchtime at the Rector Academy, the Pacific Palisades private school I refer to affectionately as Old Rectum. Quickly, we land on the topic of how well our boyfriends kiss. I insist Cal rates eight out of ten, soft lips, great tongue, and I look dubiously at Rachel when she gives geek Billy Donavon a ten. *Oh, sure.*

With a coy smile, Vanessa says to me, "Cal's more than an eight, Paula, more than a ten. Defo,"

"You can't go higher than a ten. Keep it real," Jenna says, missing the point. Van, who once dated Cal, is saying he kissed her better than me. Even though she is my BFF, we still stick needles in each other whenever we can. She hates it when I refer to her bottle blond hair, which I make sure to do a couple times a day. She spends half of school in the girls room, searching for black roots in the mirrors.

"Game level goes up," Van says, her eyes flashing in inspiration. "Count skin hits."

"The beast with two backs," I offer.

"What?"

"Shakespeare. The beast with two backs. Nevermind."

"Whatever," Van says, annoyed.

So we lie atrociously, rating our boyfriends' lovemaking ability. Those who do lie as to prowess, and those who don't do lie as to doing. It's all a freaking game. Suddenly, I wince in pain. I've had this monstrous headache for days now and it keeps getting worse. I pop two aspirin and slowly pick up on the conversation again. Rachel is prattling on about how she hopes her new jeans don't make her ass look too big.

"Way big, Rache. Sorry, girl. Like bovine," I tell her and watch her face disintegrate into despair. "Maybe you can dress in bib overalls. You know, the kind farmers wear? That would hide it."

I'm into despair, mine and everyone else's. If I feel even an inkling of guilt, I press harder. She spends the next few minutes dwelling on her elephantine ass. Then it's my turn to get some needling. Van is inspecting me with distaste. "Speaking of clothes, I just love your retro outfit, Paula. Very fashionable."

She is being sarcastic, of course. I'm wearing an old granny shift dress that goes from my Gucci sandals to my neck. Fashionable if you're talking 1890s.

"It's necessary for this afternoon," I explain. "The assembly."

Jenna's eyes widen. "Whoa. You're not still going through with that, are you?"

"I said I would."

"No way." Rachel comes back to us. "I thought you were kidding. Like massive. Massive!" She likes that word. Everything is *massive*.

"I'm going to blow this school apart," I say with resolve.

Already an expectant buzz has swept around the school that something wild is going to happen in the assembly 7th period. Only the Rude Girls know exactly what. I'm unfazed by the whispers and sidelong glances. I don't mind being the center of attention. That's what we live for, isn't it?

"You'll be expelled," Van says.

"If they catch me," I say.

Jenna laughs "Hell, Paula, my parents would kill me if I got caught for half the things you do."

I shrug as if I'm not worried though I am. This could go very badly for me. I had thought about abandoning the crash down, but an irresistible impulse has me in its grip. In a hard world, I live for the adrenaline rush you get from riding the edge between glory and disaster. I always have.

Jenna laughs. "You're way off the chain today, Paula. Totally. "

"It's this place," I tell them. "I hate it. I mean *hate*. Classrooms are unbearable. Lecture, lecture, lecture, blah, blah, blah. How can you focus on texting someone when the teacher won't shut up? Somebody's got to do something to put a spark in it."

We all laugh. Then one after the other, Van and Rachel get text messages and pull out of the conversation. Jenna soon follows suit talking on her cell phone loudly so everyone knows she is popular. I notice around the cafeteria half the people have phones stuck to their ears or are texting while chatting and eating.

I notice Jason Weismann watching me over a book he is reading. He's at the table next to us with his buddies, odd boys who get good grades—hell, great grades—and don't date because they lack even the minimum social skills or popularity to do it. A fashion disaster, he's wearing black Converse tennis shoes and baggy military pants along with a white shirt and tie. Lord God, save the boy!

When he sees me glaring back, he smiles, then goes back to his book. We used to be friends long ago, even study partners, but have since gone in different directions. He is the only one in the school who knows of my past. Creds to the boy for keeping it secret.

A couple minutes later, the Rude Girls are back debating the advantages of tanning booths verses spray tans, something that would usually interest me very much if I didn't have this monstrous headache. I undo the cap off the aspirin bottle, pop three more pills and wash them down with cold latte. All week Neil Peart, the drummer for Rush, has been inside my head ripping through *2112*.

My phone beeps. A text from Cal. The school's lunch hours are staggered and at the moment he's in Bio class. Cal's the school's Alpha male, and I, of course, the Rude Girl Queen. What we have is true love. We are Romeo and

Juliet without the warring families. I want to live with the dude for the rest of my life, the whole marriage bit. I read his message. Undying love. It feels good to read but so unimaginative. He doesn't know I plan a crash down for the assembly. If he did, he'd freak. No courage.

He texts, *You need to give me an answer about the Prom, babe, or I ask V.* I text back: *Coward.* He replies: *I'm a senior. I'm not going to miss my prom and I AM going to have a date. You, I hope. But V if needed. She'll break her date with Alex for me. SO DECIDE! Work it out by Monday*

I text back: *Dude, quit playing with your lax stick and pay attention. It's all set. I just need to clear with mom. Her rules are weird and random. She's in New York right now, so be cool. And oh btw, don't freak, but V is sitting beside me reading this. She thinks you're a tool. She's so happy to know she's second choice. Isn't that delicious??!!? Just kidding, hahaha.*

After a moment he replies: *Funny. You're the tool. Later.*

I put the phone away. Mom doesn't care about the prom. I was just jerking him around. That sounds bitchy, and it is, but these boys, even the one I love, have to be played just right or they're off after the next swing of hips that walks by. In truth, it's all about just having a good time while you can because we have to deal with so much freaking crap in our lives. I've heard the term *the Greatest Generation.* Well, we are *the Hardship Generation.* With all we have to face, our lives are tougher than ever before. Everywhere you look someone putting barriers in your way, making it hard, ordering you around, telling you you're not good enough. I have to take some control.

That's what the assembly is all about.

Chapter 2

After lunch we have two periods before the assembly. 5th is easy, Music. Though I play tolerable guitar and piano, I get A's by smiling sweetly at and sucking up to Mr. Wilson. But 6th, Mrs. Guthrie's Advanced American History class, is a minefield of nastiness. She's a piece of work. I sit in the back away from her evil gorgon stare, enlarged maniacally by her thick wire-rim glasses, text my friends and plot ways to disrupt the class. This so-called advanced class studies a few selected periods in depth. A few people pay attention but most don't. Makes you wonder about the term *advanced*. This afternoon is way daunting. She has brought in old pots and pans to talk about how to cook from scratch the way they did on the Oregon Trail. *Oh Geez!*

The cooking gear is spread out on a table beside her desk. She clanks a pan for attention. "We will start your oral reports on Monday. This will be a major part of your semester grade. We've covered three areas this semester in depth: the Civil War, the Industrial Revolution and the Great Migration West. Your topic must be from one of those three. Does everyone understand? You will not know who I will call on first so all of you must be ready."

Everyone groans. The orals will run through and beyond the day of the prom. Who wants to work on that day? But she doesn't care at all.

"You will rue the day if you are not ready," she says using her favorite expression. *Rue the day, rue the day.* It's always *rue the day.* You'd think she could come up with something else once in awhile.

"I expect a visually compelling presentation. Don't show us a picture just to show a picture. It should have some relevance. I have created a file of old photos and daguerreotypes from 1840 through 1890 on the class website. I don't want dry presentations. Put some effort in."

No one responds, but I doubt if she expected anyone to. She begins her Oregon Trail lecture by talking about a recipe for cornbread. The excitement is almost too much. I give a loud groan that causes her to pause a moment before going on. I am proud to be disliked by every teacher in the school except Mr. Wilson, but Guthrie hates me with a special loathing and cunning, pointing out my academic and moral shortcomings loudly and frequently, often with a *rue the day* attached. We have come to blows many times…figuratively. I am not going to actually hit an old lady. I do like to make her life miserable though whenever I can.

"This is a Dutch oven," she is saying, holding an iron pot high for all to see. "Women used this to cook…"

"Did you have to be Dutch to use it?" I ask with a simp smile. Not my wittiest effort.

Old Stoneface glares at me. "Very amusing, Miss Masters. I'm disappointed you could not come up with something more creative than just *do you have to be Dutch*. Surely, someone of your intelligence can do better than that."

"I'll think on it."

"May I continue?"

"Please."

She gives a shake of the head and returns to her pots and pans. From a couple desks over Jason Weismann turns and stares at me with a mixture of disappointment and anger as if I've gone after him. I mouth *what*, he frowns, I flip him off. He gives his attention back to Mrs. Guthrie's riveting presentation. Spotlight off me, I slip my Iphone under the desk and text the Rude Girls for the next half hour while the crone drones. I nearly get through to the end of class before she strikes. "Miss Masters, are you ever going to pay attention?"

I nearly jump out of my desk from the woman's piercing voice. She has a black kettle in her hand and for a second I think she might throw it at me. "I am paying attention, Mrs. Guthrie. Why, I'm positively enthralled." God, I'm a bitch, but she deserves it.

"See me after class."

"Yes, ma'am." No way am I wasting time with her. Not with the assembly coming next.

I drudge through the rest of the class, psyching myself for the crash down. When the bell rings, I rush the door. *Almost free.* Then, Guthrie calls me in her sharp drill sergeant voice. With a roll of the eyes, I return. We face each other across her desk, waiting for the class to empty, her Medusa stare piercing me to my bones. Oh, how I hate the woman. Everyone rushes out, getting out of the way of the coming fireworks. No one hangs around Guthrie's class anyway.

When we are alone, she shakes her head. "Miss Masters, you must think of your future. Your poor performances…"

"I will. I promise. Is that it, Mrs. Guthrie? Cause I really have to go."

"You have the focus of a snail darter," she says tight-lipped. "You waste my time and yours."

I shoot the needle in. "You're the one made me stay, Mrs. Guthrie. If it's a waste of time, you're the one doing it."

She doesn't take the bait I've offered. "You used to be a good student. Now you get by on charm and manipulation. It doesn't work in this classroom, though, does it? I can tell you the charm is wearing thin for the other teachers as well. You might have to do some actual work to pass this year. Do you hate school so much?"

"You got it so wrong, Mrs. Guthrie. I love school."

"You love school!" she scoffs. "You love the social life maybe, the boys and your friends, but you hate school. You need to apply yourself more. Someone with your intelligence could be getting ready for Stanford or Harvard. But I guess you know that already and don't care. Some day you may wish you paid more attention."

"I do care, Mrs. Guthrie, really. I will try harder. I promise," I tell her with all the sincerity I can muster, but she doesn't buy it. She never does.

She dismisses my assurance with a disdainful wave of her hand. "If you want to pass this class, you will make up all the work you've missed or failed to turn in."

"That's not fair. My grades are passing."

"Hardly. And worse when you add in the classroom grade."

I shake my head in disgust, then withstand a wave of pain from my throbbing headache that draws a raw hiss from me, which she mistakes for a comment on her meddling. "Can I go now?"

Something strange happens then. Her expression softens. "You know I saw you once when you were riding. What was that, two, three years ago? Long before you came to Rector."

I take a step back as if she'd slapped me. I didn't think anyone outside of Jason knew about that. It is a time I don't want to remember. After a moment, I regain my composure. "It wasn't me," I say emphatically. "Someone else, maybe. Not me. I have nothing to do with that stuff. Is there anything else, Mrs. Guthrie?"

"Sure it was. Two years ago, maybe three. I took my grandson to watch a junior show jumping event down in San Diego. You were there. You were fourteen then, weren't you? You rode that big bay horse. What was his name? My heavens, what a magnificent animal. Do you remember?"

Why is she doing this? Unable to speak, I say nothing, my anger rising. None of my friends know anything about this. No one knows. I want to keep it that way. It's not who I am anymore.

She gives an old granny chuckle. "People said you were the best rider they'd ever seen at your age, and, oh my, that horse could fly. A real Pegasus. What was his name? Yes, Quantum Leap. That was it. How appropriate. Quantum Leap."

I say coldly, "Is there something you wanted from me, Mrs. Guthrie? I have to get to the assembly. You see, I'm reading a poem to the school."

She sighs heavily as if that's supposed to mean something to me. "No, dear. Go ahead."

When I'm almost out, she asks, "Paula, whatever happened to that wonderful horse?"

The old hurt shoots through me. I grasp the doorframe to steady myself. It takes effort to keep from crying. That's not me either. I do not cry anymore. In a hard voice, I tell her, "It's none of your business."

I start out but stop again and turn back. I don't know why I tell her, but I do. "He broke his leg flying over one of those jumps and had to be put down."

"Oh my, I'm so sorry. It was not your fault." The pro forma response I'd heard a thousand times.

I feel the old surge of self-loathing. "Oh, but it was."

Her shocked face is the last I see of her for a very long time. I rush toward the auditorium and the assembly.

Chapter 3

I was not always a bad student. In fact, just the opposite. In my last school, I had a GPA higher than 4.0, on track for class Valedictorian with potential scholarships out the yingyang. I actually liked school, literature in particular, magical realism even more particularly, reading the likes of Marquez and Esquivel, guffawing aloud at the antics in *Like Water for Chocolate*. Any science class was my worst subject, but even in those I maintained straight A's.

Things change.

Back then, I had a singular passion for horses and show jumping. For me, it had priority on my time. My father had been a silver medalist in the Olympics and it was through him that I got interested in the sport. My passion took wings when dad bought Quantum Leap. He was a spectacular horse, born for the arena, a thoroughbred with speed and jumping ability. Right from the start, I exulted in what we could do together. Like we were one being.

He loved the attention and so did I. Seemingly, I lived life through him and he through me. I loved him so much. I spent more time with him than my family, even my younger brother Josh. Him I loved dearly, often dragging him along to my afternoon practices.

My last year riding, I'd been to England, Germany and Spain competing with the US Junior team and scoring three amazing victories. I was the rage of the sport. My picture appeared on equestrian magazine covers; articles abounded on web sites. The next big star, people said. They treated me as if I crapped gold, and I loved the attention.

That life, that person, crashed in November of that last year when Quantum Leap had to be put down. The blow was devastating, my grief and guilt overwhelming. Mom said she was sorry the animal had died, but we'd get another, then added succinctly I needed to move on. That was like a knife in my ribs. She didn't understand about Quantum Leap and me, or just didn't care. Move on to what? I didn't want another horse. Without Quantum the sport became a raw sore. I wanted nothing to do with it.

Dad was even worse; he was oh so sympathetic. He said he understood having gone through several horses himself in his career. He said Quantum had been like a part of the family. His attempts to give me 'closure' drove me mad. It seemed my show jumping was all that held the family together for Mom and Dad began arguing constantly, and being attorneys, neither would concede a point. Those arguments became screamers, dad left, and they divorced.

It's been nearly two years since then. In that time, my grades began a slow downward spiral. I lost interest in school. Though I kept reading on my own, never the classroom assigned books. I didn't like the rigidity and boredom of them or the classroom anymore. My mom said I had started hanging out with the wrong crowd. She didn't know I was the wrong crowd. Thus the Rector Academy this year. She hoped I'd turn my life back around. I did. I started the Rude Girls.

The assembly is on Peer Influence, Leadership and Character Building. So much BS. We all see the assembly only as a way to get out of class. No one pays attention to that drivel. Last week, I volunteered to read a poem on Character Building at the beginning so I could have access to the stage. A choir, three other student speakers and a small rock band wait backstage with me. Wildly nervous now, I stride back and forth going through every detail of the plan, popping two more aspirin, and with my stomach churning, I glance out from behind the curtains.

The auditorium is filled with students, teachers and parents. At that moment, Dr. Bramley, the fat, ruddy-faced Head Master, walks out to the podium and begins a snore of a speech on the assembly's topics. *Blah, blah, blah.* When he finishes, he says, "Next, we have Junior Paula Masters, who will read a poem on character building. Please give her all your attention. It is something important about...er... something important." He's such a wordsmith.

10

From Facebook and Twitter rips all day the message that Paula Masters is planning something wild had gone viral so the audience wakes up and applauds as if I'm a rock star. I'm seriously giddy.

Compose yourself, I say silently and clear my throat in mock seriousness. "After a Bath by Aileen Fisher. After a bath, I try, try, try to rub myself till I'm dry, dry, dry. Hands to wipe, and fingers and toes, and two wet legs and a shiny nose." I act out drying myself. "Just think how much less time I'd take, if I were a dog, and could shake, shake, shake."

I shake myself as if on a dance floor. The audience roars with laughter. I bow deeply, then walk off stage passed a stunned Bramley. His expression turns instantly ferocious.

"You ain't seen nothin' yet," I mutter under my breath.

Slipping behind the curtain into an empty cubbyhole, I draw out an overnight bag from under a table and quickly pull my dress off over my head. Anyone watching would think I'm stark naked but instead I'm wearing a flesh colored body suit. I throw on a choir gown from the bag. Donning a Marilyn Monroe mask and a black wig—Marilyn with black hair. I am all set. God help them. I leave my shoes behind and move barefoot to the curtain.

After two more poems are read by other students, Bramley introduces the choir. As they take the stage, I wriggle into the back row. One of them stares at me curiously but makes a place for me beside him. My heart sinks. It's Jason Weismann, and I'm almost positive he recognizes me. Intent on their task at hand, no one else has noticed that an intruder is among them.

"Paula?" he whispers. *How the hell does he know?* I don't answer. "What are you doing?" Alarm in his voice.

Before I can answer, the choir erupts in song. In the next few minutes, we sing our hearts out, songs about leadership I don't know. I still pitch in, but due to the latex mask getting in the way, I'm making loud, fluttering lip farts. Hearing my contribution, the audience is rolling with laughter, and the poor choirmaster is searching furiously for the source of the crude sound. Jason is scowling at me. Once again he is angry with me. *Screw him!*

When the song is finished, the audience applauds raucously, and Bramley proclaims proudly, "The Rector Academy choir. Thank you."

As they exit, I make my way to the front of the stage. People think it must be a solo, but not Bramley. He stares at me, baffled at first, then alarmed. Someone wearing a Marilyn Monroe mask might have been a clue. Whatever it is, he doesn't like it. He rushes out from behind the podium toward me just as I undo the clasps to the gown and snap it off. I'm covered from ankles to neck in a body suit, but just about everyone there that day will swear I am stark naked. Gasps and screams erupt from the audience along with cheers and whistles. It's a wild melee. Music to my ears. People are seeing what they want to see, someone in a Marilyn mask in a birthday suit.

Bramley runs at me but I hurl the choir gown at him. He trips over it and smashes his nose on the stage; his face bloodies up. As he glances about, fury shoots out of his eyes. People are still screaming and jumping. It's madness.

I am surprised a man so fat could move so fast. He springs up and dashes for me with *kill* sparking his eyes. I leap from the stage and race down the center aisle and realize hundreds of cell phones are lifted aloft to video me. *Oh, crap!*

While students cheer and parents gawk and teachers sputter in place, not one person tries to stop me. I burst out through the auditorium door. Momentarily out in the hall alone, I glance around for any one coming after me. No one. I plunge out through the school doors, work my way around back to the stage door and dash in. I am backstage again. The place is deserted because everyone is out on stage amid the pandemonium.

My shoes are gone! Someone has stolen my shoes.

I make a quick change into my dress, stuffing everything including the mask into the bag and throwing it back under the table to pick it up later. Being barefoot is a risk, but I need to make an appearance so I go out on stage where the choir and band are milling about. Still utter chaos. Bramley and the teachers have lost complete control. Blood soaked tissues are stuffed up his nose, and he is issuing orders no one is following. It's beautiful. It's perfect. The adrenaline rush has me bouncing on the ceiling. This moment is sublime, worth all the risk.

"Where are your shoes, Miss Masters?" Bramley asks sharply.

I'm caught, I'm caught. "They were pinching my toes," I offer lamely.

He glares at me but then he always glares at me. Finally, he turns and holds up his arms to the audience for silence. When someone yells out, "*Quiet*," they obey.

He walks to his microphone and stabs the podium with his finger. "Naked girls just do not strut across the stage at the Rector Academy. I want that person to step forward now."

The audience laughs at this including some of the teachers. I exchange a self-satisfied grin with the Rude Girls in the audience. I want to step forward and say, *It was me. It was me. I did it.* But I'm not suicidal and hold my place.

Of course, I get caught.

I didn't know Mrs. Guthrie had even come to the assembly, but she has found my bag backstage, the choir gown, mask and wig inside and also my French text book with my name in it. I'm not that stupid! Someone put it there; someone put the dime on me. At first, I think it's Jason, but then he'd just turn me in; he wouldn't put my French book in the bag. He's a dweeb but an honest dweeb.

A hurried board meeting is called, and with less than five minutes remaining in the day, I am expelled. But I'm not. One of them points out that they couldn't legally expel me without one of my parents present. Divorced, my father works in Europe, and my mother is on a flight back to Los Angeles right now. Neither could be contacted, so I couldn't be expelled yet. While they attempt to call my mother, I am to go home and return tomorrow morning at ten when the board would reconvene and I would be officially sent packing with my mother in attendance.

She is going to kill me.

Chapter 4

*I*t surprises me when I get home to find mom sitting out by the pool, painting her toenails bright red, cotton stuffed between her toes. The school hasn't called her yet, otherwise she would have detonated the moment I stepped out the back door. I know it will come soon enough. Maybe I can run away before it happens.

My mother looks like a sexy, blond A list actress, but, in fact, she is a high-powered corporate attorney with a big L. A. rep. When I was eleven, I made her a name plate for Christmas that said, *CAROLYN MASTERS, BIGTIME ATTORNEY.* She even put it on her desk. Those days of happy mother, happy daughter are gone. Her New York trip was to work out some sort of deal between multi-billion dollar corporations, something she does all the time.

She glances up at me. "There's just the young lady I want to talk to." She uses her lawyer voice on me. This worries me. Does she already know?

"How was the trip?" I ask, trying to get her off the topic of me as I flop down in a pool chair like I haven't a worry in the world.

"Signed the deal last night," she replies. She works on her toes with the same fierce concentration she works on everything. Documents are spread out on a deck table beside her, her cell phone on top. I stare at that phone while she talks, knowing it will ring any minute and then I'm dead. *Run now!* "My firm made lots of money," she adds. "Everyone's happy."

"When'd you get back?"

"Walked in the door fifteen minutes ago." She looks over at me and smiles. "How's that for timing?" Her smile faded. "Paula?"

"Yeah." *Oh, God, here it comes.*

"I'm not happy. You know why I'm not happy?" She pauses for a moment as if she expects an answer. First rule of dealing with interrogations: don't volunteer any info. I wait and she goes on, her tone growing harder. "While I'm trying to negotiate a billion dollar merger, one of the things I just love is your history teacher calling me in New York."

"Mrs. Guthrie?"

"Yes, Mrs. Guthrie, complaining about you. It seems you got a forty on your latest test. Only the most recent in a substantial pattern of failing scores. Your grade has fallen below passing, and I suspect it's the same in all your classes. This bad girl attitude is going to stop."

"I'm getting a good grade in PE. That'll make dad happy."

"Don't be smart, Paula. This is serious. You better take it seriously."

"I am. Guthrie hates me. And she's so boring, mom. We're studying the mid-19th century now, and she just drones on and on about it as if it's the most fascinating thing in the world. It drives us all crazy."

"I would think you would be more interested. You know you have relatives who came west back then. You're a direct descendant of strong pioneer stock."

I shrug. "Whatever."

That ticks her off. "Don't *whatever* me," she snaps. "You think when I was going through law school that every class was scintillating? That's not how the world works. It's not here to entertain you. This is your future I'm talking about."

"I am too."

Her phone chimes and I shut up immediately. For an instant, I actually consider dashing for the back door, maybe make it to the bus station and go somewhere, anywhere. Upon answering, she rolls her eyes right off; I can read that expression. It's my father. I heave a sigh of relief. They talk snappishly for several minutes then she hangs up.

"Didn't he want to talk to me?" I ask.

She frowns. "He's going to be late with the alimony again. How can you have a lawyer deadbeat for a dad?"

"Didn't he want to talk to me, mom?" I ask again.

She hesitates for a second. "Of course. I'm sorry. That's my fault, dear. I'm sure he'll call back."

"That's okay, I can call him later." I wouldn't and he wouldn't.

As I was grappling with the fact my father did not think enough of me to want to speak to me, she says, "Make sure you get home from school early tomorrow,"

"Why?" I ask cautiously

"Geez, Paula, where's your mind? Your uncles and aunts and cousins are all coming over tomorrow night. Friday Night barbecue, remember?"

"But I already have plans. The Rude Girls are going to the Hollywood Bowl to catch this hot band. It's a big night. Everyone will be there." *And my night of triumph after the assembly today.* My arguing, though, is pointless because I would soon be grounded forever.

"The Rude Girls will just have to change their plans," she said. "This is important. It's all hands on deck. You can invite them if you want."

"Not if. I don't think a Masters family barbecue is exactly what they would want to do on a Friday night."

"Why not? Ask them. Anyway you'll be here. It's your brother's birthday party. He's invited his friends."

"His birthday's not till next week," I protested.

"We're celebrating it tomorrow. You'd know that if you'd care about anyone but yourself."

"That's not fair, mom. You know I care about Josh."

She sighed. "You're right. Sorry. I do know that. But you will be there."

I am so angry I think I have popped a blood vessel. She knows if it's for Josh I will come, and that's why she combined the boring family barbecue with my little brother's birthday celebration. For a full five minutes, we sit silently while she focuses on her freaking toes, and I huff big sighs of which she takes no notice. She is not this high-powered lawyer for nothing. I am well aware she is disappointed in me. I know she wants me to be like her. I will never be like her. I could never be that strong.

Suddenly, a wave of pain rattles from front to the back in my head. Desperately, I massage my temples. *What the hell is wrong with me? What's with this headache?*

"Are you alright, Paula?"

"No, I have a mother that treats me like a slave."

She is about to respond in fury when Josh gets home from school, bounding down the back steps with his infectious grin and engaging exuberance. He is a devilishly cute twelve-year-old Down syndrome boy, and the only person who can light up my soul in dark moments like these.

"Paula!" he shouts with a wide grin as if he'd not seen me for years instead of since breakfast and runs to me, arms out like airplane wings, and hugs me. It is always the best part of my day.

"Hey, bud," I say.

"Will you come to my birthday party tomorrow, Paula? Please."

"Of course I will. I wouldn't miss it." That's that. I am proud of the level of bitchery I have achieved in my young life, but there is no way I would ever hurt this boy. I would be at his birthday party tomorrow night or be dead.

He goes over to mom and as he gives her a hug, her phone chimes again. I jump. She answers. "Yes, this is she. Yes, I know who you are Dr. Bramley. What is it you want?"

Oh, God, this is it.

As she listens, I wait like a condemned prisoner on the gallows. Her eyes shoot toward me. I don't think I've ever seen an expression of fury like that before. I am so glad I'm not incontinent; otherwise I'd be flooding the backyard.

Friday morning, mother drives me to school. Our normal silence has several added layers of tension caused in no small part by the fact my little escapade has gone viral. Though the figure dashing *naked* through the auditorium is masked, mom's embarrassment is palpable. Her one glance at me during the drive was so dark I thought she might shove me out the door at the bus station and say *goodbye*, as if I'd shot the Pope or something. It was nothing more than a prank. Still, she has grounded me forever or, she says, till I grow up, whichever comes first. She drops me off at school and tells me she will be back for the board meeting and to stay out of trouble till then. Thus begins the second day of what is already being called in Old Rectum lore Masters Disasters.

The moment I enter the school my head goes volcanic. Pain explodes off my frontal lobes, banging, banging, banging. A wave of nausea nearly knocks me off my feet and for a moment I'm really frightened. Students stare at me. They begin to spin and dissolve into nothing, being replaced by something very strange and crazy.

I am outdoors, standing in Prairie grass stirring in a breeze. I'm really there because I feel the breeze and the heat of the sun on my cheeks. Just ahead astride painted horses are three American Indians with stunned expressions. *Good God, this is crazy!*

They do not look friendly. Alarmed, I take a step back. The one in the center is the strangest man I've ever seen with a yellow slash across his bare chest. Smaller streaks on his cheeks. His hair is long and blond, his eyes blue. But the strangest thing is that he has no nose. A black scab instead. He is looking at me with such intense hatred as if he wants to kill me. *Geez, why?* Suspending the laws of gravity, he floats toward me, beckoning me forward with his hand. A voice from a deep tunnel somewhere calls out, *Come! Finish the journey.*

What journey? What the hell is going on? Suddenly dizzy, I lurch to the left and collide into a wall of lockers, back in the school hallway again, the prairie and Indians gone. That was much too real. Not a hallucination. Dazed and frightened, I try but can't understand what has just happened. Worse yet, I have crashed into freshman lockers. A small pimply boy is staring at me, bug eyed with fear as if he sees snakes coming out of my head.

"What are you looking at, rodent?" I snap and walk away.

Instead of going to class, I hang out in the girls' room trying to avoid everyone till ten when the board meeting starts. I will have to try and shift focus from the bizarre hallucination, which is scaring the piss out of me, to the little drama of my future.

Finally, 10:00 o'clock. In a small conference room, my mother and I face five people I know vaguely and principal Bramley with a white bandage across his nose and two black eyes, witness for the prosecution. I can see the glee cross his face at my entrance.

After a rehash of the incident and me giving heartfelt mea culpas—yeah right— mother addresses the committee. She torches them with a half-assed argument about my actions being an example of the school's failure to create a safe and productive learning environment for me and drops not so subtle hints of lawsuits to come. They don't stand a chance. I know right then that they are too afraid of her to expel me. It's determined I will serve an in-school suspension till the end of the year four weeks away. I think I have dodged a bullet till the hammer falls. The in-school suspension will be served in Mrs. Guthrie's classroom. Terrible! I'd rather be expelled.

"Thank you," my mother says. "I know Paula's behavior has been unacceptable. We are looking at other remedies but certainly for now we're grateful she will be able to stay at Rector and finish the school year."

Now what does that mean? Other remedies? I don't like the sound of that.

As my mother leaves and I'm left to the Guthrie Gulag, the Indian vision this morning plagues me. It scares me to death. The odd thing is my headache stopped when the prairie appeared but came back when the hallucinations ended.

I told my mother nothing about it. She already thinks I'm half-crazy. That would make me all the way crazy in her eyes. Could things possibly get worse? Yes, tonight. I have that family barbecue, something I dread having to attend. I love my relatives, but they are the last people in the world I want to spend time with, especially on a Friday night. Maybe, after Josh's party, I can sneak away and meet the Rude Girls, despite being on infinite restriction.

Chapter 5

That evening the family barbecue starts in our backyard around five when Josh's friends arrive, a few Down kids like him. We eat cake and sing a few songs, then Josh opens his presents. Eagerly unwrapping them, he thanks everyone as if their gift is the best thing he's ever gotten. I give him night vision goggles, which he puts on immediately.

"I can't see anything," he says.

I tell him, "You can only see things in the dark. Then you can see everything and no one else can."

My relatives arrive with more presents, and Josh is excited all over again. My heart goes out to him. Seeing his joy eases my trying day, one like few teens have ever endured. By the minibar, my Aunt Charlotte, a college physics professor of all things, asks me if I really ran naked through the school halls.

"No, of course not. It was the auditorium." Then I shrug. "Actually, I wore a body suit."

She laughs. "Well, you're never dull, Paula. I'll say that for you." Then she took on a more serious expression. "History was never made by well-behaved women."

I don't think she meant what I did was historic exactly. I raised my eyebrows as if I understood and wandered away. We eat hamburgers and then Uncle Dave brings out his guitar and insists I join him. This is an old family ritual. I play passably well while he is very good. My piano from years of lessons is better but not all that good. We sing, which used to be such an embarrassment for me since my singing voice is something akin to a braying donkey. Now, I don't care. I belt it out and watch my relatives try to hide their grimaces. If they want donkey, I will give them donkey.

After the fun fest, Josh's friends leave. It is early twilight, so I think I might be able to sneak out and catch up with my friends. No chance. Mother watches me with the hard eye of Big Brother, or Big Sister in this case. So as my aunts and uncles gather around the portable bar, I isolate myself across the lawn, sitting on the bench by the storage shed, sipping orange juice and trying to ignore everyone while feeling massively depressed.

Why does life have to be so freaking hard? The intense demands of school. Drugs everywhere. The pressure of having sex. Popularity always at risk. Technology ready to memorialize every bad move on YouTube or on the texting grapevine. Constant drudge duties at home. It just seems I am the only private in a world of generals. Too many people telling me what to do, leaving too little of me for me. It is just not fair.

I grimace in pain. My head aches worse than ever, and my stomach roils with nausea. Maybe I am about to pop a blood vessel in my head and die. That might not be such a bad thing. Dying would solve all my problems and make people regret how they treated me. But I'm not so sure I want my head to burst open even if I have to go back to school Monday and face Mrs. Guthrie? For sure, she will take all the pleasure out of being popular. In truth, I see no hope for me in or out of the Rector Academy. And my mother determined to find other remedies as if I am a disease.

As I look at my relatives clinking glasses and getting drunk, they all look so annoyingly happy. Well, I'm not. I have concluded this has been the worst day of my life. Everything is an uphill battle like that Greek Sisyphus we learned about in 8th grade, pushing that rock uphill just to have it roll back to the bottom and start all over again. That's me.

A warm day is cooling off. I need a jacket but I'm not going to go through the gauntlet of my relatives to get one. Wearing just a black t-shirt and jeans, I rub my arms to keep warm.

"Paula," my mother calls. "Come over here and talk to your aunts and uncles."

A couple of them smile and wave. So eager, so clueless.

I figure I might as well get this over with. Mom will not let it go till I do my family duty. Grimly, I put my smiley face on and start toward them, but as I do, they seem to drift farther away. Suddenly, cannons blast inside my head, and I shriek from the pain. My stomach floods with acid. I bend double, hands on my knees, and hurl a gush of bitter, yellow liquid splashing onto the grass. *I am afraid.* What is happening to me? Looking up, I see my relatives spinning in a kaleidoscope of heads and flailing arms rushing toward me. I fall to one knee. One last look at them. The terror on my mother's face.

Then a black curtain comes down and I am gone.

I floated in a nether world, spiraling down a black hole. I heard the words again: *Come. Finish the journey. Finish the journey.* Likely, only a few seconds passed by the time I opened my eyes and saw everyone gathered over me.

"Libby, Libby, my God, your arm is busted all to pieces!" a man shouted.

It felt like someone was banging my arm with a hammer, the pain excruciating. I stared up at them. Something was very wrong. I didn't know any of them. Mom, Uncle Dave, Aunt Charlotte weren't there. These people were strangers. Many of the men had beards and several women wore sunbonnets. *Sunbonnets!* I sat up, screaming at the searing pain in my arm. I looked at them, tears welling in my eyes.

"WHO ARE YOU PEOPLE?"

Chapter 6

I was never so miserable in my life. I lay on a quilt inside a cramped, rickety covered wagon amid several old chests, assorted garage-sale junk and a single rocking chair. Wrapped in a sling, my left arm throbbed with intense pain at every bump, and the woman driving seemed to be hitting them on purpose. My hand tucked inside the sling felt numb and swollen.

A couple of hours before, a fierce-looking man with a long black beard and the eyes of a madman knelt over me with wooden slats set to splint the break. No meds. No doctor. Get me to a doctor! I had shouted, but no one paid any attention. Someone stuck a leather strap in my mouth to bite on, and a woman held my shoulders so I couldn't move.

With a sickening snap, the man twisted my broken bones into place. I screamed, spitting out the leather onto his beard, cursing him and everyone else. In my life nothing, I mean nothing, ever hurt so much, *ever*. As he splinted me, I cried out, begging him to stop. They put me in this wagon—to wait for an ambulance to take me to a hospital, I thought, but then I heard a man outside say, "Henry, we can't wait any longer. We need to cover some miles yet today."

"She's a tough one. We're ready."

And with a jerk, the wagon moved forward.

I was scared, very scared. I didn't know what was happening. I couldn't remember how I had gotten here or anything that may have happened since I had passed out at the barbecue. On Thursday I had executed my run through the school auditorium, but when was that Thursday? For me to even be here, time completely lost to me must have passed. What was going on?

As the wagon hit another bump and pain shot through my arm, I called out to the woman driving. "God, lady, watch where you're going. Hey, you need to get me to a hospital. For Christ's sake, my arm is broken. I need a doctor. Please!"

She glanced back in at me, her face worried. "Oh, Libby honey, you know we're far from any hospital. Doc Pierce has fixed you up just fine. He says you'll be good as new."

"It hurts. Jesus! Don't you have any painkillers? At least let me use your cell phone so I can call my mother."

She gave me an expression of utter confusion that would have been comical if I wasn't hurting so much. "I know it hurts, dear, but in a couple of days it won't hurt so."

That was too much. I shouted, "You people are in big trouble. My parents are lawyers. They're going to sue your asses off. You won't have a penny left."

She sighed and went back to driving, soon singing about someone named Crazy Jane. Herself no doubt. Weird. Just freaking weird. I could not process what was happening to me. It was like tripping on bad drugs. I must have lost my memory, that much was clear.

At that moment, a man climbed in the back, grabbing a rope off a rung. "One of Captain Warren's calves got itself stuck in a mud hole," he said to me as if I cared. He had brown hair sticking out from under a battered, wide-brimmed hat. "You might start thinking about getting yourself up now. I hope you're not planning on sleeping all the way."

His face had such a hard, lock-jaw look I nearly flinched. Get up! Was the man crazy? I cut off a sharp reply because frankly the guy scared the piss out of me. This was one hard-ass bastard. I thought of a religious zealot at some commune. That might be it.

The wagon lurched sharply sending razors shooting through my arm. "Hey, you're deliberately hitting every freaking bump," I screamed at the woman.

"Do not talk to your mother that way," the man snapped. "What's gotten into you, Libby? I know you're hurt, but there's no call to take it out on your ma."

"My ma! What have you been sniffing, dude?" I shot back. "She's not my ma."

He had such a black look that I thought sure he would hit me. If I could have backed any farther away, I would have.

The woman said, "Henry, she's not herself."

"That's no reason to forget proper respect." He scowled down at me. "You show your ma respect, you hear me? No more of this squalling." He paused, his voice softening a bare fraction. "I know it hurts. Nothing we can do about that, Libby. Best you get out and walk. It will be easier on your arm."

"I'm not going anywhere," I insisted. "I'm sure not walking. Get me to a hospital."

We locked eyes for several seconds. "Suit yourself," he said with a shrug. "Bounce around in here, if that's what you want."

"If you would just get an ambulance out here," I pleaded, but he was gone.

"Honey, I know it's hard," the woman said. "But your pa's right. It would be easier on you if you would walk."

This was madness. My ma! My pa! These people had to be on something. But after a few moments in which my anger eased, I realized that, clearly, they were right. I couldn't take another bump. I had to get out of this wagon. Keeping my arm immobile, I scooted to the back and carefully climbed out.

Chapter 7

Cautiously as possible, I stepped down off the moving wagon. Being forced to walk only a couple hours after breaking my arm was abusive. My parents would cut these people to ribbons in a courtroom. The man named Henry was mounted on a horse, talking to a bearded man driving the wagon just behind.

"Yes, sir, Mr. Quarles," the driver said.

Henry glanced over at me, nodding. "Libby, you'll feel better up and about."

I was getting tired of this *Libby* crap. Still, I forced a smile and went over to him. "Look, Henry, sir, I don't remember anything. Believe me. I'm not making it up. I don't remember breaking my arm, I don't remember you, I don't even remember coming here. I know you have a job to do, but I mean really, dude. A broken arm. No painkillers. Man, you need to get me to a hospital and now."

"Not a hospital in five hundred miles I know of," he said. "Don't you worry; that arm's going to heal up real nice. Doc Pierce says so. You got yourself a real hard knock on the head, too. I suspect you'll be in birdyland for a while."

"That's even more reason to get me to a hospital." I tried to sound reasonable. "Shove this little scenario, man. Call in an ambulance or a helicopter. There'll be big trouble if you don't, I promise you."

He stared at me a moment, his eyes uncaring. "Got to get to that calf. Captain Warren is waiting." He started away, but immediately pulled back. "You were always the toughest one. I guess you're entitled to a little complaint now and then. But there's nothing for it 'cepting to buck up." Then he rode off.

Buck up! I repeated the words several times, getting more upset each time. *Buck up, buck up.* They were going to do nothing for me. My parents, probably my mother mostly, had dropped me firmly into Loonyville. I had to get out of here. As I walked alongside the wagon, I felt a suffocating cloud of confusion settling in. Nothing made sense. I asked the woman driving how I got here, but she was brain-dead, speaking about a home somewhere in Illinois. She too was following some prescribed scenario. I gave up.

I took in my surroundings. Open country. Rolling hills. We were coming out of a wide valley, climbing up a gentle slope. Below, a river, shiny and metallic, curved away from us into distant hills. Strung out along the route, I counted over 120 wagons forming a train more than half a mile long with hundreds of people walking, women and children and men, a few men on horseback, dogs roaming in and out of the line of travel. At the back rode several men and boys herding cattle and horses. Why so many wagons and people? Against the rising cloud of dust, the woman tied a red bandana on her face, making her look like a bank robber.

"Climb up here," she said. "I'll tie a kerchief on you."

I was eating a lot of dust, but said, "No thanks." I wanted nothing to do with skirting in between the oxen and the wagon. From the gist of what I'd overheard, that's how I broke my arm; my dress snagged on the tongue while climbing down and I went under the wheels. I shivered at the thought. No wonder I couldn't remember.

For the next two hours, I avoided the worst of the dust by trailing just behind the wagon and slid into a blessed, sleepwalking numbness, unable to process any of this situation. In that time, I saw nothing of civilization. No planes, no telephone towers, no roads, no houses, no towns. Nothing. That was odd in itself. Where the hell were we? And there were other odd things. An iron stove lay abandoned not far from the dirt track we followed, and a little farther on a dining table and several chairs. Who would come way out here to dump old furniture?

"You feeling any better, Missy?" the bearded man driving the next wagon back called. I'd heard Henry refer to him as Joost. First or last name, who knew, who cared? A hired man likely, certainly part of security. He smiled, showing a disgusting array of black teeth.

"Just great," I answered sarcastically. "You have a cell phone?"

He looked blank for a moment, then laughed. Hopeless.

In the late afternoon, exhausted, I'd reached my limit and went up to the woman driving. "When are we going to stop?"

"Maybe five or six o'clock, hon. Whenever Captain Warren decides."

"How much longer is that?"

"Couple hours. Maybe three."

Three hours! My arm ached, my legs ached, and my feet ached. I wasn't going to make it. After a few more minutes I asked the woman, "What's your name?"

She cocked her head at me with that sad look again. "Julia."

"You have a good singing voice, Julia." I said. She'd been going through an extensive repertoire of songs all afternoon.

She laughed. "Why, thank you, honey. You've got a lovely voice, too. Better than mine."

"Sure, I do." Singing? I sound like gravel in a cement mixer.

I studied her more closely. The bandana was pulled down around her neck now, so I got a good look at her. Maybe thirty-five, if that. Red hair and warm blue eyes. Her face was more than pretty, and strong, someone not to mess with. She was weathered like Henry, as if she spent all her time outside, which I guess she did with this gig. Hadn't she ever heard of moisturizer?

Then I noticed she was pregnant. Five or six months. *God!* Who would come out here when she was pregnant? At once, like an arc-light suddenly switching on, it came to me what all this was. One of those tough-love companies that works with troubled teens. They were everywhere. It had to be. From what I could see, there were quite a few teens out here, at least a hundred. That was it. A wagon train of bad boys and bad girls with hard ass counselors attached, and me tossed into the middle of them by my loving mother. Re-enactors no doubt, they wore period costumes and followed a well-planned scenario of some pioneer bullshit.

Bizarre, but it was the only thing that fit the facts. That had to be it. My parents had finally done it. They'd threatened other methods to deal with me, even my dad in Paris. I had a friend whose parents sent him to a tough-love camp where army drill sergeants harassed him day and night. The idea was to instill discipline in him. It worked. When he came back to school, he didn't get into any more trouble, and he told me it was because he never wanted to go back to that place. There were even tough-love schools behind barbed wire, taught by teachers with degrees in bashing heads. This wagon train to hell was just another one of those. Mother had warned me. Another remedy, she had said. This was it.

I hadn't thought I was that bad, not really. Adhering to authority was never my strong suit, but what had I done that was so bad? A joy ride last year? Some bad grades. Some conflict with teachers and with Mom. A little run through the auditorium day before yesterday or whenever? And this is what I get? I'll never forgive them for putting me here.

Yet, I still had the nagging feeling I was missing something. Where was everybody? Why was there no sign of civilization anywhere? And how could I forget so much? At supper I planned to demand that this Henry dude call my mother and tell her I was hurt. That, or I was out of here. If need be, I'd sneak off. There had to be a town or at least a highway close by.

In the evening, the authorities camped beside a riverbank with groves of cottonwoods, circling the wagons like in a Western movie. As the Quarles set up their tent and started a fire, I took a walk about the camp. I knew they wanted me to help, but what work could I do with a broken arm? Everyone was busy but me. The herds had been driven up close to the wagons, the horses hobbled but the cattle left to settle into the grass. The oxen were released into the circle to graze. Everywhere women were preparing dinner over fires. To each his own, I thought. You could take your back to nature crap and stuff it. Intent on demanding that my parents be called, I came back to the Quarles' wagons. Henry was kneeling at the fire, pouring himself a cup of tea. When he glanced at me with those unforgiving eyes, I wussed out. I decided I could wait till after we ate to confront him.

I noticed all was not bliss in wagon train land. There was tension between Henry and Julia. As he sipped his tea, their eyes met and he looked away with a frown. Maybe I was reading too much into it, but it looked like a bit of strain between them. Maybe she was angry because she was missing her favorite TV show, *The Real Housewives of Butt Creek*. I wondered if they were even married, maybe both just working a job. No, I decided. They were married. That kind of tension clearly came from married life. I'd seen it often enough.

Hanging a large pan over a tripod, Julia began heating a stew. I felt a really ludicrous pleasure that I recognized it was a Dutch oven. Mrs. Guthrie would be giddy with excitement.

"I need to wash my hands," I said.

Julia said, "Wash in the river. Take the children with you. Just be careful."

Three girls and a boy traipsed down to the water with me, Henry and Julia's children; this gig was a family operation. The oldest girl was Caroline, thirteen. There was a boy named Little George, maybe eight, who I'd yet to hear speak, and twins Seneca and Jane so blond that their hair was almost white. They said they were five. Another boy, Isaac, who was twelve, was doing something somewhere with the cattle. As we approached the stream, Caroline was cataloguing the creatures she'd caught today: several frogs, a lizard, and quite a few bugs.

"I hope they're not what we're having for supper," I said.

She laughed. "No, silly."

She had curly blond hair like me. Cute but with strange eyes, one looked straight at you but the other hugged her nose. Cockeyed. She asked me why frogs croaked instead of sang. I told her I didn't have a clue. "Do you have a thing for frogs, little girl?"

"She likes snakes," one of the twins said.

"Great. Snakes."

At the water, I said, "All of you be careful. Boy, you keep an eye on your sisters. They are your sisters, aren't they?"

The same twin, I think, remarked, "Who else's would we be?" The two of them fell into fits of giggling.

When I knelt at the water to wash, I carefully pulled back the sling from my left hand, which was still numb. What I saw hit me with the blast force of a bomb. I fell back on my ass, staring at my hand uncomprehendingly, then started screaming and screaming and screaming.

My left hand! I was missing two fingers. Two nubs were where the pinkie and the finger next to it should be. Several people came running, a couple men with guns drawn, Henry one of them. His eyes wild, he shouted, "What is it? What's wrong?"

Stunned, I couldn't speak. Julia came up and asked Caroline what happened. She shrugged. "I don't know. Libby just started screaming."

"Where are they?" Joost yelled, running up and aiming his rifle about. "I shoot them."

I found my voice. "My hand! Look at it." No one seemed to understand. I shouted "Where are my fingers?"

With a grimace, Henry turned to the other people. "Sorry, folks. False alarm." They started back, a few mumbling, "Crazy," and, "Poor girl. Her mind's gone."

Henry shook his head. "Libby, don't go screaming for nothing. You know better."

"Nothing!" I shouted at him, hysterically. "You've mutilated my hand!"

Julia helped me up, and with her arm around my shoulders, led me back to the wagon. Patiently, she explained something that I did not understand, but it had to do with a blizzard and frostbite. I thought, good God, how long have I been here? To have lost two fingers it had to have been awhile. Not hungry anymore, I climbed in the wagon and spent the next hour on my back staring in horrid astonishment at my hand before I fell into an exhausted, disturbed asleep.

Chapter 8

The next morning, I was still shaken and confused. Finding your fingers mutilated and missing would tend to have that effect. After a gruesome breakfast of biscuits and gravy and some kind of stringy meat, I asked Henry to call my parents. He did not even reply, merely shaking his head and tossing the dregs of his tea into the fire. What a bastard! I decided I'd have to take matters into my own hands and escape. Sneaking away at night should be simple enough. Finding the right time and place would be the problem. Where was I? How far to the nearest road or town?

To accomplish this, I realized I could use some allies, maybe even someone to escape with, so after the wagons started out, I made an effort to talk with a few other teens who were walking alone or in small cliques along the line of march, easily keeping pace with the slow-moving wagons. When I asked what they had done to be sent to this hell, a few laughed but most responded with big fat blanks as if I were crazy. Worse yet, when I pleaded for a cell phone, not a one could come up with an expression beyond bewilderment. Brainwashed and brain dead.

Early that morning, we crossed several streams, not even pausing but splashing right on through, then later on took hours to skirt a massive hill that was covered with red and yellow prairie flowers. Such bright colors contrasted with the dark and foreboding shades inside my head. To my stressed out mind, I was alone on some far off planet, being pursued by madness as if savage wolves nipped at my heels. I don't think I was too far wrong.

No luck enlisting other teens, I returned to the wagon of my caretakers. Caroline, the cockeyed girl, walked beside me. It was hard to pin her down about anything. I would ask her something specific like where were we, and she'd answer by showing me the frog she'd just caught. She reminded me so much of my brother Josh. Not Down syndrome, but quirky, like a wild creature herself, at home with all these animals and crawly things.

She had few friends. Only one boy that I could tell took notice of her at all. A lanky kid with an unruly shock of brown hair and an impish smile. He seemed to be the leader of a pack of real troublemakers the security people did little to curtail. Once, when he rushed by with several other kids chasing a loose calf, she watched him with such yearning she almost stopped breathing. Abruptly, he came back and gave her something that she slid into her pocket.

"Who was that?" I asked when he and the other boys went off after the calf.

"That's Putt," she said, puppy love squeezing out of both words.

"You like him, don't you?"

"We're going to get married someday."

"Really? Does he know that yet?"

She laughed. "Not yet."

"What did he give you?"

She took a snake out of her pocket. I squealed in alarm and told her to get rid of that thing. Reluctantly, she tossed it into the grass.

"What happened to my hand, Caroline? Can you at least tell me that?"

"Yes, indeed."

After several seconds of silence in which it became clear she was going to say nothing else, I said, "Well, tell me."

"You don't remember the blizzard?"

"No, I don't remember the blizzard. I don't remember anything."

"Nothing?"

"Until yesterday, as far as I know, I'd never seen you before in my life."

I was afraid I'd hurt her feelings, but she grinned. "Law! That's something."

"So what happened to my fingers?"

"You got them chopped off. You remember that?"

I shook my head.

"Pa was going to make the store bigger and I guess he needed more money to do it, so he went off to some bank far away to get the money. That's when the house and store burnt down. I remember it was real, real cold outside, snowing and blowing, I thought I was going to freeze to death. We stayed that night at the Olsen's. Cindy Olsen and me are best friends."

"Cindy Olsen and I." Did I just correct her grammar? "Never mind. Go on."

"You went in the blizzard to stop Pa from borrowing the money. Froze your fingers like they were stone. I guess that's about it."

What a fanciful story. Somehow, I lost these fingers, but I couldn't have been here long enough for it to have happened in a blizzard.

"Iris saved us all," she said.

"Saved us from what?"

"Pa says bankruptcy."

This made no sense. "And who's Iris?"

"You don't even remember Iris? She's your horse."

"I have a horse?"

"Yes, indeed. So does Isaac. No one else can ride Iris. She's so mean she won't let them."

The story was clearly part of the fanciful scenario we were expected to follow. When I asked her again if she knew where we were, she said she wasn't sure. She didn't think anyone knew for sure but the pilot, whoever and whatever that was. I sighed with disappointment. She said, "Oh, I did hear some men say we're not far from the Big Blue."

That told me nothing. We couldn't be that far from a road. Just go in one direction, say west, and stick to it. Sooner or later I'd come across civilization. I decided to go that night.

Chapter 9

I had no chance to escape that night because of the storm. It came upon us while we were still strung out travelling. It seemed as if it would never stop. Before it struck, numb with exhaustion, my arm throbbing, my fingers still missing, I had been praying for the day to end. Then, where there were pristine blue skies on the horizon one moment, suddenly there were black skies and the flash of lightning. The low kettledrum of thunder drifted to us. A soft breeze began, then grew stronger, stirring up dust and whipping the tall grass. The black clouds descended like someone drawing a shroud over us. It looked like a monster.

My insides turned over several times, fear, real fear, taking hold. Someone up ahead was frantically turning the wagons into a circle. People ran about shouting while I stood ready to scream. I had no idea what to do.

"Hurry, Libby, get the twins in the wagon," Julia yelled from the driver's seat

The twins and Little George had been somewhere else playing, but now ran back to us. At the back of the wagon, Caroline and Little George climbed in, and with my good arm I lifted each of the twins by the back of their dresses up to them, then followed. It occurred to me that this rickety old wagon would not provide much in the way of protection.

A moment later, Henry appeared and rummaged through a wooden chest. "Julia, where'd you put them slickers?" His voice was calm, but even so, I detected a hint of alarm.

"Other side," she replied. "I swear, Henry Quarles, you're getting so old, you're losing your eyesight."

The tension I'd seen between them had disappeared. "Maybe so, maybe so," he said with a smirk. "I can still see you're the prettiest gal I done ever see'd."

I thought I would throw up. Prettiest gal I done ever see'd? Come on. Really? She waved the compliment away, but you could tell she liked it.

He tossed me a raincoat. "Hellfire storm coming, Libby. Isaac is helping the other boys bring in the cattle and horses. I need you to help Joost with the oxen."

"No!" I tossed the raincoat back. The storm had me really frightened, thunder getting louder and louder. Maybe that's why I reacted so petulantly. "I just broke my damn arm, man. Can't you see that? I can't help with any stupid oxen. That's way off base. I mean, God, what are you on?"

He stared at me a long time; his eyes frozen in a steady glare.

"Henry," Julia said, the tension back.

Finally, with a harsh sigh, he slammed the chest shut. I jumped at the sound.

"We ain't going to make it if we don't each pull our weight, addled or not," he said. With a last glower at me, he climbed out of the wagon. Such a bastard. I mean, what was his problem?

Julia touched my cheek. "You're going to be just fine, Libby. I know it. May take a little time, but I just know it."

She was wrong. I wasn't going to be fine unless I could get away from these crazy people, and with this storm, that wouldn't be tonight. Then, glancing out of the wagon, I nearly wet myself with panic. A funnel cloud had dipped down to the ground and was coming straight toward us.

The wagon shook from the wind. Junk and people, squeezed into something the size of a VW van, rattled with each gust. Several times I thought we would tip over. Rain and hail drummed on the canvas, wind roared, lightning cracked explosively just overhead. The world was coming apart. I expected at any moment the tornado would lift us up into the air and tear the wagon to pieces. I didn't think we would land anywhere near Oz.

Moments later, Henry and Isaac scrambled in through the flap, shaking water from their raincoats. We settled in to hopefully ride out the storm. Henry drew the cover tight at both ends to keep the rain out, but did a poor job of it. Water still flooded in everywhere, soaking everything. My hair was wet, my clothes were wet, the quilt I tried to wrap myself in was wet. My teeth chattered from the cold. What a nightmare! If I hadn't been so frightened, I would have cried.

Next to me, Julia sat in the rocking chair, holding Seneca and Jane in her lap. I felt sorry for them, clutching fiercely to their mother, more frightened than me, if that was possible. Henry asked Julia to read aloud from the Bible. She tried but in the poor light and the constant shaking she gave up.

"It's going to be all right," she said to the twins soothingly. Her face had a Madonna-like quality. The religious Madonna, not the rocker.

"What's today's date," I asked abruptly.

"May 14th. Why?" Julia said.

May 14th. I'd lost a week. The prom had come and gone. That meant my memory of that time had completely gone. Still, things didn't add up. How was it I had lost my fingers and the wounds had healed in two weeks? I couldn't process it.

"How long's your contract for?" I asked Henry, who looked confused by the question.

Julia asked, "Contract for what, honey?"

"For me."

She gave an easy chuckle. "Oh, that's forever."

I shook my head in frustration.

"Have we lost the horses in the rain, Ma?" One of the twins asked, Seneca, I thought. She was the outgoing one.

"No, dear," Julia answered, giving her shoulders a squeeze. "They'll be safe. We'll find them."

"If we make it through the night," Isaac said, smirking at his own gallows humor.

"Isaac, don't frighten the girls," Julia scolded. "Of course, we'll make it."

The boy was hardly chastised. He was not frightened because Henry was not frightened. The boy mimicked the father. Isaac acted full of himself, while Little George was just silent. He said nothing even when he was asked a direct question. I couldn't figure whether he was slow or what. Julia had said this afternoon that he speaks, but I hadn't heard him yet. When I asked her how often he speaks, she said a couple words a month.

"Is he slow-witted?" I'd asked.

She sighed and shrugged. "I don't believe so." She clearly meant, I hope not.

Once or twice when the wind buffeted the wagon, I saw Little George's eyes bug out, then look around quickly to see if anyone had caught his moment of weakness. He was only eight. Kid, I thought, you're right to be scared.

The wind finally eased a bit, enough so that the wagon no longer shook, but the rain still pounded and water still found its way through the canvas. Caroline scooted next to me and snuggled for warmth, little of it that there was. I wrapped her in my damp quilt. Her hair was a frazzled, wet mess. Like everyone else on this wagon train, they didn't have much familiarity with shampoo.

The girl looked up at me. "I'm glad the wagon didn't squish you when it ran you over."

"Thanks. I'm glad, too, bud," I said.

I stared at them, these people. Each one looked like a fugitive from a bad reality TV show. The parents were obviously responsible for me, contracted to take care of me for the length of my incarceration or schooling or training, whatever it was. But I wondered who they really were.

"Are all these kids yours?" I asked Julia. "I assume they are. I can't imagine anyone putting such young children into a program like this one."

Quickly, she glanced at Henry, then turned back to me. "Yes, of course they are, honey, as are you."

Yeah, right. I nodded toward her pregnant belly. "My God, you have five children already, if they're all yours, and going for a sixth, what are you thinking?" I felt no restrictions about being blunt. I owed them nothing.

I saw Henry's scowl, but she warned him off with a glance and answered me pleasantly enough, "I like big families. I came from a small one. I missed not having lots of brothers and sisters."

At least her pregnancy told me this program couldn't go on much longer. She would need to get back to civilization and a hospital to deliver the baby. But then an alarm bell sounded. If they weren't going to take me back to get my arm properly set, they might not go back to deliver a baby. Maybe they were that far gone into this back-to-nature bit.

A fierce gust shook the wagon. Sheets of water shot in as one flap lifted up. Henry jumped over and tied it back into place. I had my good arm around Caroline, holding her in close. I could see the terror in her eyes. She asked, "Are you afraid, Libby?"

"No, Puddinghead," I said. "Why should I be afraid of a little rain?"

Julia winked at me.

I asked them who they were, really, hoping they'd put the reenactment scenario aside for a bit, but no luck. Patiently, Julia explained that their last name was Quarles and they all came from Springfield, Illinois, and that I was Libby Quarles. I guessed that was the character I had been assigned for the duration of this program. You'd think they could drop it for a second, once the day was done, but no. Well, I had news for them. I wasn't going to be here much longer. I was not this Libby person; I was Paula Masters, and I was getting the hell out of here.

Something clicked in my brain. "Springfield. Illinois?"

"Yes," Julia answered.

"Abraham Lincoln, 16th President of the United States."

Julia grinned as if I'd just answered the million-dollar question on a game show. "Yes, that's right, Libby. Maybe you're recalling some things now. Abe. He's our friend. You were always his favorite. When you were little, he loved to chuck you under the chin and watch you giggle. But I have to think he'd have a good laugh over that president idea."

"He's a hardworking man," Henry added. "You could always count on Old Abe. I was proud to serve with him in the militia."

"Old Abe," Isaac said, parroting his father with a rueful shake of his head.

I laughed. This was rich. "Abraham Lincoln. Springfield, Illinois. Adding him to the scenario, that's a nice touch."

The storm reared up again. I gritted my teeth to stop them from chattering. I was sure we would be airborne any second. Boom box thunder burst overhead, sending vibrations through the wagon. Caroline jumped, jarring my arm. I hissed with pain, but she was so frightened, I said nothing. I understood her fear. I thought we were going to be hurled into eternity at any moment.

I screamed out, "Where in God's name have my parents sent me?"

Julia sighed at that but said nothing. Finally, the storm eased into a steady rain, the lightning and thunder moving off. We could still hear it, though, erupting every few seconds in the distance.

"I better check on Aspasia," Henry said, unlimbering, throwing on his raincoat and climbing out through the back. Rain poured in till Isaac retied the flap.

"Who's Aspasia," I asked.

"The milk cow, dummy," Isaac said.

"How was I supposed to know, little boy?" I shot back.

"Isaac," Julia snapped. "You will not speak to your sister that way. Do you understand?"

"Yes, ma'am." He was actually contrite.

At that moment, lightning struck just outside the wagon, a deafening crack not three feet from me, blasting a hole in my eardrums, causing our hair to frizz up like Frankenstein's Bride. We all screamed. Caroline's eyes bulged white in terror. I caught the smell of ozone and burning flesh. Something alive had been struck.

Blanching with utter dread, Julia shoved the twins at me and scrambled out of the wagon moving faster than any pregnant woman I'd ever seen, followed by Isaac and Little George. The girls clung to me, jarring my arm and grinding bone. I moaned but did not scream for fear of further alarming them. Caroline was trying to close the back flap but not getting it done. We were getting soaked again. Peeking out through a tiny rip in the canvas, I saw an ox lying on its side a few feet away, steaming in the torrent of rain. Henry and Julia and the two boys stood around it, staring down as if waiting for it to rise up. I sighed with relief. I didn't want to have to tell the girls that their father had been killed.

"It's alright," I told them. "It was an ox. Henry is alright."

Eventually, everyone climbed back into the wagon. Cold and wet, we had no supper that night, and little sleep.

Chapter 10

The next morning, with the loose wood along the riverbank too wet to burn, no one could start a cook fire. I faced the prospect of going hungry again, no supper last night, no breakfast this morning. No one had a simple can of Sterno, it seemed, or any other modern equipment. Just like the Amish or something. Finally, Julia came up with a horrid breakfast of beef jerky and hard biscuits.

Henry and Isaac butchered the dead ox, sharing the meat with other families. They hung a side of that ox up on the second wagon, the one Joost drove, where it attracted hordes of flies. I thought that was utterly gross—as if I was going to eat any of that.

We had barely finished our jerky breakfast when a man rode through the camp shouting "Head 'em out! Head 'em out!"

Within seconds, the wagons were rolling, skirting the butchered remains of the ox and pushing on at a snail's pace in the mud. I dreaded another long day of walking. I couldn't help thinking this fit the definition of insanity, in a hurry to get nowhere. I hated my parents for this.

Even though it was still wet and cold, the three girls and Little George went barefoot. Not me. I'll wear shoes, thank you, ankle high pair of worn-out leather boots, hardly worthy of Wal-Mart, let alone Gucci.

Later that morning, Isaac came up to drink water from a keg on the side of Julia's wagon. He was sweating. He'd already been working hard, doing God knows what. Twelve years old and doing a grown man's work. Another crime these people were committing. Child labor. I was making a mental list.

"We got the cattle and horses," he said to me proudly. "They got run off in the storm. I figured they'd scattered to the four winds, but they was all together about a mile away. We followed Aspasia to them. She was looking for her calf."

"Crap, man, what's the deal here?" I complained in my ingratiating way. "Look at me. I'm cold and I'm wet. Why not stay a few hours and dry out the clothes, get a few hours' sleep?"

"Libby, you ain't wet at all. Captain's not holding the company up for you to get your beauty sleep. That'd take too long, anyway." He grinned. Smart-ass.

He took off his hat, a battered replica of his father's, and scratched his hair. God, I hoped he didn't have lice. "Walking, I bet, will warm you up in no time."

I shook my head. "Geez, kid, they have you brainwashed, too."

He didn't understand what I said, but understood its harsh tone. He gave a grunt, replaced his hat and said with pride, "Can't stand here chewing the fat with you. Pa's counting on me to watch the cattle this morning."

"Well, why don't you just go do that?"

He walked off, joining up with a couple of other boys, and headed back toward the horses and cattle. He would be no ally. Clearly, he was into all this.

It turned out my main task during the day's travel was to watch the twins Seneca and Jane. With Julia on one wagon and Henry out somewhere doing manly things, it was up to me to watch the little ones. Physically, I couldn't tell them apart, blond, blue-eyed waifs so small a decent wind could carry them off. In fact, clones, each with the same exact DNA, still their personalities were different. Seneca was outgoing while Jane quiet, yet both displayed an insatiable curiosity, especially Seneca, asking questions about what oxen were thinking, where Indians came from and where God lived, none of which I could answer. One thing I knew from my aunt's twins was that they often created a world of their own, exclusive to them, and no one else could enter.

Jane, the quiet one, had an abnormal fear of Indians. She still trembled at the mention of them. I thought that strange, unless you wandered into one of their casinos where they bottom out a credit card at the turn of a card. When Isaac, back for rope, teased her by saying Pawnee and Sioux were just ahead, Jane's alabaster skin grew even more colorless, and she shut down completely. I slapped the back of Isaac's head and told him to shut his mouth. He gave a yelp, and ran off. I told Jane that Indians had not been dangerous for more than a hundred years, but that didn't seem to help. Only Seneca could bring her back by guiding her out through their own little world first.

Later, I noticed them doing something remarkable. The little devils traded personalities. Seneca had been talking incessantly with Joost, at least I thought it was Seneca. When they went to another wagon to speak with a small, stout woman, the other twin was now doing all the talking. This woman addressed *her* as Seneca. Evidently, they had long since understood their uniqueness and played these ruses on everyone.

As I kept pace with the wagons, it occurred to me that the families on this operation—and therefore the security—were fairly lax when it came to watching their children, and prisoners like me. Under six or seven, they kept a close eye, but older ones like Little George or Caroline, and more importantly the inmates, were on their own. That might give me a way to escape.

By mid-morning, the sun had warmed things up. I hoped after a good hour or two that we'd stop, since we were almost certainly travelling in some kind of circle in a National Park, likely in the Midwest. In every direction was a great expanse of rolling hills with tall grass stirring in a constant breeze. Trees hugged the many streams we crossed. Several women, including a few my age, often walked out from the wagons, fifty yards or more, to escape the dust. With the twins trailing me, I went over and joined a group. Quickly, they huddled around me, attempting to console me, for what I wasn't sure. They all knew me; I didn't know any of them.

"My Aunt Lorelei got hit on her head once't," said a tall, gangly woman who seemed in her thirties. She had grey catfish eyes and brown hair pulled back in a bun, no bonnet like many of the others. "She was so addled she couldn't remember her name. Lasted nigh on to three months, but she came out of it. They always do. You will too, Libby. You're a strong girl."

A huge boy with girlish blond ringlets said in a soft, prissy voice, "Libby's not addled, Georgia. Now don't be saying she is." He was dressed in dusty jeans and a faded plaid work shirt and desperately in need of a bath.

"Well, now, I'm not saying that it's permanent," the one named Georgia replied. This was Georgia Whelan, I learned, famous on the wagon train, according to Julia, for being a canning marvel. She could can just about any fruit or veggie into jars. Big deal. I wondered if they'd ever heard of a supermarket.

Another, woman, older, with a stout, leathery face, said, "Oh, the poor dear, she looks so confused." She patted my cheek as if I were a collie. They called her Myra, which meant she was Julia's closest friend, Myra Langdon, the one the twins had talked to earlier. Her voice boomed, and the big blond guy even jumped once when she spoke.

"Well, of course," Georgia said. "If you're addled, you don't know you're addled."

"I told you she's not addled," insisted the boy, my defender.

"I'm not addled," I said sharply. "Just pissed at people talking about me as if I'm, like, not here."

It was another strange moment. They exchanged embarrassed glances. Georgia seemed to think she was the arbiter of the way people should act and was somewhat offended that I'd be so blunt.

Seneca grabbed Myra by the hand and asked about someone named Daniel.

"Oh, he's out with the pilot hunting. He'll be back in a day or two."

The women talked on about homes that they had come from with some sadness, and homes they were going to with some hope. They prattled on about daily tasks like cooking and mending and washing. Scintillating conversation. Nothing about the real world. Eventually, they returned to the wagons to knit sox or something. That just left three teen girls I'd met yesterday and the heavy-set boy. It was my chance to gather allies for an escape.

"Man, is this the pits or what?" I said to the other teens when the women had left. "When in the freaking hell are we going to stop?"

"Oh, we got a ways yet till nooning," the one called Abby answered. She was no more than fourteen, if that. Cute with a pixie face and a throaty voice. The girls dressed pretty much alike in the old-fashioned way, all in sunbonnets. Potential Rude Girls? Not likely. If my theory about this situation was right, these four were also serving time. I asked them if this was a tough-love operation.

"Tough love," Abby said with astonishment. "That's a funny thing to say. My parents are tough but fair, I suppose." Everyone agreed with that.

44

"Hell, come on. That's not what I mean and you know it." Their blank stares suggested they were worse off than I thought. I went a different way. "Have any of you got a cell phone?"

Georgia Whelan's daughter Lottie said, "You asked us that yesterday. It made no sense then and it makes no sense now. We don't know what a cell phone is."

She was fourteen, too, and a horrid little bitch. I knew this because I was one. Takes one to know one.

"She doesn't remember anything," Abby said to Lottie by way of explanation.

"I remember that," I snapped. "Forget it."

Quickly, it became clear none of them would step outside the scenario. Either brainwashed or sunk so deep into this fundamentalist crap that nothing would jar their belief system. Stockholm syndrome, I'd heard it called. Soon, the three girls returned to the wagons, leaving the funny looking boy with the blond ringlets walking beside me. One of the twins begged to be carried, so he lifted her up easily onto his back. The other begged me but with my arm still throbbing, no way.

"I never thought they'd leave," he said of the others. His voice was so soft and girlish. I suddenly realized with a shock he was a *she*.

"You're a girl!" I said astonished.

"Well, of course, I am. Why you want to say such a thing?"

"Why are you dressed like that?"

"You know Hannibal's got me working with the animals, besides the cooking."

I didn't know what she was talking about or who Hannibal was. What work made her dress like a boy? She might have been better off as one because as a girl, she was given the short stick. Her hair was frizzy and tangled; she was not at all pretty, with a florid, pudgy face. To go with that height, a head taller than me, she had muscular shoulders and wide hips. Nothing I might ever do could glam her up; a makeover was pointless. I was good, but not that good.

"So, who the hell are you?" I asked.

She giggled nervously, a high pitched sound that sent needles into my ears. She leaned in toward me. "I told Myra it was all an act. You're funning us on."

"Really?"

"I don't think you've lost your mind at all, Libby. No, ma'am, not you. Come on now. Own up to it. You're pulling my leg, aren't you?" She grinned, expecting me to admit such a stupid thing.

"I couldn't pull your leg, honey," I said heartlessly. "A team of Clydesdales couldn't pull your leg."

She flinched. In a nanosecond, her face broke into pieces of hurt and her eyes watered. I felt like an ass. That I *was* an ass hit me so hard I blinked. Why did I have to be so cruel? This was bad even for me. I hadn't always been that way.

"Sorry," I said. "I can be a bitch sometimes. Really, I didn't mean it."

She waved it away. "That's alright. I don't mind. I get it a lot."

"Not from me. Never again," I said, and meant it. "And do mind. Don't let people push you around, not me, not anyone."

"But we're best friends. So why are you shining us on?"

"Look, whoever you are, this is not meant to be mean, but I do not know you. And unless you tell me what the hell's going on here, I don't want to know you or anyone else."

That was not cruel, just the truth. Obviously the emotional type, her eyes lit with terrible revelation. "Oh, my God, Libby. You are addled. I'm so sorry. I...."

"Damn it! I'm not addled."

"Libby, I'm Sally Callahan. Don't you know me? We're best friends."

A sharp, cutting remark sprang to mind, *I would never be your best friend*, but I held it in check. I could read people, and this one was extremely lonely and fragile. I didn't need to be bitching on her. Likely she was in the same situation as I was, a juvee sent here for some kind of infraction in a too narrow world. Having friends here probably couldn't hurt. I made nice.

"I don't remember a damn thing before I broke my arm, Sally. People tell me I hit my head pretty hard, too, so there you have it." After a moment, I added, "I'm still the same person though."

"Well, you never cursed before." Suddenly, glancing over my shoulder, she gasped and a heartsick expression came into her eyes. I turned and saw a man riding toward us, drawing two horses behind.

"Who's that?" I asked.

"Mr. Hannibal Pierce." Her voice trembled with hate and fear.

He pulled up and stared at us for a moment, a small man with an Old Testament beard down to mid-chest and fierce, bloodshot eyes. He took this re-enactor crap to a new level with dirt and sweat stains on his shirt and something tiny squirming in his beard. Major gross out. Dear God, did the man ever wash? By the smell of him, I'd say not.

He said harshly to Sally, "Get back to the wagons and spell McCutcheon like you're supposed to." When she hesitated, about to speak, he rose in the stirrups. "Go on now, girl, before I take a strap to you."

Without a word, Sally set the twin on the ground and hurried off. Pierce stared at me for several seconds with a disapproving frown. Clearly, he didn't like me for some reason. The way he treated Sally, I didn't much like him either.

"You set my arm, Mr. Pierce."

"I did. I'm the closest thing this bunkum company has to a doctor."

Doctor? Him? Madness. I noticed the two horses he held by the reins, magnificent animals, both thoroughbreds.

"Fine horses."

"That they are, missy. That they are. Ambassador and Demetrius. Worth a small fortune when we get to the Promised Land."

Dismissing me, as if unworthy of his attention, he took out a small gold watch, studied it a moment, then rode off without another word. The Promised Land. How can you get there going in a circle?

The entire Quarles family and I slept in a single tent with a hung-up blanket separating the two adults. The next morning, Julia woke us up in the pre-dawn dark. Dead tired and annoyed, I rolled over, trying to go back to sleep. Caroline and the twins pounced on me, Caroline pinching my nose shut and the two younger girls playing with my ears and lips, and all having a merry time of it. Sleeping anymore this day was not going to happen.

"All right, all right, I'm getting up."

Had they left me to sleep it would have been impossible anyway because a loud and angry argument broke out minutes later between Henry and Joost, the hired man. It seemed with the terrible storm the other night and a hard long day yesterday, Joost had pulled some sort of guard duty and fallen asleep. Several horses had either wandered off or been stolen, as if anyone would come so far from anywhere just to steal a horse.

It was a stupid argument. I didn't know what Henry's problem was except that he was a bastard. They weren't even his horses. As Joost pointed out, the Quarles's animals were still in the herd. It didn't matter. Henry fired him on the spot. I heard the pleading in Joost's voice when he said he had a family to bring out and that he needed the job. Again to Henry, it didn't matter. He told the man this had not been the first time he'd failed in his work, but it would be the last.

"Gather your things out of the wagon. You are done."

Poor Joost went around camp asking everyone if they would take him on, but apparently he had a dodgy reputation for honesty and hard work, and no one offered to hire him. Sleeping on guard duty, it seemed, was worse than murder. At least they didn't shoot him. I realized these people were harder than Mrs. Guthrie, and that was clearly an achievement. A few minutes later, angry and forlorn, Joost returned with his horse, gathered a duffle from the wagon, and started out of camp. Julia caught him and gave him a cloth bag of food she'd hastily put together.

"Thankee, ma'am," he said, and then left without another word.

It was growing light, and cook fires flared up all around the camp. We ate our breakfast of biscuits, jam, and greasy meat in silence. It had occurred to me I could have slipped away and joined Joost since he was obviously returning to civilization, but I hesitated. Frankly, I didn't want to be out in this wilderness alone with the man. I didn't trust him all that much either. Still, the important thing was that there was some place to go nearby. If Joost could leave, I could leave.

Chapter 11

*I*n the heat of the late afternoon, I stood atop the highest hill within miles. A stiff breeze tossed about the gold medallion flowers and grass, and pinned my dress against my legs. A couple hundred feet below, the long wagon train crept on like a caterpillar in no particular hurry. I spotted the Quarles' two wagons about a third of the way back, Julia in her sunbonnet and red bandana, and Henry driving the second, his wide-brimmed hat pulled low over his eyes. My jailers. When I started climbing, I half expected one of them to order me back, but neither did. I thought I could just keep walking, and maybe I would if I saw a town or road from the top.

I saw nothing. Just more green hills, endless swells and undulations all the way to the far horizon. Not a telephone pole or tower. No roads or towns. Overhead was the massive 360-degree dome of sky. Not a contrail, not an airliner to be seen. Nothing. I felt the crush of overwhelming disappointment and loneliness. Where was everybody?

Nothing would compute. I knew something was vastly amiss. I wasn't stupid. Several things just didn't make sense. My missing fingers. The utter lack of technology. So much more. And today, out on the trail, we passed seven freshly dug graves. Graves for Christ's sake! I hoped they were part of the elaborate scenario of the program, but a niggling suspicion told me otherwise. Something very strange was going on. and I was not getting it.

Then, on a hill no more than a hundred yards away, movement caught my eye. Dogs! Four or five of them loping along just under the crest. My heart leapt. Finally, this at least was a sign of civilization. Where there were dogs, there were people. But as I watched them, euphoria turned bitter. Wolves! They were wolves! What could be farther from civilization than wolves? *Dear God, where was I?*

My parents had abandoned me here in this wilderness. That devastating realization now consumed my entire being. With a growing sense of despair, I started back down, back to my jailers. Passing among several boulders, I lost sight of the wagons and stopped, unwilling to go any farther. Unwilling to cry. But the urge to just fall down and not move was overpowering. Maybe, I could just wait here till the wagon train was gone, be rid of them once and for all, make my way out on foot. Maybe I was nowhere, but I had to be somewhere.

As I considered this, the sound of something approaching startled me. My first thought was the wolves! Instead, a young man was strolling down the hill toward me, someone I'd never seen before. He could be dangerous. After all, who knew what criminal activities these backwoods types were involved in? His hat sat at a slight angle. His reddish brown hair was sweaty with curls stuck to his forehead, and he had an annoying, self-assured smile. Without a word, he strode right up to me and kissed me. Took my face in his hands, and before I could say anything, kissed me. For an instant, gentle daggers threatened to undo me. I found myself responding without thinking. Then, I was furious. With my good arm, I punched him hard in the chest, shoving him backward. "Hey, dude! What the hell!"

His mouth dropped open in shock. I jabbed an accusing finger at him. "I don't know what freaking barn you grew up in, but where I come from you don't walk up and zoom on someone you don't even know. What kind of nutcase are you?"

Shocked, his lips moved but no sound came out.

"Say something, smart ass."

He couldn't. With another shove, I nearly knocked him over, then spun about and headed on down the hill, loudly leaving my final valediction. "God damn a-hole!"

I didn't need a psychiatrist to tell me my rage came from my frightening despair coupled with the humiliating fact I'd just responded to a kiss from somebody I didn't even know. My knees never went weak when Cal kissed me, nor did they this time, but something had happened. I had lost myself for an instant to a guy on first ignition, and I didn't like that, didn't like it at all. As I descended the slope, I told myself I would not look back, but I did. He was watching me go, looking at me as if I had sprouted wings.

Back with the wagons, I found Sally Callahan driving one of Pierce's three wagons. I pointed my assailant out to her as he loped down the hill. "Who is that?"

She was surprised. "That's Daniel, of course. Heavens, girl, you *have* lost your mind. He's been sparking around you ever since St. Jo." She giggled. "And you been sparking right back."

Oh, great. I understood what she meant by *sparking* well enough. He was somehow a boyfriend I'd made in the two weeks I figured I'd been here.

"Why haven't I seen him before?"

She giggled again. If she giggled one more time, I'd hit her. "I'd say you seen him lots."

"I mean since I lost my memory."

"He went hunting with the pilot a few days ago. Just got back with a deer, I heard." She grinned and winked. "I'm thinking you got a haunch of venison coming."

"Oh, goody."

As I watched, he jogged over to a wagon forty, fifty yards back, climbed up and took the reins from a woman I'd met this morning, the one named Myra, his mother I assumed.

This Daniel I didn't like at all, too brash, too sure of himself. But as I watched him, a second thought came to me. Maybe I could use him, use how he felt about me to escape. An ally who would walk through fire for me might be helpful. As he laughed at something his mother said, I hoped he would glance over at me. If he did, I'd give him a big fat grin and wave.

By the end of the long day's travel, I was suffering withdrawal symptoms. I missed my cell phone, texting my friends, having the Internet always available, the ability to do anything I wanted pretty much when I wanted. Right now, I needed to be talking to my girls and with Cal. He must be desperate. And Vanessa, that tramp, will no doubt move on him. I so needed a cell.

Admittedly, it was a pleasant evening. The sun still hung above the horizon. The air was clean with the fresh smell of the cottonwood trees that stood down by the river. In a way, I could understand what they saw in this kind of life, but that didn't mean I wanted any part of it.

After the evening meal, there was an impromptu dance, a hoedown or whatever they called it, something to keep the inmates pacified. Caroline tagged along with me. Huge Sally Callahan came in a long dress that did nothing to further her charms, Abby Rudabaugh and Lottie Whelan joined us. Two men played fiddles, another a harmonica, and a fourth a guitar, quite the band. The countless fires cast the dancers' shadows on the white canvas of the circled wagons. I marveled at their adherence to period details; their clothes, their choice of music and even their dance steps, very energetic with precise and swift movements, seemed authentic.

"Have you seen Putt yet?" Caroline asked me, trying to look over the heads of the dancers.

"Putt? Who's he now"

Lottie laughed at that. "You still got them bats in your belfry."

I gave her an icy look that didn't faze her.

"He's Daniel's brother," Caroline answered. "Remember? I told you about him."

"Oh, the one you plan to marry."

"That's him," she beamed.

"Sure she is." Lottie rolled her eyes.

And where was Daniel, the boy who kissed me today. I wondered whether he was one of the juvees like me, or part of the tough-love staff. Either way, I hoped to hook up with him. Sally was tapping her foot in time to the music. "Oh, I hope one of the boys asks me to dance," she said. "We used to dance all the time in the old country."

Lottie said, "For Saint Pete's sake, Sally, don't be whining on. No boy's going to ask you to dance, lessen it's a joke. Better you get used to it. They ain't blind."

Sally winced and shriveled. Big as a house, I thought she should be able to defend herself, but for whatever reason, she wouldn't. Not for me to do it. I wasn't her protector. When Lottie turned her attention to Caroline, though, it was different. The little bitch put a hand on the girl's shoulder. "Now, you ain't any better off than Sally. Why, look at them eyes. 'Cock-eyed Caroline Quarles' everyone calls you. You got one looking straight ahead and t'other looking hard at the back of your nose. Putt ain't no ways interested in you, so best stop looking for him."

Suddenly enraged, I grabbed her wrist and removed her hand from Caroline's shoulder, spinning her toward me. "Speak to her that way again, and I'll rearrange your face." My voice was cold and hard. I'd never been in a fight in my life, but she didn't know that. Most of us teens were juvees or parent-challenged, and probably no one outside of the admin staff knew why I was here. As far as Lottie knew, I could be a gangbanger ready to slit her throat. I added, "If you're going to be an ass, go stand someplace else."

Taken aback, she swallowed. "Sorry. I meant no offense." Like hell you didn't.

That's when Daniel arrived with two other young men and his brother Putt. Even with my arm in a sling and still hurting, I hoped he would walk straight up to me and ask me to dance, but instead he fell into conversation with two older men. There had been much talk about him today by the other girls in the company, most with the hots for him. He didn't come over to us, but Putt did. With a wide grin, he grabbed Caroline's hand and disappeared with her among the dancers, but not before she glanced back at Lottie and stuck out her tongue.

By now, with the insistent rhythm of the music, I was ready to give this barnyard dance a whirl, just so long as none of the Rude Girls ever knew about it. Much to my disappointment, Daniel asked a girl I didn't know to dance. Jealousy, the green-eyed monster, reared up in my head. Me! And anger. If he was supposed to be 'sparking' me, why had he just dissed me?

The two other young men that had arrived with him, the Hancock brothers, Jesse and Billy, were broad-shouldered farm boys I'd met yesterday. They came over to where we were standing, and Billy asked Lottie to dance.

"That arm of yours hurting too much to dance, Miss Libby?" Jesse asked.

By way of an answer, I took his arm and rushed out into the crowd, picking up the steps rather easily, ignoring the occasional shock of pain in my arm. After the second dance, I noticed Sally still standing alone, tapping her foot. "Jesse, I want you to ask Sally to dance."

"Me? Come on now. I like Old Sal, but I got no desire to dance with the girl. I got my feet to think about."

I stopped right then and walked back to Sally, taking her by the arm. "Let's show them how to do this."

She squealed with delight and we rushed in among the dancers. Belying her size, she was a terrific dancer, even graceful, making up for all my missteps. After a couple more turns, my arm began to throb, and I retreated with Sally to the sidelines.

Throughout the next hour, I watched Daniel with just about every available girl but me. He was so friendly that everyone liked him, one of those people that other people naturally gravitated to. I was surprised at how much his actions bothered me. What did he mean to me? Nothing. But I remembered the kiss from that afternoon, at once tender and fierce. And I remembered how it made me feel, like it was the first time I'd ever been kissed.

The last person he danced with was Lottie Whelan, which stung me like a needle. A jealous schoolgirl. That was me. Finally, he begged off from a group of insistent younger girls, telling them how much he'd love to stay and dance with them, but he had guard duty first up that night and could not be late. As he was leaving, his eyes fell on me. My expression must have reflected my anger and disappointment. At least, he seemed momentarily sorry and embarrassed, but didn't stop to speak, heading instead for the pasture where the horses and cattle were.

That night in the Quarles tent, lying on a pallet that seemed like it was made out of gravel, I could not sleep. I couldn't get the evening out of my mind. Any young man would do to help me escape, so why was I caught up in this Daniel fixation? I dismissed it and him. Yet as I fell into that nether state between sleep and wakefulness, I pictured him and couldn't wait till the next day when I could see him again.

Chapter 12

It seemed odd that I had a horse. Why in the world would I be given a horse? This past year in health class at Old Rectum we were given eggs for a week to care for as if they were our new born infants and then we were to write a report about our earth-shattering experience. Treasure the dumb egg, protect it and keep it safe until the end of the week when, as I suggested to the teacher, we could make an omelet. Because I was such a slacker, he bet me an A against an F that my egg would never make it to week's end. He gave me one with a specific blemish so I could not substitute. So I hardboiled it. Mr. Lopez never knew the difference.

But that was an egg. This was a live horse. Crazy!

After night camp was set up, I asked Caroline to show it to me, so we went out to the horse herd. I wanted to see how hard or easy it would be to take it and make for the nearest highway. My feelings were uneasy about this animal though. After Quantum Leap had to be put down, I had wanted nothing to do with horses ever again. Didn't want to ride them, didn't want to get anywhere near them. Anytime a memory of Quantum made its way into my thoughts, it hurt so much I almost cried. Almost. Night dreams were something different. They came often..

With the wagon train circled for the evening, chores done, tents up, fires started and supper begun, Caroline and I wandered in among the herd. A couple riders watched over it as the horses nibbled at the grass.

"There she is," Caroline said. "That's Iris."

"Oh, my God," I blurted out in horror. I'd never seen a more repulsive looking animal, a short, stocky, bandy-legged grey, as ugly as lumpy oatmeal, the ugliest horse I'd even seen. Not in the same universe as Quantum Leap.

When we approached, she raised her head, her nostrils flaring, and her eyes white in alarm as she sized us up warily. I knew a dangerous horse when I saw one and at first got no closer than a few feet. Escape on her? I doubted if she could make a mile at anything faster than a walk. I'd have to steal another.

"So, this is my horse?"

"Yes, indeed."

"Was I being punished for something?"

"Ha, ha. No, silly. Pa won't let anyone else ride her. She'll throw anyone who tries except you. No one wants to."

"I can understand why." Finally, taking my life in my hands, I went to her and tried to rub her nose, but she snorted and backed away. Maybe she knew what I thought of her.

"That's funny. Iris's never done that before with you," Caroline said. "It's like she doesn't even know you."

As the mare eyed me, I saw her confusion and fear, but also, unmistakably, her intelligence. She was trying to understand me and couldn't. Maybe, I was giving this ugly, broken-down nag too much human emotion, as if it mattered, but it was what I sensed. Paula Masters, horse whisperer.

"Easy, girl," I muttered softly, taking another step toward her. She rose up in fury, and I backpedaled quickly.

"Lord a' mercy, Libby! It's like she was the one got knocked on the head instead of you," Caroline said, astonished.

"What good to me is a horse I can't ride?"

"Maybe she's got something wrong with her."

This animal was useless. "I don't care. Let's head back."

Once again among the wagons, Caroline mentioned, "Pa said Little George and me will get our own horses when we get to Oregon."

"Yeah, sure, Oregon. Look, kid, I know we aren't going to Oregon, so you don't have to play that game with me."

"We're not?" She was confused. "Then where are we going?"

"In circles."

For a moment she looked mystified, then laughed, gave me a quick hug and laughed again. "You're funnier than you used to be."

From a distance, I spotted the Quarles' wagons, and my heart shot a mini-burst of adrenalin. Daniel was sitting on a keg by the fire, turning a slab of meat on a spit while the two families watched or worked on preparing the dinner. Actually, the men watched and the women worked. I'd not seen him all day, and I had looked. It seemed he'd ridden off somewhere with the person everyone called "the pilot" to do God knows what. Probably slipping off somewhere to get a burger or a pizza. That's what I'd do.

Caroline held me back with her hand. "Wait. There's Putt."

Sitting beside his brother Daniel, the boy had a corncob pipe stuck in his mouth like he was Huck Finn, listening as if with great wisdom to the adults talking. Since last night, I'd learned a lot more about the infamous Putnam Langdon. Everyone loved him and hated him. A trickster, a scamp, a merry prankster, he was blamed for everything wrong that happened to the company from spoiled milk to lost cattle. He kept the adults of this operation in constant fear and the children in constant laughter. I admired him because he'd actually never been caught at it.

Caroline, his chief acolyte, had regaled me with all his escapades. Her favorite was when he switched the jars containing Mr. Granby's ivory false teeth with Old Lady Branson's wooden ones. Old and doddering, neither noticed till they began eating breakfast. Except for the two victims, people laughed uproariously for days. Everyone knew it had been Putt, but no one could prove it. Only Caroline knew for sure, and she would never betray him. I wondered what he would think about my near-naked dash through the auditorium.

My one question was whether he, in fact, was Daniel's brother, or like me, a juvee given a family pedigree and placed here to have his evil ways wrestled away. If that was the case, the program was not working for him anymore than it was for me.

Caroline yanked a long blade of grass, raced along the shadows of the wagons, and actually got on the ground. She slithered forward like a thief stealing into camp. With the grass, she rose up behind Putt and tickled his ear. Not noticing it was her, he swiped at it absently with his hand. Leaning her head close, she made a sound exactly like a bee, then pinched his earlobe. In alarm, Putt jumped almost into the fire. Everyone laughed. Screaming in delight, Caroline ran while Putt grabbed a nearby bucket of water and gave chase. Barefoot, she was fast, but he finally caught up and drenched her.

With feigned sternness, Julia ordered, "Now, you two stop that carrying on. Caroline, you go into the wagon and change that dress."

Myra Langdon scolded her son, "Putt, you go down to the river and fill that bucket up. You're the one emptied it."

"Yes, ma'am." With freckles crawling across the bridge of his nose, he was blessed with the most innocent of faces, perfect for a little con man. Here was my ally.

Julia saw me at the edge of the wagons. "Now, there she is. I told you she hadn't been swallowed up by the earth. Come, Libby, sit beside Daniel."

Chapter 13

As I approached the fire, Julia and Myra grinned at each other, the matchmakers. At hearing Libby, my scenario name, Daniel glanced back, raising his eyebrows in mock fear as if expecting me to throw something at him. I took the stool beside him. I was unaccountably nervous, looking straight ahead and saying nothing. A good thing my nervousness often seemed like aloofness to others.

Daniel playfully asked, "You're not going to hit me again, are you?"

"I didn't hit you."

"You most certainly did." With a mock grimace, he rubbed his chest. "Yesterday afternoon on the hill. You pack quite a wallop, too. Practically killed me."

His eyes did not waver from mine. I said, "You really know what you're doing with that spit? You do all the Langdon cooking?"

He didn't take the offense I meant, smiling easily. "Not all, but some. My own fault. Langdon family rule. You shoot it, you cook it. Fitz and me been hunting for days looking for buffalo, but couldn't find nary a fresh track. Then yesterday morning we come across this buck, and I shot it."

Myra chuckled. "Like most Langdon family rules, too easily broken. My girls and I do most of the cooking."

I did not believe in love at first sight, but admittedly I had felt something, a fine dizziness at first seeing him yesterday. There was a part of me that wanted to drag him off into the trees along the river right now, but I needed to be careful. In reality, this fellow could be...well, I didn't know what he was. A simple reenactor or a tough-love counselor. Who could know? I didn't. And any kind of romance ain't going to happen. But that didn't mean I couldn't play him. Get him to help me. And enjoy it while it lasted.

For dinner, we had Daniel's venison, beans and rice, cornbread, and some mustard greens. I found the gamey taste of the meat hard to choke down, but I was so hungry that I ate my fill, especially of the cornbread and rice. Dessert was a surprise, a delicious apple pie with such light crust it flaked off on my tongue. All washed down with strong tea. I asked if we could score some ice cream, it would go great with the pie, but I got a blank stare from everyone. I was getting tired of people treating me like I'd lost my mind.

Julia put a hand on my arm. "I know it's your favorite, Libby, but we have no way we can make ice cream out here."

Now, I couldn't stop thinking about ice cream. The rest of the dinner talk was mostly about farm animals—how enthralling—and about the long, long journey ahead. Indeed, if you're going in circles, the trek could be endless. And about being in Pawnee country. Those are Indians. Strange indeed.

"Since there's no real Indian danger, why circle the wagons?" I asked. "Just playing the game, I guess."

"Well, that's a relief, Pa," Isaac said with a smirk. "Don't have to worry about no Pawnee no more. And Sioux up ahead? Guess not them either."

"Leave her be, son," Henry said.

Julia said, "It makes a corral for the animals. Everyone keeps the oxen and a couple of their horses inside." I gave her a sarcastic thumbs-up. She glanced at Henry, then stared down at the plate of apple pie on her lap.

"Why are you here?" I asked all of them. "I mean you all must have real homes somewhere. Why be out here living in a wagon?"

No one answered for a long time. Then Henry, of all people, said, "I guess we come to see the elephant."

Wait! What freaking elephant!

Mr. Langdon removed the pipe from his mouth and tapped it on his hand. "I suppose that does explain it. We're all on this road so's we can see that elephant."

"What elephant?" I asked, astonished.

Everyone laughed. This was maddening. I tuned the conversation out after that, thinking how utterly weird all this was and what a story I would tell the

Rude Girls when I got back. Out of the corner of my eye, I studied Daniel, how he would listen so intently when someone was talking to him, as if this person or that person had the most important thing to say he had ever heard. To him, everyone merited the same full measure of respect. He was so unlike the boys I knew back in Pacific Palisades. He could not be a juvy. With a rifle, he had to be staff. I was disappointed in that.

Abruptly, I was drawn back into the group by the arrival at our campfire of the wagon train's leader, Captain Warren. These people were just incredible! Like an Old West gunfighter, he wore two ancient pistols in his belt. In fact, most of the men wore handguns, which was unnerving. This sure couldn't be California. Daniel had a rifle propped against his leg, as if he might need it quickly. Did they expect black ops helicopters to descend on them at any moment?

Julia poured Captain Warren a cup of tea, and he squatted by the fire, pushing his hat back on his head. "This is good tea, Mrs. Quarles. Taste like it's got a spot of lemon in it."

"Thank you, captain," she replied with a nod. "I put a dab of extract in each pot."

"Well, it surely is good."

Lemon extract in tea. Wow, I was learning something important here.

About fifty, he had a genial manner with warm brown eyes and a broad, fleshy nose, but I told myself to make no mistakes with him. This was the enemy. As the leader of this rolling prison, he was my chief jailer. Ultimately, he'd be the one I was escaping.

"Going to be a tough crossing tomorrow," he said. "River's up and moving fast, but I figure we can make it across in three hours and be on our way."

"To the next river crossing," Henry said with a harumph. It was the closest he could come to making a joke.

Warren smiled. "You're right there. Fitzpatrick says we will cross more than a thousand rivers before we get where we're going. I think maybe he exaggerates, but not by much." He took a sip of his tea and paused over his next words. "Pawnees are bad. They steal horses when they can, so we need to keep up a sharp vigil. But soon we'll be coming onto Sioux country. They're worse. Much worse. They will likely kill us as look at us."

Everyone seemed to take this seriously. This would make a good reality TV show, except not with me in it. He went on. "Fitz says there's one in particular causing all kinds of trouble for travelers. His name is Brings Thunder, and he's one mean Indian. Sometimes hunts whites alone. You don't want to be caught out with him because he kills quick and rides on quicker. Even got Fitz worried. You children don't want to stray too far from the wagons."

Pawnee and Sioux. Sure. I gave a little chortle that got everyone to glance my way.

"Can't the army do something?" Sam Langdon asked.

"Not enough army to patrol out this way. We'll need to take care of ourselves."

What silly talk! Let them play their game, I thought. It meant nothing to me. I'd be gone soon enough. That's when he said something that had my heart racing. "After we cross tomorrow, we have a straight run up to the Platte. We're less than a day out from Fort Kearny. It's a new military post. Should reach there tomorrow afternoon sometime. They got a sutler's store, so we can stock up on items we might need for the long haul."

Abruptly, I turned my head and fixed my eyes on him. That meant we would be stopping someplace where there was civilization. A military post! A phone. A hospital. I could even refuse to go on, or run off till they had gone. I was aching to see my parents and Josh and my friends again, and now I would. Finally, the answer had presented itself. Get to the army post.

Escape.

When Captain Warren moved on to another campfire, I whispered to Daniel, "Meet me down by the river. One hour."

When twilight had come, I waited for Daniel by the river. I wanted to enlist his help for tomorrow in case Captain Warren or Henry gave me problems when I tried to get away. On the other side of the river, the crest of a saddleback hill was etched sharply against the paling sky. From camp came the sound of someone tuning a violin. Another dance? Didn't these people ever get tired?

In the growing darkness, I thought of my family, my father over in Europe, my mother and brother at home, all going through their daily lives without me, as if I had never existed. As much as I argued with my mother, I loved her and missed her. And Josh I missed so much. Did he think I had abandoned him? That thought made me tear up. What had mom told him about me? That I had failed the family and had to be sent away for everyone's good? I tried telling myself they were only a short airplane hop away, but some dark sense told me they were much, much farther. I had to get away and get back home.

Suddenly, something out on the river caught my eye. A small crib with a baby in it was floating downstream. I gasped. Dear God! Who would do something like that? I waited as it neared the bank, then frantically waded out and with my good arm snatched the baby out of its cradle. It was just a wooden doll. I sighed heavily in relief.

"What are you doing?" Daniel called from the bank.

I jumped, giving a squeak of alarm. "You scared me. Geez."

"You'll drown out there."

I held the doll up and splashed back toward shore. "This was in a cradle floating down the river. I thought it was real for a second."

He took me by the elbow and guided me higher up onto the bank. That touch sent off Fourth of July fireworks in me. I didn't need a Teen Vogue article to tell me I was falling for this guy. Breathless and momentarily brain-locked, I clung to him like an awkward ninth grader.

When I managed to get the stupid grin off my face, I said, "You needn't worry. I was hardly out far."

"I'll always worry about you, Libby." Holding my shoulders in his hands, he stared at me, clearly on the cusp of leaning down to kiss me. Do it. Do it! Instead, he released me and stepped back. "They say you can't remember a thing."

I sighed. "Nothing of this wagon train anyway. A few days maybe."

"You don't remember about you and me?"

I shook my head. Better not lie about that. Too easily found out. Even in the pale light, I could see his frown. Quickly, I added a workable lie, "I feel a connection to you, as if you are important to me. Are you?"

I felt a twinge of guilt using his feelings for my own purposes. What I knew already about him was that he was popular, well thought of, and he was capable. I mean, he shot a deer, after all.

"Yes, I think so," he answered simply. "We were important to each other. I hope we still are."

I nodded and said softly, "So do I. Tell me about us, Daniel."

It was a subject he warmed to quickly. In a rush, he told me how we had met in St. Jo when the emigrants came together to form the Warren Company. How his mother and Julia had been childhood friends, so when meeting up again, their families quickly became close. How we soon fell in love, or at least he did. Now, he guessed he had to start all over again.

I put my hand on his chest. "Are you saying you're in love with me?"

"Yes. It's no secret."

It was what I wanted to hear. No scenario here, and that made everything simpler. "Then you would never hurt me, would you? You would help me if I needed it, wouldn't you?"

"Of course."

"Were we lovers?" I asked, a little playfully.

"Yes, we were lovers."

"I hope you used a condom."

"A what?"

"A condom, farm boy," I said, suddenly upset. Oddly, if we had made love, even consensual, which I'm sure it was, it felt like it took place without my consent if I couldn't even remember it. "If you made love to me, you better have used a condom. I do not want to get pregnant. My mother would really freak."

His bewildered expression dissolved into one of alarm. "No, you misunderstand, Libby. Laws, we did not, er, make love. I was sparking, courting. That's the lovemaking. That's all. I took no advantage. I swear."

"You sure?"

"Yes." He gave a wicked grin. "I think I'd remember it, even if you don't."

"What? You don't think I'm pretty enough?"

"Well, yes, I…I do, but…."

"Well, what did we do?"

"Do?"

Now, he was confused. I tugged playfully at the button on his shirt. "Yes, do. Did you, like, even kiss me? Did you think enough of me to even do that?"

"Yes, we kissed," he said, "a lot."

Surprising him, I put my hand on the back of his neck, drew him down and kissed him. His hands slid down my back to my ass, and he pressed me to him. Sexual voltage surged through my body. I felt his hammer and tong growing larger against me and wondered if his aw-shucks restraint would hold if I pushed him further. That would complicate things too much, and after a bit I forced myself to push him back gently with my good arm.

Sighing, he thrust his hands in his pockets. I could tell he was frustrated.

"Be patient with me, Daniel."

"Patience," he coughed the word harshly.

"Daniel, when we get to Fort Kearney tomorrow, I may need your help with something. Will you help me? Will you promise to help me?"

He focused on my request. "Yes, of course, Libby. Anything."

I kissed his cheek. "Thank you. Now, I want to be alone for awhile. There are some things I need to clear up in my mind."

"I'll stay with you. You shouldn't be out here alone at night. It's not safe."

"I'll be all right. Just go." When he hesitated, I said sharply again, "Just go."

It took him a moment more but he left. When he was gone, I stepped to the water's edge. Darkness had fully settled, a panoply of stars spreading across the sky much more strikingly than in Pacific Palisade. A damp chill rose up from the water. Birds sang, crickets chirped. At that moment, my longing for home was so strong, so overwhelming, that it felt like a clamp on my chest. My memory contained only three days here. That was enough. Tomorrow, I would be on my way home.

Then a premonition hit me hard: I would never see my family again. The belief so strong I gasped. I looked around in desperation, as if answers were out there in the darkness somewhere. No! I would see them again. I would. I considered walking away now. I might make Fort Kearny by morning and be done with it. It couldn't be that far. But which way was it?

Suddenly, movement on the other side of the river drew me back to the moment. Three shadowy figures advanced slowly along the opposite bank, frequently stopping, then moving on again. Maybe, they came from a nearby town. I could shout out to them and ask for help, but their odd behavior frightened me. Just one more bizarre thing in this bizarre world. With growing fear, I slipped cautiously away from the trees and hurried back to the wagons.

Chapter 14

Fort Kearny was just over the next ridge, Putt announced to the group. According to Captain Warren, the military did not allow us to camp within three miles of the fort. A precaution against terrorists, I presumed. Nearly a hundred of us from the wagons churned up a big dust cloud. I was riding double with Caroline on a gentler horse than Iris, flanked by Daniel and Putt on bay mounts. Anticipation had welled up in me so much it gave me the hiccups. The freaking hiccups! Daniel thought it hilarious. Caroline and Putt shrieked with laughter.

Walking in front, Henry strode stiff-backed like a high school principal leading his students on a field trip. I couldn't imagine what the soldiers would think when all these reenactors came over the rise as if out of the nineteenth century and marched down on them. Immediately when I got to the fort, I planned to claim sanctuary, stating I didn't belong with these people. Claim I'd been kidnapped, if I had to. After they saw these ragtag fundamentalists, they would surely take me in, or at least allow me to call my mother. But when we topped the crest and I saw Fort Kearny laying before us, my heart broke apart.

"My God," I whispered, devastated, pulling up on the horse.

"What's wrong?" Daniel asked.

I did not answer. Below was no military post. Sprawling along a huge brownish river were several rustic buildings, maybe twenty. Men in odd uniform dress—or undress, more like it—lounged outside two long mud-brick structures that had grass roofs. There were no highways. No cars. No MPs. Only horse drawn wagons coming and going.

We moved on down to the buildings. When I saw the "soldiers", my alarm grew even worse. Soldiers? Hardly. More reenactors. And slovenly ones at that with unkempt hair and beards. Rough men more like convicts than soldiers. Several were even barefoot. Hygiene was clearly not a priority here. How could this be a military post? The answer was, it was not. My disappointment was overwhelming.

Henry led a group of us up to one of the flat buildings. "I'm told this here's the sutler's store," he said. "Now don't buy all the poor man's stock. We need to think of other emigrants."

In a daze, I could barely move. I couldn't comprehend this. The store just didn't look right, no building standards at all, roughhewn wood, no electric or telephone wires, but a small glass window near the door.

A couple soldiers passed by in their frightfully old costumes. "You folks come to swindle Old Man Parsons?" one asked, laughing.

"That's the idea," Sam Langdon said with a friendly grin. Had everyone gone mad?

I told myself someone here had to have a cell phone at least. Prudence dictated that. You had to be able to call 911 for medical emergencies. You had to! I would get my hands on one, even if I had to beg, threaten or steal.

Daniel helped Caroline down, then held me by the waist and set me on the ground. "I hear they got some mighty pleasing…"

I strode past him into the store.

Inside, I expected to see a few vending machines and racks of chips, candy, other odds and ends, but there was none of that. It was a junk store. Shoddy camping gear. Tin cups and plates. Tools like picks and shovels. Oddly colored glass tumblers and thick wine glasses. Brass candlesticks. Wooden toys like wagons, horses and soldiers. And a couple dolls like the one I found floating in the river last night. On the floor by the counter lay a stack of smelly furs.

But nowhere a phone.

A middle-aged man stood behind the counter, grinning with a mouthful of crooked, yellow teeth. Spread out before him were a pile of beef jerky, hard stick candy in a jar and a stack of flat biscuits. There were also two tumblers of what looked like lemonade. Several people lined up at the counter to pay a coin and drink from the same two filthy glasses.

Daniel came up beside me. "You want some lemonade, Libby?"

"I think not."

I went up to the clerk and tried to get his attention. He was helping a woman with a bolt of cloth, while parceling out candy to children and lemonade to others. A multitasker. I noticed a newspaper on the counter, the New York Herald, one of those old reproductions like a front page of the stock market crash or the bombing of Pearl Harbor. It seemed well used, but was not chemically faded enough to be a good replication.

I scanned it quickly. March 12, 1848. The big headline was: *Victory! Mexican War Ends!* Another: *Fremont Court-Martialed.* The rest of the stories were local New York news, mostly society things like a soiree held at Lafayette Place that only a chosen few were invited to. I knew New York society was the nineteenth century's equivalent to reality TV, people everywhere followed it, so whoever worked up this paper knew history.

"Will you look at that," Myra Langdon said eagerly, picking up the newspaper and studying it. Two other women glanced over her shoulder. She shoved it at me. "Read it aloud for us, Libby. You got the best schooling."

"You read it," I snapped.

"Well, all right, but you know I don't read like you."

With the eagerness of someone who'd been stranded on a deserted island for the last twenty years, she began stuttering over this reproduction as if it were real. Several people gathered about her. A grown woman reading no better than a third grader seemed odd. I got tired of waiting for the clerk and pushed to the front of the line.

"Libby Quarles, you wait your turn," Georgia Whelan, the famous canner of fruits and veggies, demanded.

I ignored her. "Sir, please, I will give you a hundred dollars for the use of your cell phone." He glanced at me with a seriously baffled expression.

"Don't mind her," Georgia said to him. "She recently got a knock on her head."

I shot her a death glare, then turned back to the clerk. "I'll give you five hundred dollars for the use of a cell phone."

He looked at me, puzzled. "A what, missy?"

"Jesus, a cell phone! You've heard of a cell phone," I shrieked.

Everyone in the store stopped what they were doing to stare at me. My voice trembled. "Please, sir, you must have a cell phone."

"I got good products here, young miss," he said. "You might find it somewhere. Who knows? Just look around a bit."

My blood drained out of me. A sudden overwhelming desperation took hold. In my mind I saw that pack of wolves on the hillside now upon me, savaging me. I could hardly deny it anymore. Something was wrong, very, very wrong. The man said something else, but I barely heard him. Tears welled up in my eyes, and I pushed my way back from the counter.

"Libby, lemonade's only a nickel," Daniel said. "I can get a glass for the both of us."

I screamed at him, "I don't want any God damn lemonade!"

Henry was coming toward me, scowling. I rushed from the store. Outside, I leaned against the glass of the front window, wiping my eyes and trying to gather my senses. Nothing fit. Nothing would compute. I groped for answers, anything that would explain what was going on, but found none. Maybe, I'd missed something inside, I thought in desperation. Maybe there was more to the store than I'd seen. Something else. I turned to look through the window and then I received the greatest shock of my life, of a thousand lives. Something so horrendous it struck me down right there and left me dead in my heart and mind.

I saw my reflection.

I was looking at someone who wasn't me, looked nothing like me. I moved back a step to make sure it was my mirror image. It was! Oh, dear God, it was. I, Paula Masters, was gloriously blond and pretty. This creature was not. She had a plain oval face with a straight nose, dull brown hair and colorless grey eyes that stared back at me with freaky alarm, like she came from a madhouse.

She had…I had!

A nightmare had wrapped me in its black tentacles. I stumbled back from the window and began screaming. I don't remember stopping.

Chapter 15

That reflection in the store window hurled me into oblivion. My mind could not handle it. After Fort Kearny, I was unable to speak, barely able to perceive the world around me. Brain lock. Catatonia. A waking coma.

In the days since my awakening here, I had come across many clues to my true situation, but my mind couldn't grasp them. How do you go from the twenty-first century to the nineteenth in the blink of an eye? How does your mind accept such a thing? It can't. Not even when you get hit over the head with it, which was what happened to me when I saw someone else staring back at me from my reflection in the store window. Then I knew. That newspaper was real. It was 1848.

When these people took up their journey again, I sat in the rocker in the wagon Julia drove. Mile after mile swept by in one slow blur. With my mind and heart numb, I processed the world slowly and disjointedly, sometimes picking up something that occurred in the morning and slotting it into the evening. My mind became a Picasso painting.

Julia fed me. Gave me water. Walked me out with the other women to help me release my bowels. She told me how much she loved me. I guessed she was this creature's mother, all right. Several people came to visit me. Caroline, my 'sister,' talked to me as if nothing was wrong at all, dropping bugs, frogs and snakes into my lap. I made no reaction. But Julia got angry with her. "Caroline! If I've told you once, I've told you a thousand times, do not play with snakes. They are dangerous. You hear me? And stop bothering your sister with those things."

"Yes, ma'am." Caroline said something else, but I did not process it till later. She said, "Mama, I do know the difference between a good snake and a bad snake."

After a few days or maybe a few hours, the word *cholera* floated about in the air like a smothering fog. Terror was attached to it. It did nothing to break my stupor.

The twins were always around playing, acting as if I were part of their games, and occasionally sitting in my lap. They tied ribbons in my hair and around my ears and my good arm. One of them stuck two ribbons up my nose like I was running pink snot. I think it was Seneca, but by the time I processed it, she had been gone for hours. I couldn't tell them apart anyway. They laughed hysterically as I sneezed out the ribbons.

Once again, I sensed fear thick in the air and it all centered on cholera. Myra was talking to Julia. "Lord, Lord, the cholera is raging everywhere around us," she said breathlessly. "Two companies farther up the road and one behind have been hit hard. There's many dying and us in the middle. Oh, Julia, it's going to hit us."

"We don't know that for sure."

"Why can't nobody do nothing?" Silence followed maybe for a few seconds, maybe into a different conversation later, but it seemed to all fit together. "I worry about Sam. If the cholera takes him, what would happen to me and the children?"

"God forbid it should, but you're a strong woman, Myra. The boys are old enough and strong, too. You'll manage. No good can come of worrying yourself sick."

"That's easy for you to say, Julia. You're educated."

"That won't keep the grim reaper away. Or get me enough work to support my family if the Lord takes Henry."

"All this for Oregon," Myra said derisively.

"Yes, for Oregon."

Caroline was laughing, but I couldn't tell if that was at the same time Myra was speaking about cholera or some other time. Henry, my nineteenth century father, stopped a couple times to tell me he was sorry, real sorry, he couldn't allow me more schooling. He knew I was real smart, like my ma, but I had been needed, just like Isaac, to keep the business afloat. This was more excuse than apology, and more than he would have ever given if I wasn't out of my mind.

Even Isaac came to visit me with Putt. They talked to me and each other about horses and rifles and Indians, eager to see the wild Sioux.

At camp each night, the Quarles family would put me out by the fire in the rocking chair, kind of a circus attraction, and Sally Callahan, Lottie Whelan, Abby Rudabaugh, and several others came by to offer me encouragement and commiserate with Julia.

One morning, Daniel climbed into the back of the wagon and took my hand in both his and said he wanted to marry me. When I processed that bit of data, I was thinking, I knew it already, dude. Not very ballsy to say it when I'm brain dead. He talked of his dream, of him and me starting a ranch out in Oregon Territory with a gristmill, blacksmith shop, orange orchard and vegetable garden. Sounded charming. And five children. You've got to be kidding!

Truth was, he loved Libby Quarles, not Paula Masters. This Libby creature was popular. Everyone liked her for who she was, not her golden looks, because she didn't have any. People cared about her more than anyone ever did Paula Masters in the twenty-first century. There, they cared about my image and Rude Girl status. Libby, everyone loved. I could never live up to that.

Where was she anyway? What had happened to her? Why was I now her? I had no answers. Even if my brain circuitry had not crashed, I would have no answers.

I kept hearing the word Oregon as if it were the Promised Land, the place everyone had to reach. *Come. Finish the journey.* Those words I had heard twice. Once in the hallucination with the weird Indian and then when I crossed over from my time to this one. Was that it? Was that why I was here? I had to finish Libby's journey to Oregon, then I could go home? If that was true, in my heart of hearts, I didn't think I could make it all the way to Oregon.

As the days grew hotter, thunderstorms frequented the afternoons, nuclear eruptions of rain, wind and noise, I still felt safe in my cocoon. Often, I couldn't tell phantoms from reality.

A floating butterfly the size of an eagle, a golden sunset one evening by the fire, Putt and Isaac in the wagon with me trying to tickle me back into the world, but failing to waken my mind. With his finger and an ink bottle, Putt wrote something on my forehead, which made Isaac laugh hysterically. Great. People were writing graffiti on my skull.

"Come on, Libby, old girl. I know you're in there. Come back to us," Putt said. "You're too good a gal to get lost in your head. I know you can hear me. You come back, I promise to tell you all my secrets, like how to make a cow's milk curdle in the teat."

"That ought to bring her back," Isaac said sarcastically.

Putt shrugged. "You come up with something then."

"Forget it. She's got the mind of a rock. Let's go."

Nothing worked. My mind had gone to some dark, safe place where it could heal its wounds and maybe never come back as long as I remained in this century. I didn't respond to anyone. I perceived the sheer superficial knowledge of existence, which was like a TV flickering in front of me. I did wonder once or twice what Putt had written on my head.

Then something happened that drew me back to reality. Barnaby Pierce, the son of the estimable Hannibal, came to see me. He climbed into the back of the wagon, glancing about to make sure no one was watching. "You truly crazy, gal?" he asked, laughing nervously, the strong smell of cow crap invading my nostrils. I felt an overwhelming sense of disgust.

In the front, Julia was driving the oxen, singing a song that had some pleasant familiarity. She turned around. "Why, Barnaby Pierce, what are you doing here?"

He waved at her. "Hello, Mrs. Quarles. Just visiting Libby."

"Well, that's sweet of you. Go on. Talk to her. Do her good."

She turned back around and took up her singing again, leaving me helpless with this toad.

Squatting, he leaned in toward me and whispered, "Well, ain't you the pretty one, Libby. I figger you'd make a man the perfect wife now. Can't talk back. Don't put up no fuss or fight when a man gets his urges. Yes, sir, the perfect wife." He giggled. "Maybe, I'll marry you now."

I made no response at all, hardly aware of him except for the overwhelming odor. He held his hand in front of my eyes and waved it. There was nothing for me to see.

"Haw!" he barked. "You damned hollow head." He struck my head with his knuckles. "Haw!" Then he groped my breast, guffawing. "Haw, haw."

That's what did it. I came smack out of my stupor, grabbed an iron skillet hanging by a hook, and cracked him on the side of the head so hard the pan rang like a bell and knocked him clear out of the wagon. I dropped the skillet and retreated back into my cocoon of protection, but only this time I was faking. Julia glanced back and saw just me sitting alone.

Back to reality, I had to sort out what was going on and what to do. Thank you, Barnaby. I knew I was in the nineteenth century on the Oregon Trail, 1848. There were no cars, no airplanes, no iPhones, no Blackberries, no Internet, no TV, no movies, no modern doctors, no modern hospitals, no wonder drugs. And no Josh, Mom or Dad.

Of all the possibilities that I had grappled with to explain my situation, being abruptly hurled more than a hundred and sixty-five years into the past had not been one of them, not a hundredth on the list, not one millionth. But here I was. That was now undeniable.

With an eye on Julia's back, I rummaged quietly through a chest, searching for a mirror. At the bottom, under some folded clothes, I found one, a wood-framed oval ten inches in length, and drew it out. Swallowing a deep breath, I held it up to my new face. A groan escaped me, my worst fears realized. I was plain. Really, really plain. A face only a mother could love. There was not the hint of make-up, the skin reddened from so much outdoor living. The best I could say, it was a pleasant face. It didn't give offense.

On my forehead under the loose hair were the backward words Putt had written. I reversed them in my mind: *Loco Libby*. That rascal. I found a piece of cloth and wiped my forehead clean

I didn't want anyone to know my mind had returned till I had a chance to wrestle with my extreme circumstances, which left my heart empty and desperate. Clearly, the situation was grave. In this century, in this time, if you wanted to travel anywhere, say, like to Oregon, you had to walk or ride a horse or in a carriage. Not even trains out here yet. Distances were greater, vastly greater. According to Mrs. Guthrie, a two thousand mile trip took as long as eight months, not four hours by air, and I had nearly that far to go. No choice.

In my time, the idea of walking that far would have been beyond absurd. We wouldn't even walk down the block but used a car instead. I knew this about the little Oregon hike we were on: I couldn't do it. No way! Come. Finish the journey. No! Get me out of here!

Whatever cosmic force had put me down in this alien time, by design or randomly, I had to survive till I was sent back. Aye, there was the rub. I did not think I could do that. Especially with no one to help me. On my own to live or die. And, oh, how I knew I could die here. My broken arm, which still could hurt like hell, told me that much.

Grappling with all this, a chaos of emotions amped up inside my fragile psyche. Fear, sadness, confusion, anger, longing, among many others, but mostly anger. A growing anger. Why me? I would not accept this. Right then, I swore one thing: I would see my family again. Not the first clue how, but this I would do. I would survive, and I would make it back. The thought of missing my younger brother growing up or making amends with my mother or not reclaiming my father was unbearable.

I glanced at myself in the mirror again and sighed. Ah, the worst of it. I didn't know who I was anymore. Was I this Libby creature I saw in the mirror or Paula Masters? How do you flaunt your world class looks, if you look like a day-old muffin?

Chapter 16

That evening in camp, Julia had Henry move the rocking chair out by the fire for me. Everyone was working, cooking or setting up the tent. Julia was stirring a pot of stew while keeping the spit turning on a couple rabbits. I got out of the rocking chair, went to the fire, and took the spit from her. "Here, let me help."

Julia was taken aback. "Libby?"

"Yes." It was time to find my way among them.

After a moment, she asked, "Are you all right now?"

"Yes."

The twins ran over and hugged me. One asked, "They said your mind went on a trip."

"Yes, to a place where girls wear ribbons in their noses."

Both shrieked with laughter at being caught out for their little prank.

Julia asked, hopefully, "You have your memories back?"

I knew she wanted me to remember the family before the trek began, but I could not lie to this woman, nor tell her the truth, that I never had those memories. "No, Julia. Sorry."

If I thought things would change with understanding of my true situation, it didn't. The days still had a deadening sameness. Each morning, stumble out of bed before daylight, desperate for a Starbuck's cherry latte, gather livestock, prepare and eat breakfast, yoke the oxen, then walk, walk, walk, walk in blistering heat, followed by sudden thunderstorms, set up camp, and then do it all again the next day.

My duties still consisted of helping Julia with chores and watching the twins. In the time since I'd been with the Quarles family, I'd come to realize those two were possessed of amazing balance and agility, kind of like talented, young gymnasts. Once, they did something so surprising, I was too stunned to stop them. Too small to climb up into the wagon back without help, one of them put her foot between the wheel spokes and rode up till she could latch onto the wagon bed and scramble to the back and in. The other girl followed right behind. Furiously, I scolded them and told them never to do it again, knowing, of course, they would.

One morning, we passed an encampment of about fifty wagons with twenty fresh grave markers laid one after the other. Immediately, fear raced through our company. I saw it in the alarmed stares.

"What is it?" I asked Julia.

"Cholera." Her voice cracked. She was terrified.

It took about three seconds for that to hit home. In my century, at least in developed countries, the disease was no problem, but here, now, it was a deadly pestilence that swept whole groups of people away. In this age, there was no defense against it. I tried to remember what I knew about it. Very little. You came across the mention of it all the time, mostly in middle school health or history class, but I couldn't remember much about it. We swung out wide to avoid them altogether. We could feel sorry for them, but no one wanted to go near them.

I tried to push the sight of those graves out of my mind for the rest of the morning, unsuccessfully, but by nooning, I had convinced myself that if the company was careful, we might be able to avoid the disease altogether.

As we were getting ready for lunch, a small incident made me stop worrying about cholera for the moment. It involved Henry. That man could arouse my anger and frustration like no one I'd ever met. My initial take on him had not changed by the fact he was of the nineteenth century, and not just a twenty-first century whacko. Either way, he was a mean, uncaring S-O-B, as inflexible as a crowbar, and I hated him. He had become the living symbol of my misery.

The children had been scrounging for loose wood along the riverbank to use in the cook fire. Little George ran back crying, an inch-long splinter stuck deep in the meat of his hand. It had to hurt, and I winced at the sight of it. When Julia reached to pull it out, he turned away screaming.

"It'll be okay, bud," I said, trying to help.

At that moment, Henry came up and grabbed him by the shoulders. "Stop this, boy. It's just a splinter. You're a Quarles, so stop this caterwauling, you hear me? You ain't wearing no petticoat."

Stifling his sniffles, Little George stared up at his father. "Yes...yes, sir."

Terrorized by his father, those were the first words I'd heard him speak all week. Henry? What an ass. While the boy's mind was distracted, though, Julia drew out the splinter. At least she had a little common sense. Too late, Little George snatched his hand away and almost screamed again, till his father cut him off with a glare. The boy wiped his nose with his sleeve. I could tell he still wanted to cry, but Henry was having none of it.

"Where's the wood, son?" he demanded.

Back to his silent ways, the boy didn't reply. If I had a father like that, I might not want to speak either.

Henry looked askance at him. "Weren't you sent to fetch firewood? Well then, go get it, son."

Holding his hand, Little George ran off. I worried the simple wound would become infected, and with no antibiotic around, I decided when he got back to wash his hand with alcohol. There certainly would be alcohol in this outfit somewhere.

When Henry saw Julia staring at him, he frowned. "He has to learn," he said, then walked away.

"What's his problem?" I asked Julia.

The question upset her. "Your father is touchy right now."

Touchy? Touched, I'd say. He was always ready to argue with anyone and hold his ground except with Julia. He gave in to her, and that made it worse. How she ever ended up with such a loser was a mystery, and I realized that may have been his problem: he knew she was too good for him.

Over the next couple days, the Warren Company skirted two more wagon trains stopped dead by cholera. Too many sick and dying to move on. They had to wait it out. This caused me to think about my own survival. Not wanting to be so vulnerable to the disease, I began to consider stealing off on my own to get away. In the close environment of a rolling community with many people providing a breeding ground for an outbreak seemed the last place I should be. But go where? And I had to admit these people were important to me. The twins, Julia, Caroline, Little George, and even Isaac had come to mean more to me in a few short weeks than all my friends in my own time. Odd, that was. Maybe it said too much about Paula Masters I didn't want to think about. And there was Daniel. I could not deny my feelings for him, even if I didn't know exactly what those feelings were.

I had to survive then, here and now. The nineteenth century meant horses. In the twenty-first century I wanted nothing more to do with them. Now, I had to come back to them. At least, if there was anything I knew about and was good at—very good at—it was horses. So I decided I better deal with Iris. I could not help comparing her to Quantum Leap. No comparison. One barely suited to pull a milk wagon, the other a super horse. Remembering Quantum always brought back the day he died. It was a memory that laid waste to my emotions.

When I was riding juniors, I had a rival, Clayton Fellows, a year older than me and jealous as hell. The problem was that for us to have a rivalry, he had to win something, and he couldn't. I won all the time. I was that good. One day, after we finished working our horses in the ring, he challenged me to a run through a course so tough the senior riders didn't even practice on it. It was to be scrapped that afternoon. Always competitive, I accepted. He went first and his run through was terrible, his horse pulling up at two jumps, knocked down another. He was in so much despair I should have just told him to forget it. But I had to show off.

I made it through the first part of the course as if it was the Kentucky Derby. Quantum Leap was flying. I chanced a glance over at Clayton, who had his jaw open in alarm. Next was a triple jump I should have slowed down for, but instead, in my hubris, I pushed my super horse faster. Stupid, stupid, stupid. His jump over the first of the three was too long, which made the middle jump impossible. It was a water jump. He crashed through the rails and landed in the water, slipped and crashed to the ground, throwing me. I heard the horrible snap of his leg and his shrill screams. I still hear those screams. He was put down within the hour. He had been such a beautiful animal, and I killed him. I never wanted to get near a horse again. Now, I had to, even though this one was the ugliest, meanest, and most useless horse God ever created.

Despite still having one arm in a sling, it was time for me to teach Iris which one of us was boss. Cautiously, Daniel saddled her for me. When I swung aboard, she reared up, shooting daggers of pain through my arm.

"Stick with her," Daniel called.

"Get real," I said, leaping off her back while I still had only one broken bone.

Daniel hurried over and after a quick glance at me said flatly, "You're not hurt."

I replied angrily, "I know I'm not hurt."

Iris was pawing the ground like a bull about to charge.

Daniel said, "Strange. Like she doesn't even know you."

"Everybody keeps telling me that." She knew I wasn't Libby, but no horse was going to get the better of me. I went up to her and we stood nose to nose. She didn't move, just stared. Discretion being the better part of valor—I could not do this with my arm in a sling—it would have to wait. I said softly to her, "We aren't done, Iris." She snorted her hot breath on me.

Chapter 17

When Captain Warren called a halt to the day's travel, camping at a spot close to the Platte River, I was exhausted, ready to crash, but these people still had life in them. Most nights there were prayer meetings, especially with cholera all about. And entertainment of all kinds. With no HD TVs or movie houses or theme parks, they still found ways to amuse themselves. Dances, readings, little plays, games, or groups of people gathering just to talk.

Julia had one of these ways. Several weeks before, she had shown me her prized possession, a small treasure chest she brought out of the wagon into the fading twilight. People young and old had gathered round our campfire in expectation. I was curious. Julia lit a lantern, hung it above her on the wagon, and sat in her rocking chair. Then she opened the chest. I couldn't have been more surprised. She had books! Five of them with dark leather bindings. She took them out one by one, brushing each one off carefully, and then set them back in.

Before she did, I saw the titles. Some I recognized and others I didn't. *Pride and Prejudice*. Read it in the tenth grade last year. *Godey's Lady's Book*. Never heard of it. In fact, it was magazines bound together. Dickens's *Oliver Twist* and Longfellow's *Evangeline*.

The last one was blank, no title. Asking her permission, I took it back out of the chest and flipped it open. It was in a foreign language I didn't recognize at first, then it came to me: Latin! Julia could read Latin. I indicated the book. "What is this?"

She smiled. "Ah, that is Ovid."

Ovid. I didn't know much about his work except that he was an X-rated Roman poet. That she had such a book was surprising. Most would have been shocked at what I held in my hand if they knew what it was. But then few people around here could read Latin, and I doubt if they had ever heard of Ovid.

"These your favorites books?" I asked.

She glanced at them. "I suppose. I couldn't bring my library. Books weigh too much. I left them with my sister. I chose five to take with us."

I wondered what that conversation with Henry had been like when he told her she'd have to leave her books. With a sigh, she picked up *Pride and Prejudice*. "Now, where were we? Ah, yes, Mr. Darcy has asked Lizzie to dance." People gathered closer.

While Julia read, I sat on the grass, Seneca and Jane snuggling in with me, and Caroline leaning against my back. She held Little George. Julia made the reading dramatic, lowering her voice slightly when men spoke, and adding inflection to her voice to match the scenes. It was far more enthralling than I thought possible.

A few minutes into the reading, Caroline whispered to me, "Here comes Mr. Darcy."

I glanced back to see Daniel approaching. Nodding to Julia, he sat next to me, not touching but close. He said nothing, just listened as intently as everyone else. Knowing I was in his century for an unknown amount of time, my relationship with him, by necessity, had become infinitely more complicated. I didn't know yet how he'd fit into this new reality. I wasn't exactly like Libby and he'd noticed. I doubt if she'd had as sharp a tongue or was as manipulative. So maybe he was reconsidering what the word *us* meant. When he nudged me at something witty Elizabeth had said to Darcy, as if I had said it, I realized I had nothing figured out about him yet. I had to decide, quickly, what *us* meant as well.

After the reading, he suggested we take a moonlight walk, but I begged off, telling him I was too tired. I did not want to be alone with him till I had worked out the Daniel puzzle. I trusted him, but not myself. Needing time away from both him and the Quarles family, I made a bed in the wagon for myself but couldn't sleep. As I lay there, I heard Henry's loud snores from the tent blend in with a harsh chorus of snores from around the camp. I heard the river's gentle murmur and from far off the howl of a coyote or wolf. The distance to my own world was the width of the universe. No one could imagine how alone I felt at that moment. I could not keep the tears out of my eyes.

"Josh, I didn't abandon you, buddy," I whispered. "I swear to you, I'm coming home."

Shutting my eyes, gritting my teeth, and flexing my fists, I tried to will myself back, but that didn't quite work. To bring about my return on my own seemed impossible.

From outside the wagon, I heard a footfall and felt a surge of fear. I sat up grabbing the old iron skillet and wondering if I should call out. As the sound came closer, I got ready to swing.

"Libby," someone whispered. "Libby."

"Daniel?"

He appeared at the back and I set the skillet aside. "What are you doing?" I asked, keeping my voice low.

"I just got off guard duty," he said. "I saw you getting in the wagon earlier, so I took a chance you were still awake. I had to see you."

"Well, I'm awake now."

Nervously, he shifted his weight from foot to foot. "Sorry. Something's troubling you, and I suspect it's not a little thing."

I could hardly confide in him. "What are you talking about?" I demanded too harshly.

"Are you losing your feelings for me?"

Obviously, he still loved Libby very much, and maybe she loved him. As for me, clearly, there was no way I could fall in love with someone that lived two centuries before my own. I might be whisked back at any moment, and then what would happen to that love? Love transcends time? Not really. The telling thing, though, was I did have strong feelings for him, more than I did for Cal, who would not be born for...Oh, Jesus! This stuff was driving me crazy.

"No, of course not," I said.

He nodded, accepting that with an easy sigh. "If you tell me to go away, I will, but I care about you. I don't like seeing you so worried about things. If there's something else wrong, then, you can tell me."

I took his hand. "Thank you, Daniel. I will remember that. But this problem I have to work out on my own."

After staring at me with such longing, he said, "You know, I am always struck by how beautiful your hair is in the moonlight."

The boy must be blind. I gave him a coy smile. "There is no moonlight inside this wagon. You trying to sweet talk me, sir?"

He laughed and reached out again. I said sharply, "Don't. Not now."

He shook his head. "You've changed some, I'll warrant."

"Sorry I can't be what you want."

"Oh, you're exactly what I want."

We settled into an awkward silence, me in the wagon, him standing just outside. I felt lost between universes. I whispered, "Daniel, come inside."

In one leap he cleared the backboard and came into my embrace.

Chapter 18

The next day, we got our first case of cholera.

It had been an ever present threat for days with wagon trains ahead and behind suffering from the disease. When survivors came to the Warren Company asking for help, we kept them at a distance but placed what we could out on the prairie for them. No one knew what caused the disease. I did. But what could I do? As a girl in 1848, I'd have a hard time convincing anyone I had special knowledge of anything. I decided, though, to go to the company's only doctor, Hannibal Pierce, and tell him what I knew. How could it hurt?

Pierce had no training in medicine. In fact, he was only a farmer from Tennessee who had gained a reputation for treating animals, then people started going to him for help, and he had some success, or at least that's what people said. Since no one else in the company had a better background in doctoring, Pierce was it. He saw himself as a tireless healer, and tireless I supposed he was. He had not done a bad job setting my arm, but about disease he knew nothing. Who did at this time? Still, I could not get my mind around a person without much schooling, let alone medical training, calling himself a doctor.

Georgia Whelan had been the first to catch the disease. She rode on a pallet in her wagon, filling up a slop bucket that one of her children had to empty regularly. Lottie drove the wagon, while Millie, at twelve, was inside caring for her mother. The rest of the children walked alongside, looking somber and afraid. If Georgia died, it would play hell on this family, because Mr. Whelan had trouble controlling his children, especially Lottie. Without his wife, I knew it would be hopeless. I caught up with Pierce outside her wagon with Mr. Whelan, giving him instructions on her care.

"Mr. Pierce, sir, can I talk with you for a minute?" I asked.

He looked alarmed. "Is someone in your family ill?"

"No, we're all fine. I just remembered a couple of things about cholera that might be helpful. I thought I should tell you."

He scowled. "You came to tell me?"

"Well, sir, yes, sir, everyone should be boiling their water, at least for drinking and..."

"You want I should make tea for everyone?"

"No, no, I was just..."

His frown deepened. "I got no time for this. Now run along."

"I just thought..."

He turned on me. "I told you to get. You try my patience, girl. You got no business meddling in what's none of your affair. Now, go afore I talk to your pa." He went back to Mr. Whelan as if I didn't exist. "Let the missus rest for now, and I'll be back tonight for treatment."

What possible treatment that would be, I couldn't imagine.

That evening after supper, Caroline and I carried a bucket of dishes down to the river to wash. I saw Daniel standing a ways off among a few cottonwood trees, and he was crying. At his age he was more man than anyone I knew or had known, so to see him standing there bawling was scary; something very bad must have happened.

When I hurried to him, he turned away. I put a hand on his shoulder. "Daniel, what is it?"

He wiped his eyes. For a moment he couldn't speak, then he straightened up, faced me and said, "It's Putt. He's got the cholera."

It took a second for his words to register, then shock set in. Not Putt. It hit me harder than I would have imagined. Where was the doctor? Get him to a hospital. But there were no hospitals and no doctor except, dear God, Hannibal Pierce.

"He'll be all right. You know Putt. He's probably even putting us on a little."

"He's dying."

I liked and cared about Putt and didn't want him to die. With what I knew, which wasn't much, I actually could do something to prevent it, but should I become involved? "Daniel, will you take me to him?" I asked. He hesitated, and I said, "Please." After a moment, he nodded.

I told Caroline I had to go somewhere and for her to finish the dishes. Apparently, she didn't know about Putt yet, because she laughed. "Yeah, I know where you two are going."

Daniel led me back through camp to the Langdon tent and held the flap open for me. When I stepped inside, I walked into a bloody scene right out of the Dark Ages. Even after realizing I had somehow been planted here in the nineteenth century, a subatomic part of me hoped that there was still some other explanation. What I saw destroyed any last doubts.

Pierce knelt over Putt, bleeding him.

The tent smelled of stopped up toilets. A single lantern hung from the center post. In shadow, on a pallet of blankets and quilts, Putt lay so shriveled he looked like an old tobacco leaf. My heart crumpled. I couldn't help him. I could not fix this. Worst of all, his wrist was draped over a pan and his blood was draining out into it. My knees grew weak and I fought to keep from passing out. It was all too overwhelming. I nearly freaked and ran and would have if I had anywhere to run to. I had never had to deal with these kinds of things before. What dress to wear, what boy to flirt with, what needle to stick in Mrs. Guthrie, sure, but not this. My mind screamed, when was I going to be taken out of this dreadful nightmare and sent back to my own time? Here, cutting people open and bleeding them passed for doctoring? I wanted to go home.

With his eyes closed, Putt looked dead. "Is he...?" I asked Daniel.

Slowly, he shook his head. Did he mean no, he wasn't dead or I don't know?

Pierce held a little half-moon knife that dripped crimson. At my entrance, he glanced over at me and frowned. Tobacco spittle stained his beard and the dirt and filth of the trail clung to his clothes. He had not even washed his hands. Myra, Putt's mother, sat beside him, holding his hand. Normally, her face had strength, but now that had all drained away. Sam Langdon stood over his son, his harsh features heavy with worry, watching as Pierce slapped Putt's wrist a couple times, and the blood flowed more quickly.

"No," I blurted out without thinking. "Stop. Please, stop."

Putt opened his eyes and looked over at me, smiling weakly. He tried to speak but couldn't. The two men scowled at me. I didn't care. They were killing him. I thought bleeding had gone out in the Middle Ages. Pierce went back to his mutilation.

I was desperate. I'm no fool. I knew a teenage girl had no standing here, but I had the benefit of knowledge they didn't have. I knew about bacteria and the importance of cleanliness and how draining someone's blood was lethal. Unless I could do something, Putt was going to die for a certainty. I spoke more calmly, "You can't bleed him. That makes him weaker. You have to stop. That's the worst thing you can do." *Please listen to me. I'm from the twenty-first century.*

Ignoring me, Pierce continued draining blood into the pan. The boy's father made no move to intervene. It would have been foolish to think he would. I didn't know what to do. I repeated my plea and again they ignored me. I became frustrated and shouted, "This is Dark Ages crap. Please, stop! You're killing him!"

"Get that crazy girl out of here!" Pierce demanded.

I looked to Daniel for help, but he was caught up in his own agonies. I couldn't walk away and let Putt die. I just couldn't. Not knowing what else to do, I started for Pierce, but Daniel caught me by the arm.

"You have to stop this," I cried out.

"Take her out," Langdon ordered.

As Daniel dragged me back, I struggled frantically, yelling like a madwoman. "You butcher. You're killing him. What are you going to do with his blood? Drink it, you damned vampire?"

Pierce stared at me with bloodshot saucer eyes. He was truly surprised. Finally, taking care not to further injure my arm, Daniel got me outside. Clearly, in the nineteenth century, women did not act this way. I had only made things worse. I thought he must hate me for it.

"I'm sorry," I said weakly.

He shook his head. The light from a nearby fire lit his face, and I saw anger mixed with sorrow. Was he angry at me? I was disheartened that I had failed Putt. A few weeks ago at Rector Academy, I was trying to decide who to let take me to the prom. Now I was trying to figure out how to stop a deadly disease from taking the life of a friend.

People around the fire were staring at us. They'd heard me screaming. I could see fear on their faces, and I knew why. Once this disease struck, as it had here, it would start reaping its grim harvest. Few families would be left untouched. I didn't know if I was strong enough for this. Maybe this creature Libby was. As it stood, I was literally the only one who could help Putt. No 911 call here. No paramedics rushing in to save him. Just me. I had the knowledge. It felt like a slab from Stonehenge had been hoisted onto my shoulders. I didn't like it, I didn't want it, but I had it. So I had to try again.

"Please believe me, Daniel, when I tell you bleeding will make it worse," I said, trying for a more reasonable tone. "He'll die if Pierce keeps that up."

"It's cholera, Libby. I've seen it before. I'm no doctor, but I do know you got to get the sickness out of him. That's why Doc Pierce is bleeding him. Everyone knows that."

I placed a hand on his chest. "No, that's the old way." I searched for how to make him see reason and found one. I lied. "Back home in Springfield, our doctor was trained in Boston at Harvard Medical School. Dr. Pitt. Dr. Bradley Pitt." It was the first name that popped into my head. Making it up as I went, I added, "All the newest research. He always said bleeding was the worst thing you can do. It steals the patient's strength and spirit. Just the things he needs to fight the disease. In fact, it makes the disease stronger."

Daniel didn't respond to what I'd said immediately, twisting on it awhile. He was not stupid, but medicine in this age, as in mine, seemed a territory beyond the common person. He probably didn't know what to believe. Finally, his eyes fixed on me and he said the magic words, "Did Doc Pitt ever say how to cure cholera? It's for sure that old fool Pierce doesn't have any idea."

"Well, you know what? He did. In fact, he was able to cure all his patients of it. The miracle of modern medicine."

Now, I was in trouble. I shouldn't have said that. I didn't know the first thing about curing cholera. Just stopping bad treatment didn't mean that leaving Putt alone was going to cure him. Desperately, I tried to remember what I had learned about the disease in health and history classes. You couldn't study any period in history without coming across this pestilence. Mrs. Guthrie, where are you when I need you?

Daniel fell silent for several seconds, staring at me while I considered what to do. Abruptly, he took hold of my shoulders. "People die of the cholera, Libby. Once they get it, they die, Doc Pierce or no. If this doctor told you how to save Putt, tell me. Please, tell me." In a barely audible voice, he added, "I don't want Putt to die."

He waited for me to tell him how to cure cholera. Something I didn't know. Soon, when I couldn't come up with anything, he would grow angry and tell me to go to hell, and he'd be right to do it.

At that moment, Pierce and Mr. Langdon came out of the tent. Pierce dumped the pan of blood into the grass. "I'm sorry, Samuel," he said, putting a hand on the other man's shoulder.

"There's naught else I can do. It's in God's hands now. I'll know more in the morning."

I hated him. How could he be that maliciously ignorant, 1848 or not? With no notice of us, he headed off while Langdon after a glance our way returned inside the tent.

Daniel said softly, "Libby, tell me what to do. And I pray to God you got the right of it."

I had to come up with something. I searched my brain. What did I know about cholera? It wasn't a disease that my friends or I worried about, but it was one that still swept through Third World countries from time to time. Mrs. Guthrie, earlier in the year, had talked about it along with smallpox, the plague and typhoid. As I recalled, it had a lot to do with hygiene.

"For one, boil your water," I told Daniel. "Don't drink any water that hasn't been boiled."

"What good will that do?"

"Daniel, you asked, I'm telling. Boil your water before you drink it."

"So give Putt boiled water?" he asked skeptically.

"Geez, no. Everyone must drink only boiled water, but let it cool first, for heaven's sake. Got it?"

"Yeah. Is that it? Boiled water?"

"No, there's more." Dr. Paula Masters. This was crazy. I'm freaking out here. What had Mrs. Guthrie said? I didn't remember any big vaccine like for polio or smallpox or a thousand other diseases. So how can I help Putt? Then it came to me. Mrs. Guthrie in front of class. Replace the electrolytes. That was it. The victim was dying of dehydration from constant, virulent diarrhea, so replace the lost water and electrolytes. But what the hell were electrolytes? Gatorade! Not a chance of that here. But you could also find them, according to her, in baking soda and citrus fruit. Thank you, Mrs. Guthrie.

"Do you have any lemons, like at the Fort Kearny store? Can you make lemonade?"

"Lemonade, Libby?" I knew it sounded crazy. At my scowl, he said, "Well, no, but Mrs. Rudabaugh bought some back at Fort Kearny. I guess I could get one or two. And I think Ma has some extract. I think that's made of lemons."

"And baking powder. Mix it in water. I want Putt drinking that and lemonade all night long. That's what Dr. Pitt would tell you, and he's never wrong. Start now. Wake him up to make him drink. Make sure the water is boiled. Do that, and he may have a chance."

I didn't know if Mr. Langdon would go along with the plan. It seemed crazy even to me, but Daniel nodded, hesitated a moment, kissed me on the cheek, then rushed back inside the tent.

I had done what I could. I hoped it was enough. Offering up a prayer, I walked back to the Quarles' wagons.

The next morning, Putt died.

Chapter 19

Grey clouds hovered overhead and a drizzle fell as Julia, who'd just returned from the Langdon tent, told us of his passing. We were sitting at our breakfast fire as it sputtered in the thin rain, too worried to be hungry. "He's gone," was all she said with infinite sadness. I couldn't believe it. Caroline ran into her arms, sobbing, and Isaac stood up, poured his tea onto the ground, and walked off toward the horse herd. The twins and Little George were dazed.

Julia kissed Caroline on the cheek. "You know, God wanted that boy by his side. He wanted his laughter up in heaven and He just couldn't wait any longer."

Squatting at the fire, Henry exchanged a look with her I couldn't read. "I'll let Isaac be for awhile," he said. "Plenty of time before we start out."

"Why are you going on? You can't go on now," I insisted.

"Can't help that boy now," he replied simply.

I wanted to scream at him, but I doubted even that would break through his rock hard exterior. Putt was gone, and he had the sympathy of a gnat.

Wrapped in heavy coats or blankets draped over their shoulders against the morning chill, the emigrants huddled around a hundred breakfast fires or had gathered in small groups, worried, wondering who would be next. Heartbroken and feeling the same dread, I glanced at the Quarles brothers and sisters and prayed not them. Please, not them. Right now, I couldn't make this impossible hurt go away for them or for me. I wondered if this was what it was like living in the 1840s.

"There's something else," Julia said, looking at me. "Doc Pierce is saying the boy didn't have to die. He's blaming you for it, Libby."

"Me?"

Henry said angrily, "What did you do?"

"Nothing." I swallowed hard. "I just told Daniel what I knew."

"What you knew!" He sucked in through clenched teeth. "So what is it you think you know?"

"I told him about..."

He banged his metal cup hard on a rock, splashing his tea. "I don't want to hear it. I better see if I can fix this." He stood and stalked off toward the Langdon's tent.

Had I really caused Putt's death? I didn't think so, but that didn't matter. He was dead and that left an empty hole in my center, bad enough, but Pierce's value to the company meant he could throw us out. For the life of me I couldn't figure what else I could have done.

Julia said, "I need to help Myra prepare the body for burial. Can you get us ready to leave, Libby?"

I nodded. In slow zombielike movements, Caroline helped me pack the wagon. For a second, I thought I ought to go see Daniel, to try and set things right between us and console him, but then I let my cowardice get the better of me. I couldn't imagine a worse thing for me to do right now than to barge into the Langdon tent where Pierce was proclaiming to everyone that I had killed Putt.

I heard a soft moan come from Caroline. She held a frying pan with burnt bacon from our breakfast, doing nothing with it, tears flowing down her cheeks. I took the pan from her and dropped it in the dish bucket. "I'll get us ready. You watch the twins."

A few minutes later, Henry returned to grab a shovel out of the wagon. He stopped in front of me as I was kicking dirt on the fire. His face held rage barely under control. "Dang it all, Libby, the boy had the cholera, not the sniffles. Why did you interfere?"

I was too stunned to speak at first, I could hardly explain to him about bacteria and hygiene and electrolytes. "To save his life."

He was so upset his hands white-knuckled around the shovel. "Well, you sure didn't."

That hit me like a fist. So hateful. What an utter bastard. When I started to speak again, he cut me off. "Pierce wants to throw you out of the company, and therefore us."

"He can't do that," I offered, weakly.

"Yes, he can. Maybe he thinks you ought not to practice medicine like you was a doctor. Captain Warren wants to see you and me after the burial. He will decide then. God help us. No family can make it by themselves out here."

He turned abruptly and walked off. I wished at that moment I could just get on a horse and ride off. I noticed Caroline shivering and wrapped my good arm around her. I wondered what I could possibly say to Captain Warren to keep him from tossing the Quarles out of the company, but I could think of nothing.

Putt's funeral was held in a grassy field near the rutted wagon track. The entire four hundred or so in the company had gathered. The drizzle had grown into a steady, light rain; the thick clouds overhead left the day grey and miserable. Julia was with Isaac somewhere. As I shepherded Caroline, Little George and the twins through the crowd, I received hostile glances, everyone clearly thinking I'd killed poor Putt. I stiffened my back and made it up to the front beside Daniel, hoping at least he didn't blame me. I touched his arm. "I'm so sorry, Daniel."

My voice fell at his sudden glare. He did blame me. It was unfair, but he had the right. It was his brother lying over there in the shroud, and I had meddled. My thoughts, though, were with Putt. I expected to see him among the crowd up to some devilment. I felt my eyes well up with tears.

There was nothing else I could say to Daniel that wasn't trite. Being a caring, concerned girl was tough for me. I wasn't used to it. Being an uncaring bitch was easier. If you have no feelings, you have no hurt. Over the last year at Rector Academy, I'd been so ego-driven, so self-centered, nothing bothered me unless it was an espresso delivered cold. I cared about no one except my brother Josh. My saving grace was that I knew it. I worried over trivial things: the right makeup, the killer dress, which boy to date. Not this. Not this. This hurt.

With his eyes bloodshot and his face covered in stubble, Daniel looked as if he'd not slept in days. I had such a surge of feeling for him, I wanted to wrap my arms around him. A smear of dirt smudged his cheek, but when I reached up to wipe it off, he pushed my hand away sharply. "Don't."

He walked over to the other side of the grave to stand with his father and mother and little sisters. The service began.

Since Captain Warren was the elected leader of the company and also a preacher, he began the service by reading a passage from the Bible, then spoke to the crowd. His voice was strong and clear, kind of like a TV evangelist. I didn't listen, numbed by it all. Around us, many of the men and women had tears in their eyes. Putt had left his mark.

When I came back to Captain Warren's sermon he was saying, "We stand in the presence of the Almighty ready to deliver our son and friend Putnam Langdon unto His good care. Putt has gone to his endless rest far too early. We know God works in strange ways. We do not challenge. We do not claim to know the wisdom of those ways. After all, when he calls, we all must come. Who can take Putt home now but God? Putt's soul is free, his suffering done. Oh, Lord, receive our beloved son and brother and friend. In God's name we pray. Amen."

Henry and Daniel and several other men then lowered the body into the grave and shoveled dirt over it. It was done. He would reside there alone for all eternity for we were moving on. Everyone dispersed back to their wagons except for those few involved in my so-called trial: the Langdons, the Quarles, Captain Warren, Doc Pierce, and another man I didn't know.

At first glance, this man was unremarkable looking, ruddy faced with a straggly beard, and shaggy brown hair sticking down from under a black, broad-brimmed hat. He wore a fringed buckskin shirt, frayed plaid pants, and moccasin leggings. Smoking a small bone pipe, he struck the pose of a patient banker. Then I noticed the piercing grey eyes, like a hawk's searching for its next meal, and his left hand gnarled like a claw with two missing fingers just like me.

I guessed this must be Tom Fitzpatrick, the man Sally called "the pilot," the one who knew the way to Oregon. And, suddenly, I realized I had heard of him. He was a famous mountain man we had studied in middle and high school history classes. Everyone here said he had sand, meaning he was someone with character. As pilot, he was often scouting ahead or hunting with Daniel, so I had not seen him till now. Though he had an amused expression, I could not tell if he was for me or against me.

"Let's make this quick," Captain Warren addressed us. "We need to get moving. Doc Pierce has made charges about Libby in regard to Putt. Some serious ones, and we need to decide what to do. I asked the Langdons to…"

Impatiently, Pierce interrupted him. "Get to the point, Captain. Medicine ain't no child's game and no female's neither. It takes a man's mind, one what's got experience in the matter. I been treating people for nigh on thirty years and I got some fair knowledge about what to do."

"Then spell it out, Hannibal," Captain Warren demanded.

"She done it. She twisted Daniel's mind with her words, like women do. He tried some of that silliness on the boy." He paused a moment, glancing at Daniel and his parents. "It killed the Langdon boy. I tell you, Captain, something's got to be done."

"Daniel, is this true?" Captain Warren asked.

He nodded. "Yes, sir. She was only trying to help. She didn't mean no harm." His voice had a catch in it, so he paused, then said more firmly, "My brother was real sick and like to die anyway. I was ready to try anything"

"That mumbo jumbo done killed the boy," Pierce insisted.

"Likely as not cholera killed the boy," Fitzpatrick said. "I never heard of lemonade killing anyone. Or baking powder for that matter."

Pierce was having none of it. He reiterated my many sins, which included pride, envy and vainglory, telling everyone how I tricked Daniel into following such bizarre treatment. "She took away the boy's chance to survive. I had him on the road to recovery."

Fitzpatrick asked, "So what is it you want us to do, Hannibal? Hang her?"

Pierce hesitated long enough to make it clear he considered that option a good one. "No, of course not. I want her exiled. Throw her out of the company."

The entire Quarles brood stood with me. Protectively, Julia put her arm around my shoulders, and Henry stepped forward. "No one is throwing my daughter out of the company."

"We'll see about that," Pierce replied testily, turning to Warren. "Captain, we got the cholera among us now. Already this morning, three more come down with it. They can't be thinking lemonade is going to cure them. Boil water! That's just pure crazy. We got to send this girl away so the people will know that what she did and said was wrong."

With a sigh, Captain Warren removed his hat and ran his hand through his hair. "What have you got to say for yourself, Libby?"

Everyone looked at me. I wish I could have come up with something more profound, but I just reacted. "Man, this sucks."

They might not have understood the words, but they understood the tone. Not exactly a stirring defense, but what was I going to say? I'm really from the future, and I understand this disease better than you do? I had been a poor student in the last year but even I knew about bacteria and hygiene.

Pierce said, "See there? Did I not tell you? Pride goeth before a fall."

"Goeth? What does that mean?" I snapped. Not smart to antagonize him further, plus it was petty. This defense was not my finest moment.

Shaking his head, Captain Warren turned to Daniel. "You have anything to add, son?"

Myra answered for him. "No, sir, my boy doesn't. I've heard enough of this. This girl had naught to do with my boy's death. It was the cholera that took him and nothing more, and that's the end of it, Captain. Now, let's get moving so we can grieve in peace." Her face was set and I doubted if any of the men wanted to contradict her. I loved her for that.

Captain Warren turned to me. "I guess that settles it. Libby, we got cholera among us now. You must not go around doctoring people. You're just a girl. You're no doctor."

I was about to come back with *Pierce sure as hell is no doctor*, but I felt Julia's hand squeeze my shoulder. Fitzpatrick smiled. "And if you got to give someone lemonade, don't tell 'em it cures everything from warts to gout."

Chapter 20

The wagons pulled out fifteen minutes later, rolling over Putt's grave, obliterating any tangible evidence he had ever existed. It was done so wolves or Indians wouldn't dig him up.

I could understand wolves, but could not imagine why Indians would want to do that, but then that was the belief at the time. We left him behind, far from home and family and friends. It was a beautiful spot, filled with wildflowers and the Platte River flowing by.

The leave-taking cast me down as far as I had ever been. Wanting nothing more than to lie down and mourn, I had to push myself to take each step. Caroline walked beside me. I could not imagine how she bore it. After all, she was in love with him. In the drizzle, she frequently glanced back at the spot as it receded farther and farther, till finally it was lost. When she began to cry again, it undid me; my own emotions hit critical mass. Putt's death, stranded in this time and place, the prospect of never seeing my family again, all grew too much for me. I took Caroline in my arms, both of us crying in great sobs. The wagons rolled by, people staring. I didn't care. We bawled so loud it must have scared half the buffalo and Indians on the plains.

Julia stopped her wagon and lumbered back to us, wrapping us in her arms, not such an easy task with the girth of her pregnancy. By and by, every other wagon behind us passed and then the horse herd and the cattle, and we were alone on the prairie, but Julia didn't seem to care. She would have stood there all day, if need be. Soothingly, she called us daughter, over and over. I loved my mother, but at that moment, I would not have minded having Julia as a second mother. Caroline cried herself out first, and then I stopped. Julia gave us another squeeze and said, "Let's go. We need to catch up."

It rained all day, harder and harder. By mid-afternoon, everyone was soaked and looked sad and bedraggled. Putt's death left a somber pall over the company. When the rain became more intense, I climbed inside the wagon with Caroline, Seneca and Jane. Through a slight opening in our drawn-up canvas, I could see Henry now driving the wagon behind us with Isaac beside him, both hunkered down in their slickers, Little George's head occasionally popping out from behind them.

Once I'd said that my generation in the twenty-first century had it hardest of all. I already knew now that wasn't true. After all that had happened, I kept thinking on the words, *come. Finish the journey* and hoped it was how I would get back to my family. Get to Oregon. Once I did, the journey would be complete. Now, more than ever, I wanted out of this dangerous, sad, sad time. Please, can I go home now?

"So, you remember nothing before you broke your arm?" Julia asked suddenly, glancing back at me through the little canvas opening. She wore a slicker; rain water dripped from the brim of her hat.

"Not a thing."

"Well, I guess I should tell you who you are then."

"I'd like that." I threw on my own slicker and hat and climbed onto the seat next to her.

Throughout the next hour, she taught me about "my family" and our home in Springfield, Illinois. Back there, Henry had tried farming and running a general store. Remarkable that they knew Abe Lincoln. Remarkable. I asked about him. He was not even President yet, of course—the Civil War was still more than a decade off—though he'd just finished a term as a member of Congress. Just think, I could go to Illinois right now and actually see him. That would be a trip and a half. Mrs. Guthrie would be so jealous.

Astonishingly, Lincoln and his wife Mary almost came on this journey with the Quarles. It was in the planning stages. Lincoln had been offered the position of governor of Oregon Territory by newly elected President Zachary Taylor, but after long thought, he declined and saw the Quarles off a couple months ago. Julia held her finger and thumb a centimeter apart. "They were this close to coming, but Abe's ambitious. In the end, he wanted to stay in the States."

She was a surprising woman. For one thing, she had a great love of books. I didn't think anyone in this situation, pioneers on the Oregon Trail, would have even a passing acquaintance with books, but that was silly. Of course, they did. Some anyway. And she was well-educated, something unusual for a woman of the time. Her father was a literature professor at a small college on the Mississippi where she and her sister had taken classes.

"Your arm still hurt?" she asked.

"No, not so much anymore."

"Good. You should be able to get rid of that sling in a week or two."

I glanced at it, saw my mutilated hand. "Julia, how'd I lose my fingers?"

"Can you call me mother? I am your ma."

I already had a mother and had to draw the line. "I'm sorry. I really am. To me, I've only known you a few weeks."

She shook her head sadly. "You went out in a blizzard, that's how. It was the worst storm to hit Springfield in living memory. I was so angry with you I could have killed you myself."

As the story went, the Quarles owned a farm, but drought two years running broke them financially. They sold it and bought a general store in Springfield, doing well at first, so much so that Henry wanted to expand, but none of the banks in Springfield would loan him money in a poor economy. He travelled to a bank in Decatur, thirty some miles away, that promised money in exchange for the deeds to both the store and the town lot as collateral, everything they owned.

A few hours after Henry had gone, the blizzard hit. The weather worsened throughout the day, and Julia worried that he might have been caught out in it. That night disaster struck. They lived in the back of the store. Somehow a fire started and the store burned to the ground, taking the entire inventory with it. Julia barely got her children out. They faced financial ruin. Once Henry signed the papers for the loan with the high interests, they would owe more than they could ever pay back, even if they sold the lot immediately. They'd have nothing left but debt.

"You were very foolish," she said. "You could have been killed." But I heard pride in her voice. "That night you saddled Iris and went after your pa, right into the teeth of the blizzard. You didn't tell anyone you were going. If you had, I would have stopped you. As it was, I was sure I'd lost you, too. The snowstorm was so fierce, it stopped all travel for several days. I had no way of knowing what happened to you or Henry."

"Did I reach Decatur in time?"

"You did." She stared at me for a long second. "Many times you could have stopped at farmhouses along the way and taken shelter, but you kept going. You're more stubborn than an old mule. You get that from your father. If you were on any other horse than Iris, you would have perished. She got you through."

"Iris?"

She smiled. "That's a tough little mare. You two were meant for each other."

"Iris, Goddess of Discord."

"Yes. That's how she got her name." From habit, she gently shook the reins with no visible effect on the oxen. "Anyway, like I was saying, you found your pa before he borrowed the money, but your left hand was nearly frozen off. The doctor had to amputate two fingers to save it. We'd been talking about emigrating to Oregon for a long while, so instead of taking out the loan, your pa sold the property for just enough to set us on our way. That's all due to you and Iris. And so here we are on the Emigrant Road."

Libby was something, but she wasn't me. How was I going to live up to her? What she had done I could never have done. People expected much of her, almost nothing of Paula.

Where was she anyway? Why didn't she come back so I could go home?

For the next few days it rained steadily. So wet and muddy, it seemed every hour wagons got stuck, men shoving at the back and extra oxen and ropes to get them moving again. Miserable hardly described it. Food was scarce, not because we didn't have it, but because we couldn't cook it. Mostly we ate dried beef jerky and hard biscuits every freaking meal.

But that was only the backdrop to the worst thing I ever experienced. Cholera. It swept through our wagon train, taking weak and strong alike, old and young, men and women. You could wake up well in the morning and be dead by nightfall. We buried them along the side of the road, and then we kept going. Families left behind sons and daughters, brothers, sisters, parents. No one was exempt.

Since the disease was ravaging three companies on the Platte's south bank, Fitzpatrick suggested we cross to the north side and get out of the sick zone. The river was more than a mile wide, but not very deep. Getting stuck in the river bottom was the problem. Several extra teams of oxen had to be yoked to each wagon to pull it through the muck. It took us six hours, then Fitzpatrick led us on another five miles to a spring known as Ash Hollow.

That evening, two tents were strung together to hear Captain Warren do more preaching, and with cholera in camp, every family attended. Afterward, as he did every night, Hannibal Pierce made his rounds with his knife and blood pan, and there was nothing I could do to stop him. I had never fought for important things like this before, not in my world. Most things had been given to me. To get Mom to buy me a new Gucci bag or an Armani sweater, I might have had to manipulate her more than usual, or to get a better grade. I might have had to work extra hard to persuade a teacher to my side. The irony here was, like Cassandra, that Trojan prophetess, I actually knew what to do, me, Paula Masters, but no one believed me.

For awhile, I tried to give Pierce the benefit of the doubt; his ignorance was the ignorance of his times. That didn't make it any easier, though, as more bodies were wrapped in shrouds and buried; twenty-eight in the four days since Putt had died. Pierce worked tirelessly—I had to give him that—trying to save everyone, but he saved no one.

I saw him coming out of the Whelan tent. Tall, gawky Georgia Whelan had been the first to come down with the disease, but still hung on. I glimpsed her through the tent flap, Lottie and the other children kneeling over her. She looked like a skeleton. She'd been bled so much I knew she didn't have a chance. Pierce's face was worn and haggard. His hands, which he seldom washed, were caked with dried blood. He gave me a sullen glance.

"You are working too hard, Mr. Pierce," I said, trying a friendly approach.

He glared at me with his grim reaper eyes. "If there's any justice in this life, Libby Quarles, you will be the next person struck down with cholera. Surely God will not protect the wicked."

I was stunned. It was such a hateful thing to say. I couldn't fathom hating anyone that much, let alone someone hating me that much. In response, my inner nasty came out. "Hannibal Pierce!"

"Doctor Pierce to you."

"Hannibal the Cannibal."

"What's that you say?"

"Hannibal the Cannibal. If God struck down the wicked, you'd have been dead a long time ago." I left him standing there, his mouth agape. It was a childish, feel-good moment that accomplished nothing.

As the cholera got worse, I feared everyone in the company would perish, including me. I was certainly not immune. Only a couple people taken ill had so far survived, a nearly 90 percent mortality rate. That was high, but not by much, especially with Pierce running around with his knife. Henry didn't like it, but Julia went from tent to tent among the sick. I wanted to go with her, but at first, Captain Warren had forbidden it.

Finally, with so many falling ill, he relented, allowing me to accompany her as long as I didn't start thinking I was a doctor. So I emptied slop buckets—a wholly unpleasant task—and washed the sick. In a way, I was amazed that I was doing these things I would have never imagined doing in my old life. Now, I had to. Either help or be swept away by the disease, though I didn't think we were helping much. Oddly, some people were afraid of me. Others, ever the wits, called me, "Dr. Lemonade."

Every time I thought to give up because of exhaustion or just fear of contamination, someone reached out and begged me not to leave them. I was there when poor Georgia Whelan breathed her last. Lottie burst into tears and ran from the tent. Julia closed the woman's eyes. Mr. Whelan was too stunned to speak, to even function. He sat on a stool, rubbing his bald head like it itched. His other children hovered nearby, uncertain what to do. Julia parceled them out to different families for the night. Everyone we saw that day had been bled by the industrious Mr. Pierce.

No matter who had died, come morning the wagons rolled out. The company did not stop for anything. The dead were buried, the sick were hauled along. Captain Warren's cry each morning, "Head 'em west!"

It was the third day after crossing the South Platte when Caroline came down with the disease.

Chapter 21

The weather had not been good. Again, it was raining hard in the morning and off and on in the afternoon. For the rest of my life, I would never be able to experience a rainy day without thinking of the cholera epidemic of 1848 that swept through the emigrant wagon companies. When the rain slackened, Caroline and I got out of the claustrophobic wagon to walk. As usual, she was barefoot.

One moment Caroline was beside me, the next she wasn't. When I glanced back, I saw her lying on the ground, unconscious. I screamed for Julia and then frantically rushed to the girl. Instantly, Henry bounded off his wagon and ran to us. He scooped her up in his arms. When he glanced at Julia, I saw terror in his eyes.

"Get her in the wagon," she said. "I'll make a bed."

Caroline awoke. "Have I got the cholera?"

"I don't know, honey," Julia lied. "Might be just a touch of the croup."

I could not bear to see Caroline die, too. It would be like watching Josh die. Henry laid her in the wagon, and Julia wrapped her in a quilt, brushing her hair back from her eyes and whispering something to her I couldn't hear.

When Julia climbed out of the wagon, I grabbed her wrist so hard she winced. "Please, let me take care of her," I begged. I swore to her if we got started with a baking powder and salt solution quick enough, it would save her life. And, yes, some lemonade. I didn't know that it would, but felt she was doomed otherwise.

"You're talking crazy," Henry said, infuriated, coming out the back of the wagon. "I'm in no mood for this. Go get Isaac. He's with the horse herd. Tell him to get Doc Pierce over here. If God takes her, it won't be because we didn't do what we could."

I stood my ground. I should have been afraid of him, but I wasn't. He could hit me. I didn't care. "Pierce is a butcher," I insisted with a little panic in my voice. "We need to boil our water for drinking and make sure everyone stays clean, very clean. We need to prepare big pitchers of lemonade and baking powder water for Caroline. She will have a chance."

His fists clenched, Henry stepped toward me, but Julia stopped him with a gentle hand on his arm. "No," she said softly. Then more forcefully, "I think we ought to listen to Libby. I've been reading things. I think she might be right. At least about staying clean."

Henry was astounded. "Reading things. You're not talking sense. Those are just the girl's crazy ramblings. That's all. You can't think there's anything to them. You would not bet your daughter's life on them. Reading things," he growled disgustedly.

Julia's back stiffened. "I know Hannibal Pierce isn't going to save my daughter. He has not saved anyone yet. I don't want that man coming anywhere near her with that knife of his. Henry, I read it last year. There are new medical discoveries made every day."

He sagged a little as if he was a balloon losing air. By his reaction, it almost appeared as if she had struck him. Something she had said had a powerful impact, but I couldn't begin to guess what it was. She pressed on. "I know doctors in the east have given up on bleeding as doing nothing but harm. Henry, please, see reason."

"See reason! This is crazy talk." He stood for the longest time slapping his hat against his leg over and over again. All the wagons had passed us. We stood alone in the prairie as the wagon train got farther and farther away.

Seeing Henry frustrated, I suddenly knew exactly what caused the tension between them. Simply put, she was educated and he was not. He barely read and she'd had a university education. Not a good mix for two people trying to connect. Finally, he turned to me with a ferocity that gave me a shudder and asked, "You should know your place, Libby. Tell me, how do you know all this? How do you know how to fix cholera?"

This was the telling moment. Caroline's life depended on my answer. Of course, he would never believe the truth. *Well, I'm from the twenty-first century, you know.* That would sink Caroline's chances.

"I just know," Weak!

"That's not good enough."

I was a manipulative bitch, as Vanessa often said to me. It was a compliment. So I did what I did best, I lied, again. "Back in Springfield, I met that new doctor, you know, the one across town. He'd studied at Harvard Medical School. He told me how to cure cholera."

Henry didn't know any new doctor in Springfield, primarily because I had made him up, but he couldn't be sure that he didn't exist. And fortunately, Libby, it seemed, had a reputation for honesty.

"So you remember now?"

"Some things."

Julia placed a hand on his shoulder. "Trust her, Henry. Please. I know she's right."

I could tell he didn't want to. It was too radical a step. But he finally nodded. He had been beaten the moment Julia mentioned she had been reading.

"Oh, Lord, let her be right," he whispered.

Despite the damp, Julia and Isaac got a fire going and I got busy boiling water. That done, I made concoctions for Caroline to drink using extract of lemon and baking powder, several batches, guessing at the proportions but figuring it had to at least be drinkable. We washed her, and all through the rest of the day and night, filled her with liquid. Over and over again. I was desperate to get water into her, clean water. I knew that much.

She'd crap it out. We'd pour it in.

I made Isaac dig holes far from our little camp to dump the slop buckets. I made everyone swear not to drink any water that had not been boiled first and to wash often. A regular autocrat, that was me, but they did it, even Henry. But I could tell by his watchful gaze that I had better be right, or I'd need to find a new family.

Caroline spent the entire night in cycles of sleep and wake, evacuating her bowels and drinking the liquid, then sleep again. Twice she refused to drink, but I forced her. Where had my certainty come from? Was it just from the comparatively vast knowledge I had, or was it Libby's fortitude?

In the morning, Tom Fitzpatrick and Hannibal Pierce rode back to see how Caroline was faring. It was a chilly morning with heavy dew, but the sun was already out. The family, except for Caroline and Julia, hovered around the campfire for warmth as we ate a simple breakfast of bacon, biscuits and tea.

"How's that girl of yours?" Fitzpatrick asked Henry.

"Still with us."

Pierce reached in his saddle bag and drew out the blood pan and knife. "I'll draw blood. She made it this far. Might just get her through."

When Pierce started to dismount, Henry held up his hand. "No need, Pierce."

"But it will…"

"We don't need it," Henry repeated firmly.

Fitzpatrick smiled. "You using Dr. Lemonade's Fabulous All-healing Elixir, then?"

"We are."

I was surprised Henry was backing me, but then he and Pierce had run-ins before. Indignant, Pierce stuffed his pan back in his bags. "God help you and that girl." He spun his horse about and rode off.

Fitzpatrick watched him go a moment. "Man's got a permanent burr up his arse. Pardon my French, Miss Libby. No need for you to break camp. We're only about five miles up the road. Captain Warren's staying put for a day or two. Drying out. Besides, too many sick. We can't outrun this disease." His face darkened. "I'm afraid we will lose many. So no hurry catching up to us. Maybe some Pawnee or Sioux about, so watch yourselves."

"Thanks, Fitz," Henry said. "We'll be along when we can."

Fitzpatrick glanced at me. "I'll tell the captain about your wondrous healing, Miss Quarles. If it works for Caroline maybe it will work for others. Maybe we can do something about this damned pestilence." He tipped his hat and rode off.

In the afternoon two days later, when we drove our two wagons up to the encampment, Caroline rode out on the seat with Julia. She was weak, but feeling much better. Everyone was surprised. During the rest of the afternoon, people came to see her as if an archangel had come down to earth. She wasn't the first to survive the cholera, but everyone thought this one was because of me.

Tom Fitzpatrick gawked at her. "Well, don't that beat all?" he said. "Dr. Lemonade cures her first patient. How are you feeling, Miss Caroline?"

"Tolerable, Mr. Fitz. Better than being dead. That lemonade was good, but I didn't like that other stuff very much."

He laughed. "I bet not. What real medicine ever tastes good?" He looked over at me beside the wagon. "Well, Libby Quarles, the word is spreading. You best come along with me. I think you're going to have some new patients and be a very busy girl for awhile."

Thus began an appalling three-day battle against the Fates. With Julia, I went from tent to tent, carrying a pot of salt and baking powder solution and one of lemonade to start people on my treatment. Caroline's recovery had people desperate for any way to save their loved ones. I explained boiling water was essential. We showed how to prepare the salt and baking powder solutions, and if they had citrus extracts, which most did, told them to use that as well. Afraid I was a bit of a drama queen. Each time I gave them the brew and they looked at it skeptically, I said, "Use it and live. Don't and die. It's your choice."

Caught up in my own mystique, I told them about the wonder doctor in Springfield who took me under his wing and taught me how to heal. Now everyone thought I was a miracle worker. I let them think it. But really, this was simple. You boil freaking water! You drink liquids. You replace electrolytes. The remedy was logical, and it worked.

That first day I did not get to bed till long after midnight. The next morning, a couple more people died. Cynthia Rudabaugh, Abby's six-year-old sister, and the daughter of Newton and Rebecca Rudabaugh, and then Wilson, ten, their son. Silas Hartsook, husband of Mary, father to four boys. James and Lily Tyler, recent newlyweds, she pregnant. I felt the loss of each one. I now had a personal stake in each sick person in this company.

But for the first time most survived.

The second day was the crux of the battle. With a cadre of women, Julia, Myra Langdon, and others, I went from tent to tent, urging each family to stick to the regimen. Myra bore me no ill will for her son's death and made that clear to everyone, saying, had they used my treatment earlier, Putt would still be here. I feared Daniel did not share the same sentiments. Later that day, two more died. Ann Walker, mother of seven, and Joey Nelson, boy of four. But by the next morning, we started to get the better of the beast. Some slight improvement was seen in most patients. That was the hardest and longest day of my life. Once when I thought Jonathon Parrish, a sixty-year-old man, had died, I fled back to my tent and collapsed in tears till Julia came to tell me the man had not passed, but was breathing better and taking down soup with his medicine.

The third day no one died.

The fourth, the wagons pulled out again.

Chapter 22

*A*s I was treating people, a strange thought came to me. Had I altered time? On the Oregon Trail that year, cholera ripped through emigrant company after emigrant company, leaving thousands dead. My anachronistic knowledge had saved many in this company who would otherwise have died. How would that change the future? Did I care? Not at all. As we pushed along just north of the Platte River, I was so exhausted after so many long nights that I walked in a kind of somnambulant state. What was the line from the Frost poem? Miles to go before I sleep. That was me.

Travelling along a series of marshes, the oxen made slow going. They were never fast anyway. Julia decided she needed a break from the constant driving, and while Isaac and Henry drove the two wagons, she walked with me up one of the hills. So heavy with child, she struggled all the way to the top. She had to be no more than a month or two away from giving birth, and the company was not even halfway to journey's end. I wondered what kind of man would drag his pregnant wife out in this wilderness to give birth. Henry was hardly alone. At least four other women were also visibly pregnant. Incredible! I asked her why they had not waited. She waved the idea away. "Myra's a good midwife. I'll be fine."

"Did you even want to come?"

"I go where Henry goes."

Despite her words, I could see a flash of sadness in her eyes. She hadn't wanted to come at all. I wondered if that was also a source of the tension between them. We stood overlooking the Platte River and the road ahead. Maybe five miles away was the glitter of white sails, another wagon train.

"I didn't want to leave my family and friends," she said finally, by way of explanation. "I may never see my sister or my father again. That's a hard thing to accept."

"Then why come?"

"I told you, I go where Henry goes." She thought a moment, then shook her head. "No, it's more than that. In the end, I wanted to go, too. We all know we're making history. I daresay most of us in this company believe it. All the Oregon companies think that."

History. You did make it, I thought. I studied you people in class. "Well, you're right."

She gave me a hug. "I'm proud of you, Libby. No mother could have a better daughter."

Except I wasn't her daughter. "Thank you. Too bad Henry doesn't feel the same."

"Oh, he does. Don't think he doesn't." She brushed the hair out of my eyes. "You've carried adult responsibilities for a few years now but this…what you've done… well, your father and I are proud."

It felt good, her praising me. I got little of it from my real mom, but then I didn't deserve it from her. The low hill was covered with red and yellow flowers. She picked a couple and stuck them in her hair. I helped adjust them. "Perfect," I said. We started making our way down the slope toward the wagons.

"Your memory starting to come back?" she asked.

I shook my head. "Sorry, no. I still don't remember anything before breaking my arm."

"Then you've never met any doctor who told you about cholera, did you?"

She had me. If I couldn't remember beyond a couple of months ago, then how'd I remember this doctor in Springfield? I'd lied and got caught at it. What she didn't know was how good I usually was at it. Telling the truth was important to her, especially between people you cared about. People like her didn't lie, especially to family. I was in trouble.

"You're right," I said, finally. "I lied to you and I'm sorry. I knew how to cure cholera, but couldn't tell you how I knew. I don't really know myself."

Another lie. "Who would believe that? Henry wouldn't. Saving Caroline's life was more important. Maybe it was just God's will."

"Of course, it was. That showed me you're still the same Libby. But lying to your father or me, don't make a habit of it."

"No, ma'am. I promise I won't." And I decided at that moment, I wouldn't. Unless, of course, I had to.

In the Warren Company, forty-three people had died of cholera and were buried along the way. The worst of it was the parents who had to bury so many of their children and leave them behind. I hated witnessing it. It impacted everyone worse than me, because they lost family and friends, and I lost people I'd only just come to know. But they handled it better. Death and hardship was a part of their lives, like the wind and the sun. No family, including the Quarles, was without the tragedy of lost children. They had escaped any loss from this disease, but long before they joined the Warren Company, Henry and Julia had buried three children. It was all too common.

No one wanted to get bled anymore, and that upset Hannibal Pierce. It made him furious with me. He would not even acknowledge my existence. His son Barnaby would, but his acknowledgement was a leer and a sneer, both of which he had perfected. Now, people came to me for every little ailment. As the new "healer," I cleaned a few cuts and scratches, tried to get people to practice better hygiene. Beyond that I didn't have a clue. It was madness to pretend otherwise.

Paula Masters, aka Libby Quarles, the great healer, reigned for just two more days, right up until the moment I was dragged with Julia into the Spence wagon to treat a sick boy, and I had no idea what was wrong with him. He was about five, freckled with a shock of red hair that reminded me of Putt. He had a fever and his neck and jaw were swollen, as if he'd been punched, but there was no discoloration. It wasn't cholera. I knew that much.

Julia and the boy's mother stared at me waiting for the great healer to speak. I stared down at him desperate for some answer to come to me. None did. I looked at Julia, pleading for help. She smiled and told the boy's mother, "Just a damp cloth and rest, Nell."

"Well, I knew that much myself," the woman said.

As we were walking away from their wagon, I asked, "What was wrong with him?"

"Mumps. Maybe it's time for Dr. Lemonade to retire."

"Maybe it is," I replied.

The next morning, I was up early, fixing breakfast with Julia and Caroline, who was much improved, and with the twins flitting around us like buzzing flies. Before the wagons pulled out, Daniel and Tom Fitzpatrick rode by on their way out to hunt buffalo. When they tipped their hats, Daniel gave me an unreadable gaze. I watched him the entire way out of camp.

A sharp voice startled me. "How do, Miss Quarles? Dr. Lemonade, I should say." It was Mr. Whelan prancing by at that moment, an empty bucket in his hand and looking anything but the bereaved widower. He waved his small hand, giving me a syrupy smile.

"Dr. Lemonade has retired," I shouted after him.

He, like everyone else, was treating me as if I was the second coming of Jonas Salk, the famous doctor of the last century—or is it the next century— who came up with a cure for polio.

Julia said scornfully, "He's sure in a jaunty mood for a man whose wife just passed. You'd think that man would be a little more introspective with six children to care for."

For me, the following week was the same old aggravation. Constant chores, barely checked hostility from Henry and endless walking. Hot dry days in which dust stirred up by wagon wheels caught in my throat like stuffed rags. Then stinging rain while the wagons crawled through sucking mud. I even had to pitch in to free wheels when they got stuck.

Worst for me was the lack of anything remotely resembling decent shampoo. How much can you ask a girl to take? My hair was Libby's hair. Not a lot to work with. A little shampoo could put some sheen to it and make it auburn. A better word than brown. Maybe I could be blond again with a little coloring. Did they even have hair coloring now? And little opportunity for a bath. Keeping clean with rough soap in muddy Platte water, especially when you had to maintain decorum and stay mostly dressed, was a trial.

Much to my disappointment, Daniel avoided me as if I had leprosy. Usually having two boyfriends could be a problem. Having them from different centuries was beyond a problem. Cal and Daniel. Cal had his own car. Daniel his own rifle. Choices are sometimes easy. Owning his own rifle made Daniel in the here and now more desirable than all the cover boys with a thousand cars in my time. His skill with that weapon dwarfed any remembrance of Cal and his car. Something happened, though, that took our relationship and tied it in a blue ribbon. I found Libby's diary.

During a sudden cloudburst, I was riding in the back of the wagon with Seneca and Jane, who were playing with their dolls and talking to them in a language all their own, which sent both girls into peals of laughter. Curious to see what I, Libby, personally owned, I rummaged around in the chest that held her and Caroline's things, which was mostly clothes neither would wear on the trail. At the bottom, I found a small book and took it out. There was no title. Just hide covered with the thick smell of leather. I opened it and realized immediately it was a diary, Libby's diary. Feeling guilty, I glanced at the twins, but wrapped up in their own world, they weren't paying attention to me. Why should they? It was my chest. My diary. Still, I felt uneasy when I started reading at a point where she and Daniel met.

April 28, 1848
His name is Daniel. We joined up with him and his folks two days ago when we first got to St. Joseph. His ma is old friends with my ma. We got no emigrant company to travel with yet and Pa and Mr. Langdon went off to find one. No one wants to go it alone in Indian country and people say it is Indian country all the way to Oregon. I do not like the sound of that.

Daniel went with me to explore the town. I had never seen the like. Loud noises came from just about everywhere with the constant hammering in blacksmith sheds and the hawing of those mules and creak of wagon axels and the streets crowded with men, horses and mules and one big emigrant train passing through. I saw several children peeking out from the back of wagons as they went by. Little urchins Daniel called them with a laugh, about to embark on the great adventure. He had a nice laugh. He touched my elbow when he took me into the mercantile to buy us lemonade.

April 30

We crossed the Missouri this morning on the ferry to join up with the Warren Company, which is camped in a meadow on the far side. With our two wagons and the Langdon's two that put the company over one hundred wagons in all. I imagine the biggest company ever. Pa and Isaac attended a lot of meetings in which resolutions got passed and regulations made. They've been here a week. They say they're waiting for the grass to grow before starting out. Doesn't sound like they know what they're doing.

May 1

We started out this morning. I guess the grass grew overnight. We have stopped for lunch. They call that nooning. We have made ten miles already on good road and forded two rivers. I believe it will not always be so easy. Oh, Lord, I am daunted by what lays ahead. Ma says it's 2400 miles before we complete the journey in a place called Oregon City. Seneca and Jane are terrified by the tales of killings and scalping and it worries me some, too. I got to stop writing. I have got chores to do before we start out again.

I just came in from being with Daniel. I am writing this under the Lantern inside the tent while Ma is reading. Pa is out standing guard. Not five minutes ago, Daniel kissed me. Oh, oh, oh.

May 3
Daniel kissed me again last night. I should be writing about the journey, but I only want to write about him. Now, I have to make this a personal diary. Many of us are writing journals for family and friends back in the States. But I don't want anyone to see this.

May 4
Joyous, beautiful kisses again. Many times this night before we parted. He makes me feel like I'm grown. Many girls my age are already married. Maybe me too. It's been only a week and I think I am in love with him. He is nearing twenty, already someone who could take care of himself. People respect him.

May 7
Travelled only ten miles today since it rained quite steadily and the wheels bogged down in the muck. There was a sick fellow laying side of the road. No one knew him. He could barely speak. Some wanted to take him along, but the man refused. Said he wanted to stay right where he was so he could die in peace. Dr. Pierce did what he could for the man, bled him, made him comfortable, and we went on our way.

I think he loves me. Not Dr. Pierce, the man scares me a little, but Daniel, though he has never said it. Oh, I hope so.

Reading this, my own heart came too sharply into focus. A wave of emotion welled up inside me. Libby, who was lost God knows where, loved Daniel and I had her body. Were my feelings for Daniel, which I could not deny anymore, her feelings or my own? They hurt like my own. I could not pass a moment without thinking of him, could not eat or sleep. And I could not abide his ignoring me, but didn't know how to fix it. Strangely, I admitted to a feeling of jealousy for Libby. I mean, who did Daniel love? Her or me? Neither of us right now, it seemed.

As I slid the diary back under her clothes, I wondered what happened to all her hopes and dreams. Would she ever be back to fulfill them?

Chapter 23

A few days later, I did away with the sling. It felt good to have the use of my left arm again, if only in a limited way. It allowed me the edge I needed in my war with Iris. I had figured out how to tame her. Not by force—I doubted that could be done, and I was no rodeo rider—but by guile. As mean as she was, the nasty little beast loved to be groomed. No one knew that because no one dared get close enough to her. Though cautious, I started brushing her at least an hour each day. She was as hard as Sally to glam up, but that didn't mean neither one was worth the effort.

I noticed little by little she began to accept me and even look forward to my coming.

Eventually, she allowed the saddle and me aboard and that was it. I rode her every day, farther and farther out. I was not foolish enough to ride so far out that I lost sight of the wagon train. I was under no illusion as to how dangerous it was in this time. When we studied the mountain men in middle school, someone gave a report on Jed Smith. I remember the manner of his death.

Riding out alone from the wagons he was leading to Santa Fe, he ran into five Comanche while crossing a stream. They killed him without a by-your-leave. I did not want to ride out too far and run into a band of Sioux and face the same fate.

On a glorious, warm Friday evening, Sadie Warren, aged sixteen, the captain's daughter, married Lemual Mason, aged twenty-one. Sixteen was the marrying age, it seemed. A lot of young, recent brides on this trek. It didn't slip my razor sharp brain that I was of age. A proud Captain Warren conducted the ceremony in the shade of the trees along the Platte. Everyone was there. Daniel stood as the best man, and I was one of the bridesmaids. Sadie was pretty, but as severe a girl as I'd ever seen. She never smiled. She took to religion even more than her father did. Lem was almost as stern, but probably, being male, they called him serious. They made a matching pair. I imagined their children would have the humor quotient of a ferret.

During the ceremony, I glanced at Daniel a couple times, wondering what he was thinking. His usual half-smile of amusement was missing, his expression hard to read. When I caught his eye, he looked away. Captain Warren pronounced the couple man and wife. The groom kissed the bride. People cheered. It was done. Standing next to me, Sally cried so loudly everyone stared. It was embarrassing. "It's so beautiful, Libby. Oh, oh, it's so beautiful."

"Okay," I said and tried to move away from her, but she followed me.

"Someday it will be me, Libby. I swear, someday it will be me that gets married." She spoke with such intensity, I stared to see if she was all right.

"Yes, I'm sure it will," I said. Well, it could, I thought. Men outnumbered women ten to one in Oregon, so why not?

Her luck, though, had not been so good in the wagon train. She had made eyes at every single male in the Warren Company from sixteen to sixty, but not one of them was interested. Besides, being bigger than any of them didn't help. Men just ignored her. Even so, she was the most feminine girl I'd ever met, dainty in fact. She said men wanted to visit her at night or slip out into the bushes with her, but she refused. Good for her.

As we walked from the wedding back toward the wagons, I told her she would find a man when she got to Oregon. I truly felt sorry for her, but at the moment, I just wanted her to stop crying.

"I'm sure you're right," she said, not convinced, wiping away her tears.

After the ceremony, the newlyweds slipped off to their tent where they were given a good hour before much of the company showed up banging pots and pans. The couple's parents dragged them out in hastily thrown-on clothes.

"Chivaree!" everyone shouted.

The party lasted well into the night. Fiddles and harmonicas. One man from New Orleans had a Spanish guitar. The same old band. I laughed and danced with several men, picking up the steps quickly, really enjoying myself for the first time since I arrived in this century.

As it grew late, the newly married couple slipped away, and most people went back to their tents, leaving twenty or so men and women by the fire as the impromptu band slipped into playing slower, sadder songs. I recognized Shenandoah but none of the rest.

After awhile, I asked for the Spanish guitar and the man from New Orleans handed it to me. "You play?" he asked with an odd Southern accent.

"A bit, but it'll be a little hard with only three fingers and a couple of nubs," I said, taking the instrument and strumming a couple of chords. I was not very good. I was not as good as this fellow, but that had never stopped me before. Playing with one hand, I managed to punch out a good rendition of *500 Miles*, one of my Uncle Dave's favorite barbecue sing-along tunes. The melancholy melody just about had everyone, including me in tears.

If you miss the train I'm on,
You will know that I am gone.
You can hear the whistle blow
One hundred miles.
One hundred miles, one hundred miles,
One hundred miles, one hundred miles,
You can hear the whistle blow
One hundred miles.
Lord, I'm one, Lord, I'm two,
Lord, I'm three, Lord, I'm four,
Lord, I'm five hundred miles
Away from home.
Five hundred miles, five hundred miles,
Five hundred miles, five hundred miles,

Lord, I'm five hundred miles
Away from home.
Not a shirt on my back,
Not a penny to my name.
Lord, I can't go a-home
This a-way.
This a-way, this a-way,
This a-way, this a-way,
Lord, I can't go a-home
This a-way.

My voice was far better than ever before, actually good, angelic even. Libby's voice! I felt a tingle of excitement. I could actually sing! Julia had a look of utter amazement and Henry's jaw had dropped open. When I finished, everyone clapped enthusiastically, even him. Grinning, I stood and bowed with a flourish.

Myra said with a tear on her cheek, "That song told it all, Libby. You told it all."

"Don't that beat all," Henry said, pulling at his beard. "She ain't never had a single music lesson in her life. Not for two hands or one. How'd you play that, Libby?"

"I don't know," I said. "It just came to me."

Not much of an answer, but what was I going to say. I'm not Libby? It was troubling though seeing Julia watching me with far deeper curiosity, as if puzzling out some great mystery.

Chapter 24

*P*eople made a racket getting ready for bed. One couple, the Warrens, argued about where the newlyweds would live in Oregon. From another tent, I heard a father chastising a boy for losing a knife. In a shrill voice, Lottie Whelan was telling her father she was not going to be mother to all her brothers and sisters. No one could have a private argument on the trail; everyone heard everything. I figured that was about to happen with Daniel and me.

Throughout the chivaree and afterward, I'd been hoping he would come to me, but except for the one dance, he ignored me. I'd had enough. I approached him as he stood by his family's camp fire, drinking from a small jug I assumed was filled with spirits with the Hancock brothers, Billy and Jesse. A half-moon in a clear night sky gave a shadowy darkness to the prairie surrounding us.

They fell silent as I came up. "I want to speak with Daniel," I said.

"All right," he replied, but just stood there.

"Well, if you want to discuss this in front of these two bozos, that's fine with me."

In fact, neither brother was a bozo. I liked them both, but I was angry, mostly with myself for caring about a hopeless relationship. I drew him away to a spot near the Quarles wagon.

"What is it with you?" I asked harshly. "You're treating me like I went out of my way to kill Putt. I did all that I could for him. I cared about him. You know that. And my treatment worked with others so it…"

He said something so quietly, at first I couldn't hear him.

"What?"

"I said, I know, Libby." He fell silent for several seconds. "I know. I should have spoke up for you, but I didn't. I know you didn't kill Putt. If anyone did, it was me. I knew that stuff Pierce was doing was not helping. I knew it, but I didn't say a word."

I was surprised. "It wasn't your fault,"

"It was. I should have been quicker with your drinks for him. I waited till after midnight."

I took his hands in mine. "Nothing could have saved Putt. When I saw him, it was too late. I'm so sorry. The cholera killed him. Please, don't think otherwise."

After a long time, he nodded, but still seemed unconvinced. Taking him in my arms, I leaned back against the wagon, pulling his head down to my shoulder. Here was the strongest young man in the company, the best shot, the most virile, and he was weeping on my shoulder. We stood like that for several minutes till we started talking about other things, mundane things, like hunting and horses and how I was doing with Iris.

Then gently, he kissed me on the lips and pressed his body to mine, his hands slid into my hair and his tongue explored. I felt a thrill corkscrew down my spine. I wanted more of him. He kissed my eyelids, my neck and shoulders. Then I heard giggling. A moment killer.

Instantly, we pulled apart. The twins were hanging out of the wagon enjoying our performance. "What are you two doing out of the tent?" I whispered in mock harshness. "Get back there now before your mom and dad find you gone. Now go."

Still giggling, they scampered down from the wagon and dashed into the tent. I wondered how many other people had heard us.

When the wagons pushed out early the next morning, Julia surprised me by telling me that in another week I was to celebrate my sixteenth birthday. That came as a shock. I was not even as old as I thought I was. This would be my second sixteenth birthday in the last few months. How totally strange that was. Right now, Libby Quarles was fifteen, Paula Masters, sixteen. So how old was I really?

With a knowing grin, Julia told me that once I was sixteen, I could expect a lot more beaus to come around and maybe get a few marriage proposals. Paula Masters was never short of "beaus," but Libby Quarles seemed to have, or have wanted, only Daniel. That counted for a lot, though. His looks were certainly magazine-cover worthy in his rough way, but he had a lot more to him. And I was about to have someone propose to me. That was what Sally said.

"Who?" I asked her, as if I didn't know. Daniel had been hinting at that very thing.

"Sorry. I swore I wouldn't tell. He'd kill me. Oh, Libby. You will be so happy. I wish it was me."

"So do I."

Of course, I couldn't marry Daniel, but this was not exactly like being asked to the prom. He would not expect me to refuse, and I didn't want to hurt him, but I had to.

All the rest of the day I wondered when he'd ask. As it was, the proposal came that evening but with a shocking turn of events. It was at Chimney Rock, a pillar some five hundred feet tall, rising out of the landscape. We camped that evening three quarters of a mile away, and with a couple hours of daylight left after dinner, Sally and I decided to explore it. Daniel and Mr. Whelan came along for protection, both armed with rifles and pistols. This would be Daniel's chance. I anguished over how he would take the rejection. No doubt, Whelan wished for free time away from his six children, who were driving him crazy. After their mother's death, they had gotten worse. His beard had been trimmed recently, and he looked neat in a clean brown shirt and bowler hat. I thought it looked funny out here on the prairie.

"That's a right pretty dress, Miss Quarles," he said with a silly grin as we hiked toward Chimney Rock. He was making it difficult for Daniel to get me alone and pop the big question.

"Thank you, Mr. Whelan," I said and gave Sally a roll of the eyes.

Daniel chuckled. I don't know what he thought so funny. If he was going to ask me to marry him, I wanted him to at least feel a few more nerves. Against my own better judgment, I began looking forward to the moment. How would he do it? On one knee maybe. A heartfelt declaration of love. At the least, it would mean some big time romantic sparks. Nothing wrong with that. A little part of me wished I actually was from this era, so I could accept.

A few other groups had gone out from the wagon train earlier and passed them heading back. Finally, the great tower loomed above us and we began climbing. Sally gave me about the two-hundredth knowing look, so I demanded, "What?"

"Oh, nothing, nothing." She giggled. Infuriating! Daniel and I should have come alone.

The base was fairly steep, so we made our way up carefully. On the rocks where people had carved their names, we planned to do the same. Mr. Whelan had brought a hammer and chisel. A man of foresight. We chose a large, unmarked boulder. When it came my turn, I carved in "Paula Masters," which surprised everyone. Then, I added, "Libby Quarles." I didn't want to rob her of her immortality.

Daniel asked, "Who is Paula Masters?"

"Just an old friend."

"She die?"

"No," I replied sharply. "Why would you think that?"

He gestured to the etched name, as if that was an answer, then shrugged. We went on up to the needle where we could go no higher. It went straight up another couple hundred feet. No climbing that.

"Too steep for you ladies, I'm afraid," Mr. Whelan said, puffing out his chest. Yeah, right, I thought. Like you'd scamper right up its sides if we weren't here.

"We better start back," Daniel said. "It's getting late."

Mr. Whelan took out a gold watch, making sure everyone saw it. "Yes. Near 9:30. We've waited too long as it is."

We were in a long twilight, getting near the dark end of it, and had a lot of prairie to cover to get back to the wagons. For the first time, I thought about Indians skulking around at night. Still, as we headed back, I went out in front about twenty yards as if in a hurry, but in reality, it was to give Daniel space to ask me the big question. Finally, I heard his footsteps coming to catch up. This was it. Smiling pleasantly, I turned around.

"Right pretty evening, isn't it, Miss Quarles?"

I stared, horrified. It was Mr. Whelan. Go back, go back, I thought. Give Daniel his chance. Then I had a terrible thought. Quickly, I looked to Daniel and Sally holding back. In the waning light, I could just make out her giddy smile and his amused expression. Oh, dear God.

"I would like your permission to speak with your father, Miss Quarles," Whelan said hesitantly. "I feel we can reach an understanding."

Oh, dear God! "About what?" I almost shouted it.

"If he is amenable, it would be a great honor to ask him for your hand in marriage."

I reverted hard back to being Paula Masters. "Are you tripping out, dude?"

He blinked. "Miss Quarles?"

Going ballistic, I said, "I'm sixteen, no fifteen, only one year older than Lottie. You know, your daughter! And you're freaking eighty-five. This is perve territory, dude."

"Hardly that old." He tried to smile but couldn't quite pull it off. He was discomfited, his constant blinking annoying the hell out of me. "I am but thirty-six, er, thirty-four. Some older than you, but I'm settled. Are you not soon to be sixteen? That's certainly marrying age. You see…" He cleared his throat. "You see, I am in need of a wife, and you will search long and hard to find a better husband. I have built up …I have solid business…"

I interrupted him. "I'm telling you, sir, I am not looking for a husband."

Like a bad dream, he went on as if I hadn't spoken. "I will provide you with a good home. I will always put food on the table."

He handed me a ring. I realized with alarm he had to have taken it off his dead wife. I dropped it in the sand. He picked it up and brushed it off. He straightened his back. "As my wife, you will never lack anything. When we reach Oregon, I will make a success. You will see. You will be so rich you will make other women feel small. I will put gold on your arms and diamonds on your neck, and when you walk by, people will say, there goes William Whelan's wife." Suddenly, he smiled and stopped blinking. "What do you say, Miss Quarles?"

He had six wild children, including Lottie, not my favorite person, and needed a wife to take care of them. That much was clear. But it was sure as hell not going to be me. It would be a horrible thing to do to poor Libby. I would someday be whisked back to the twenty-first century and she'd be left in a marriage with this guy.

Then it got worse. To my horror, he bent down on one knee. I grabbed hold of his shirt with both my hands and yanked him to his feet. "Geez, get up."

My sudden grab threw him off balance. He stumbled forward, tumbling us both to the ground. He fell right on top of me, knocking my breath out. Mumbling apologies, he scrambled up, brushing himself off. Somehow, he'd left the ring in my hand.

Daniel rushed forward and helped me up. "Are you all right?" he asked.

"Oh, man. Oh, man," was all I could say.

"I'm sorry, Miss Quarles," Whelan said hastily. "I don't know what happened,"

"Hold your hand out," I ordered him.

Confused, he did, and I plunked the ring back into it. "Thank you for the offer, sir, but I can't marry you." I turned to Sally. "Let's go."

When we got back to camp, Sally and Whelan went to their separate wagons. I punched Daniel hard in the side. "Did you know about that?"

He held up his hands in innocence. "No, I swear. I did worry there for a bit you might accept such a fine offer."

I shoved him and walked off. Inside, the wagon and found the diary. I found a pen and ink bottle in a small chest.

Libby's diary, June 20

I must keep this journal going. My responsibility now. I had a marriage proposal today, and I will say no more about that. Not much else I want to say except I miss my family. Julia says we covered twenty miles today. That's way more than usual. I can believe it. I walked most of it with Sally, Abby, and Lottie, far out from the wagons to avoid the clouds of dust churned up by the wheels. The heat was oppressive, surely getting up to a hundred.

Teenage girls talk pretty much about the same things in any time period: boys; looking good, which is not so easy on this trek; and sex. For these girls, sex was a stolen kiss behind the wagons and maybe a hastily groped breast.

Just after the nooning, Seneca became ill with a stomach ailment. I worried it was something with no cure, which was just about everything, but Julia said it's because she drank muddy river water. She made the girl vomit to get rid of it. That did the trick. Seneca was up and out of the wagon in less than an hour.

Libby's diary, June 21

Daniel was almost killed by Indians earlier today and I'm sick about it. More and more he goes out on his own to hunt, like he's Tom Fitzpatrick or something. Today, he ran into a band of Cheyenne, a hundred or more, he said. They took his horse, pistol, rifle and clothes, leaving him with nothing but a pair of short britches and then let him go. When he made it back to the company this evening, his embarrassment was clear from the blush of his skin, all his skin.

Everyone geared up for an attack by the whole Cheyenne Nation. "Lock and load," men cried out. "They're a comin' to take our scalps," someone warned. Sure enough, near sunset, the Cheyenne appeared in the far distance, but what looked like a horde to me turned out to be no more than twenty. My first glimpse of wild and lethal Indians had me awed and scared out of my wits. I was sure that any moment they'd come rampaging through the wagon train.

Incredibly brave or stupid, Fitzpatrick rode out alone to talk with them and somehow convinced them to return everything but Daniel's pistol. When Fitzpatrick returned his clothes to him, Daniel looked as if he wanted to crawl into a hole. Now everyone is calling him "Cheyenne" Langdon. He doesn't like that much.

Libby's diary, June 22
Before starting out this morning, Little George caught two fish. The boy was beaming with pride. Still he gave only grunted responses when we praised him for it. During nooning, Julia cooked them up. Hot again today.

Libby's diary, June 23
On this day, another person died. The way things turn so quickly from ordinary to deadly scares me to my bones. I don't think I'll ever get used to it. It happened like this: when we woke up in the morning, we learned some cattle had either run off in the night or been stolen by Indians. Daniel, Jesse and Billy Hancock, Barnaby Pierce and several other men rode off after them while the rest of us started out on the trail. A couple hours later, Mr. Whelan raced his horse in like the Sioux Nation was on his tail just to bring us the news that one of the boys drowned. People were furious with the fool because he didn't know who. Right off, it seems, the men split up to search for the cattle and the drowning had not occurred in Whelan's group. He had been so eager to be the one to bring us the news, he hadn't waited to find out which boy had died. I wanted to boot him into the Platte. I prayed it wasn't Daniel.

It was Billy Hancock.

Poor Billy. I felt ashamed at my sudden elation when I learned it wasn't Daniel. I didn't want Billy to drown, but, Dear God, I didn't want it to be Daniel. Poor Jesse. When the men returned with the missing cattle, which had only drifted off a short way after all, they had the body with them. Jesse was blank-staring as if his brain had shut down. Daniel told me that while crossing a small stream, Billy's horse threw him and his boot caught in the stirrup. He was dragged through the water and drowned before anyone could get to him. We will bury him in the morning and move on. Jesse is inconsolable.

June 24
Very late. I write by lantern inside the wagon. The others are asleep in the tent. It's hard writing just a day after such a tragedy. Daniel was shaken by the loss of his friend, so I spent time with him till long after dark, huddled together in the lee of his wagon while a persistent drizzle fell. We talked, oblivious to the wet and the lateness. He didn't exactly blame himself for Billy, but he was the first to reach him and felt that, if he could have been faster, he might have saved him. Holding on to him, I told him not to blame himself. I finally let him go when Myra came out of their tent to get him, demanding if we knew what time it was. He kissed my cheek and went in.

Unfortunately, tragedies such as this one have not been unusual. I find it difficult to deal with how hard this journey is, both emotionally and physically. Sometimes I think these people are crazy and other times amazing. Not much difference between the two, I suppose. Even after a long bone-wearying day, even after hardship and tragedy, these people still move on the next morning, relentless, determined, as if desperately trying to distance themselves from the pain of it, and maybe, also, the reminder of their own mortality. I see in their eyes that it takes its toll on them. It sure does me.

Chapter 25

Not long after Billy Hancock's drowning, Daniel finally asked me to marry him. Maybe the brush with death again had made him long for something more. The wagon train that afternoon was passing Scott's Bluff. With Seneca and Jane on our backs, we hiked up to the crags at its base. Always armed, he carried two pistols in his belt and a rifle. As we explored the bluff, the wagons crawled leisurely along a couple hundred yards away, dust lifting off the wheels. The day was hot and the sky endless. From their perches on our backs, Seneca and Jane were playing their favorite game, trying to fool Daniel as to which twin was which.

"Now that's hard," he said, giving it some thought.

"Guess. Who am I?" Seneca pressed. She was on his back.

"I know," he said playfully. "You're one of them ornery Quarles' girls."

"Yes, but which one, Daniel, which one?" she persisted, excitedly.

Stopping, he pulled her off his back and held her by the scruff of her dress with one arm, her legs running in place, squealing with delight as he puzzled over her. "You're Jane."

Both girls laughed hysterically. "Yes!" Seneca said. "I'm Jane."

Daniel swung her onto his back again.

"You little liar," I scolded with a mock frown. "I can tell you two apart now."

"You're our sister," Jane said. "You're supposed to."

I pointed to Seneca's left eye and winked. She had a barely visible red blemish in the shape of a Z just above it. Maybe the only physical difference in the twins.

I touched it gently. "The Mark of Zorro. That's how I can tell you apart."

"What's a Zorro?" she asked.

"He wears a mask and fights bad people. He helps good hardworking folks like the Langdons and the Quarles. He is the best sword fighter in all of California."

Daniel glanced at me with an amused smile. "A mask, huh?"

"Sure."

Suddenly, he set Seneca on the ground, shifted from foot to foot, then said, "Seneca, Jane, I want you to be quiet for a minute so I can speak to your sister about something mighty important. And I want you to promise not to listen. You promise?"

Both girls nodded.

"Elizabeth Mary Emma Quarles," he began. I didn't even know I had a middle name and it turned out I had two of them. He descended to one knee. Oh, Lord! "I love you with all my heart. I've loved you since the first day I saw you in St. Jo. I want to live the rest of my life as your husband. Libby, will you marry me?"

For some time, I'd half expected this to happen, but still it set my blood racing. I swallowed and couldn't respond at first. So many reasons why I couldn't accept this.

The twins shouted in unison, "Yes!"

"He's not asking you two," I said.

"Well, say yes," Jane said.

No way could I marry him, yet I heard myself saying, "Yes. Yes, I will marry you."

Immediately, I cursed myself for being an idiot. I could not marry someone I would soon leave with no hope of ever seeing again. But Libby did love him, too, so it would be okay, and I could not take it back now. As he rose to his feet, he had a broad grin on his face. He kissed me while the twins laughed and cheered.

"Daniel, I will marry you, but not now and not here. When we get to Oregon." I saw his grin fade. "Can you wait?" I asked.

After a long moment, he said, "I guess I will have to." He kissed me again to the delight of the squealing twins, and then we headed back.

That evening we celebrated our engagement with a big dinner between the Quarles and Langdons during which half the company came by to congratulate us. Funny how things in life fit together. Daniel asked me to marry him and I accepted, but I did not think I'd be in this century long enough to see it done. Then, that night, as if by ordination, a stranger rode into camp that would play such a big part in both our lives and in time giving me an avenue back to my own century.

He came during one of Tom Fitzpatrick's stories at Captain Warren's campfire, where he often told tales of his fur trapping days, which tended to draw a large crowd. Being well into Sioux country, several men asked Fitz what he knew of them. "Well, now, I'm partial to the Arapaho and never had me too many good experiences with the Lakota, any tribe of them. But seeing as how I'm the Agent to all the Plains Indians now, I got to look at all of them with equanimity, even those folks. I figure you men want God's own truth in the matter, and so I tell you that they are tough men, no people to fight if you can avoid it."

Fitz paused, taking another draw on his pipe. "They can be mighty friendly people when they're not trying to take your scalp."

Light was waning, and a few stars had appeared in a still grey sky. I leaned against Daniel, taking his hand and squeezing it. At that moment, Fitzpatrick rose from his stool and took several steps forward, gazing beyond the wagons at a swathe of hills to the west. Something had caught his eye. We all looked in that direction. A rider was etched against the twilight sky crossing a nearby ridge and heading our way. After a moment, Fitz muttered, "Well, I'll be damned."

Hurriedly, the men retrieved their rifles. Trust of strangers out here was not a plentiful commodity. A few minutes later, horse and rider ambled into the circle of wagons, a freshly killed antelope looped over his saddle. I studied him curiously. A black man in dust-covered fringe buckskin, a long rifle cradled in the crook of his arm, a wizened look to his dark, leathery face. No one to be trifled with. He dropped the antelope on the ground in front of Fitzpatrick and announced, "Now, folks, I brung you some meat. I done heerd you all had old Fitz as your pilot and hunter, so I figgered by now if you ain't lost, you'd likely be starving."

I knew who it was. Jim Beckwourth. Like Fitzpatrick, this was a famous mountain man and scout. Not only had I studied both men in Mrs. Guthrie's class, I'd done a report in middle school on Beckwourth, an ex-slave. I recycled it later in Mrs. Guthrie's class because she particularly liked him. I'd score easy points, I'd thought. She gave me a D. I found it incredible he was right in front of me now, incredible that mountain men like him, Jed Smith, Jim Bridger and Tom Fitzpatrick were still alive. Well, not Jed Smith.

"Oh, now we're saved," Fitzpatrick said in a high-pitched voice, mocking him.

"Fitz, you are looking mighty long in the tooth, old son." Beckwourth slipped from his horse. "You gots to be pushing eighty now, ain't you?"

Fitzpatrick's eyes flashed. For a moment, as they stood facing each other, belligerence was written all over their faces and violence seemed certain. I squeezed closer to Daniel. What was it with everyone in this time, always ready to fight? Then Beckwourth gave out with a bellowing laugh and Fitzpatrick joined in.

"Ladies and gentlemen," Fitzpatrick said. "I'd like to present to you the biggest liar on the plains, Mr. Jim Beckwourth."

"Liar? I got me the best horse, the surest rifle, the prettiest wife and the ugliest dog west of the Mississippi, and probably east of it, too. I can out trap any man in the mountains including this old has-been Tom Fitzpatrick. I wrestle grizzly bars for fun and eat tree bark for supper, though I do prefer good buffalo meat. That there's the By-God truth."

"And out drink," Fitzpatrick added.

Beckwourth grinned. "That too."

I was thinking what a report I could write for Advanced History now.

"What are you doing here, Jim?" Fitz asked. "Last I heard you were up north with the Crow."

"I was. Came down to sell buffalo hides at Fort Laramie. Now, I'm headed to Californy."

Fitzpatrick shook his head ruefully. When he spoke, it was with great sadness. "Now I knew you were getting on in years, Jim, but I didn't realize just how far gone you were. I hate to be the one to tell you, old son, but you're going the wrong way." He pointed west. "If you be coming from Fort Laramie, well, California's west, not east."

Beckwourth nodded and did not reply at first. A cold expression came into his eyes and his tone was hard. "Had business with the Pawnee." What business, he didn't say, but from his demeanor my guess was the Pawnee didn't fare too well in it. "Now, I'm to Californy. Some fellow found gold there." He turned to the rest of us and said loudly, "Gold's been found in Californy. You can pick it up off the ground. The hills shine with it. You just got to have big pockets to stick it in is all."

That caused a stir. Shouting gold among the emigrants was like shouting water among people dying of thirst. You got a rise.

"If you think there's lots of emigrants on the Holy Road now," Beckwourth added. "Next year they'll outnumber the stars. I'm getting there ahead of the crowd."

I could tell in that instant many of these emigrants, too, wanted to be first on the scene. I was seeing the fever spread through the company that very moment, every adult glancing at each other, and erupting in a hundred excited conversations. The news would change everything.

"Figger to catch on as pilot somewhere," Beckwourth said.

Captain Warren, who'd been listening intently, said, "Mr. Fitzpatrick is our pilot. We are well satisfied with his service, but he will be leaving us in a few weeks to take up his duties as Indian Agent. You are welcome to travel with us and pilot us afterward, but we are heading for Oregon."

"Now, I may do that. Lot of miles between here and the turn off to Californy. Don't want to worry you none, sir, but when we get to Fort Hall, there might be a few of your wagons headed south to the goldfields." He spoke to his audience, most of the company now. "It's a hard trail, hard trail. Deserts that ain't seen water since Noah's time and mountains that touch the sky. You heared of the Donners? Well, folks, don't you worry. Old Jim will get you through."

Captain Warren bore a troubled expression. "We'll cross that bridge when we come to it."

"Anything up ahead we need to worry about?" Fitzpatrick asked.

"Yep. Got some news of the Indian variety." To milk the moment, Beckwourth took off his chewed up hat and for several seconds wiped his forehead with a checkered handkerchief. With everyone intent on him, he finally said, "Lots of Sioux activity around Fort Laramie. Several bands down from the north. Wild ones of the mean kind. A regular little war going on with the Pawnee. Raiding each other's camps, stealing horses and carrying off squaws. They ain't attacked no whites yet, but my guess is they will, sooner than later."

"Not likely, Jim. Sioux are not at war with us," Fitzpatrick said.

"You bet these people's hair on that, Tom?"

I knew very little about Indians except that in my day they ran casinos. Last year, Cal, Alex, Van and I went to one south of LA. Using fake IDs, we got drunk, especially me, and lost tons of money I didn't have, nearly two thousand dollars on my mother's credit card. We trashed our rooms—not cool—and ordered room service we couldn't pay for. For more than two hours, the Indians scared the piss out of us with vague threats, then told us to get off their land and never come back. That they let us go, even with my being such a primo bitch during the whole affair, was surprising. I still can't figure out why they did. When my mother found out about the casino bills, she had a cow, then paid them and grounded me forever. Maybe that was when she and Dad started seeing me as a problem.

Now they were more than 180 years away.

Alarm was rippling through the emigrants. In a way, I could understand it. Since I'd been in this time, I'd heard tale after tale of Indian atrocities. Massacres, scalping, torture. Even the most superficial look at these stories showed they couldn't possibly all be true, but try as Fitzpatrick might, nothing could change minds when people were scared. And Indians made them scared. I had no illusion. In this time, they were extremely dangerous.

Fitzpatrick studied Beckwourth a moment. "You got something else. Tell it."

The black man drew in his breath. "Brings Thunder is out and about."

A grim look came to Fitzpatrick's face. "You're sure?"

"Saw him at Fort Laramie a week ago."

Fitzpatrick turned to Captain Warren. "We better double the guards."

Captain Warren announced, "I heard of him back in St. Louis. Keep your weapons nigh and your powder dry, boys."

Curious, I made a mental note to find out who this Brings Thunder was. I remembered Fitzpatrick mentioning him once before during one of his tales with an edge of hate and maybe fear in his voice. Anyone who had Fitzpatrick frightened got me frightened.

The next morning, I wrote again in Libby's diary.

Libby's diary, June 27

As I write this sitting inside the wagon, chores done, waiting for the captain to start us moving, the sun is rising over a far bluff in crimson and orange swathes. Rain today, I bet. I plan to ride Iris some today. She is getting used to me. Fitzpatrick says we may get in twenty-five miles, if it doesn't rain too hard.

Last night, a strange rider arrived and caused a stir with news of the California gold strike and a warning about possible hostile Indians ahead. Once, he looked at me and did a double take, as if he recognized me. For some reason, I think he is important to me. I don't know why. This man's name is Jim Beckwourth. Incredible! Mrs. Guthrie would pee with envy.

Chapter 26

A couple days later, the Sioux came.

They were not at all as I had expected. It was the evening of my birthday, well, Libby's birthday. Rain had fallen earlier. When it finally stopped, the sun came out, and we celebrated my second sixteenth birthday. Odd that. Once we found enough dry kindling and buffalo chips to start a fire, Julia baked a yellow cake with the Dutch oven, then the twins spread lemon icing over it, getting as much on themselves as the cake. The cake was hard and crusty on the outside, doughy on the inside. Julia was not exactly a great cook. Not quite Sara Lee, but I appreciated the effort and sincerely thanked them all. Caroline stuck on a single candle.

Julia and I also fried a ton of pancakes for our breakfasts over the next few days and had them stacked on plates cooling as we ate our dinner. Just after seven, the Langdons arrived for cake.

"We come to congratulate the birthday girl," Myra said.

Daniel said playfully, "Sixteen. No more excuses now. Adult things will be expected of you." He winked. I blushed.

Sally arrived a few minutes later with a shy wave. After I handed her a piece of cake, she sat off by herself next to the wagon, so she could duck behind it if she saw Hannibal or Barnaby coming. Neither wanted her having anything to do with me. Captain Warren and his wife and daughter came by with Tom Fitzpatrick and several others, but not Beckwourth. For some reason, he was avoiding me. Every time I went to Captain Warren's wagons, they'd say he'd just rode off. I'd even saddled Iris to look for him, riding out alone a few hundred yards and getting soaked in the process. I thought that when I returned to my own time, I could go to Mrs. Guthrie and tell her all

140

about her Mr. Jim Beckwourth. His avoiding me didn't make sense, but then what did?

Except for the cake, this was not much of a birthday party. Gifts were in short supply. Henry wasn't much for celebrations, and people didn't seem to worry too much about birthdays. But they had nothing against cake. Daniel did surprise me with a new bridle for Iris he'd been working on for the past month. Seeing how eager he was for my reaction, I did my best to appear excited and whispered to him, "I'll thank you later."

That's when Jane screamed at the sudden appearance of the Indians, two men and two women on foot arriving at the wagons as if conjured there. Julia wrapped the twins in her arms. Quickly, a hundred rifles were aimed at the Indians. They were not marauders; they came to beg food. For some reason, this disappointed me. I didn't know what I had expected, noble savage, that kind of thing, but it wasn't beggars.

When Fitzpatrick insisted that they meant no harm, the guns were lowered. He said they were Lakota from a nearby band. Wearing scruffy buffalo robes, the two men were lean, early forties by the look of them, skin weathered to a dark hue. A strong, sweaty musk clung to them.

The leader had an empty eye socket. Fascinating and grotesque, I found myself continually looking away, then back to it. Old One Eye did not seem the least self-conscious about it. The women were clothed in buckskin dresses and leggings, both stocky and strongly muscled with broad, florid faces.

Giving a gap-toothed grin, Old One Eye pointed to Julia's belly. "Hoksicala," he said and laughed. His laugh was deep and pleasant. When he indicated with crude sign language that he wanted food, Julia muttered, "Oh, dear."

She just couldn't turn anyone away hungry. She had baked those pancakes for the family to eat for days, but ended up giving them all away, along with a daub of molasses in a small jar. Old One Eye grinned again and made a speech no one understood, not even Fitzpatrick.

Hands out, they went from campfire to campfire, turned away at some, but receiving bread and jerky at others. The people of the company had no fondness for beggars of any kind, especially if they were able-bodied. To them, life meant hard work, and they did not like someone riding free on someone else's labor.

Kindness was a different matter. These emigrants could be more compassionate and kindly toward someone in need than most in my own time. In this case, though, even when Fitz explained that to the Lakota food was to be shared, it didn't sway any minds.

Finally, walking away with tomorrow's breakfast, Old One Eye glanced back with an unreadable expression at Julia and me. Feeling a roguish impulse, I gave an exaggerated wave.

The next day, the Sioux came again, many, many more of them and this time with savage purpose. During nooning when the wagons had circled, Daniel and I rode alone, heading up a long gradual slope toward the crest of a low hill. Under a cloudless sky, the prairie stretched for endless miles, undulations with stunted grass baking under a fierce sun. Studying the ridge just ahead, Daniel leaned forward in the stirrups then back, his hands fidgeting on the reins.

"Should I go away?" I asked him.

He jerked as if I'd jabbed him with a needle. "Why do you say that?"

"Maybe you want to be alone with your thoughts. You're thinking about Lydia Watson, aren't you?"

"No, of course not."

"Ah, a guilty reaction, if I ever saw one."

"Why would I be thinking of her?"

"Oh, I don't know. Because you like her. She's pretty. You and she are always snuggling up to each other, giggling like little children."

"We don't snuggle. She comes over. I can't just tell her to go away."

"Why not? I do."

"It would be rude."

"I'm one of the original Rude Girls. You can like Lydia all you want if that's what you're worried about. It means nothing to me."

He drew his horse to a halt, gazing at me. "Libby, you're talking crazy. Why would I be sparking Lydia Watson when we're going to be married and I'm riding up here with you? Not her. And I do not giggle."

I laughed. "Oh, Daniel, you can admit you like her. I see how you look at her. It's all right. I don't own you."

In frustration, he shook his head. "We're engaged, woman. How do I look at her?"

"Like she's, oh, so pretty, prettier than me. I understand that."

"No one's prettier than you."

"Now I know you're lying." Libby was not pretty. "You're such a liar, Daniel."

He sighed deeply and fell silent. By this time, we'd drifted pretty far from the wagons, nearly a half mile off and very near the top of the ridge. He looked at me askance. "I swear, Libby Quarles, you are more different than any girl I ever met. Quarles is a good name for you."

Laughing, I took his hand and placed it on my cheek. Our horses were so close together that our legs touched. I knew he felt the sudden shudder that passed between us because his chest lifted big time, and his face flushed. My own breathing sped up. Neither of us moved. He ran his fingers along my cheek to my lips, then with the other hand drew me to him and kissed me. Electricity shot up my spine. With all that juice, I was sure I could light a city. I felt the world rumble.

Then, abruptly, we broke apart. The earth really was shaking, deep tremors, as if rising up from the center of the earth. Daniel's hand was still on my neck. "What is that?"

I shook my head. How would I know?

A look of worry crossed his face, and now I was afraid. The horses stumbled apart as the ground shook more. A California girl, it came to me. "Earthquake."

In school we got under our desks. What were we supposed to do here? I was suddenly terrified; the din grew as if a 747 was going to come over the crest of the hill straight at us. A cloud of dust rose from the other side, and I realized it was no earthquake. I had no idea what was coming, but I knew it wasn't good. "I think we better go."

Before we could move, they came. Buffalo! A massive, dark wave more than half a mile wide on the ridge, bearing down on us.

I screamed in terror, "My God!"

"Ride!" Daniel screamed.

Bursting to life, we spun our horses toward the wagons. To my surprise, Iris flew, her ears pinned back, her strides lengthening, ever swifter. God, she was fast! In a few strides I had outdistanced Daniel and glanced back.

"Keep going," he shouted.

I slanted to the right till I was well out of the oncoming tsunami and watched the herd in horror as they headed straight for the wagons. I prayed the Quarles, all of them, would be safe. Then something sent a chill down my back. Several women and children had been walking out from the wagons and were running back, Caroline among them, and I could see she wasn't going to make it. The buffalo would swamp her long before she reached safety.

Standing on the wagon seat, Julia waved frantically at her, shouting something that could not be heard over the roar. Daniel raced for her and leaning down snatched her up from behind without breaking stride. I yelled a cheer so loud I could actually hear it over the din. Turning his horse out of the way of the onslaught, he brought her over and handed her to me. She hugged me.

I reached out and put a hand on Daniel's forearm. "Thank you."

He nodded and then rode hard back into the melee, dashing for the wagons.

I screamed at him, "Where are you going?"

I had no desire to follow, especially holding onto Caroline. I watched terrified as he disappeared into the dust cloud. My heart was swallowed up in a dark hopelessness. He would be trampled to death. The great herd was seconds away from the wagons, women and children screaming, running, just ahead. Three men broke out on horseback, waving blankets in an attempt to turn them. Henry was one of them. This was suicide.

The roar grew monstrous. Henry and the two other men waved frantically, fleas trying to stop an ocean. They were engulfed. One man went down underneath. Caroline screamed and I turned us both away. When I looked back, I couldn't see any of them. Henry had disappeared in a sea of black.

Amazingly, they had managed to turn some of the beasts aside, or maybe it was the wall of white prairie schooners that turned them. Whatever it was, most of the buffalo changed direction, taking a big swing toward the west. That left maybe two hundred that tore into the wagons, a collision of dust and fury.

Several wagons spun 180 degrees; two toppled in great crashes. I heard screams above the din.

The animals were almost on the Quarles wagons. At the last second, Isaac was helping Little George into the back, the twins pulling on him, and Isaac clambered in afterward, as if that rickety thing would provide protection.

Caroline moaned, "Libby." I held her.

Julia turned the oxen directly into the massive herd, and the buffalo split like water around an island. The Quarles' wagon shook and shook but remained upright. From nearly a hundred yards, I could see how huge the beasts were, as big as SUVs, gnarled black fur, black horned heads, bulging eyes white with fear. Their hooves were pounding inside my chest. Beyond the wagons, they plunged into the river. I took in a gulp of air, realizing I hadn't been breathing.

But the danger was not done. Something was chasing the buffalo, and now we saw them coming out of the dust cloud. I got my first look at one of the most feared and lethal Indian tribes of American History, the wild Sioux in their pomp, in their splendor, on the chase.

Riding with a power and beauty I had never imagined possible, some thirty Sioux pursued the buffalo, whooping and hollering, letting loose arrows with a frequency and accuracy that was amazing. Handling their mounts with only a rope halter, they rode bareback with such wild abandon that they and their ponies seemed one being. They were clad only in breechclouts, their muscular bodies glistening in the sunlight, sweeping past us in a pounding blur and splashing headlong into the river after the buffalo. There was something primordial about it all. Within seconds, forty buffalo were trapped on an island in the river, and the slaughter began.

For me, agony tore at my soul. Daniel was nowhere in sight, likely dead under the buffalo hooves, and maybe Henry as well. That would mean disaster for the Quarles and Langdon families. And for me. With Caroline quietly crying, I chucked Iris toward our people.

Chapter 27

The scene looked like a tornado had swept through a trailer park. People were dazed, staring at overturned wagons, wandering through debris fields of household goods. I was beside myself with worry for Daniel. After depositing Caroline with Julia, I frantically searched for him. The Langdons had no idea where he was either and feared the worst. Then I saw him about a half mile to the east with two other men herding some cattle and horses. Furious, I rode out to him.

Hearing my own voice raised to a hysterical pitch, I shouted, "Damn you, Daniel, for riding off like that. I thought you were dead. Your parents thought you were dead. Some of us care about you, you know, though I don't know why."

He gave me that amused expression for just a moment, then realized making light of my anger was a bad choice. "You're right. I'm sorry. I should have come back right away. I saw the cattle and horses running off and just followed them."

I said nothing, just spun Iris around and headed back to camp. This was terrible. I kept asking myself what I was doing. Dear God, I had fallen desperately in love with someone from a different century. This was madness.

As it turned out, we were lucky; we only lost one man. Henry had survived. He had been swept along with the buffalo herd, smartly going with it instead of against it, finally making his way to safety, as did another of the trio who had attempted to turn the herd with their blankets.

Fortier, the guitarist from New Orleans, was the unlucky one. He'd gone down under the pounding hooves. Unlucky for his wife and children also. She would have almost no way to earn a living, so likely she would have to marry quickly for the sake of the children. After the funeral, she wanted to sell me the guitar—said she had no use for it now—but Henry vetoed the idea, saying we did not have the money to spend on such useless things. Jerk!

With so much cleanup and repair to do, Captain Warren decided to camp where we were. After we'd set up as best we could in the mess, Old One Eye showed up at our wagon, beckoning us to follow him. Henry, Isaac and I waded out after him into the Platte to "Slaughter Island," where over the years, the Indians had trapped and killed hundreds of buffalo, thus the name. Indian women were arm deep in blood, carving up the beasts. A few other families from the wagons had come out as well, too curious to be scared.

Nothing in my life of fast food places, coffee shops and cafeteria lunches could have prepared me for butchered buffalo carcasses surrounded by clouds of flies and yellow jackets. Old One Eye led us to the massive body of a cow, where three women worked. The youngest one, no more than my age, sliced open the belly. As blood and entrails slopped out, my stomach grew queasy, but it didn't bother Isaac, so I wasn't going to let it bother me. Gritting my teeth, I forced myself to watch.

One of the women cut off a teat and drank the milk, passing it to the others. The youngest one handed it to me. Thinking of all the bacteria it must contain, I grimaced but took a drink and hoped my stomach would keep it down, then passed it along. As the women quickly skinned the beast, they snacked on pieces of raw meat, chatting constantly among themselves and to us, though none of us could understand them. Didn't matter. We had established a friendship for that moment in time.

They moved on to work at butchering a bull next. Then, shockingly, one cut off a testicle and offered it to me, indicating I was to eat it. Are you kidding me! No way. My eyes must have bugged out wider than the monster that ate Tokyo, for she urged me on. Milk from the teat was one thing, but buffalo balls was too much. Closing my eyes, I took a tentative, tiny bite and handed it quickly to Isaac with a smug challenge, but he gave me a snarky expression and bit right into it. Old One-Eye gave us a huge cut of meat, and we returned to camp with our bloody haul.

I thought, of course, this would be the last time we saw Old One-Eye but it wasn't. When he came back a couple of days later he put the Warren Company on the verge of an Indian War. But that was two days hence. The night of the buffalo stampede, I lay in bed, keyed up from the day's events and fearful that the great herd would come back and crush us in our flimsy tents. I thought about what had happened to poor Mr. Fortier, now nineteenth century roadkill, and the Indians, oh, the Indians, these Lakota, as Fitzpatrick called them, chasing the buffalo with such skill and daring. I thought of myself as a good rider, better even, but I couldn't do that. No one I'd ever seen could do that.

It kept coming to me that I had seen a massive buffalo herd and wild Indians chasing them, and oh, man, that was like being caught in the middle of my own Spielberg/Lucas Imax 3D epic. Up until then, I'd only seen a few buffalo on TV, but in the here and now along the Platte River, I'd seen thousands, huge beasts, and it left an adrenaline bomb repeatedly going off in my chest.

This was a couple decades before the great slaughter that nearly exterminated the herds. Right now, no hordes of people hunted them for their fur, killed them for their horns, or brought them down just for the hell of it. So in 1848, they were there by the thousands upon thousands; by 1878, I knew they would be gone.

Libby's diary, June 28
As I write this, a sunset rains gold across the western sky. My attempt at poetical description. Enough of that. It has been a long, hard day. Travelled at least twenty miles, and I walked each one. Felt no worse for it. I guess I'm getting stronger. Fitzpatrick says we are about sixty miles from Fort Laramie. I will hate to see him leave us there or shortly after, which he will do since he's the new Agent of the Plains Indians, tasked with keeping them peaceable. Should I tell him how that goes? It won't matter, so I won't.

The plan is to spend a couple days camped near the fort to rest, dry things out and finish repairs on the wagons. Everyone is eager to get there. The trading post must do a booming business. A couple other emigrant companies are near us heading there as well.

A thunderstorm came just after supper and we prepared for it by tying down the wagons with stakes. Some shaking, but we're getting used to it. The storm brought hail the size of golf balls, but it quickly ended. All this is hard, but maybe I'm getting used to it.

I must go. Daniel has come for our nightly walk.

The brief friendly relation with the Sioux ended abruptly the next day when Old One-Eye rode into camp with several other Indian men during the nooning. One-Eye wore a black stovepipe hat, like the ones Lincoln wore, or would wear with a large feather stuck in the hatband. I wondered where he got the hat. It made him look taller. They were there to barter goods, bringing buffalo robes, deer hides, moccasins, and a string of seven ponies. They wanted tools, food stuff, and something we couldn't give, something that would cause the trouble.

Henry traded two kitchen knives and a polished obsidian stone for two pairs of calf-length moccasins, which he gave to Caroline and me, and we put them on immediately. Oh, my, those moccasins felt good. All the while during these transactions, One Eye kept an eye on me, nodding with a pleased smile when I stomped around in my new footwear—*tres chic*—and kept watching as Caroline and I raced down to the river. His constant interest was starting to make me nervous.

Sally came to watch the trading. "What's going on?"

"I just got some new shoes," I said, more pleased than I should have been. "And that old Indian dude is giving me the hairy eyeball."

As if to prove my point, One Eye addressed Henry, gesturing conspicuously toward me.

Standing by the fire, Julia said, "I don't think I like this, Henry. With all those horses, I got a feeling he wants to make a trade for something we will not part with."

Several people, including Mr. Whelan, had gathered to barter with the Indians and stopped to listen. One Eye spoke again, pointing to Sally as well. It became pretty clear what he wanted. Horses for her and me. Henry chuckled, "Well, you suppose we can get a few more horses out of the bargain for these two girls?"

A few men laughed. Julia was indignant. "Henry Quarles! This isn't funny."

"No, ma'am, I guess it ain't." But it was clear from his wry smile and a wink toward Isaac, he still saw the humor in it. I sure didn't.

Just then, Captain Warren showed up with Fitzpatrick and Beckwourth and just behind them, Pierce, his finger in the trigger guard of his rifle.

"What's going on here?" Captain Warren asked, pushing through to the front. "We don't need trouble."

Whelan was quick to answer. "Seems this old Injun wants to buy himself a wife, captain. Maybe even two. Those horses are for Libby and Sally."

Fitz spoke to One Eye in sign language. When he told us what the Indian said, I was doubly embarrassed. He offered five horses for Sally and just two for me. Why so many for her? Like I'm meatloaf and she's steak?

Immediately, Henry and Pierce stood protectively beside us. One Eye looked fierce enough, but the implacable glare of the other warriors on horseback caused icicles of fear down our backs. This did not look promising. I didn't want a blood fight, but One Eye seemed determined.

Daniel finally arrived, working his way through the crowd to me. "What's going on?"

"One Eye wants to buy me and Sally."

He glanced around at the standoff. "If things go bad, run to your wagon."

I wondered for a brief second what would happen if Henry took the ponies so he could get rid of his brain-addled daughter, but, of course, he refused. He would not be able to face Julia if he had done otherwise. Hannibal Pierce, however, accepted.

He held up seven fingers to signify he wanted all the horses for Sally, and the chief nodded, the stovepipe hat bobbing. There were gasps and angry shouts at Pierce.

"This not funny, Pierce," Captain Warren said.

"Who's joking?" He shoved Sally toward the Indians, walked over and took the reins of the horses. He loved horses more than people. He could care less what we thought about him.

For a moment, everyone was too stunned to speak. Then came another eruption of protests. Henry found his voice. "Now hold on a minute. You can't sell her. You got no right."

"I got every right. Sally's my family. Mind your own," Pierce said, gesturing toward me. "If I's you, I'd get rid of that one, too. Her mind ain't never coming back." He chuckled. "But, then, I already done got all the redskin's horses."

I snapped, "You son of a bitch!" Shocking words for a female of these times, but then I was not a female of these times.

He glared at me, but said nothing. Sally was halfway between One Eye and us. The Indians couldn't know what was being said, but they knew something was going wrong, and a fight was coming. I saw several notch arrows into their bows. The two that had rifles eased them into position. Women herded the children away. Julia was already lifting Little George into the wagon with the twins. He didn't want to go, but she smacked his behind and shoved him in.

Casually adjusting his stovepipe hat, One Eye nudged his horse forward and reached down for Sally, but she backed away.

Captain Warren walked over to Pierce. "Give the Indian back his damn horses, Pierce." A lay preacher, he never cursed, so we knew he was riled. "You're not selling this girl. Whatever rights you got, it don't include buying and selling people."

"Start easing back to the wagon," Daniel said to me.

For some reason, scared as I was, I could not leave Sally. "No."

The Indians exchanged several angry words with our men, each side shouting at the other, while Fitzpatrick frantically tried to calm things. "Give it up, Pierce," he said, coldly. "If things go bad, I'll shoot you down first."

Isolated, Pierce fumed, but would not give in. "Talk about no right. It was a fair and square deal. The girl's my kin. These are my horses, and that Indian has got hisself a wife, and he's welcome to her. More trouble than she's worth."

His patience gone, Captain Warren stepped up his face not an inch from Pierce's. "If you don't give the horses back right now, we're going to do it for you. Then we're going to throw you out of the company. You can deal with this Sioux on your own. I don't suspect he will be happy, that's sure."

Pierce finally saw he had no choice. The Sioux would eat him alive alone out here. Angrily, he spit and handed the reins to the captain. "Here, take 'em and be damned."

While Fitzpatrick explained the situation in sign, the captain tried to give back the horses, but One Eye refused. Now we were in for it. Several men raised their weapons. A lot of people were going to get hurt. Likely us, if not now, later. This Sioux would not forget the slight.

That's when Sally did something extraordinary. "I'll go," she said so softly at first few heard her. She repeated louder, "I'll go. It's all right. I'll do it."

"There you go," Pierce said to Warren, snatching the reins back, then turned to Sally and said, "Now, that's my girl."

Sally scooped up a handful of dirt and threw it in his face. "I ain't your girl, you piss pot of a man. Keep your damn horses. I don't never want to see your ugly face again."

She had crossed some divide in her mind, made one of those decisions that determined the course of a life. She faced all of us and said, "I'm going with him."

She reached up to One Eye, who took her arm and with a mighty struggle swung her up behind him. Tipping his stovepipe hat to us, he turned his horse and rode off, followed by the rest of the warriors. As they galloped away, she called back to me with a laugh. "Ha, Libby, I will be married before you. You can come to my wedding."

Seeing her go, I experienced a crushing sadness at losing such a good friend, but for the first time since I'd met her, she seemed happy, as if released from jail. Maybe I was reading too much into it, but I didn't think so. Several men wanted to go after her, but Beckwourth said, "You do and a lot of you won't be coming back."

"Ain't no Sioux Indian going to scare me off from doing what's right," Whelan said. "They ain't that tough."

"Mr. Whelan," Fitzpatrick said, "Out here on his land, he's the toughest fighting man in the world. You wouldn't stand a chance."

Whelan straightened his back. "I'm not afraid of any man, leastways no red man."

"Didn't say you were."

"Captain," Whelan persisted. "We need to do something."

Captain Warren waved him away, "Give it up, Mr. Whelan. The girl made her own choice, and the devil be damned. She's no longer welcome in white society. Not our concern now. I don't like it. It sticks in my craw. But not our concern."

When Whelan started to protest again, Captain Warren's dark look shut him up.

"If she'd been taken by the savages that'd be different," the captain said to everyone, "we'd ride to the ends of the earth then, but we all saw, she went of her own will. Now, boys, we've wasted enough time. Let's get this company moving."

I saw in the distance One Eye and Sally and the other Indians riding over a ridge and disappearing from view. The thought that settled in my brain consisted of two simple questions. How could life push such choices on us? And how One Eye kept that hat on his head as he rode?

Chapter 28

At the end of the day when we camped ten miles from Fort Laramie, everyone still spoke about Sally Callahan and the Indians. A few people had gathered at the Langdon wagons next to ours to talk the matter up. Julia and I could hear them as we cooked cornbread in the Dutch oven for tomorrow's journey. Within a mile of us, I could see the white sails of prairie schooners from another company and the smoke from hundreds of campfires.

I was beginning to understand that relations between Indians and whites in the nineteenth century were more complex than the somewhat politically correct version of my own century. The opinion I heard most was stated by Henry, "Indians are savages." I thought this typical of the man, inflexible, a hard view of things, all black and white and nothing in between.

Surprisingly, on this journey, women began to speak up more often, as if they'd already achieved the equality of later times. Myra quickly supported the prevailing view. "They'll kill you if they get the chance."

I wondered why Julia didn't take part in the discussion since she was probably the smartest person in the entire company and certainly possessed more wisdom than all of them put together. But she didn't speak in groups much. She seemed content to worry about her own family, and unless real help needed, let others do the worrying about whether Indians were savages or not.

"They don't hate Indians so much as fear them," she explained to me as we set out plates for supper. "All the logic in the world is not going to argue that fear away."

"I suppose."

"But fear becomes hate pretty fast."

She lifted the lid off the Dutch oven, pressed her finger down on the corn-bread. "Almost done."

The twilight was cooling things down. It was becoming a pleasant enough evening.

"When he was a young man," she said, "before we even met, your pa fought against the Sauk and Fox in Black Hawk's War. He lost a brother and a sister in that one. So he's got reason to hate. Not good for a person to hate, but it's what people do. The Indians, too. They're people, just like us, just as good, just as bad. Many of them hate us, and they got reason, just like we got reason. Black Hawk sure did, but don't say that to your pa."

Black Hawk? I should have known what she was talking about, but high school American History only went so far. I did understand love and hate, or thought I did. In my life I'd known both, but those things seemed petty now compared to what people experienced in this age.

I had thought I loved Cal, but I didn't. I never wanted to love Daniel, but I did. It had me aching to see him the moment I awoke in the morning till I went to sleep at night. My hate for Mrs. Guthrie, too, now seemed childish next to what I felt for Hannibal Pierce. Mrs. Guthrie was just a teacher trying to do her best, and now I respected her for it. Pierce was a scoundrel who sold his sister-in-law for a few horses.

"But we're only passing through their land," Julia continued. "We are no threat to them."

In no hurry to continue, she poured herself a cup of tea and sipped it. She seemed to have a point to make, and so I waited patiently. "What happens when Oregon and California fill up? Someday, maybe fifty years from now, we white people are going to want the Indians' lands. Then what?"

Sooner than that, I wanted to tell her, much sooner. Julia saw their side of it, though few of the men did, including Henry. Maybe they couldn't afford to. Once the struggle with the Indians began, no one here knew exactly how it would end. But I did, of course.

"Do you hate them?" I asked her.

"No, but I fear them." She glanced at me as if to issue a warning. "Only a fool would not fear them. From what Tom Fitzpatrick says, there is reason for fear, especially with these Sioux."

I nodded, then impulsively kissed her cheek.

Inside the tent that night, Jane too was bothered by what had happened with Sally. We shared a pallet. I knew something was wrong by the way she kept turning restlessly, unable to sleep.

"Libby," she finally said, "would Pa ever sell me to the Indians?"

"Oh, honey, no, never. Why would you even think that?"

"Well, Mr. Pierce did."

"Your Pa loves you too much. Besides, he couldn't get even a donkey for you."

She knew I was teasing and laughed, but it sounded strained. "Why did Sally do that?" she asked. "She never saw that man before."

"I think maybe she didn't like her life here."

"But she left her family."

"Pierce was no family of hers. Besides, not all families are as good as the Quarles," I said, but wasn't sure I meant it. How could any family that had Henry Quarles in it be all that good?

She gave a serious nod. "Is that why she done it? She don't like Mr. Pierce?"

"Did it, is that why she did it, and doesn't like Pierce. Yes, that'd be my guess."

She seemed satisfied and shifted her weight and soon fell asleep. As always after a long trying day, I was exhausted, but this time I couldn't sleep. I looked over at Caroline and Seneca on the other pallet—Isaac and Little George had taken to sleeping in one of the wagons. The two girls had their knees pulled up into a fetal position. One, I couldn't tell which in the darkness, mumbled something in her sleep.

I watched them for awhile. Sweet kids all. I wished they were really my sisters, as I wished Isaac and Little George were my brothers. I'd grown fond of them, even Isaac. I supposed if I had to be stuck in the nineteenth century with a family, it could have been much worse. As I lay there, my hands folded behind my head, I listened to the night and soon heard distant laughter coming from somewhere far off. Curious, unable to sleep, I got up, threw on a dress and slipped out of the tent to see who it was.

At first, I couldn't tell where the laughter was coming from. The night was moonless with a spectacular field of stars above, and the Milky Way spread thick across the sky. A pleasant coolness settled in the air. Pulling a shawl tighter around my shoulders, I set off toward the river where I saw a small campfire amid the trees.

Several men, among them Daniel and Henry, were passing a jug around and listening to Beckwourth tell a tale about the Indians. Standing back in the shadows, I listened. He was speaking about the Lakota named Brings Thunder, the Sioux superman that all the other Indians and whites feared.

According to the mountain man's outrageous way of spinning a story, this fellow could run faster, ride harder, and swim farther than any man alive, including Beckwourth, and for once Fitz didn't challenge him on it. No one was better at stealing horses or killing his enemy. That Indian wrestled mountain lions and could lift a live bear above his head.

Beckwourth's voice went to a near whisper as everyone leaned in closer to hear him. "It's true. Brings Thunder moves like a ghost. His enemies never heared him a-coming. He has the ability to fly 'cause he kin go hundreds of miles in just seconds, showing up beside an enemy like he come up out of the ground. Until five years ago, no one had heared of him. Then, like he'd falled out of the sky, he showed up on the plains. The Lakota respected his courage and took him in. Soon, he became a great and famous war leader amongst them."

Hearing of this Indian's exploits, I began to feel uneasy. Something about what was being said sent up red flags. I moved closer to the fringe of the crowd.

Then Beckwourth told a miraculous tale about how Brings Thunder got his wonder horse, an Appaloosa, while leading a raid against a large Blackfeet encampment on Dog Creek. Alone, he snuck into the center of the enemy village by making himself invisible and got right up to the chief's lodge with the Appaloosa tied outside. As he was about to snatch him, the tipi flap opened and the chief came out.

Instantly, Brings Thunder made himself into a prairie dog. The Blackfeet chief sniffed the air as if he could smell his enemies, but only caught the prairie dog's scent. The other Lakota warriors chose that moment to drive off the horse herd, causing the alarm to be sounded.

Immediately, the chief grabbed his bow and rushed to the Appaloosa just as Brings Thunder restored himself to human form, shocking the man. But being no weakling, this chief fired an arrow that bounced off Brings Thunder's chest, then charged with his war club. Brings Thunder struck back with a bolt of lightning from his fist, killing his enemy.

Unexpectedly finding himself in the middle of a hundred angry Blackfeet warriors, he jumped astride the Appaloosa and rode out of the village. When he reached his warriors, they were driving the horse herd away, whooping wildly. This was their downfall. The whole village of Blackfeet warriors closed in on them and some Lakota were killed. To stop the pursuit, Brings Thunder spun his horse around to face the Blackfeet alone, firing more lightning bolts. That stopped the Blackfeet and allowed his men to escape. Who wanted to face the power of a summer storm?

One warrior, though, rushed to within a few feet of Brings Thunder, and with an old dragoon pistol, fired. At the last second Brings Thunder, no ordinary man, saw the bullet and turned his head aside. He watched the bullet pass right in front of his eyes, felt its searing heat, and for an instant thought it had missed him. Then, he felt the gush of blood drain into his mouth and down his chin to his chest.

Beckwourth leaned his head back and laughed. "Folks, that bullet took his nose clean off. Left nothing there, not even a nub. Brings Thunder had the nosebleed of all nosebleeds. Well, he swung his war club and bashed that Indian's head down into his chest so he could see his own heart beating, then old Brings Thunder rode out of there so fast on that Appaloosa no Blackfeet could keep up. All the while, he was screaming, 'Where's my nose? Where's my nose?'"

As everyone laughed, I gasped as if the ground had split apart beneath me. My ears swelled with ringing. No one else fully believed the tale, but what if it were true, really true in all its particulars. I knew some of it was. This Brings Thunder must have been the blond Indian I'd seen sitting astride his horse with two other warriors at the other end of the portal on that long ago

Friday morning when I had stepped through the school doors and found myself out on these very same western plains.

That was too big of a coincidence. It had to be the same person. How many noseless Indians were there? Nothing would stop me from speaking to that man. For him to be waiting there for me, he had to have something to do with wrenching me into this century. Blond-haired, blue-eyed, he was no Indian. Perhaps, he could fly. Had some vehicle that he used. Perhaps, he had a weapon that was far more destructive than a simple hand gun. Perhaps it was true, and if so, this man was my ticket home. At least, somehow, someway, he had to know something, to have answers about how I got here and how I get back. I gave no consideration to the possibility that I was wrong about him. If there was only a 10 percent chance that Brings Thunder could help me, then I had to treat that 10% as if it were a hundred. Because the other 90 percent got me nowhere.

Pushing past the men into the firelight, I said with assurance, "Brings Thunder is no Indian."

Everyone was startled. Beckwourth scowled at me. "Now, how would you know that, Miss Quarles?" The tone, especially when he said Miss Quarles, was not pleasant.

"Brings Thunder has blue eyes," I said. "You left that out. He has blue eyes and blond hair. He's no Indian."

Beckwourth's scowl turned to fear. I realized then that he was afraid of me. Me! Why? "Now how would you know that?"

"I know."

What he did next completely surprised me and everyone else. Without another word, he stood up and walked to his horse tied nearby, swung up onto it and rode out of camp into the darkness.

"Wait! Mr. Beckwourth!" I called, running after him. "Wait! Please! I need to speak with you."

Daniel caught up to me and took me by the shoulders. "Stop, Libby. Stop."

"Let me go. You don't understand."

"You can't run out there at night. It's too dangerous. You'd likely fall into a ravine and break your fool neck or run into a savage. He'll be back."

I knew he was right, so I returned with him to our tent where I said good-night, leaving him standing there, then slipped out again when he had gone. For the next several hours, I hid in the shadows around Captain Warren's wagons where Beckwourth spread a bedroll. Embers glowed from a hundred dying fires. The camp was silent except for a jumbled chorus of snores.

When Beckwourth finally returned sometime after three in the morning, I was still there. As I approached, he drew his knife in one swift motion. I squeaked and took a step back

"What are you doing, girl, skulking about at night?"

"Waiting for you, Mr. Beckwourth?" I sputtered. "I need to talk with you about Brings Thunder."

He was furious. "I ain't wanting to talk to you. Now go on with you. Go spook someone else."

He dumbfounded me. "Why do you not like me? Everyone likes me."

He stared for a long time and I thought he wouldn't answer. Finally, he said, "Something wrong with you." He picked out each word carefully. "You're a spirit, a ghost. Something wrong with you. I ain't afraid to say it. Evil in you."

I was shocked. I can be bitchy, and proudly so, but evil? I cackled, "By the prickling of my thumbs, something wicked this way comes."

"You mocking me, girl?' He still held his knife, a large bone handled weapon. He could stick me and no one would know it was him. They'd all think an Indian had done it.

"No. Look, I am not evil, but think what you want. I don't care. I need to get some information from you, so talk to me, or I swear every cup of whiskey you drink will taste like piss. Stick me with that or talk to me."

He thought about it a long time, then finally slid the knife back in his belt. "We talk. Then you leave old Becks alone." He glanced around and pointed out toward the Platte. "Let's go off aways. I talk to you out there."

Out there? Out by the river? Alone? But when he walked out of the circle of wagons into the darkness, I followed. He stopped at the same spot by the river he had told the story of Brings Thunder, a place far enough away where he could easily kill me and throw me in the water, and no one would know.

"Who are you? What are you?" he asked. "You tell Old Becks the truth or I tell you nothing."

The truth. Why not? "I'm not Libby Quarles. My spirit was moved from where I was into her body. I don't know why. I don't even know if there is a why. But I'm not evil, at least not in that way. I'm a girl just like her. I miss my family, my real family, and I want to get back to them. I think Brings Thunder helped bring me here, so maybe he can get me back. That's the truth, Mr. Beckwourth. He, maybe, can get me back to my family. The only evil in it was what was done to me."

I knew that sounded nutty in the extreme, but he nodded, accepting it as if I'd merely said I was a girl from St. Louis. "You got a dark obscuration hanging about you. You are evil. I ain't fooled by you saying it otherwise."

"I spoke truthfully. Now it's your turn. I need to find Brings Thunder. Can you help me?"

"Whites call him Blue sometimes because of his blue eyes. He trades buffalo robes and deer hides with whites, that is if he lets them live long enough to do it."

"What else?" I asked. "You better have something else."

Just above a whisper, he said, "All right, but you leave me be then." He paused, gathering his thoughts or lies. "I know'd them Lakota. I know'd his band tolerable well. So believe me, girl, I know him. He hates you white people worse than he'd hate a snake in his lodge. His hate is a great thing. The obscuration around him is the darkest I have ever seen. Worse than you by a country mile."

He glanced around again as if someone were listening. "Yes, ma'am, he may be white, but he hates whites all the same. Back when he come to the Lakota, he married up with one of their women. They had a daughter, you see. A blue-eyed, black haired little scamp. He loved that girl more than his own life. For a time he was almost a human being. Last year while he was raiding into Blackfeet country after that horse, that girl of his died of a white man's disease, whooping cough. He knew it was coming. She'd had it for a long time."

"I don't see..."

"Shush, let me tell it. Where'd the Lakota get that whooping cough? From these emigrants what been coming along the Holy Road for years. White man's disease kilt his girl. No doubt there. Right or wrong don't matter. He blames you folk for it. He plans to kill as many of you as he can." He gave a skittering laugh. "He trades with you whites at the fort, then kills you. Man, woman, child, don't matter none."

"I'm sorry about what happened to his daughter, but he surely can't..."

He held up his hand to stop me. "He don't want your sorrow. By the time he found his band after the Blackfeet raid, they had moved hundreds of miles from where the girl died. She had been placed on a scaffold like they always do. Brings Thunder rode back alone to be with her a final time. He was no prize before, but that worsened him mightily. Since then he has kilt many whites. Any emigrants what wander away from a wagon train, he cuts them up good. Trappers, hunters, traders, he catch them up and kills them slow." He paused. "Same he do to you, he get you alone."

I shivered at that.

"You know what he said to me? He says he wants his daughter back. I ask him will he stop killing whites then. He laughs and says, no. I tell him, well, he can't have her back, she dead. But he says he can get her back. I say how? Raise the dead? He don't answer, just smiles like he knowed something no one else knowed. Now don't that beat all?"

"Why didn't he kill you?"

He laughed. "I ain't white."

Of course. "Do you know where he is?"

When he shook his head, I felt my heart sink. All that talk and I was no closer to Brings Thunder. Beckwourth fell silent after that, listening to the sound of a bird making chortling calls. I was going to get no more from him. I now had an idea about this Brings Thunder person. I would have to stay on at Fort Laramie and find someone to help me search for the man. In my mind, I was saying goodbye to the Quarles family and this company. And Daniel. Damn, Daniel!

"Thank you, Mr. Beckwourth. I appreciate your helping me," I said, turning to go.

"Don't rightly know where he is," he said, "but I do know where he's going to be."

My heart lurched. I swung back to face him.

"You don't want to meet him. He's a bad, bad character."

I took an aggressive step toward him. "I don't care if he's Jack the Ripper. I need to speak with him. Tell me."

"Maybe you two should meet. I spoke to him just this noon, scouting out this camp site. He was travelling alone, so he's out there somewhere, right now, but I wouldn't recommend you go looking for him." He cackled at his little joke. "If you want to see him that bad, why, I suppose you can come into Fort Laramie tomorrow. He's bringing in some buffalo hides."

I never felt such elation in my life. For me, those words *Fort Laramie tomorrow* meant I had a chance, a small chance but a chance, to go home.

Chapter 29

The next day before noon, the wagons plunged across the shallow river and rolled on past Fort Laramie's high adobe walls another two hundred yards before circling up. Not only was another wagon train company camped nearby, but also a sizeable Indian village sprawled not far from the walls themselves.

According to Captain Warren, the layover would be a full day and a half, time enough to repair wagons, dry out belongings, wash clothes, bathe in the river, write letters back home (my letters home would be a long time in the delivery), bring diaries up to date, and trade at the post. After we set up camp, seemingly half the company headed for the fort. I couldn't contain my eagerness—I was wired—but Henry insisted we Quarles stay together, so I had to wait for Caroline and Isaac to finish chores. I'd kill them if I missed Brings Thunder.

At the fort, our party mingled in with the traffic making its way through the front gate beneath a blockhouse erected to defend the entrance, odd because Indians moved in and out freely, as well as traders, fur trappers and emigrants. I had Seneca by the hand and Jane walked with Caroline, both twins wide-eyed with wonder.

If you're talking Los Angeles circa twenty-first century, there weren't many people here, but for the prairie in 1848, this place was teeming, a hundred and fifty to two hundred men and women, white and Indian, bartering hides, slabs of meat, whiskey and trade goods out of wagons or on blankets, the Walmart of the Plains.

Ahead of me, a man struggled to push a wheelbarrow heavily loaded with jugs of what Isaac said was pure poison disguised as mountain whiskey, as if he would know. "Put hair on your chest," he said.

"You can barely handle lemonade," I said snippily.

"What would you know about it?"

"You two quit that bickering," Henry demanded.

There were no soldiers. Fitzpatrick explained that it wasn't that kind of fort, just one for trading, but the army was negotiating with the owner James Bordeaux to garrison the place next year. Their job would be to protect the emigrant wagon trains, something he, Fitz, had been recommending for a long time. This was not his last stop with us. He would travel with the Warren Company another couple weeks before turning south toward a place called Bent's Fort. As the government's Indian agent he had the entire Plains Indians, north and south, to deal with.

Henry nodded toward the twins. "Keep them girls close. I don't want you or Caroline to stray far from me."

"We won't," I replied. Unless I have to. "Where's the trading post?" That's where Brings Thunder would be.

Fitzpatrick nodded toward a two-story adobe building just inside the gate. It had a homemade sign nailed above the door that read, *Trading Post, James Bordeaux, Bourgeois*. In front of it, men were packing a wagon with kegs, hides, blankets, kettles, pots and pans. When Henry, Caroline and I entered with the twins, Captain Warren was at the counter, examining a rifle. Several emigrants had gathered around to gawk. With Seneca by the hand, I searched the store for Brings Thunder, but he was not here. I despaired the man would show.

Everyone was talking excitedly about the rifle, sharing opinions based more on its shiny sleekness than any knowledge of its capabilities. The clerk, a small, dark man who spoke with a heavy French accent, was giving his sales pitch. "She is called Sharps. First model. Only 1500 made. Tres précis, *mon* ami. You kill beaucoup buffalo. Be mighty hunter, eh?"

As Captain Warren aimed at imaginary targets, Whelan shook his head in wonder. "That's some shooting piece, Captain. What are they going to think of next?"

That's when the room fell silent, starting like a ripple on the outside moving toward the counter. We all turned toward the door where a huge man stood, over six feet tall, his figure etched in light.

Brings Thunder had come.

Everyone—I mean everyone—stood frozen. I was afraid and so was Seneca. She pressed close to me. I can't say what others were feeling, but the look of the man made me uneasy to be sure. He wore hide leggings, a breechclout and a tattered suit vest. His skin had been burnt to the color of leather. His blond hair was greasy and braided in a single strand down his back. And he had no nose.

On one shoulder, he carried a large stack of pelts and hides as easily as if it were a bag of feathers. My knees grew weak at the thought of approaching this man. With blue eyes cold as river ice, he was staring at Captain Warren. "You have my rifle, sir," he said. His English had a distinct British accent. "Place it back on the counter."

Captain Warren pointedly held on to the rifle, cradling it in his arm. Shaking his head, Brings Thunder gave a geese honk of a snort through the scabby hole in his face and walked to the counter while people shuffled quickly out of his way. He dumped the hides in front of the clerk. "These skins pay for the rifle, Bordeaux. That was the deal we had."

Frightened, Seneca tugged at my hand. "Let's go, Libby."

"Wait, honey."

The Frenchman had a nervous smile when he spoke, "Oh, *mon* ami, we had no handshake. You say maybe you buy rifle. This man has coin. He and I shake the hand."

Brings Thunder shoved the hides closer. "My rifle."

"Sorry, friend," Captain Warren said, cradling the Sharps. "I just bought it."

"Is that how you see it?" Brings Thunder asked softly. It felt like the temperature had dropped twenty degrees. I sensed that nothing restrained this man, not civilization, not morality.

This didn't suit my purposes at all. Captain Warren had a pistol stuck in his belt and the rifle in his arm, not a man to brace easily. He would not back down. I didn't want to see the captain hurt, but definitely I didn't want anything to happen to Brings Thunder. I had convinced myself he had somehow been caught up in the same cosmic maelstrom that sent me here; he had to get me back to my own time.

Dragging Seneca, I pushed my way up to him. "Mr. Brings Thunder?" I said tentatively, knowing this was hardly the best time.

Henry put a hand on my shoulder. "Hush, Libby."

"Contest!" Bordeaux suddenly shouted, "Winner gets rifle."

"Shooting contest," Pierce added excitedly.

"No, no." Bordeaux waved the suggestion off. "No shooting. I do not pay for bullets. Use the knives."

Brings Thunder and Captain Warren looked at each other and nodded. I moaned. A knife fight!

"We go outside," Bordeaux said. "No blood on trade goods."

Outside, both men removed their boots and stood barefoot. I wondered, what was this? The Frenchman began explaining the rules as everyone on the grounds quickly gathered. Each man got three tosses of the knife. The closest to the other mans' foot without drawing blood buys the rifle. "Agreed?"

They both nodded.

Brings Thunder took out a bone-handled knife, the blade about ten inches long and caked with dried blood. Human or animal? Captain Warren's knife was smaller, shiny and clean. Climbing up on a bench for a better view, I watched with Seneca from the porch. The girl buried her head in the side of my dress, and I felt guilty for keeping her here, but I had to see this through. Too much was riding on this for me. The wind had picked up slightly; a dust devil swept across the square and died out amid the crowd.

"Begin," Bordeaux announced loudly.

Brings Thunder spread his legs to shoulder width, and Captain Warren's toss hit the ground a half inch from the white Indian's foot. A few men cheered.

"Good one, Captain," Whelan said. "That's a winner."

"Likely," Pierce added.

Bordeaux measured with a string, tied a knot in it, then nodded to Brings Thunder. Standing with his legs wide, the captain waited, his jaw set tightly and his lips mashed together in a harsh grimace. My guess was Brings Thunder could get inside the captain's throw. He did, but not in the way I'd thought. The man flipped his knife several times, then threw, sticking it with a sickening thud deep into the captain's foot. Captain Warren let out a scream of pain and danced around for several seconds with the knife sticking out.

A few men laughed. Several shouted, "Foul!"

Unconcerned, Brings Thunder said, "A pity. I have lost. You can buy the rifle."

"Damn you, Indian, you done that on purpose," Pierce shouted, and several men joined in the chorus.

Of course, he had, but Brings Thunder was not at all worried. Calmly, he bent down and yanked his knife out of the captain's foot, and this time the captain's screech was so loud it echoed off the adobe walls. Whelan and Pierce caught him as he teetered. Angrily, he shrugged them off. His hand slid to his pistol.

"Captain, you draw that, he'll kill you." Fitzpatrick strode quickly up to him.

"He did that just for the hell of it," the captain said, wincing as blood seeped into the ground from his foot.

Fitzpatrick shook his head. "Maybe so, but you folks want to fight your way through Sioux country?"

"If we have to," Pierce answered.

Even wounded and angry, the captain was more reflective and dropped his hand away from his pistol. Also, his adrenaline was wearing thin, and by his expression it was clear the severe pain of the wound was overtaking him.

"Get me my damn rifle, Bordeaux," he commanded, and the Frenchman rushed inside. Seconds later he returned with the shiny new Sharps and handed it to him. Surrounded by several men, he limped out of the fort, leaving red tracks in the dirt.

Now was my chance with Brings Thunder. I lifted Seneca up on my back, and with my bowels churning, strode toward him.

Chapter 30

*A*fraid of Brings Thunder, any child's bogeyman, Seneca buried her head in the back of my neck, and I was leading her to him. He was heading for his horse at the rail near the gate.

I stood in his path. "Mr. Brings Thunder, sir, I need to talk with you, please. It's important. I know you know me. We are the same. We came…"

I jumped out of the way or he would have walked right over me. He grabbed his reins and began leading the horse to the gate.

"Brings Thunder," I called, following. "I know where you come from."

He turned on me. "You know nothing, Wasinca."

Abruptly, when he saw Seneca, his eyes softened as if a cold wintry night melted into the warmth of a summer day. He reached out to touch her hair, but when she whimpered, I stepped back quickly. He smiled, almost human, but the missing nose made that impossible. He just looked plain scary, and nothing would change that.

"Who is this" he asked. I felt Seneca shift away and bury her head into my hair again.

"She's my sister. Leave her alone."

"Those blue eyes," he said, "They remind me of my daughter's."

"You have to talk with me, sir," I pleaded. "You know me. You must know me. I want to go back to my own time, and you're the only one who can get me back." Did he understand? Was I all wrong about him? A distinct possibility, but I had to proceed as if he did. Bafflement did cross his face, followed by a quick nod. I sighed with relief.

Then he said, "I can't go back. Why should you?"

"Because I'm not supposed to be here, because I don't want…"

He gave a brisk wave of the hand. "Not here. If you want to stick your head into the bear's mouth, I will meet you in an hour at the Laramie fork. We can talk all you want there."

After a final glance at Seneca, he turned and mounted his horse, riding quickly through the small gate.

A half hour later, I snuck out of camp while Julia and Caroline were preparing lunch and Henry was off somewhere. To go unseen, I hurried along the banks of the river and into the Sioux village where several women sat scraping buffalo hides. They seemed to be the only ones working. A number of men loafed by a fire, blankets draped over their shoulders, eyeing me as I passed. Several children ran up to me and tagged me with play tomahawks. Toys or not, they still hurt.

Outside the village, I walked quickly the mile to the fork of the North Platte and Laramie Rivers, wondering what would happen to Libby if I could get out of 1848 and back to the twenty-first century. Would she return, or had she died when the wagon ran over her, and I had replaced her at just that moment? I hoped she would come back from wherever she was and retake her body. In the weeks I had been using it, I had come to like it and her. She was tough, a lot tougher than Paula Masters, and people liked her. But I was going home. Nothing would stop me from getting back.

When I reached the appointed spot, Brings Thunder had not yet arrived. A copse of tall trees with heavy undergrowth stood where the rivers came together. A flock of birds flew out of the branches as I came up, but a crow remained, cawing at me for invading its territory. Waiting, my stomach churned with a violent queasiness. I was afraid. It was not lost on me that I was meeting someone who killed whites like a one-man cholera epidemic, taking his revenge for his daughter's death on every one of us. How this man was involved in my situation, I did not know, but I intended to discover to what extent if any. I had seen him that day in school, waiting for me on the other side of the time portal, beckoning me to him. What was he? A fugitive of time? How much control did he have over the process?

It was also foolish to be so far away from my people. This was the heyday of the wild Sioux. It was no comfort that I could see the white gleam of the fort walls a mile off and the circle of our wagons beyond. They might hear a gunshot, but not a tomahawk blow to my skull. Still, I stayed rooted here, determined to wait till Brings Thunder came.

The sound of horses startled me. Five Sioux warriors rode on the opposite bank heading toward the fort and village. Two of them had dead antelope slung over their horses. Immediately, I ducked down, but they had seen me, abruptly changed direction, and with a burst of speed, splashed across the river toward me.

My heart pounded like an hammer against my ribs. I rose and stepped out of the brush to face them, my knees barely able to hold me up. My God, I was scared. Not ten feet away, they pulled up five abreast and stared at me. I saw myself being scalped and my body thrown in the river. The end of me.

Running would get me dead the quickest; I knew that much. In my childhood, I had watched enough TV and old movies to remember a couple words that might be Sioux, so I raised my hand in greeting and said in a voice cracking with super soprano squeaks, "Hau. Hoka Hey, Crazy Horse, Sitting Bull."

They stared at me for another beat, then burst into laughter. Five wild Indians laughing hysterically at me. Funny was not what I expected. Then they argued among themselves about, no doubt, who gets to split the girl's skull with an axe. Another rider was coming hard for us, and the Indians fell silent as he approached. It was Brings Thunder.

He pulled his horse up with a savage jerk, shouting something harshly to the Sioux hunters. One of the men yelled back angrily, and I thought for a moment violence would come of it. Whatever was said, though, the five Sioux clearly didn't want to challenge him about it, and abruptly they rode off for the village.

For a few seconds Brings Thunder watched them go, then turned his gaze down at me. His scab nose dripped. The bloody knife he used to maim poor Captain Warren hung from his waist. In a scabbard was a shiny, new rifle, the Sharps they had fought over. Somehow, within the last hour, he had snuck into camp and stolen it. If he could do that during daylight, the thought of what he could do at night became a chilling prospect.

Now, standing in front of him, my chest heaved with panic. At that moment, I didn't think I would survive this encounter.

"You are out here alone," he said, amused, but the humor had a sinister darkness to it.

"Yes," I managed.

"Foolish."

"You plan to hurt me?" I asked, trying to keep my voice firm, but with only marginal success. He didn't answer. Not good. He slid off his horse. When I backed up, he looked at me, again amused.

"I know who you are," I said.

Still, he didn't respond, folding his arms over his chest, waiting for me to go on. I felt I only had a few seconds to get this right or die. I said quickly, "I know everything about you."

After a moment, he gave a disconcerting laugh. "I come from Oxford in England, a place an ignorant girl like you could know nothing about. I was a lecturer in Natural Philosophy, you know that? My knowledge is so vastly greater than yours, you cannot imagine it. You know not particle one about me, about what I was or who I am. You play a silly game. It is going to get you killed."

My heart sank. He didn't recognize me. I wasn't Libby yet the day I came through when he first saw me. I needed to tell him something that, as a scientist, he would know was from the future. "The speed of light. It's 186,000 miles a second, give or take a mile or two. How's that for knowledge?"

His eyes widened. He cocked his head, looking at me curiously. "Neat circus trick. Too fast by 25 percent, by the few current assessments, but curious."

"I told you. I know where you really come from, so I know you can help me."

What he said next surprised me. His stare grew distant as he spoke. "My daughter had blue eyes, you know, like your sister. A brilliant blue, like a sky so deep you can see the heavens." He nodded several times.

"I'm sorry about your daughter," I offered.

He seemed not to hear me. "I had wanted a boy. I was disappointed when she was born. But she tried harder than any boy to learn the skills of a warrior, and even though her mother tried to teach her the ways of women, she wanted only boy's play. She could run faster and shoot the arrows straighter than boys her age. When she was four, I had taught her how to use a child's bow. She was already sick then. You know so much, did you know that?"

I shook my head.

"Before she was even two, she could speak English and Lakota, going from one language to the other as easily as stepping from one stone to the next crossing a creek. She'd speak Lakota to my wife and then English to me."

I should say something, but thought any more sympathy from me would be unwelcome. It startled me when he laughed. "Is she a good runner?"

"Who?"

"Your sister. Is she smart?"

"She's smart. Yes. And she runs like any five year old. She can climb like a monkey."

Falling silent for a few seconds, he stared at me. I thought he was considering what to do with me. Here was a man whose pastime was killing white people, and here I was, a mouse who had come up to the cat. I needed to turn this conversation to my favor. "Mr. Brings Thunder, you know who I am as much as I know you. You recognized me at the store. You are the only one who can help me. That's why I had to talk to you." I waited for a response but he said nothing, his expression unchanged. I took a deep breath and asked him, "I don't belong in 1848. Did you bring me here?"

He frowned. I waited for him to say something to give me hope, but he just stared at me with those cold eyes, as if he were a starving bear and I were a fish flopping around on land.

I went on. "I belong in the twenty-first century, not the nineteenth. Do you know who or what brought me here?"

For the first time, I saw a spark of life in his eyes. What it meant I couldn't begin to fathom. "The twenty-first century. So far in the future," he said, a hint of amusement in his voice.

I began to feel frustrated. He would not give me a straight answer. I said, "I saw you before. You were with two other men on horseback. You kept telling me to come forward. To finish the journey. I would have appeared from nothing in the prairie. A bird flew in between us, and gone back to nothing."

His eyebrows knitted together. "That apparition six months ago had yellow hair."

Six months ago? "That was me. This is not my body. This is just the one I was given. I almost stepped through time then." I paused, hesitant with the next question. "Do you know how I came here? You must."

After a long moment, he nodded his head. "Yes, I know."

My heart leapt for joy. "Why did you take me? I wasn't the happiest girl in the world where I was, but I didn't want this."

"Why not you? We wanted you. We saw it would be good."

"Good? Good for who?"

He shrugged. I saw that little sparkle come to his dead eyes once more. He was enjoying this. Playing with the mouse. I saw that but had no choice but to go on.

"Were you brought here from another time like me?" I asked.

"Yes, of course."

"In what century did you live?"

"You are not to know this. Do not ask it again."

"Can you get us back?"

"I do not want to go back."

"Can you get me back?" I pressed.

"Perhaps. I will give this much thought." Abruptly, he turned to leave.

"Wait. You have to help me get back."

"Keep going on the Holy Road. I will come to you."

"How long?" When he didn't answer, I grabbed his arm. "How long?"

He turned on me suddenly, punching me in the chest, knocking me on my butt. My chest bone hurt terribly and I rubbed it. Bending down from his great height, he pressed his noseless face an inch from mine. The nose was dripping. Nauseatingly. His breath was foul, and an overwhelming rage burned from his eyes. "I want to cut your throat, white girl, and watch you bleed to death." He rose and leapt onto his horse. "One week, I will come. If I can send you back, I will."

For several minutes after he rode off, I sat in the grass, unable to move. I shivered from fear. The only thing that seemed real about the entire meeting was his threat. When I calmed down enough to get up and start back to our camp, I felt drained. I was missing something. That gnawing suspicion plagued me. Was Brings Thunder telling the truth? No, not all of it, but what was he hiding and how much was true? Would he really help me? I didn't know, but he was the only chance I had.

One week till I would go back home to my own time…maybe. It would be the longest week of my life.

Chapter 31

*B*eyond Fort Laramie, the land was dry sand hills with stunted pine and cedar called the Black Hills. In the old days when I was a good student I was far better in history than geography, but I knew these were not the Black Hills of later historical importance. Those were somewhere in South Dakota, though South Dakota would be a while yet coming into existence.

A snow-topped mountain loomed in the distance ahead. "Laramie Peak," Daniel said, flipping through a leather-bound guidebook as we rode together out from the wagons.

"Where will we be the seventh day out from Fort Laramie?"

"Hard to say. Still beside the river."

I rolled my eyes. "That's helpful. We're always beside the river."

Daniel was talking, but my mind was on Brings Thunder. Even though this was only the second day into the week, I looked for him on the horizon. Eventually, Daniel realized I wasn't listening and fell silent. He didn't seem to mind. I liked that. Most boys his age would have had their egos bent out of shape and start pouting. To him, riding silently with me was as much a boon as talking with me. Yeah, I liked that. Leaving him would be the hardest thing I ever had to do. I loved him; for me there could be no doubt. I knew the depth and strength of that love would never be matched again in my entire life, but I had to leave. I had to go home.

Later at that day's nooning, Captain Warren painfully hobbled over and gave Seneca and Jane a fur ball of a puppy from a litter his mongrel dog had borne. The captain's wound was healing slowly, and I feared he'd die from it. There was no way to stop infection once it took hold, and worse, Pierce was treating him. I told the captain to make sure he kept it clean and pour alcohol on it—there was enough of that about, and he said he would. He never said a thing about the missing Sharps rifle.

And that stupid puppy! Looking more like a raw hotdog in search of a bun, the little rodent charmed the twins instantly. The girls fawned over it like it was the cutest baby. They looked to Henry pleadingly, who said he'd let them keep it only if Little George agreed to help take care of it, and the girls then pleaded with their brother. I could tell the boy's initial reluctance was feigned, and he quickly agreed with a solemn nod.

"You can never have enough good dogs, sir," Isaac said, placing a hand on Little George's shoulder, as if he, Isaac, was a wise old adult.

I said, "Oh, give me a break."

"Well, you can't."

The twins ran off with the pup to play, and Little George followed. Later, I saw him trying to train it to heel, but the pup was having none of it. Far too young, it just ate and crapped and ran off every chance it got, keeping Little George and the twins busy chasing after it.

Libby's diary, July 6

The sixth day out from Fort Laramie. Made fifteen miles. Waiting for Brings Thunder. Where is he? The sun is still broiling as I write this on a lap table Daniel made for me from an old barrel top. We are waiting to cross the North Platte at the Mormon Ferry, but a large company of three hundred wagons are ahead of us, and so we sit in the heat. They are having a bad time of it with wagons tumbling over into the water. Captain Warren came by minutes ago and said the other company will take the rest of the day and then some. He's walking with a pronounced limp and quite a bit of pain.

When Caroline asked him about the people who ran the ferry, he explained they called themselves Latter-day Saints and ferried here to raise money for new Mormon emigrants to come to their paradise in Utah. I have to put my pencil down. Julia has asked me to help start supper early since we won't be crossing today. Mrs. Guthrie, she has a Dutch oven. Ha!

After supper, Daniel and I climbed to the top of the highest bluff. A couple hours of daylight still remained, so we had stunning views, spread out over a great distance. Snowcapped Laramie Peak appeared no nearer. Off to the west, we could see two wagon companies across the river and circled for the night. Daniel took my hand and turned me toward him. He didn't know it, but this might be our last night together. Now on the verge, perhaps, of returning to my own time, my own family, my feelings were complicated. I could not get around the thought that in my own time, where I truly belonged, Daniel had long been dust, his life lived out more than a century before I was born.

He had an intense expression and took my face in both his hands. "Ah, girl, you are so pretty. It's your face I see the last thing at night and first thing in the morning."

"Daniel…"

"Libby, I love you."

There it was. When a boy said that to you, as he had been for quite a while now, and meant it, and you loved him back, it was the greatest feeling in the world. He was more than just a kiss in the night; I would give him more. I determined to give myself to him, fully, in body as I had in my soul. Give Libby's body to him. After all, we were nearly married, or would have been.

His intensity dissolved into a half-smile as he kissed my cheek lightly, then my eyelids, then my mouth. The thrill of it shooting needles of pleasure through my body. A gust of wind swept over us. My hair shifted and my dress flapped. He stepped back and stared at my figure. He seemed to come to a decision.

"Marry me tonight, Libby. Captain Warren can marry us." His voice rose in excitement. "We can do it. Why wait? We can do it tonight."

I should have expected it, but still the question surprised me. I wanted to say yes, but couldn't. Couldn't do that to Libby. She had a right to make her own decision if she came back when I vacated the premises. What a fraud I was. Truth was I wanted to marry this boy, this man. I didn't want to leave him behind? This dilemma plagued my soul. Desperately wanting to stay with him and desperately wanting to go home where Josh and mom and dad were. Hopeless.

He knew my answer. His eyes reflected his disappointment. "My God, Libby, what in the world are you thinking? You look like I hit you over the head with a frying pan. Marrying me can't be that bad."

"Don't be angry with me. It has to be Oregon. Not now. Not here. When we get to Oregon."

I witnessed his face change from disappointment to anger, all in the blink of an eye. He did not speak for a long time, then said, "We won't get to Oregon City for four more months, hard months. I think of us as married now. There's no other woman for me. There never will be."

"I know. I feel the same way. Truly, I do. I love you now and always."

He was about to speak but I stopped him by placing a hand on his lips. My voice was a choked whisper. "Tonight I will sleep outside alone. Come to me then."

If I was going to leave him, I wanted one night with him, one night to last a lifetime.

I woke before dawn of the next day filled with our lovemaking. Daniel still lay beside me on the blanket gently snoring. He had found us a spot about half a mile from camp in a copse of trees along the riverbank. Foolishly, we had no fear of Indians or wild beasts. If I was more poetic, I would have called it our Garden of Eden. I will never forget the moonlight, the cool night air, the sound of crickets, the gentle rush of the river, and Daniel sliding his hand under my shift. Nothing in my life ever felt so good as that hand. We lay down together on the blanket and made love, married by God, if not by man. Daniel was hesitant at first, but eventually got it right, becoming better and better throughout the night.

Then, as I sat up, the import of the day hit me. This was the seventh day when Brings Thunder would come and show me the way back, and I was filled with a terrible anticipation.

I shook Daniel. "Wake up, cowboy. We need to get back to the wagons."

After a quick breakfast, the company began crossing the river on ferries that were hardly stable, a slow process over swift water. The Quarles' wagons were among the first to board. Once across we followed Fitzpatrick another five miles to the new campsite on a stream called the LaBonte, where we were to wait for the rest of the company. Most of the men stayed back with the horses and cattle, while Julia and the other women set up camp to prepare lunch. I could tell how worried she was. River crossings could easily be fatal. Drownings were common.

We heard from each succeeding group that arrived how it was going. Captain Warren had planned to take no more than half a day, but the loss of three wagons to a capsized ferry had pushed that estimate back further till it became apparent we would not be moving again this day. Fortunately, no lives were lost, but all the belongings of those poor families were swept away.

As Julia and Caroline kept a fresh pot of tea going and biscuits baking, I stood out by the creek watching Jane, Seneca and Little George play with their puppy. I was grateful for the simple task since it gave me an opportunity to keep an eye out for Brings Thunder. Above in the trees, birds set up a constant chatter of whistles and caws. Since I was standing in the shade, I just hoped they wouldn't crap on my head. One made a high-pitched trilling that sent the puppy into a frenzy, scurrying off each time with the children racing after him, laughing. Little George would scoop it up before it got very far. Each time, Seneca would scold the pup for his attempted escape.

With a sheepish nod, Mr. Whelan joined me in the grove, his mooncalf eyes on me. Since his wife fell to the cholera and I had refused his marriage proposal, he had begun to look more and more slovenly. There was a thick layer of dust on his brown shirt, but I wasn't going to brush it off. His presence made me uncomfortable and it annoyed me. I had no time for this.

"A pleasant day to you, Miss Quarles," he said.

"And to you, sir," I said, coldly.

He was nervous and managed only, "Those children sure like that pup."

"Yes, they do."

"Have you given any more consideration to the conversation we had at Chimney Rock?"

"Mr. Whelan, I thought the matter settled. Anyway, you must have heard Daniel and I are engaged."

"I have heard something of the like. Yes, but I figured to make sure."

I frowned at him. "It's sure."

Shifting about, he appeared tongue-tied after that. I did not feel it my duty to help him out and said nothing. He was just a sad, sad man overwhelmed by rampaging children he could not handle. Presently, his attention latched on the pup, and he began laughing at its antics. I turned away, anxiously scanning the hills for Brings Thunder. It was already well into afternoon and he had not shown. Why he hadn't, I didn't want to consider. That would mean he had lied and didn't plan to help me at all. More likely could not. My nerves were becoming frayed as the minutes ticked by slowly. One thought took the prominence of a supernova inside my head: if he showed, I might be sleeping tonight in my own bed in the twenty-first century, making all this just a dream.

But Daniel was no dream, the Quarles were no dream. I would remember them always.

Something moved in the distance. My heart jumped into my throat. A rider on the crest of a hill about three quarters of a mile off was coming this way. With a quick glance at the children—Whelan was with them, surely they would be safe—I shouted to him, "Watch the children," and walked quickly toward the rider, waving to get his attention. He didn't see me, so I ran toward him, waving frantically now.

I stopped abruptly. From a half mile, I could tell it wasn't Brings Thunder at all, but Jim Beckwourth. I felt everything sag inside me. Drained, miserable, thinking the man wasn't coming, I returned to the grove in a state of numbness, telling myself over and over not to give up. There were still hours of daylight left.

At the creek, Whelan was tossing rocks into the water. The children were gone. Alarmed, I shouted, "Where are Jane and Seneca? Where's Little George?"

"Oh, they ran off after that pup."

"You damned idiot!" I shouted, unable to control my sudden fear. "Where?"

He flapped his mouth for several seconds before pointing. "Just up that arroyo yonder. Not far. Just a minute ago. Don't worry. They'll be fine, Libby."

I moaned, running after them with Whelan following. "Don't get so upset, girl," he said. "They'll be fine."

The arroyo sloped sharply upward, quickly becoming a difficult climb over rocks and boulders. Scrambling hand over foot, I called out, "Little George! Seneca! Jane!" but got no answer.

After another minute we came out onto a level grassy stretch. What I saw made my heart come apart. Little George lay in the dry creek bed, a bloody swathe cut across his head. Six Indians on horseback were riding off with Seneca and Jane.

"No!" I screamed. I hurried to Little George. He was groaning, still alive. Thank, God.

Running past us, Whelan drew a pistol, firing off three quick shots. One of the Indians folded over on his horse, but kept astride.

"I hit one! I hit one!" Whelan yelled with almost schoolboy delight.

Another of the Indians turned and road swiftly back toward us. I recognized Brings Thunder coming up on us like a horseman out of Hell. He had one of the twins in front of him.

Whelan stumbled backward, turned and ran. Brings Thunder was on him in an instant, swinging his war club. I turned away.

When I looked back, Whelan was still running. Somehow, he had ducked the club.

"Run, Libby!" he cried.

As he disappeared down into the ravine, I stood over Little George, shaking with fear. I wasn't leaving him. Brings Thunder pulled his horse to a halt twenty feet away and stared at me with arrogant contempt, holding fiercely to the struggling girl I thought was Seneca.

"Seneca! Don't struggle," I called out.

It was her for at her name she stopped moving, looking at me helplessly. I had no doubt he would kill her if she became too much trouble. "Don't struggle. I will come for you. I swear to God I will come for you."

He gave a chilling laugh. "Yes, by all means. Who knows? I still might help you."

I looked into the heart of evil. "You son of a bitch!"

"Oh, I am that, and you," he said, pointing to Little George, "you have seen to the death of that boy and given me these two girls to replace my own."

Why he didn't kill me at that moment was hard to figure till I realized for someone like him, he could hurt me worse but letting me live. My hurt was as exposed as a bare breast. Little George, laying at my feet and the girls taken, all my fault. No one else's. He saw the anguish I would harbor forever, for it was folly to think I could get the girls back. To him, killing me now would spoil his fun and be a mercy, and this man had no mercy in him.

Though no longer squirming, Seneca was crying. As he whirled his horse around and rode off, she screamed, "Libby, help me!"

That cry shattered my heart.

Chapter 32

*I*t took several hours for the wagons to cross the river. By the time Captain Warren could lead twenty men out to pursue the Indian raiders, they were already three hours behind Brings Thunder. Both Fitzpatrick and Beckwourth went with them, and if the Sioux could be tracked and caught, those two would be the ones who could do it. The worst part was that Henry and Daniel had set out immediately, well ahead of Captain Warren's bunch.

I had done that. Two farmers in pursuit of six Lakota warriors led by that psycho Brit. If they caught up with them, it would be the end of Daniel and Henry. Isaac had wanted to go, but Henry said he had to stay and protect the rest of the family. The boy puffed his chest out and carried a big pistol in his belt now, like he was grown.

There was no way to rationalize it. I had brought disaster on the Quarles family. I could never have imagined the level of pain and anguish that caused me. I sat on that old stool by the wagon as the company's women came to support Julia in her own anguish while Caroline fed them cornbread and tea.

Few things could stop the wagon train from its inexorable move forward, but the kidnapping of Seneca and Jane did. We would not be moving for days till they were found and brought back. Julia was in and out of the wagon with Myra, taking care of Little George, while several women helped with chores, setting up our tent, cooking, and hanging out our wash on lines stretched between wagons. They talked about Indian raids in general and how lost white girls were raised by Sioux. I wanted to shout at them that the girls weren't lost, but kept my mouth shut for once.

As knots twisted my stomach, I heard Little George complaining he wanted to get up, but Julia insisted he rest. His head had taken a glancing blow from an Indian war club and bandaged by Hannibal Pierce, who then went off with

Captain Warren. Pierce had wondered aloud at the aftereffect of Little George's injury, citing how the Quarles family had a history of going batty after a knock on the head. No one thought it funny.

Neither Julia nor anyone else openly blamed me for this tragedy, but they had to be thinking it. They hardly knew the worst of it, how I had brought it all about, had brought Brings Thunder's attention onto the company. I knew now even if Brings Thunder could help me get back to my century, which I doubted, he was not someone I could control and manipulate like I could people in the twenty-first century. In my arrogance, I had thought I could, but I was wrong.

I had promised Seneca I would come for her. As I sat there in my little bubble of misery, I decided I had to at least try, as mad as that sounded to me. Against Brings Thunder and the Lakota, I felt sure the men, even with Beckwourth and Fitzpatrick, would fail. What could I do that they couldn't? I knew it was hopeless, but I could not accept things as they were. If I had to die here in this time attempting to get those girls back, then so be it.

Calmly, I got up and went to the Quarles' other wagon. Inside, I rummaged through a chest of Isaac's clothes. Though only twelve, he was about my size. I found a pair of checked pants that fit, and discarding my dress and petticoat, put them on, tucking them into my moccasins. I put on one of his grey cotton shirts.

As I was hooking the belt, Isaac appeared at the back and gave me a gaping look of outrage. "What are you doing?" he demanded.

"Go on with you, Isaac," I snapped at him. "This doesn't concern you."

"I'd say it does. You're wearing my pants." He shouted, "Ma! Ma! Come quick."

Moments later, Julia showed up with Myra and several other women. "Oh, dear," she said.

"You can't stop me."

Julia stared at me with infinite sadness. "Haven't I suffered enough for one day, Libby?"

"I'm sorry. I don't want to hurt you."

She turned to the other women and said, "Give me a minute alone with my daughter, please."

I knew the arguments she would make and was ready for them. To my surprise, she made none of them. Quickly she said to Isaac, "Go saddle Iris for your sister. Hurry now!"

Confused, he ran off. She called after him. "And throw some biscuits in a flour sack for her."

I climbed down from the wagon. "I'm sorry. I have to. I could not bear another moment unless I went."

"I know. It was not your fault, Libby. It wasn't. Many a time, the girls have wandered off on me."

I shook my head because I knew she was wrong.

"Just like your pa," she said. "When he sets his mind to something, nothing on God's earth can stop him from doing it. You're a mindful child until it doesn't suit you. Nothing I can do about it, is there? You rode through that blizzard to fetch him, so this is just another blizzard I'd say. I know if I stop you, you will just go later. There're a couple hours of daylight left. Hurry now, so you can find your pa before dark."

When I nodded, she climbed into the wagon and a minute later returned, placing a wide-brimmed straw hat on my head and tied a red kerchief around the top and my chin to hold it in place. "Wouldn't want that pretty face of yours to burn."

Then she kissed me. Tears ran down her cheeks. My eyes watered, but I couldn't allow myself to cry. What she gave me next was not the usual mother-daughter gift. It was a long-barreled pistol much like the one Isaac carried. It weighed a ton.

I tried to give it back. "I've never fired a gun before. I wouldn't know how."

"You have. And you're a pretty fair shot. It's a Colt Paterson. It'll come back to you. You can't go out into that country without a weapon."

It was sleek and shiny. I stared at it. "Julia, it doesn't even have a trigger."

"You need to cock it. Do it now."

I did. When it clicked back, the trigger appeared. She gave me a handful of cartridges which I stuck in my pocket.

"Find your father. You should be all right then. If you get lost, just come back south and you'll cross the Oregon Road. You get into trouble, give Iris her head. She'll take care of you."

There was nothing else to say. An hour after Captain Warren's group had left, I rode out of camp after them.

I became lost in ten minutes.

As soon as the camp was out of sight, I saw an endless panorama of hills and arroyos ahead and nowhere to go. I had assumed a group of twenty men on horseback would be easy to follow, and they probably were for someone like Beckwourth or Fitzpatrick, but as I pushed on with Iris at a strong canter, I found I couldn't tell a hoof print from a hole in the ground.

Still, I wasn't turning back. I continued on in the same direction I thought they had headed, deeper into the dry hills of future Wyoming. As I got farther into this alien wilderness, I hoped to leave behind the terrible anguish of what I'd done, but the feeling clung to me like sunburn.

Out ahead, the prairie rose toward a high ridge, miles and miles in the distance. As Iris picked her way nimbly over the rocky terrain, I felt an overwhelming sense of urgency. I had to find Captain Warren's party in a hurry. Getting caught out here alone at night would be a terrible mistake. Maybe Libby was pioneer enough to take care of herself; I was not.

After more than an hour, I reached the crest of the ridge, hoping the men would be in view. The new vista that greeted me was huge beyond believing, a world of lunar landscapes reaching far into a hazy distance, ravines that looked like giant claw marks in the land. As I searched for the captain, my stomach sank. I saw nothing. I was alone. Utterly alone. What a fool I was.

Then, just as I kneed Iris on, I spotted them. They were maybe four or five miles off, tiny figures coming up out of a ravine, raising a dust cloud that I was sure if I could see, every Indian within miles could see. Quickly, they road over a ridge and disappeared again.

"Wait!" I yelled foolishly, but, of course, they were way too far ahead to hear. Dear God, I'd found them and lost them in the same instant.

My idiotic shout was a monumental blunder for at that moment I noticed off to my right a half mile away three Lakota warriors astride pinto horses, watching me. A moan of sheer despair escaped my lips. My bowels were suddenly roiling as if overcome with dysentery.

Fighting the urge to kick Iris into a full-out gallop, I let her pick her way down into a gully where I lost sight of the Indians, and we wound our way through a maze of those little ravines for a few minutes, expecting at any moment to see the three warriors above me or ahead of me blocking the way. Once out of the gullies, I chucked Iris into a run. I didn't see the Indians, but knew they were about, maybe tracking me. I could visualize my hair on a scalp pole.

For the next fifteen minutes, Iris and I ate up terrain. It was tough ground, but she handled it as if she were part mountain goat. When she started to lather, I slowed down, knowing enough to realize out here pushing your horse to exhaustion was a bad idea. To the west was a range of mountains, purple in twilight shadows. I figured I had about a half hour of light left to find the men. On a gentle downslope, we came to a small stream barely five feet wide with small fish swimming near the surface. While I let Iris drink, I got down to tighten the cinch. Leave it to Isaac to saddle the horse wrong. Something like a hoof print caught my attention and I squatted to look at it. Paula Masters, Indian scout. Stupid. It meant nothing to me. It left me vulnerable.

I was kneeling there when I heard a sound that sent terror spiking through me. A blood-chilling war cry. Not thirty yards back, the three Lakota warriors were bearing down on me, eyes ablaze with ferocity. One got off an arrow that swooshed past my head. Full of dread, my instinct kicked in, and I swung up on Iris, screaming, "Go!"

She did. We splashed across the stream just ahead of them and up the other bank. They'd closed quickly, barely ten yards between us, as I darted into a dry creek bed. It narrowed all at once, forming a canyon that left only a thin strip of sky overhead. In the shadows, Iris took the shrub and dried wood debris like a slalom racer. The canyon walls echoed to the pounding of her hooves and those of the horses behind.

I glanced back and was surprised to see the three Lakota falling behind, not far, maybe twenty yards now, but Iris was outrunning them. For half a moment, I experienced a rush of exhilaration, then she stumbled. It was a terrible moment, but she regained her footing and instantly shot back up to speed. The lead pursuer, though, had gained to within a couple strides. He leaned forward with his war hatchet in his hand readying to split my head open.

I suddenly remembered I had the gun stuck in my belt. I drew it, cocked it and fired. Sparks from the errant bullet flew off the canyon walls. That I had a weapon and I had fired it didn't seem to faze the warrior. He swung the club, I ducked and it glanced off my left shoulder. I shrieked in pain. For a moment, the arm went dead, but then the feeling came back. The blunt end had struck, not the sharp end, which likely would have taken a piece of my shoulder and knocked me from my saddle.

We hit a long straight away of about fifty yards, and in that space Iris pulled ahead again. There was no give in her. Lathering and breathing hard, her pace was unflagging. How I loved her at that moment. She was a plug ugly horse, but she was fast. My God, she was fast.

Around the next turn, the canyon narrowed even more and darkened. I could still see objects, but barely. Soon, very soon, it would be too dark for even Iris, and the Indians would have me. I needed to escape this death trap and pleaded with God that there would be a way out. My first real communication with Him in years. In the next instant, I saw how that prayer was answered. The way was blocked. A dead end. A ghastly joke.

As dread lurched into the front chambers of my brain, I saw debris that had been deposited in flood after flood to form a perfect dam ahead, about five feet high. No way through. In the center of it, scalded white, was a giant animal head, bigger than anything I'd ever seen, bigger than a buffalo by twice. I had never truly thought of death before, at least not my own. But here it was, and in the dreadful notion of it, I was overwhelmed by an incredible loneliness. So far, far away from anyone I ever loved or who had loved me. To die here and now, forsaken by God.

With the Lakota behind me screaming war cries that froze the heart, I pushed Iris right at the dam. Incredibly, this horse did not balk, but charged it and took it with a jump that would have made Quantum Leap proud.

"Iris, you beauty!" I shouted. I grinned and slapped her neck with pride.

I did not look back, but knew my pursuers had not made it over. After another hundred yards or so where the canyon walls widened and gentled upward, we slowed and climbed out onto a ridge where I saw the boundless twilight sky and stars already making an appearance. My chest was heaving and Iris was breathing hard. I glanced around to see if the Sioux followed. In the dying of the light, I saw them coming up out of the canyon far off, a couple hundred yards or so away. We were separated by several arroyos, and the three figures calmly sat on their horses and watched me. I was safe for the moment. I considered that maybe the prayer was answered after all.

I thought to wave to Sioux, but that would be childish hubris. I waved anyway, but they gave no response. I guess I'm not in Los Angeles anymore. I turned and headed down onto a wide plain in search of Captain Warren.

Chapter 33

*D*arkness fell. Moonlight made things too bright and me too visible. Behind me, I felt the Sioux warriors closing in and half expected to feel the sizeable hurt of an arrow in my back. My shoulder was throbbing in pain and a sense of hopelessness settled in quickly. I knew they had to be near. Cresting a small hill, I saw a couple fires a mile off and headed for them. God, let them be Captain Warren and his men and not Indians.

As I drew nearer, I sighed with relief. It was the men from the company, camped by a single cedar tree that nestled in close on a creek bank. I dismounted and walked Iris in the last few yards, past two guards who were watching Pierce and Beckwourth arguing, and not for anyone approaching. At least, Pierce was arguing. Beckwourth was piling dried scrub onto the fire and seemed unconcerned. Fitzpatrick and Captain Warren and the other men were listening intently. I was surprised to see Daniel and Henry among them.

"I thought you was supposed to be this great pilot, Beckwourth," Pierce was saying heatedly as I came into the firelight. "And here you go building fires and letting the Injuns know where we are. Even I know'd not to do that."

Beckwourth exchanged an amused glance with Fitzpatrick, then asked calmly, "So you know the Indian, do you, Mr. Pierce?"

"I know'd a fire going to give away our position."

Beckwourth shook his head. "Well, maybe so. Could be you're just the man to find those two girls." With a dirty cloth, he adjusted a metal teapot on the fire and smiled at Pierce. "As for me, I plan to sit here a spell and boil me some water for tea."

"The Indians already know you're here," I said, walking in among them. They couldn't have been more startled if I'd been leading an elephant instead of Iris.

"What the…," Pierce muttered.

Henry and Daniel shot to their feet and rushed over, grabbing me as if testing to see if I was real.

"Ow!" I twisted away as one of them grabbed my bruised shoulder.

"Libby! Dear God," Daniel said.

Henry's face was drawn and pale. "What are you doing here, Libby? Crazy. Crazy."

"Seneca and Jane were my fault. I'm here to help get them back."

Pierce lifted his head to the heavens. "Lord, help us. This just about tears it."

"You shouldn't have come," Captain Warren said, frowning with disapproval. "This is no place for a girl."

I ignored his comment. "You might as well have a fire, sir. The Indians know you're here. Three Sioux have been watching you for several hours."

Hands on hips, Pierce accused, "Oh? And how would you know that, missy?"

"I saw them. One of them got me on the shoulder with a war club."

Hearing that, Daniel winced and put his arm gently around me.

"And they just let you waltz on in here?" Pierce asked.

"Iris outran them."

Beckwourth eyed me like I had come to eat his young. He and Fitzpatrick were the only ones who could stop me from going by just refusing to go themselves. Without at least one of them, we were hopelessly out of our depth in this country. But I doubted that would happen.

Captain Warren gazed at me sternly. "Well, it was foolish, you coming, Libby. It puts an extra burden on all of us. You'll be going back tomorrow." He turned to Daniel. "You take her back." He hesitated a moment. "You and Jesse. I can't spare any more men to protect her."

I saw Daniel's disappointment. By now I knew him well enough to understand he felt deeply about the twins, but also saw this as a grand adventure and didn't want to miss it. I straightened up. "I'm not going back. You'll have to tie me to the saddle, and even then I'll come back first chance I get. Those girls were my responsibility. I know Brings Thunder more than any of you. I've spoken with him more than once. I can help. Either way, I will not go back."

At first, they seemed stunned.

"What kind of talk is that for a girl?" Whelan said, expressing what they all thought. Fact was, nineteenth century women seldom went against what men said, at least publically, and never young girls. They always obeyed.

The men looked to Henry, who, merely shrugged.

Pierce shook his head derisively. "Quarles, can't you control your daughter?"

"When I've a mind to," he answered. "Right now, I've not got a mind to."

It seemed for an instant that Pierce was going to say something else, but Henry was no Milquetoast, and when it came down to it, Pierce was afraid of him and kept his mouth shut.

Henry addressed the men. "I appreciate all of you coming, putting yourselves at risk out here to retrieve my girls, and I know how you feel about Libby being here. But I'll take my daughter with me. I know firsthand no one's going to get her back to the company unless she wants to go. She's got a mind of her own. No whupping I ever give her has changed that." He gave Pierce a hard look. "And no one else is going to touch her."

He paused as they all took that in, staring from me back to all of them. A few men shook their heads in exasperation and bewilderment. "She comes, Captain," he added. "I'll see she's no burden to anyone, but I can tell you this from experience. When times get hard, there's no one tougher than Libby. It don't factor she's a girl. Others might become a burden, she never will."

I couldn't believe he said that about me...well, about Libby. I felt a warmth for him I never had before. I hoped to God nothing happened to him or Daniel or any of them in this trouble I had caused.

"Will the Indians attack us?" Jesse Hancock asked, putting an end to the discussion about me.

"Count on it," Beckwourth answered.

"But why?" Barnaby Pierce asked hopefully. "They haven't bothered us before. In fact, they've been mighty friendly, you ask me."

"'Cause Whelan shot one of them, boy," Hannibal Pierce answered his son.

Whelan responded with the ire of the unjustly accused, "They was attacking me. What was I supposed to do? Sing them a lullaby?"

"You did right, Mr. Whelan," Fitzpatrick said, eyeing Pierce. "No one saying otherwise. A party our size, no Indian is going to particularly like. As long as you folks stay on the Holy Road, they don't bother you much. As most see it, you're passing through. But soon as anyone comes north, especially a party as big as us right now, into the heart of their country, they don't like it. Don't like it at all. None of the tribes do. That's like dropping a hornet's nest inside their tipis. It's going to stir them up."

Captain Warren set a night schedule for sentries, but left me off it. I didn't argue the point, hoping they'd do a better job than the two on guard at my approach. Most of the men crawled into their bedrolls along with their rifles, but a few sat about the fire still talking in hushed tones with Beckwourth, Fitzpatrick, and the captain about our prospects, which no one seemed to think were good, even though we had two of the most famous mountain men ever with us. Though a little fuzzy about the details, I knew the two men's life spans and that they both had major achievements yet to make. If I got them killed on this ride, would that change history?

Sitting beside me on our blankets, Daniel tried to reassure me. "Don't worry. We've got guns and there're twenty of us. We'll get out of this pickle."

"I know we will." I knew nothing of the kind. I rubbed his back. "You should have seen Iris today. I've never seen a horse do what she did. I had a horse a couple years ago I thought was the most magnificent creature God ever created. I loved him so much. His name was Quantum Leap. He could jump so high people thought he was flying. But Iris is a match."

"I'm just glad you're safe." Daniel smiled and winked. "If there weren't so many people around, I'd..."

I made like I was fanning myself with my hand. "My, my, Mr. Langdon, you do give a girl the vapors."

He laughed and we lay down, separated by a good two feet, of course, and tried to get some sleep.

Throughout the following day, the sun bore down on us as if it had measurable weight; the blue shimmer of prairie quivered under it. In the giant expanse,

I experienced that same sense of loneliness I felt yesterday, as if nothing lived out here, that any people with a real connection to me were as distant as the Andromeda galaxy. In fact, I was the alien here.

Progress through this difficult terrain of ravines and steep hills was not easy. Fitzpatrick had ridden on ahead to look for sign while Beckwourth maintained us at a canter, but I feared Brings Thunder and his band were getting farther away. I even chaffed at the short rest at noon—take a lunch break while pursuing kidnappers?

As we pushed on in the afternoon, I rode near the black mountain man. He seemed to be asleep in the saddle most of the time, occasionally waking up and pointing out sign for my benefit. He seemed more amenable to me since I told him who I really was. He was the only person on the planet besides Brings Thunder who actually knew me. Well-armed, two long revolver pistols were stuck in a leather belt and a rifle rested in a scabbard on his saddle.

Alongside him, Captain Warren rode his favorite black mule George. I could tell his foot was ailing him, but he would say nothing about it. He favored mules over horses and had three. They had better endurance, he said, if a might stubborn sometimes. He couldn't have been happy about events. Beside his ailing foot, we were a long way from the wagons now and getting farther. Each day we pursued the Indians, the company would get no closer to Oregon. Everyone worried they'd get caught in the mountains in winter. No one wanted that.

Once, when we crested a hill and saw miles of prairie with not a thing moving, certainly no band of Sioux with the twins, Henry asked, "Mr. Beckwourth, are we really going to catch them?"

"Should. If we's persistent enough. We got a long way to go."

"Will we be able to trade for my girls?"

"No. Don't figure we will. We'll have to steal them back."

Daniel and I exchanged worried glances. If we tried to steal them back, Brings Thunder could kill them and maybe a lot of other people would get hurt.

"Why'd he steal them, Mr. Beckwourth? Why my girls?" Henry asked.

"Don't have any idea." He glanced at Henry, then at me as if rolling over a decision in his head. When he turned back to watching the trail, he said, "He ain't no common Injun, ain't no Injun at all. A Lakota would keep both girls but I feared he's just ornery enough he won't."

"Then what?" Henry asked, a tremble in his voice. He knew. So did I.

Beckwourth was not one to soften the truth. "Sir, he may kill the one he don't want."

I moaned at the thought, saying the words, *please, no,* over and over to myself.

Chapter 34

The Sioux attacked the afternoon of the fourth day. We'd travelled more than a hundred miles from the North Platte River, reaching the foothills of the Bighorn Mountains, as Beckwourth called them. Sage and rock had given way to fields of grass, red buttes and high standing hills with patches of pine and cedar, their distinct smell hanging in the dry air.

We rode with little talk. Everyone feared an Indian attack, though there'd been no sight of them since I came into camp. I said three Sioux, but Beckwourth said there were maybe fifty warriors round about. That made the tension worse. As we rode, the men nervously watched the ridges.

"Fifty? I don't see them," I said hopefully, riding up beside Beckwourth.

"That's 'cause you ain't looking." He insisted there were plenty of sign, but I just couldn't read them. "Like you can't read your letters so books make no sense to you, only it's the land you can't read."

He was about to explain when potbellied Newton Rudabaugh let out a yelp. I followed his gaze and saw five Indians in nothing but breechclouts, sitting their horses atop a ridge two hundred yards to the left, calmly watching us. Rifles at the ready, we kept moving.

"Don't waste a shot," Beckwourth said. "They's too far. Keep going easy like."

"If they want a fight," Barnaby said, "we can give it to them."

"We don't know for sure they have any mean intentions toward us," Beckwourth said. "Likely as not they do, but if they want to let us ride on, then we let them let us."

Most of these men were just farmers. But this was the nineteenth century, and farmers could handle weapons and had done so all their lives. I told myself I was safe with these men. I even felt we had a chance of getting the girls back. I had

197

almost convinced myself, but the rational part of my brain practically shouted we were in mortal danger, and the chances of getting the girls back near nonexistent.

Beckwourth said, "You folks see those trees off to the right, that big clump by the creek? If we need to ride hard, go for that. We get in there, we can hold them off."

"There's only five of them," Pierce said. "Let's go after them."

"Where there's five, there's fifty." Beckwourth replied.

"They'll try us," Whelan said. "You'll see if I ain't right."

"Maybe they won't attack," Rudabaugh said. Frightened, his voice quivered and his hands shook. He was so nervous he farted, and despite the awful tension, everyone laughed.

"You trumpeting a charge, Rudabaugh?" Pierce said.

In spite of my worry, I laughed hysterically with everyone else. I thought we must be causing the Indians a lot of confusion, wondering if we were all mad. Abruptly, everyone stopped laughing. Four more warriors rode slowly over the crest of the ridge and down the slope at us waving blankets.

"What the hell they doing?" Whelan muttered.

"Keep steady," Captain Warren ordered.

That's when another ten Sioux appeared in a long single file and came down the slope out in front of us, blocking us from the copse of trees. I counted them. Twenty-two now, half of them armed with rifles. Likely not all of them. No Seneca or Jane among them.

"When I say ride, you boys ride," Beckwourth said.

"But the Indians are between us and those damn trees," Pierce said.

"Yes, sir, they are," Beckwourth replied. "We ride through them."

Whelan moved his horse up next to mine. "I'll see you through, Miss Libby."

I thanked him. Daniel to my right, Henry behind, all with the sacred task to see I was not hurt. I preferred they saw to themselves, but I was so scared I said nothing. My biggest fear was that Iris would outdistance everyone and I'd be the first one to hit the wall of Indians.

At the very edge of rifle range, a few of the Indians started firing. Beckwourth called out, "Hold, hold. Not yet."

As the few shots flew by or peppered the ground in front of us, we ambled our horses slowly ahead as if on a Sunday ride. Then Beckwourth shouted the order, "Ride, boys, ride!"

As one, we spurred our horses into a headlong gallop right at the Indians. My heart was pounding furiously. Flashing in and out of my brain was the phrase, "Into the valley of death." Our men started firing, random shots that did little good, but got the Indians to split apart. As we rode through the opening in the center, I saw several of them notching arrows and loosening them at us. A few whizzed by me like twigs in a hurricane.

Amid the pounding of hooves and the war cries and men yelling, I heard a scream and a gurgling sound right next to me. Whelan had an arrow sticking out of his throat. His eyes rolled back in his head, and he tumbled from the horse.

"Keep going!" Daniel shouted.

I hadn't planned on stopping.

Once through their line, we made for the grove of trees, now less than a hundred yards away. The Indians pursued us. Iris shot ahead. I glanced back at Daniel, and that's when he went down onto the hardpan. Already twenty yards ahead, I reined Iris around. Stunned, Daniel rose up on unsteady feet. The Indians were almost upon him. Dear God, no!

Henry grabbed my reins. "You can't help him."

"Let go!" I shouted.

I jerked away from him and just as I was about to start back for Daniel, Jesse Hancock rode up to him, holding his arm out. Daniel swung up behind him as Henry got off a couple pistol shots at the Indians, then we whipped our horses around and rode hard for the shelter of the trees.

In among the grove, chaos reigned. Everyone scrambled for a spot from which to fire. In the next few seconds, we unloaded on them, turning them back. They rode another couple hundred yards till they were far out of range and there milled about. I helped Daniel hobble in behind a tree. He was badly hurt. A broken ankle maybe or a severely sprained one. Not usually fatal unless you were in Indian country and your horse was lying a hundred yards away screeching in pain with a broken leg. Beckwourth took aim and ended its pain.

When I got Daniel's boot off, his ankle was already swelling up. Grabbing a shirt from my saddle bags, I dashed to the creek, dipped it into the cold water and brought it back. After I wrapped the soaked shirt around his ankle, certain it was probably not cold enough to do any good, he sucked in sharp breath and nodded at me.

"It'll be fine, Libby," he said. "It ain't that bad."

It was bad. Smiling, I nodded as if I believed him, but my thoughts were going through a severe adjustment. When he went down out there, I felt like I went down, too. What I had worried might happen if I allowed myself to fall in love with him was now a hard reality. I had to accept the strength of feeling I had for this man, and realized I could not live without him. It was as sobering a thought as I had ever had.

Jesse came over and knelt next to us. "How's the leg?"

"It's all right, Jesse, thanks," Daniel said.

"I thought Libby had gone down," he said with a grin. "My mistake."

The firing had ceased for now. The grove offered little real cover should the Indians attack. If they came in full force again, we were dead. I could see by the hard set on the faces of the men that if that happened, the Sioux would pay dearly for our lives. Right now, the Indians held their position some three hundred yards out, talking among themselves in plain view. Henry and Captain Warren came back to Daniel and me.

"How's the patient?" Captain Warren asked.

"Patient's fine," Daniel said firmly. "Just a little sprain. I'll be fine in a minute or two." He patted the pistol on his lap. "I'll watch Libby."

Captain Warren touched the ankle and Daniel winced. "Looks like you'll be stoved up for a week or two. Might even be worse off than my foot."

"Here they come!" Someone shouted.

Henry and the Captain dashed back to the edge of the grove. Howling their chilling, wild war cries, the warriors rode at an oblique angle, then swung across our front some fifty yards away, firing their rifles and arrows. Their maneuver gave us no target to fix on, but offered little accuracy for them. Several bullets struck trees and cut through the branches with a crack. Hugging the ground with Daniel, I felt like a fugitive from the law of averages.

"Cease fire!" Captain Warren shouted when they were once again out of range.

They repeated this maneuver two more times. They fired, we didn't. We were wasting too many cartridges and hitting nothing, so Captain Warren kept saying, "Not yet. Wait till they come at us."

The only one hurt this round was Jesse Hancock who took several splinters in his cheek when a bullet exploded the tree bark next to his face. I spent the next fifteen minutes picking them out. He said ouch with each one and winked at me, "Thanks, Libs, you're a sweetheart." Libs!

The Indians again watched us from their safe zone three hundred yards away. I could not claim to be an arms expert, but I did know that the single-loading rifles our men had were not all that accurate. Beckwourth, though, had one as good as the one Brings Thunder had taken from Captain Warren, and he was an expert shot with it. He could have picked off any one of the warriors from this distance, but he didn't. I wondered why and was about to ask him, when Pierce yelled, "Here they come again!"

Not all of them, just one warrior, lean and muscular, a single eagle feather in his hair and screaming his banshee war cry.

"What is he doing," I muttered.

"Crazy," Daniel said.

Captain Warren ordered, "Hold! Not yet. Hold. Let him get closer."

I noticed Beckwourth hadn't taken aim. The warrior came at us. A hundred yards, then fifty, then twenty.

"Fire!" the captain shouted.

The volley sounded like a single cannon. An instant later when the smoke had cleared, the Indian was still astride his pony, coming hard. Too late, the men fumbled at their rifles to reload. A few drew pistols and fired. The Sioux swung his war axe, which glinted in the afternoon sun, and crashed at full speed right in among us, taking Rudabaugh down with a glancing swipe to the head. Blood spurted out from the gash.

The Indian rode right on through us without a shot touching him, across the creek and out into the meadow beyond where he was joined by five other warriors. With a last whoop they rode to cover, disappearing through a funnel of small hills. The Sioux in front of us also withdrew beyond the high ridge.

Now we had warriors in front and behind. Even I knew this wasn't good.

Chapter 35

The day wore on, afternoon changing to evening. Rudabaugh was alive, but he didn't have a clue where he was. "You got the hardest head I ever seen," Pierce said, wrapping a bandage on it.

The sun, which had been brutal, shifted down beyond the Bighorn Mountains, almost instantly dropping the temperature several degrees. We tried to ignore poor Mr. Whelan lying about a hundred yards away, buzzards circling him. There was nothing we could do for him now but bury him if we got the chance. Occasionally we heard gunshots and the loud whooping from over the ridge, keeping tension high. We all knew that our position here was untenable. We had water close by, but our food would run out soon enough, and then what?

"Where's Fitzpatrick?" Captain Warren asked Beckwourth. "He should have been back by now."

Beckwourth shook his head, indicating he didn't know.

After about ten minutes in which only silence came from over the hills, Pierce said, hopefully, "I think they're gone. You think they're gone, Beckwourth? I think they're gone."

"Why don't you ride on out there and find out, Pierce?" Beckwourth suggested.

"Like hell, I will."

Night fell. A brilliant panorama of stars filled the sky and later a quarter moon. It would have been beautiful on any occasion other than this. Beckwourth called it a stalking moon.

I didn't like being the one stalked. We'd just finished a supper of hardtack and beef jerky. My stomach jumpy, I could only handle a few bites. With Henry looking on, I gave Daniel a kiss on the cheek. "Thank you," I said softly. I didn't know exactly why I was thanking him, but I meant it.

"Libby, you know I'd break both legs for you."

"Now's no time to be sparking my daughter, young man," Henry said, forcing playfulness more than feeling it.

Daniel smiled. He was not in so much pain, he'd said, just throbbing in his ankle, which was monstrously swollen, at least twice its size. My water wrap had been a bust. A little while before, he'd tried to put weight on it and hissed in pain. Henry and I got him quickly back on the ground.

As the night deepened, I tried to sleep but couldn't, and neither could anyone else. Not surprising. We expected the Indians to burst out of the darkness with their banshee screams at any moment. Around midnight, Beckwourth, Captain Warren and Pierce came to check on Daniel. They'd been talking, and I hoped they'd come up with a plan to get us out of this pickle, for clearly Daniel could not go on. That meant the group would have to split up.

Henry said, "We can't sit here forever."

"We know that, Quarles," Pierce said. "You got a way to get us out of here, 'cause if you do, please, by all means, tell us."

"We got about the same number of men," Henry said. "What with part of them behind us, we're larger than any one group."

"So?"

"Let's not sit here and wait for them to come to us, let's go after them. We hit them, drive them off, then we got a chance."

"Thank you, General Quarles," Pierce said sarcastically.

It wasn't a bad idea. Captain Warren was giving it some thought. Be aggressive because doing nothing would be our end.

Beckwourth shook his head, firmly. "No, not a good idea." He exchanged a look with Henry that I did not come close to understanding, but Henry seemed to accept it. "Leastways, not yet."

I asked, hopefully, "You got something in mind, Mr. Beckwourth?"

"No, not at all, but let me go have a look first before any of you frontiersmen does anything."

My eyes widened in alarm. He was going out alone into the night with all the Sioux around. I would not have done that in a million years.

"I should be back in a couple hours." With that, he slipped quickly out of the grove, and his silhouette was lost to us almost immediately.

No one even tried to sleep after he left. Henry had a guard shift just before dawn, and when I saw him get up and move to the edge of the little camp, I nestled into Daniel's arm. He too was wide awake, his rifle resting in the other arm.

We talked in hushed whispers. He was certain we'd get the girls back, but I was just as certain he could go no farther. After a while, he told more of his plans for when we married. His farm in Oregon would have a mix of dairy cows and beef cattle. He'd open most of the acreage to a money crop like oranges, while I planted and tended a garden for food crops, like corn and potatoes. I snorted derisively at that suggestion. Me planting a garden!

Then he mentioned again how he fell in love with me the moment he saw me in St. Jo. "You stood out," he said, "a girl so pretty my heart bled. You were standing up to a store clerk who had tried to cheat you on the purchase of hard rock candy for you brothers and sisters, and that did me in. I was in love."

I didn't remember because that hadn't been me. Exhausted, mostly from the constant tension and fear, I finally fell asleep to the smooth, sweet tones of his voice speaking of Oregon.

When I woke again, likely less than an hour later, it was still night, but off to the east the first shards of morning had appeared in the sky. The grove was in a turmoil of activity. It seemed everyone was up but me. Beckwourth was back. "The Indians are gone," he said, repeating it several times for those like me who couldn't believe it. I could not exaggerate the joy I felt when I heard that, like being told you're dying by a doctor then, oops, it was a mistake.

"Don't know if they'll be back," he added, "so I suggest we get moving before they do."

There was no immediate response, and I wanted to shout, what's the matter with you people. Let's get out of here!

Captain Warren looked at Henry with a deep frown. By his expression, I knew what was coming. "Well, the pinch of the game has arrived, Quarles. We come about as far as we can. We're more than a hundred miles away from our own families. We got Whelan dead and Daniel badly injured. I'm sorry it's so, but those girls of yours could be anywhere within a thousand miles and more, and we got the whole Sioux nation to ride through trying to find them. It's a hard pill to swallow, but we have to go back. Nothing more we can do."

Blood staining his bandaged head, Rudabaugh spoke haltingly, "I'd go to the ends of the earth with you, Henry, if we had a chance. This…" He gestured to the grove. "This just showed us we don't."

"Like trying to find two particular fish in the sea with sharks swimming all about," Captain Warren said. "We're heading back."

"Then go," Henry replied sharply. "I'm going on."

"I'm going on, too," I said immediately. Henry glanced at me, but didn't contradict me.

Captain Warren shook his head ruefully but said nothing either.

"Me, too," Daniel said.

"No, you're not," I told him firmly. "You're going back."

"You'd only slow us down, Daniel," Henry said. "You need to watch out for my family. Make sure my wife goes on with the company. We'll catch up when we get Seneca and Jane. Can you do that for me, son?"

Accepting the reality of his situation, Daniel closed his eyes and nodded. I squeezed his hand.

No one could look Henry in the eye, not even Jesse Hancock. It was unfair to blame them, though I did. From their point of view, we were already dead. One man and his sixteen-year-old daughter just could not ride about in this vast Indian country and survive, and anyone who went with them would suffer the same fate. If we ever found the girls, we could not force the Sioux to give them back, even if we had a thousand men.

Henry turned to Beckwourth. "What's your pleasure, sir?"

I wished Fitzpatrick were here. He'd go with us, but he was likely dead somewhere. I knew we had no hope without this mountain man. He rubbed his chin in thought.

"You got a contract with those going to California," Captain Warren said. "With Fitzpatrick God knows where and maybe dead, we are without a pilot."

Beckwourth glanced at me. Then he turned to the captain. "Hell's fire, Warren, ride south to the Platte, then just follow the setting sun. It's not like you're going to get lost. We'll all be along in a few days."

Before they left, Jesse Hancock gave me the last of his rations, saying he'd share with others. "You ever tire of that Daniel cuss, I'm the man for you."

I smiled and thanked him. Daniel gave a final squeeze of my hand. "You should not be going. You know that. You should not."

Captain Warren called, "Come on, Daniel. Give her a pat on the cheek and let's go."

Instead, he kissed me, then hopped on one leg to Whelan's horse and lifted himself into the saddle. Earlier, Captain Warren had sent several men out to bury poor Whelan in a shallow rock grave. Now, as they rode past it heading back the way they'd come, no one even glanced at it.

Beckwourth, Henry and I headed north.

Chapter 36

For the next four days, under a bare sun so hot it felt molten, Beckwourth, Henry and I followed the trail of Brings Thunder's band in a generally northeasterly direction, crossing the hundreds of streams that poured out of the Bighorn Mountains. At least we thought it was his band. Beckwourth spent the time teaching me to read sign. Though I wasn't the most apt pupil, I began to recognize small animal tracks, which were in abundance: the skunk's tiny little almost-human footprint, the raccoon's looking like a small human hand, the coyote's canine claw. I was becoming a regular Daniel Boone. Or Jim Beckwourth. We even came across grizzly track, though I didn't see one in the flesh. Plenty of deer and elk appeared but no bear.

When we forded a creek, no more than a trickle of water, Beckwourth dismounted and motioned me to join him. Kneeling, he pointed at a wide swath of hoof prints in the soft earth. Even I could make them out.

"There are a lot of them," I said.

"How many you figure?" he asked me.

I had no idea. "Forty?"

"Not bad. Two bands done come together," he explained. "Ones what attacked us joining up with Brings Thunder's boys back a-ways. You can tell by the size of this patch and how deep the prints go. Deeper tracks mean hoof prints one on top t'other. Fifty ponies crossed here, maybe more. Don't like it at all. Not one bit. Party that big got no fear."

"How far ahead are they?" Henry asked. His hand was swathed in a dirty bandage. Somehow he'd cut himself that morning slicing a piece of pemmican for me. I rinsed it with clean water, then winced when he took his grimy bandana and wrapped it around his hand to staunch the bleeding. When I objected, he brusquely waved me away.

"No more than half a day. We done closed pretty good on them," the mountain man said. He took the time to light a pipe. Getting in the first couple of puffs, he looked up at Henry, a deep concern in his eyes. "This country is very dangerous. Arapaho, Crow, Gros Ventre, not to mention the Sioux we been following."

"You knew that when you came with us. You getting scared now, Beckwourth?"

"I been scared. Any man not is a fool."

"You want to leave, leave."

"Didn't say that at all, Quarles. Just saying this is damn dangerous country."

He mounted his horse and started out along the trail, and we followed. He'd been uneasy since that morning when we came across an isolated buffalo carcass. Our appearance had scattered a pack of wolves and buzzards battling over the meat. Tangled hair and scraps of hide lay scattered about. When we came up, the wolves milled about yelping some fifty yards away and the buzzards circled above.

As we rode on, Beckwourth found perplexing sign, the tracks of four ponies that broke off from the larger band and headed directly north.

"What are they doing?" Henry asked the mountain man.

"Damned if I know."

We found a good stream and camped for the night, then set out early next morning to try and pick up Brings Thunder's trail. When we did, it was much more than we bargained for.

What we came upon was one trail after another coming together like tributaries into a mighty river. A massive trail of hoof prints lay out before us, one that stretched more than fifty yards across.

"What's going on?" Henry asked.

Looking troubled, Beckwourth stroked his beard. "Seems a big gathering up ahead. Sioux, Arapaho, Cheyenne."

"I can see that," Henry snapped. "But what the hell are they doing that for?"

Beckwourth just shrugged. "Buffalo more than likely. Tongue River ahead. They'll camp there."

When we came upon it, the Tongue River was lined by long stretches of thick trees and underbrush, but in several places the bushes were beaten down by travois being dragged across. Fifty yards farther downriver, several horses stood in the water drinking. Crossing, we pushed through the bushes and saw a vast Indian village spreading out a half mile or more.

"You think the ones attacked us are here?" Henry asked Beckwourth.

"I do."

"My girls here?"

"They're here. Let's go say hello."

When he said that, my heart leapt into my throat. Was he mad? Just ride in? But what else were we to do? So, the three of us rode our horse at an easy walk straight toward the village.

Chapter 37

$\mathcal{A}$s we entered the Indian encampment, the Indians stopped what they were doing, frozen for an instant. then several men came warily toward us. I felt my intestines erupting with tiny explosions, thinking of poor Mr. Rudabaugh passing gas.

"You should know I'm adopted Crow," Beckwourth said hesitantly. "I have a Crow wife."

"So?" Henry said glancing at him.

"They may not welcome me. Like I said before, the Sioux hate the Crow, and I'm kind of Crow."

I thought this was not exactly the best time to mention such new information. "Would they even know you?" I asked.

"Not a lot of black men wandering this country. They know me," he answered.

I searched the Indian men fast approaching for at least one friendly face but saw none. Suddenly, a man wrapped in a grey blanket and wearing a red cap broke into a grin and rushed toward us. No Indian, he was thin with a heavy black beard. He could hardly weigh more than a 120 pounds and a lot of that was grime.

"Beckwourth," he shouted. "*Vieux fou*, what are you doing among the Lakota, *mon ami?*"

"Fonteneau," Beckwourth greeted him, hopping down from his horse and embracing the man.

"I am hearing you go to California," Fonteneau said. "Headed that way myself. They found gold, you know."

Surprisingly, the Indians seemed friendly enough, as if the Frenchman had given his seal of approval. Beckwourth motioned Henry and me down, and when we dismounted, the Sioux men squeezed around us. Instantly, I became wary, but all they wanted to do was shake hands with us, over and over again. I doubted if that was a Sioux thing, shaking hands—no doubt learned from white men like this Fonteneau—but importantly, it showed we were welcomed for the moment.

Fonteneau introduced two important chiefs, Crow Killer and Buffalo Horn. From the way the Frenchman nodded obsequiously to Buffalo Horn, he must have been the bigger chief. A short, barrel-chested man with thick muscular arms and a square jaw, he wore just a breechclout over stumpy legs. As I stood back a little, watching them, I removed my bandana and hat to wipe my face and my hair tumbled out. I heard gasps and chatter and laughter. It seemed they hadn't known I was a girl.

"Ah, la belle *fille*, you are welcome. All of you are welcome," the Frenchman said. "Come to my lodge. We eat."

As he led us deeper into the village, he said, "You're just in time for big buffalo hunt tomorrow."

"We're not here for the buffalo," Henry said.

"Is Brings Thunder here?" Beckwourth asked quickly.

Fonteneau's eyes darkened in fear. "*Oui.* He come yesterday. What you want with him?"

"Did he have two white girls with him?" Henry asked.

Looking ill, Fonteneau didn't answer right away.

"Did he?" Henry repeated sharply.

"I did not see them, but others have told me he has taken two white girls. You know these ones?"

"They are my daughters."

"And my sisters," I said.

"Ogallala will not see it so," Fonteneau said. "The two girls belong to Brings Thunder now."

"Like hell they do," Henry growled. "I'll kill the bastard first."

The Frenchman flinched and said in a hushed voice, "Be quiet, *mon ami*. Say nothing of this now. We parlay later."

The Indian village had a raw, earthy smell. Smoke lifted from hundreds of fires, and strips of meat hung like washing on ropes stretched from lodge to lodge to dry. When we reached Fonteneau's tipi, a pretty Indian woman in her late teens appeared from beneath the flap and took our horses. Stooping, we entered into dim light.

At first, I wanted to cough. Smoke from a small fire in the center filled the tipi with a fine haze. Several things hung from the lodge poles, including three metal cups, a pistol, several knives and a pipe. We sat on fur hides. Immediately Henry asked if the twins were all right.

"*Oui*. I should say so," Fonteneau answered. "I have heard this. He has both girls and they are alive."

"How do we get them back?"

The Frenchman shook his head as if Henry had just asked how to fly to the moon. "He take girls," he said. "They belong to him now. The Ogallala think that is fair thing."

"Like hell they belong to him," Henry shot back angrily.

Fonteneau held up both hands in a gesture of surrender. "I tell you only what the Lakota think, not what I think. Try to take them from him, and you will be killed, girls killed. Can you fly like a bird? Make yourself ghost? Brings Thunder can do this. *Merde*. He will kill you, and the Ogallala will help him."

"You will not help us?" Henry asked harshly.

He shrugged, and I wondered what that meant.

Beckwourth lit his pipe and offered it to Fonteneau, who took a deep inhale on it, his eyes closing with pleasure, and said, "Ah, bon. American tobacco."

"Yes, sir. I got me a bag full in St. Louis a while back," Beckwourth said. "You should see that place. They got pretty near everything there now." He received the pipe back. "Have you heard anything of Tom Fitzpatrick?"

"Not in months," Fonteneau answered.

Beckwourth looked worried. "Funny."

Henry fumed. "What are we going to do about my girls?"

"We will go after them," Beckwourth answered. "Don't you worry about that, Mr. Quarles. Don't you worry about that." He turned to Fonteneau. "Friend, we will take them girls back one way t'other. When we do, the Indians going to smell a rat. They put that smelly old rat on your head, maybe. You help us, we can fix it so they smell no rat at all."

The Frenchman thought long about this. His wife came back with three bowls filled with chunks of meat and handed them to us. My stomach churned with hunger, and I ate ravenously, hoping this was buffalo and not rat meat.

It was only after the meal that Fonteneau answered. "We will speak to Buffalo Horn. Maybe he can do something. That is all I can do."

Using Fonteneau as an interpreter, we went to see the chief. It took some time for Henry and Beckwourth to convince him to help. He was afraid of Brings Thunder I thought. Eventually, he said he would speak to the Brit about giving the girls back for trade goods and horses. Where we would get these things, I couldn't guess. Such an easy resolution seemed unlikely. Then he gave us a long speech about how he was a friend to the white people and was ready to help good relations between our people for all time. Straightening up, he nodded to us and left for Brings Thunder's lodge.

I wondered how long his friendship would last when whites began coming into his country in great numbers in the coming decades. Then we might not be such good friends.

In the afternoon, Buffalo Horn returned to Fonteneau's tipi to report Brings Thunder agreed to think on it. He would give his decision after the buffalo hunt. As I saw it, he was just stalling and did not intend to return the girls. I told Beckwourth and Henry my suspicions and suggested we come up with a plan B.

"A plan B?" Beckwourth said curiously, then understood. "Yes, I think a plan is needed."

"You have a smart daughter, *mon ami*," Fonteneau said.

About to say something in reply, Henry grimaced when he accidentally nudged his bandaged hand against a lodge pole. When I asked to look at it, he curtly waved me away.

"We got to be careful here," Beckwourth said. "If we try something before the buffalo hunt, he may harm your girls."

"Can I see them?" Henry asked Buffalo Horn. Fonteneau translated the question.

The Indian shook his head. "No, he keeps them in his lodge. He did not allow me to see them. They are well."

I frowned. If he didn't see them, then how the hell would he know?

He pondered something a long time, then when he finally spoke, he set the framework for all that was to follow. "Brings Thunder is no Lakota. Many like his power, but no one likes the man. As a man, I do not believe he is to be trusted. He has too much white blood for that. It is dangerous for you. He has friends. That is my judgment. That is what I think."

The three of us stayed in Fonteneau's lodge with his wife and two young children, a boy and a girl, both under four. The woman's name, I learned, was Black Cloud Woman, which seemed odd since she was so friendly, always smiling with her perfect white teeth, something Fonteneau did not have. Objects of curiosity, we were invited to other lodges to eat. The three of us went despite Buffalo Horn's warning of danger. Everywhere people offered us bowls of tasty meat. After becoming bloated from stuffing ourselves, I made it a point, as did Henry, to still take a bite or two, making appropriate sighs of delight.

In each place, the hosts passed a pipe around, though never offered it to me because I was female. They were not used to me speaking up as I did. Women in council. Maybe, something peculiar to the white race, they may have thought. As we went from place to place, I noticed two more bands arriving for the big buffalo hunt tomorrow, adding more lodges to the already enormous encampment.

In late afternoon, a quick thunderstorm washed away the raw odor for a while. I slipped away from the others and wandered through the village, hoping for a glimpse of the girls, but after an hour, and no sight of them, I made my way toward the river. The problem was, I could not see how we were going to get Seneca and Jane back. Brings Thunder would not give them up, and if the Sioux did intervene, it wouldn't be for us but for him. I felt ill at the prospect of losing them.

"Libby! Libby Quarles!"

I turned and saw a huge Indian woman lumbering toward me, a big grin on her face. For a second, I thought she was going to tackle me but instead she engulfed me in a giant bear hug.

"Sally Callahan!" I said, astonished.

"Libby, Libby, my God, it's you. They said another white woman was here. I had to see."

I felt a surge of warmth. "Sally, I thought I'd never see you again. Look at you."

"A regular Indian."

"Do you want to come back? You can come with us."

In her excitement, she talked so quickly I could barely keep up. "No, never, never. I am happy here. My husband treats me good, like I'm a real person. I think he loves me. Me! Can you believe that?"

"Of course I can."

"And these people are the nicest people I've ever met. I'm not one of them, but they treat me like I am. They even gave me a new name. I'm called something that means Eagle Feather. You can call me Feather."

I wondered if that was Indian sarcasm. She went on. "My husband is a great hunter and provides for me and his mother and father. I get along with them much better than I ever thought possible."

"I'm glad, Sally. I've been worried about you. Come. I want to hear all about it." I took her hand and led her along the riverbank. After telling me excitedly about her life, she sighed, breathless and stared at me. "You haven't run off and married yourself an Indian man, have you?"

"Seneca and Jane were taken by the Sioux," I said. "Henry and I are here with Jim Beckwourth to get them back."

She put her hand to her mouth in shock. "Oh, no."

"Brings Thunder took them. Have you heard of him?"

Her face drained of color. "Yes, I've heard of him. Everyone has. They say he has great power."

"I fear we are not going to be able to do this alone. Can you help me, Sally, er, Feather?"

She didn't hesitate. "Anything."

"Right now, I don't know," I answered truthfully. "I don't know what we're going to do yet. Nothing will happen till after the hunt tomorrow. For now, can you see if you can find out where Brings Thunder's tipi is? If you've seen one, you've seen them all."

"I'll find out. I swear it."

We followed the river upstream for another couple hundred yards, moving among the trees and underbrush till we'd left the encampment far behind. We had come out onto an open area and traversed down a gully to the other side, when I started with shock. Standing above us on the ravine bank was a huge Indian in just a breechclout and moccasins. His face cast in shadow, I still knew who it was.

When Sally saw him a second later, she jolted like she'd been tasered. That noseless face would shock a company of marines. He pointed a finger at her. "You, white cow. Get thee gone."

Trembling, Sally held her place beside me. I love you for that, Sally. When he spoke again, his voice had an arctic chill. "Leave us, cow. I will not tell you again."

"Go, Feather," I told her. "I'll be all right."

"Feather!" he laughed. "Who said the Indian doesn't have a sense of humor?"

She stumbled backward a couple steps, then turned and ran.

Brings Thunder said, "She is so pitiable, that one. I will have to kill her someday."

"You're a monster."

His eyes closed, savoring my words. "So I am, so I am."

"You like being the bully boy, don't you? Where I come from we'd say you're one sick puppy."

He squatted down, observing me with an amused expression. Striving for an air of superiority, he missed the mark greatly. A scab for a nose would tend to do that.

"Mister, I don't know if you have any humanity left. Maybe not. But if you do, you must give the girls back. They belong with their own family."

He stared at me emotionless. I knew my plea had fallen on ground so barren nothing would ever grow. He shook his head. "I know what you're thinking. You see me and say, you, sir, come from civilized society. How can you justify what you're doing? Oh, yes, very much yes, I do come from a civilized society. The future, the past and this, the present. More than anyone, you know I do. But, you see, civilization has so many rules. Why should I live by someone else's rules?"

"So you live by your own."

"No. You seem to pride yourself on being intelligent beyond your gender's usual incapability. I'm surprised you haven't figured it out."

"You live by no rules. No morality. No humanity."

He clapped. "Very good. Give the girl a lolly. I knew you'd get it. It is so liberating."

"You are just playing with me. I'm heading back." I started up the opposite bank.

"I will give you a choice," he called to me. "I have the power to send you back to where you belong. I shall do that tomorrow, should you choose to go."

I turned back abruptly. "Choose to go? Of course, I choose to go," I shouted at him. He had hit my raw spot and knew it.

"Don't you want to hear the other choice? I shall return you to your own place or return my captive. One. Not both."

"You bastard." I should have known. My conscience went hyper because I didn't immediately dismiss it. The idea of going home and abandoning the Quarles and the girls and even Daniel flittered once, twice, three times through my head.

"Give the girls back," I said emphatically. "Both of them."

He beamed. "Very noble indeed. Now, there's morality. Humanity. Then that's what shall happen. Except I said captive in the singular. You see, one is my daughter, the other a captive. You can't have both. One will replace the beloved child you killed. This is final. I said you choose. So which one is it? Jane or Seneca?"

I felt like a mouse being teased by a cat, one paw-nudge after another.

"I suggest you choose quickly. I only have need of one. If you don't choose, I will kill the other, a swift blow to the head. No pain. I'm not a cad after all."

I was no fool. Of course, I knew he was lying. He had no plans to return either, but I had to let him think I believed him, that I was playing his game. Even so, I did not want to do this, pick one to save and one to give up, but I needed to prolong the game for now. Seneca or Jane? How could I choose one? Finally, I said, "Seneca. Give back Seneca."

He nodded. "Ah, and so it shall be. I will keep my promise. Tomorrow, I will tell them you have chosen Seneca to be saved, Jane to be abandoned."

The sound of that nasal chuckle plagued me long into the night

Chapter 38

The next day we joined the buffalo hunt with Crow Killer. Henry didn't want to go, hoping to get the girls while most of the encampment was out, but Beckwourth said if we didn't go, Brings Thunder would stay behind to protect his prizes. I had told them about my encounter with him, at least the parts I could tell. We were all in agreement. He would never give either girl back. If they escaped, we had to bring it about.

Early in the morning, out of earshot of Fonteneau, Beckwourth whispered to us that he had come up with a plan, and after he explained it, it seemed to me to have about the proverbial snowball's chance in hell of succeeding. Henry thought it would work, though mostly because he wanted it to work. Unfortunately, it was the only plan we had.

It was simple. Once we saw Brings Thunder caught up in the hunt, we'd steal back to camp, snatch the girls, and make a two-hundred-mile dash back to Captain Warren's company.

"Won't some of the warriors still be in camp?" Henry asked Beckwourth.

"Not with the buffalo running. Every man jack of them will be out there and most of the women following to do the skinning. We should, I say should, only have his wife to deal with. That won't be easy, though. They say she's not altogether right in the head."

"That makes two of them," I said.

After a quick breakfast of antelope meat, we saddled our horses and joined the Indians as they left camp, travelling with Crow Killer's and Buffalo Horn's men. I searched for Brings Thunder but could not spot him. Neither did Henry, but with so many hundreds we couldn't have seen everyone who'd left camp. The day was overcast. I wore an extra shirt of Henry's, but the Indians, clad in just breechclouts, seemed bothered not at all by the chill. Henry was already sweating, his eyes glazed and his face haggard.

"Are you all right?" I asked.

"Fine," he muttered.

About a mile from camp, they broke into hunting parties of twenty to thirty each. I wore my straw hat tied down, and I carried my pistol in my belt, a regular Calamity Jane, confident aboard Iris that I could ride the wind. In mass, the women and children followed us with their skinning knives. We crested a ridge and came upon a stunning sight, a vast buffalo-filled plain as far as the eye could see, the beasts grazing on all the short grass.

Crow Killer said something to me and I looked to Fonteneau, who was nearby. "He asks if you are ready."

"Yes," I patted my pistol and the Indian laughed and said something else that I didn't get a chance to have translated, because it had begun. No particular signal was given, yet, all across the plain, the hunting parties as one started to gallop toward the herd. As I chucked Iris forward, the mare was caught up in the excitement and wanted to get out ahead of the party. The wind pushed back the brim of my hat.

"Stay close to me," Henry yelled above the horses' hooves. "Don't get caught in the herd. When the Indians ride hell bent for leather, we'll go for the village."

"We must find Brings Thunder first," Beckwourth called. "We must know he is with the hunt."

At first the buffalo seemed not at all alarmed, scruffy old bulls and huge hairy cows looking at us as if we were leaves fluttering in the wind toward them. Then the ones directly ahead of the hunting parties broke into a lumbering gait of alarm that rippled slowly through the entire herd, building up to a massive slow wave. A gap opened in the herd, and despite what Henry had said, all of us rode straight into it. The Indians seemed at home, but for me it became a game of survival very quickly with hundreds of beasts all around. Silently efficiently, the Sioux fired their arrows with an accuracy that was astounding.

Finally, the entire herd broke into a wild stampede racing at top speed, and I found myself in the middle of it. A great dust cloud rose and visibility shrunk to only a few feet, separating me from Henry and Beckwourth. The din reverberated in the hollows of my chest; Iris's nostrils flared. As I tried to maintain speed, a bull suddenly turned and charged. Iris dodged nimbly, never losing pace, quickly getting ahead of him.

In spite of the terrible danger, I experienced an overwhelming excitement. Every synapse in my brain fired on high alert. I gave a primal yell. As the buffalo squeezed in so close on either side, a big-assed bull lumbered in front of us, blocking the way for escape. God, don't let Iris fall. But the next instant she did. The bull running in front suddenly disappeared as if swallowed by the earth, then the ground vanished beneath me and we tumbled down into a hidden ravine. Iris crumpled to her knees, and I went over her head, slamming into the ground. It knocked the breath out of me, and the world sputtered in flashes of brilliant, prismatic lights.

Stunned, I sat up to see a scene of utter chaos. Buffalo tumbled into the ravine like a waterfall, coming right at me. I spun aside to escape one beast whose horns dug into the ground inches from me. They were falling all around me. Some got up and struggled up the steep bank. Others lay writhing and bellowing in agony. Iris scrambled up, and I fell in behind her, scratching and clawing to the top. My head buzzed as I swung back up in the saddle, and before being trampled, we shot back into the racing melee. The herd was still running, but on this side of the ravine an island of space had opened up in the black tidal wave. I wanted no more of them and reined Iris back and worked my way out. Finally, the buffalo had gone past and seconds later the dust cloud lifted.

It was then I saw him, Brings Thunder, about two hundred yards to the left, unmistakable as he charged his horse after an isolated bull, his rifle in both hands. He fired and the animal went down. Without waiting, he raced on to the next and the next, reloading his rifle for each shot. I saw three fall in the space of two minutes. His blood was up. Now was the time to go.

Trailing the herd for the next fifteen minutes, I searched for Henry and Beckwourth. Time was running out on our plan. Finally, I sought high ground and waved my hat, hoping they would see me first, before Brings Thunder did. They did, riding out of the herd toward me.

"I saw him," I shouted as they came up.

"You're sure?" Henry asked.

"Yes. It was him."

"Then we go," Beckwourth said. "I know his lodge. Hurry. We can get ahead of them by half a day."

More people were in the village than I expected, many women already returned from the bloody fields and even a few warriors.

"Don't like it," Beckwourth said. "We snatch up the girls now, won't be much of a head start. Brings Thunder be after us in an hour, less maybe. Ain't enough. We'll have the whole damn Sioux nation on us lickety-split."

"Can't be helped," Henry said. "It's got to be now. You can back out if you want, Beckwourth."

"No call for that, Quarles. I ain't abandoning you two tenderfeet to the loving embrace of the Sioux and their friends."

We hurried to Fonteneau's lodge and dismounted. "Get our things, Libby," Henry ordered. "We'll pick up Seneca and Jane and be back before you can count to sixty."

When I entered the tipi, it was empty, Fonteneau's wife must still be out on the plain skinning buffalo carcasses. I rushed about gathering our bedrolls and gear, securing it to our saddles, and then swung up on Iris. I sat there waiting, counting, and holding onto Henry's and Beckwourth's horses. I had this awful feeling that things had been running south all along, that Brings Thunder had been playing us for fools. Especially me. Even if he had some connection with my leap through time, it was clear he had no intention of helping me get back.

When Henry and Beckwourth didn't return, I went in search of them, leading their horses. I found the two men caught in a wild, hectic scene, Henry running from lodge to lodge, screaming for Seneca and Jane and Beckwourth trying desperately to appease several irate women and a few scowling warriors.

"What happened?" I shouted as Henry sped right past me into another lodge.

"They ain't here," Beckwourth answered. "Brings Thunder's wife was, but not the girls. He knew we'd come. He moved them."

"To where?"

He shook his head, signing with a big, fierce-looking warrior to keep him at bay. "Don't know Elk Woman, Brings Thunder's wife, waved me off and not very hospitable like. This ain't good. This ain't good at all. Lakota going to be powerful mad."

I wanted to scream.

With sign language, a big warrior communicated something, then walked away. Beckwourth rubbed a hand over the stubble of his beard distraught.

I pressed him. "What'd he say?"

"He said the white girls are not here. He said if they are among the living, he doesn't know where they are. Only Brings Thunder knows."

I could not accept that they were dead and neither could Henry. Brings Thunder had them someplace. Finally, we retreated to Fonteneau's lodge.

Beckwourth was worried. He insisted we had no choice now. "No one can predict how the Lakota going to react to a thing. They ain't like no one else. They could be mightily irate about you running around like a mad bear scaring their women and children and old folks. I suggest we get out now while we can."

"Ain't going nowhere. I'm not leaving without my girls," Henry replied. "You take Libby. You two can make it back."

"I'm not leaving," I said firmly, folding my arms in front of my chest for emphasis.

"You two are foolish," Beckwourth said, staring at us for several seconds, then abruptly strode out. We heard him riding off. So much for Mr. Jim Beckwourth, mountain man legend. Inveterate storyteller. Boaster. Coward.

Henry and I exchanged glances but said nothing for a long time. Then he said, "I'm proud of you. No father could be more proud of his daughter. I wish you had gone back with him. But I'm proud." He winced as he flexed his bandaged hand. "I'm so sorry I got you into this."

"You didn't."

He seemed to understand what I was thinking and grabbed my arm with such force it hurt. "It was not your fault, Libby. That's just crazy. You are never to say that again, do you hear me?"

I nodded, more coward than Beckwourth. I couldn't explain how I brought Brings Thunder to the Quarles family, how he saw a replacement daughter there. So I said nothing.

At that moment, the tipi flap was thrown back and Crow Killer and Buffalo Horn stepped in, both men scowling at us as if we'd betrayed them. Probably to them, we had.

Chapter 39

Give Beckwourth credit. He had not left us in the lurch, but had gone to find Crow Killer and Buffalo Horn. As they stood in Fonteneau's lodge, their faces grim, Henry paced back and forth, running his good hand through his hair. The warriors and the women were returning from the buffalo hunt, their excited chatter pervading the village. It had been a very successful hunt. I hoped their good mood would be fortunate for us.

Buffalo Horn said he had called for a council of elders to settle the matter of Henry's actions and the status of the girls. They could decide anything from death to expulsion for us. Whatever was decided, he warned, we must abide by the council's decision, even if the verdict was death for Henry, otherwise Beckwourth and I would also be killed. We nodded. A lie, of course. If the elders decided the girls belonged to Brings Thunder, I wouldn't abide by it.

So, in deepening twilight, we found ourselves at the huge council meeting of Lakota, Arapaho and Cheyenne elders, held in public, a very unusual circumstance according to Beckwourth. It seemed everyone was a chief. Half the massive village had shown up, sitting so far back among the lodges I didn't think they'd be able to hear. Brings Thunder came wearing a wooden nose strapped to his face with rawhide, making him look with his frenzied blue eyes like a madman from a Chucky movie or an insane Pinocchio.

Henry and I sat among the younger warriors and women, all falling silent while the chiefs spoke. First, as translated by Fonteneau, each related a story of the day's hunt, the blessings of Wakan Tanka and the spirits of the buffalo, and thanking all for their good fortune today.

Eventually, Buffalo Horn spoke and came to the point of the matter. "I am Lakota. I am of the People. My fathers were warriors. My sons are warriors. We are the land and the rivers and the sky. Did not Wakan Tanka make them all for the use of the Lakota and the Arapaho and the Cheyenne? The white man travels on it, on the Holy Road to Or-ree-gone beyond the setting sun. He trades with us and gives us many good things."

Swiftly, he held up a rifle and fired it. Several people started, including me. I glanced around. People were now even more riveted. "No Lakota must think the whites are an easy people to make war against." He patted the rifle. "This is the white man. They are a dangerous people. Make no bad judgment. Some want to be our friends. They know the Lakota are great warriors and do not want to fight us. It is better to be friends than enemies with them. The Blackfeet are enemies, the Snakes, the Crow. Not the white people. If they come in friendship, we must give them friendship."

He paused to let his words sink in, then he turned toward Brings Thunder and addressed him directly. "Brother, you have taken this man's children. We are not at war with him. He comes in friendship and you steal his children. This is a bad thing. Do you wish to prevent the Lakota from being friends with the white man? You are a white man. Do you wish us to be at war with them? You have the chance to return his children to him, which would be a right and good thing to do. Do as you wish. I cannot tell you this or that to be done. But you take the People along with your decision. If you do not return them, this will bring harm and dishonor to the People."

Crow Killer followed with much the same argument, but shorter and much less forceful. He also said he hoped there could be good relations with white people that would last lifetimes. I felt a sense of guilt. Here in the 1840s, still at the beginning of relations with the Indians of the West, people of good will well might believe that friendship was possible. I knew it wasn't.

Lasting peace treaties wouldn't last. It would be a dream of a few that was blotted out like the last flicker of a campfire in a summer rain. One side would lose utterly, and the other would sweep over the land like that summer locusts and seize it for their own. But right now, Libby Quarles, emigrant girl on her way to Oregon, wanted only to get her sisters back.

226

I looked at the Indian faces to get a sense of whether Buffalo Horn's argument had won the day but couldn't tell. I glanced at Beckwourth with a questioning expression. He shook his head.

It was dark when Crow Killer finished his speech, and Brings Thunder stood. Everyone fell silent; not even the dogs and night animals out on the prairie seemed to make a noise. Seeing him illuminated by the fire with his God-awful wooden nose, I was chilled to the bone. He stared straight at me. "I hate the white people. I don't want peace with them. I know them. Yes, I am one of them. That is how I know them. They have done me more harm than all the Blackfeet or Crow could." His words were slow, forceful, each one sharp as a knifepoint.

Then he turned to Buffalo Horn, his voice a snarl of sarcasm. "He gives us many good things. Yes, he gives us disease. Our enemies the Mandan were once a great force. We fought them and they fought us. Then they all died. The white man gave them smallpox. He builds permanent lodges that take root like the tree and allows no one else to pass over the land. Soon the air, the earth, and the sky will be theirs and there will be no place for us. The way, the only way to stop this evil, is for the People to kill every white man he finds. Kill the women who bear the children. Kill the children who grow into white men and women. They all must die."

I felt sick. This man would murder the girls before giving them back.

"I have good reasons to accuse the white people of injustice," he went on. "All the land beyond the sunrise he has taken from our brothers. Those that still live are pushed onto small bits of land and starve from no hunting. That's what awaits the Lakota. The white man's heart is black. He has no regard for the People. Everything I have told you is true."

Reservations. He knew the future. Of that there was no doubt. He waited a long time. The silence grew. When he spoke next, his voice was soft, as if a different man had taken possession of him, a reasonable one. I feared this one even more. "I have decided what to do with my two children. I will return one of them, as some of my brothers wish."

There was a general sound of agreement and nods of the head around the gathering that this was just and proper, a Solomon-like decision. Whichever girl

227

was left would not be the first white child raised by the Sioux. The council also decided that Henry's actions were to be forgiven as of no great matter. We left the meeting in a state of depression. Back at Fonteneau's lodge, Henry asked Beckwourth in desperation, "What if we steal the girls tonight and make our escape."

"We don't know where them girls are. They might not even be in the camp. You go looking through their tipis again, that would make the Lakota mighty annoyed."

Henry was frustrated. "I will do what needs be done, damn it!"

Beckwourth gave a helpless shrug. "Then what? Likely they'd give Libby to the squaws to beat till she drops. You and me? Dead. And how will that help them girls of yours?"

Henry stared at him a long second, then shook his head. "Anyone ever tell you you're a sour fellow?"

I tuned them out, not giving up, but losing hope, thinking about what the two girls must be going through so far from their family. It was a hard thing to dwell on. Five years old. They probably didn't know we were even here. Would he return Seneca now as I had said? That decision would haunt me for as long as I lived, that I had picked one.

The next morning Henry shook me awake before dawn and whispered, "Libby, get up. Something's happening."

Fonteneau was still snoring heavily. Beckwourth was already gone. Following Henry outside, I stumbled into the early morning twilight to see the Indians breaking camp. Eastern skies were lit with shafts of bright yellows and reds as Black Cloud Woman brought several horses near to begin the work of tearing down the tipi and packing their belongings. Finally, Fonteneau came out scratching his unruly hair and mumbling. He'd stayed up late celebrating, as had all of them, yet, here they were up and leaving before first light. What was causing them to leave so quickly?

"What's going on?" Henry demanded.

The Frenchman shrugged. "I guess we're leaving."

Most of the Indians had their lodges down, things already packed onto travois. By necessity, they'd learned to do it quickly and efficiently. In scores of small bands, they were heading off in different directions. Henry went a little crazy then. It was a terrible thing to see how he ran through the remaining camp searching for the girls like a madman. Fonteneau struggled to keep up with him, to keep him from accosting anyone. The Indians treated him with forbearance and a little disdain but no belligerence. They understood he was crazy and why.

It was clear Brings Thunder had lied to everyone. He was not returning either of the twins; he was escaping with both of them. It was as hard a thing to take as I'd ever experienced.

"Pa, please," I shouted at him, using that term for the first time. "Stop. This won't help them." I grabbed his arm and he turned on me with a frenzied look that had kill written all over it.

"Listen to her, *mon ami*," Fonteneau said. "The People do not like Brings Thunder for long time now. He has become beaucoup crazy. He go own way. Alone. Always alone. You can find him. Wait for Beckwourth."

Despite his threatening glare, I held onto Henry's arm till he relaxed. The sigh that followed came out of utter desolation. "Find our horses, Libby," he finally ordered. "We're not going to let the man out of our sight."

I ran off to the dwindling horse herd. When I got back with Iris and Henry's bay, Beckwourth was there. We were almost alone on the prairie now with hundreds of travois in the distance heading away, and the twins may not even be among them, because now we knew they weren't with Brings Thunder.

Desperately, Henry asked Beckwourth, "Where are my girls?"

"Wish I could tell you, Mr. Quarles. If he don't got them, they got to be somewhere. Some other band, or maybe he done already stashed them up in them hills. These days, Brings Thunder's got few friends, but he still has some."

"We follow him then."

So, hour after hour, through that long day, we followed Brings Thunder and his wife from a mile behind as they pulled a single travois and herded several horses northeast along the Tongue River. He could see us easily, but that didn't seem to concern him.

By late afternoon, I considered the possibility of failure. A massive wave of hopelessness settled on me, a poisonous cloud. Good doesn't always win. Even with Beckwourth's knowledge and skill, we were sadly overmatched by the situation. What would happen to Julia and the Quarles family if we lost them? I knew the answer: they'd persevere. But the hurt would last forever. And that included me.

Finally, we had some luck. Sometime in the evening, when the heat began to ease, Fonteneau rode out of the hills as if chased by a thousand screaming Sioux, hallooing from too far off for us to make out what he was saying. When he got near, we heard him shouting.

"We found her! We found her!" he shouted.

When he pulled up, he gasped between breaths, "*Mon ami*, we found her. We have the girl. She is alive."

Henry was dumbfounded at first, then said, "What are you saying? You have both girls?"

Fonteneau became pale. "Oh." He sputtered then said, "Both? No. We have one girl."

"Which one?" I demanded.

Fonteneau's face now drained of all color. "*Merde!* I don't know."

Chapter 40

*I*n fact, Sally Callahan had found her. Feather. Travelling with her band, she had seen a flash of movement in the hills above them, and to her, it looked like a child. She decided to investigate and found the little girl hiding amid the scrub pine. Sally didn't know which twin it was because the girl wouldn't speak. But whichever one, she did recognize Sally and clung to her as they returned to the band.

When we caught up with them, my heart broke to see her. Heartbreakingly, she was emaciated so much so I thought a strong wind would carry her away, her body covered with the dirt of days alone in the wilderness, and her hair thick with tangles. When Henry dismounted, the girl raced from Sally and threw herself at him. He picked her up and hugged her as she wept. Then, she saw me and jumped into my arms, crying, burying her head in my shirt. She hadn't said a word.

It was Jane.

"Jane, honey, where's Seneca? Do you know where Seneca is?" Henry asked.

She shook her head as if to say she didn't know. No matter how gently we asked, though, she would not speak.

"Can we backtrack her trail?" I asked Beckwourth.

Surprisingly, his eyes had watered as he stared at Jane. He shook his head. "No, too long, too dry, too much wind wiping out sign. Nothing to track."

With Jane still in my arms, I hugged Sally Feather fiercely and thanked her. I told her somehow, someway, we would see each other again. I didn't believe it, but desperately wanted it to be true. Her band kept going on, and we set out to regain Brings Thunder's trail. Jane rode on Iris with me. Just before dark, we set up camp back beside the Tongue. We had one miracle, now we needed another.

Next day was cool and cloudy, better than the constant summer heat. As we rode along, Henry showed signs of illness, sweating too much and going through fits of coughing. I tried to get him to stop, but he refused, saying it was only a bit of the flux. "It'll pass. We can't afford to let that man get away from us."

As it was, we fell miles behind while Henry dashed countless times into the brush to relieve his loose bowels. Something was wrong with him. I looked to Beckwourth for help, but he just shrugged. In late afternoon, Brings Thunder's trail disappeared. Dry rock doesn't hold sign well and we'd fallen too far behind. He was our only connection to Seneca.

Beckwourth was frustrated. "They're dragging a damned travois, for Christ's sake. They can't fly. Not really. I'll find something to show their passage. I swear it."

The rest of the day we tried to regain the trail but found nothing. Night made it impossible to see tracks even if they were there. It was like Brings Thunder, his wife and their horses had disappeared. Henry wanted to push on even for another couple hours because a full moon had risen.

"Don't be a fool, Quarles," Beckwourth said. "That's the moon up there, not the sun. If we come across anything, we'll likely miss it. Plus, your daughters need rest, and so do I, even if you don't."

"We go on for now," Henry said firmly. "I can damn well see. You do what you must."

We went on for the two extra hours. I understood Henry's need to keep going, but he wasn't thinking straight. He'd go all night if he could. The person I didn't understand was Beckwourth. Why was he putting up with this? He had helped us far beyond any responsibility. Captain Warren and the others had turned back, but he was still with us. What drove him? It was as if this was something personal for him. Don't ask, I told myself. Leave well enough alone.

We found a clear creek where we replenished our water and pitched camp for the night. As I wrapped Jane in a blanket with me, I felt that sense of hopelessness coming on me again. This time it was bottomless. Henry was getting sicker. So determined to push on, he would not hear of taking time to recover. We had no trail to follow and no idea where Seneca was, and Jane still not speaking. I did not sleep so well that night.

Next morning, Beckwourth said we should continue to push northeast along the Tongue River in hopes of crossing Indian sign. From his tone, I could tell he was not happy with the way things were. When we finished saddling and packing our gear, he finally had it out with Henry. "I'm with you as long as need be, Mr. Quarles, I am, but I got to say you are slowing me down.

You are slowing me down to a crawl. It is impossible to find your girl this way. You got other family, Mr. Quarles. You need to be thinking of them some. If I was…"

"Do not lecture me on my family, Mr. Beckwourth," Henry cut in angrily. "I know full well I have other family. Right now I have a daughter to find."

"And you make that harder. This country is big, bigger than any of you folk can imagine. The way we go now it could take ten years and still not find her. What happens to the rest of your family then? What happens to Oregon?"

Henry said quietly, "I would give up Oregon to get my daughter back, sir."

"I know you would, Mr. Quarles. I know you would. But this ain't working. On my own, I might find her. Like this, it will never happen. You, sir, should go back. Let me go on alone."

He waved the suggestion away. "I'm not going to abandon my Seneca."

"I'm not saying you should. I can move faster without you. I got the best chance of finding her, the only chance. Let me. You go back to your family. I will find the girl, if she can be found, and bring her back to you."

His head bowed, Henry stood holding the reins to his horse in his good hand, flipping them against his thigh. I ached for him. Though it was the only logical thing to do, he couldn't bring himself to nod in agreement. I didn't want to stop either. For nearly a full minute, he stood frozen in place. I knew his heart was telling him he would be abandoning his daughter, while his head was saying he had to leave it to Beckwourth if he was ever to get her back.

Finally, almost inaudibly, he said, "You go on."

Immediately, Beckwourth swung up into the saddle and rode off, leaving us behind. We stood there feeling desperately alone now, watching that spot on the hill for a long time before it disappeared over the crest a half mile farther on. Henry's jaw worked as if he were chewing something. He couldn't come to grips with what he'd done. We were heading back. It was the right thing to do, but it didn't feel that way.

Three days later, travelling south, Henry, Jane and I reached the foothills of the Bighorn Mountains. Pine trees filled the steep hillsides of a narrow valley in which we found ourselves, pine scent heavy in the air. It was late afternoon, the valley cast in shadows. Even so, it was stiflingly hot. Jane shared Iris with me, sitting in front. As we passed, we picked berries off the bushes of a slow moving stream. They had a slightly tart taste.

"I hope these aren't poisonous," I said.

"They're not, Libby," she replied.

That was the limit of her conversation the entire day, but she was speaking. A few words only, but slowly coming back to us.

I didn't know where we were going and neither did Henry. We were heading south, all we knew to do, but I feared becoming lost in this maze of valleys. Unskilled tracker that I was, I'd still recognized sign of bear and mountain lion. I didn't want to face either. Henry was not doing well. He slouched in the saddle, his illness finally catching up to him and in the last couple hours getting dramatically worse. Still, he would not stop, he would not rest.

Three times I asked him if he was okay and three times he just waved his hand, his bandaged hand, surely the source of his illness. Sepsis was setting in, but he kept saying it was fine. The term bacteria would have had no meaning for him. In the twenty-first century it was unheard of for someone to die from a simple cut, certainly in developed countries. But in the 1840s, it was common enough. Wounds became infected, blood poisoning set in, people died.

I rode up alongside him. "We need to stop, Henry. Jane needs a rest, and so do I."

His eyes glazed, he said, "Not yet. We need to find Seneca."

"We need to stop. I need to take a look at your hand."

He snapped at me. "Just do as you're told, girl."

Clearly, he wasn't thinking right. If he were my real father, I likely wouldn't have been any more obedient. I jumped down off of Iris and set Jane down.

"Pa, we need to rest a bit. Just a couple of minutes. Please, Pa."

He weaved atop the horse a moment, then said, "All right. Just for a couple minutes."

When he climbed down, he crashed heavily into my arms, and I dragged him over to the stream. He was in a bad way, his breathing labored, his forehead burning. The first thing I had to do was tend to his hand. Unwrapping it, I nearly choked at what I saw. The hand was swollen and oozed blood and pus, and it stunk. A wave of nausea rushed through me. Jane's eyes bugged out.

"He'll be all right," I told her. I didn't think that at all. Blood poisoning. Dear God, I didn't want to bury Henry here. I sent Jane down to the stream to wash out the bandana for his forehead. When I touched the wound, he shrieked with pain.

"Sorry."

He stared at me with a dazed look. "You ain't Libby. Your hair's blond."

"Sure I am." I replied uneasily. "Your loving daughter."

"Who are you?"

Jane rushed back and held the bandana on his forehead.

"Seneca," he said to her, "I knew we'd find you. God's will."

The girl's face blanched. She fell back, scooting away like a wounded animal.

"Jane, come back here," I ordered. "I need your help. Keep the bandana on his forehead."

After a moment, she came back, her shoulders slumped making her seem even smaller.

"When it gets warm, wet it again," I said. "Try to keep it cool."

She nodded. I gave an easy laugh. "He just said I wasn't Libby. Asked me who I was. Did you hear that? Your father's sick. He barely knows who he is. He'll probably think you're Caroline next, and I'm Isaac."

She mustered a giggle at that and seemed to revive.

"Henry, can you understand me?" I asked.

"Course I can understand you."

I told him I had to cut open the wound to let the poison out, which sounded like I really knew what I was doing. I didn't. I felt sure, though, if I did nothing, he would die.

"It's going to hurt worse than anything has ever hurt in your life." That probably wasn't great bedside manner, but he nodded. There wasn't a thing on earth I wanted to do less than cut open a swollen, pus-ridden hand.

Jane and I started a small fire and put water on to boil in the teapot and scalded the knife in the flames. I soaked a couple of strips of cloth in the boiled water. When the knife had cooled, I realized I had wasted enough time. Jane turned away as I placed the blade to Henry's hand and cut. His scream echoed through the valley.

The next two days, we lay up at the creek. Too sick to travel, Henry slept most of the time thrashing about, his forehead beading in sweat from fever. I did not think he would make it. I probably should have amputated his hand, but that I could not do. With my Paterson Colt, I tried to hunt. I got off a couple shots at a rabbit and even one at a deer but hit nothing. The animals were never in any danger. So we were stuck with biscuits and pemmican, which I fried up with bacon grease in a tiny skillet. Add berries and tea, and it was a fine meal.

By evening of the second day, Henry was feeling better, not well, but well enough to travel, he said. Since it was so late, we decided to stay one more night and start out early the next morning. His hand was wrapped in one of the clean strips, which I changed each day. The swelling had gone down; the wound was healing. Another miracle for Dr. Lemonade.

That last night by the fire, I held Jane in my lap. We'd pressed a couple of times for her to tell us what happened but knew it would do no good. She would tell us when she was ready. Since she had not known the land, we didn't feel she could tell us anything helpful anyway. I knew a lot of the pop psych stuff, at least what gooey TV talk shows said about how to handle people who'd undergone trauma. When I told Henry some of the stuff, he said, "Well, that's all sweet and such, but I think we best just use love and common sense with your sister."

When she did open up to us, it came with no prodding from me or Henry and poured out like a tipped barrel of water. Between bites of pemmican that last evening by the creek, I was telling the story of *Twelfth Night*, reducing it to a children's tale set in a 1840s emigrant train. I noticed Jane's eyes welling up.

Since this part of the play was funny, I knew her mind was not on it. I nudged her gently. "You know, Viola loves pemmican."

She studied the meat in her hand for a moment, then started crying. "I ran away. I ran away from Seneca. I left her with those bad men."

Like a bolt, Henry reached over and snatched her up into his arms, wincing at the pain this caused to his hand. "No, no, no, dear, sweet Jane. Don't say that. You saved her life. You saved Seneca's life. That bad man was going to kill her and keep you. You understand that? You running off saved her life. And we will get her back. I promise you, Jane, she will be coming back. So don't ever say you left her there. You saved her. Understand? Jane, say you understand?"

Finally, wiping her tears, she nodded. "I understand."

He hugged her and she buried her head against his chest and cried. After a time, we were able to coax the story out of her. Long before Brings Thunder came to the Indian encampment on the Tongue River, a few other Indians took the girls up into the hills to the north. Seneca and Jane were never in the Sioux village. One day, the Indian she rode with fell behind while he relieved himself in the bushes. He'd left her standing beside his pony. Only a small girl, she could make no trouble for him.

But Jane had what people called gumption. She pulled the pony's head down by the halter, and clinging to his neck when his head rose back up, she climbed onto his back. A slick move I'd seen both her and Seneca do before. The Indian saw her too late and came out of the bushes, running. She turned the horse, and kicking for all she was worth, rode off. She pushed the animal at full speed for a long time.

Eventually, she realized that the others were not far behind, so she ditched the horse, sending it on its way with some well-thrown pebbles to the backsides. From high in the hills, she saw four Indians pass below, one of them with Seneca in front of him. For the next many days, she wandered the wilderness, keeping alive by eating berries, till Sally found her. It was an amazing story. After she told it, a great weight seemed to lift from her, and she fell fast asleep. Exhausted, more emotionally than physically, I soon followed.

Later that night, I was awakened by a strange sound and realized it was someone crying. Jane was asleep in my arms. I saw it was Henry, buried in his blanket, his body wracked by muffled sobs. That sight gripped me so deeply I could not even think about getting back to sleep. The poor man. Seneca was surely lost, and even though we were doing the right thing by leaving whatever chances were left to Beckwourth, that could not have set well with him. It had to be tearing his insides up. It was mine.

Chapter 41

$\mathcal{T}$he next day, we travelled south through small valleys and passed hills dotted by stunted pine. All along the way, the Bighorns loomed to our right. We entered a canyon and traveled a few miles before its walls narrowed to a few feet amid a jumble of pine trees and foliage. I could see it opened up on the other side. The silence and shadows of it were foreboding. I wanted to turn around and not go through there. I glanced at Henry, but he seemed unconcerned, so I said nothing. When Jane, sensing my unease, glanced up at me, I forced a smile, chastising myself for letting my fears take hold, but out here fear was a good thing. It meant alertness; it could mean survival.

Jane didn't buy my reassuring smile. I had her spooked now. As our horses ambled toward the shrouded canyon gap, my pulse began racing. I imagined bear or mountain lion or, more likely, an Indian raiding party waiting to spring upon us. I whispered to Jane, "Get behind me."

In the saddle, she scrambled nimbly from in front to behind. I placed my hand on the butt of the Colt in my belt. Even though I couldn't hit anything with it, just the feel of it gave me some comfort. Twenty feet to the trees, ten, then in among the heavy foliage of a narrow deer track that weaved through the tangle. Spooked, expecting an attack at any second, I frantically searched the shadows for danger.

"What are you doing?" Henry asked, curious.

"Nothing. Nothing," I answered, a little embarrassed.

"Well, stop it. You're giving me the jitters."

The canyon walls curved sharply to the left and began to open up to a wide valley leading out of the foothills and onto the prairie. I sighed with relief, further chastising myself for letting my imagination run wild. In the next instant, as we made the final small twist out of the tight defile, I received a stunning shock. Just ahead, Brings Thunder sat his horse, waiting for us.

Jane screamed and squeezed into my back. I could feel her shaking violently. Not ten feet away, the man leaned forward insouciantly, smiling as if he'd just come across old friends. The hideousness of his scabby nose and cold eyes sent dread and hate deep into my bones. Unbidden, the thought of getting back to my own time flashed once more across my mind, but I dismissed it immediately. Selfish! He was not here to help me; he had never been here to help me.

"We have unfinished business," he said. Shirtless, he had a streak of blue and white paint across his chest, and he wore red uniform trousers from who knows what army and an eagle feather in his braided hair.

Henry aimed his rifle at him. "Hold it there, you bastard. Where's Seneca?"

The man was unconcerned. "She's safe."

"She is only safe with me. I should kill you now and be done with it."

"I will trade Seneca for that one." He pointed to Jane.

"Quit playing games." Henry cocked the rifle. "Where's my daughter? Tell me now or I send you to perdition."

Brings Thunder gave an easy laugh. "You just rode right past her." He gestured behind Henry. "See. There she is, trussed to that pine." He called out, "Wave to your father, Seneca."

I did not look. My trust in him had long ago been used up. But Henry did. As he turned, Brings Thunder drew his pistol and shot him.

I screamed, "No!"

The man got off a second shot as Henry was falling to the ground. His riderless horse sped by causing Brings Thunder to skitter out of the way. That gave me an instant to draw my Colt, cock it and fire. A dark plume of blood and gore erupted from his chest. Still astride, he stared down at the wound, then at me with an expression of utter disbelief. I shot him again. This time he fell from his horse.

Jane and I scrambled down. She ran to Henry, while I walked calmly over to Brings Thunder. He was still alive. I felt no mercy.

"Foolish girl," he said weakly, red froth spurting from his mouth as he groped for his pistol next to him. "I was going to send you home. I still can."

He got the gun and lifted it toward me.

"You evil son of a bitch," I said. "You never could. But I'm going to send you to hell."

I shot him in the face, right in the nose hole.

Henry was alive. Turning to look for Seneca had saved his life. The first bullet dug a furrow out of his chest as it passed by. The second bullet missed completely. I staunched the blood with a cloth strip.

"Find Seneca," he urged. "He said she was here."

"He was lying. She's not here."

"You have to look for her," he urged frantically. He sat up. "Go."

"Stay here. Don't move," I said. Jane and I searched the hillside for our sister, she wasn't there. The bastard had lied; he always lied. Nothing he had ever said was true.

I got Henry on Brings Thunder's horse, and we rode off a distance to get away from the body that would soon be attracting all sorts of scavengers. I didn't think any Indians had come with him but wanted to get clear of him anyway. We picked up Henry's horse on the way and made camp about five miles farther on at a stream I had recognized from our journey north. There, I set about tending to Henry's wounds.

Pushing the horses to their limit and ours, it took us three long, long days of riding, sunrise to sunset and beyond, sixty to seventy miles a day, before we caught up with Captain Warren's company on the eastern slope of South Pass. Even though weak from illness and wounds, Henry had taken no time to rest, urging us on late into the night till falling into an unseen ravine became a real danger. I couldn't imagine how he stood up to it.

As we approached South Pass, the horses were played out, even Iris, and so too was I with an exhaustion that settled deep into my soul. I dreaded what we were about to tell Julia. I didn't want to see her agony when she found out that Seneca, if even alive, was still among the Indians. We'd likely never see her again. But we had Jane. So joy and tragedy in one breath. It was a terrible thing for a mother to face. Nothing on this journey was easy for a mother. Or a father for that matter, but this?

South Pass was a high valley in the Rocky Mountains, twenty miles wide, with great snowcapped peaks flanking it. At thousands of feet in elevation, a distinct chill hung in the thin air when we finally saw the encampment ahead. The last rays of the sun struck the white canvas of the wagons.

Holding her giant belly Julia hurried out from the wagons to meet us with Isaac, Little George and Caroline, and at least a hundred people following. If we weren't bringing such terrible news, her fast, pregnant waddle would be comical. In the time since we'd left, she had ballooned enormously.

With a great wail and arms outstretched, Jane literally leapt from Iris into Julia's arms. Henry climbed wearily down from his horse and placed a hand on his wife's shoulder. It was a loving gesture, the limit of his public affection. Over Jane, she glanced questioningly at him. He gave a barely perceptible shake of his head. The color drained from her face and she held even more fiercely to Jane. "I am so glad, so happy you are safe, my dear child."

"I'm Jane."

Julia forced a small laugh. "I know you are, honey. And I'm so happy to have you back."

"I didn't want to leave Seneca."

"I know, honey, I know."

Henry squeezed his daughter's shoulder. "We'll get your sister back."

I couldn't tell whether he believed it or not. Maybe he did. Beckwourth was still looking after all. People gathered in closer as if to give comfort just by their presence, and Julia needed them all. Joy and tragedy was shared. It was hard to accommodate the two emotions in the same space. My eyes welled with tears, and I looked away. Caroline and Little George were crying. I hugged them both, hugged Isaac, who squirmed with embarrassment, but I caught a sniffle coming from him as well.

I saw Daniel running out from the wagons and pushing his way through the crowd. Immediately, he hugged me. "Are you all right?"

"Yes," I muttered.

Captain Warren asked, "What news of Seneca?"

"Beckwourth is on the hunt," Henry answered with a far more confident tone than I knew he felt. "We were holding him back. He could move faster than the four of us, so we came back for now. It seemed the best thing to do for her."

"It was. It surely was," the captain said.

Pierce stepped forward, agitated. "Wait a minute now. Beckwourth done contracted to take some of us on to California. We ain't that far from Fort Hall. A man's word's got to stand for something. He can't be wandering all over the country looking for that girl. She's surely lost. I'm sorry as can be to say that, Quarles, but surely she is."

"Shut up, Pierce," Captain Warren said.

"I'm just saying…"

"Well, don't." He turned back to Henry. "Any word on Fitzpatrick."

Henry shook his head. "Nothing."

After I ate some hot food, I put on a coat against the cold and walked with Daniel. He still had a pronounced limp from his ankle injury. As we passed camp-fires, people greeted me with a newfound respect and not just a little bit of awe. Henry had told the story of how I'd killed Brings Thunder, and even Hannibal Pierce looked at me differently. Daniel wanted to hear the details, how I shot such a notorious bad man, but I couldn't speak about it. I told him I did not want the killing of someone, even a bastard like Brings Thunder, to define who I was. That was so twenty-first century. Still, I didn't want to talk about it.

We said little then, but once out of camp, his arm went around me, and it felt comforting. I desperately needed that comfort. The unearthly glow of snowcapped mountains under a starlit sky did not match the bleakness I felt. I thought continuously of Seneca. Like Henry, I couldn't think of what else I could have done, and yet the feeling that I had failed her gripped me so strongly it overwhelmed me.

Later that night in the Quarles' tent, the temperature was near freezing. As I slipped dog-tired under the double blankets with Jane between me, I heard Henry beyond the canvas divider telling Julia about Seneca. Even though they whispered, their voices carried. The level of hurt in his voice was excruciating. Caroline was crying softly.

The last thing I heard before falling off was Julia asking, quietly, "Is Oregon worth it?"

Chapter 42

The next day we came off South Pass, traversing down through the clouds of a snowstorm, even though it was July. As we got lower, it turned quickly to cold rain. Even bundled in coats and slickers, everyone got soaked and the cold seeped into our bones. Along the way, we passed the bleached skeletons of mules and oxen, a sure sign of the toll the trek had taken on other companies, not just ours. That night we spent shivering in the wagons because the wind was too great to set up the tents.

The next day we made it off the pass into barren, dry country. The heat was oppressive. Each day, we waited for Beckwourth's return, each day losing a little more hope. No one talked openly about it, but few people had faith in him finding Seneca. Not that they didn't respect his frontier skills, but it was like finding a needle in a thousand-mile haystack. Some, like Hannibal Pierce, said he would not be coming back at all because he was purely and simply a scoundrel. He would be off somewhere with his Crow woman most likely, having forgotten about his obligations.

I didn't think so. In fact, I'd come to trust him completely. I just didn't think he was capable of the impossible, bringing Seneca back to us. That broke my heart. To keep Julia's spirits up, Henry remained outwardly confident, but I could tell he had given up hope of ever seeing his daughter again. He often exchanged looks with me in which he couldn't hide the bleakness in his eyes. I could not imagine how it would feel to lose a child.

But losing both parents had to be just as bad. One evening, I noticed Lottie Whelan sitting by herself next to a small fire, absently stirring it with a stick. She was fourteen, the oldest of the Whelan children, a hellion who'd run with Putt. Her mother had been taken by the cholera and her father by Indians. She now had the responsibility of her five siblings. Tonight, staring so sadly into the fire, the girl's face was not that of a hellion, but a child struck hard by life.

Something that had happened on South Pass drove home to me her situation, caught between childhood and adult responsibilities. Up there was a spring that sent two streams down the mountain, one headed west nearly a thousand miles to the Pacific and the other east in an even longer journey to the Missouri, the Mississippi, and eventually the Gulf of Mexico.

At least that's what Daniel fancifully told a group of us girls, who were filling up containers of water from the spring the morning we packed to leave.

Lottie had rushed back to her wagon and wrote a short note about her parents' deaths and how they were on for Oregon just the same, addressing it to her grandparents in the East. She stuffed it into a bottle and set it afloat in the stream. It likely wouldn't make it off South Pass, let alone back East, but she did it anyway.

In the days that followed, Daniel and I grew even closer, went from awkward lovers to real intimacy. When we could steal some privacy, we kissed and groped and fondled and caressed. There was so much more urgency to it, living life to the fullest. More and more, I had to admit I really liked him. Love, yes. That was a biological thing. But like, you had some control over whom you liked and respected. He was so confident, even cocky, while at the same time kind and funny and solid. In a dangerous nineteenth century world, solid was good.

I read a book once that began this way: he was born with the gift of laughter and a sense that the world was mad. In a way, that was Daniel. He was one of those people who could see the humor in everyday life. Always a ready smile on his face.

In the evenings when he and I were together, he talked about our marriage that I knew would never happen. I felt so guilty. To me this was our marriage. The few months we would have together. He said when we arrived in Oregon City he would file on good farmland and we'd start our life together. Me, a farmer's wife! God, would Vanessa scream. The Rude Girls. I hadn't thought about them for a long, long time. I wasn't sure anymore that they ever existed.

Daniel and I'd first live with his folks to help them settle and then build our home on our own 640 acres adjacent to his family's spread. The Quarles had already agreed to settle in the same area. Well, I wished them all well. My journey finished by then, I couldn't imagine I'd be there.

"I've been thinking," he said as we stood beside the Big Sandy River, him standing behind me, his arms wrapped around me.

"That sounds ominous."

"I was thinking about California," he said with an edge of excitement in his voice. "Jesse and me been talking. There's gold nuggets just lying on the ground there, Libby. I could fill my pockets. A man could get rich in just one day."

Abruptly, I shook his arms off and turned to face him. "I doubt that."

"It's true. Jesse says the first ones there are going to be rich."

I was upset. Now, he wanted to go to California with Jesse Hancock instead of on to Oregon to marry me. I hated the idea but instantly realized it might be for the best. I asked evenly. "So, you're breaking up with me?"

"No, no. I love you with all my heart, Libby. I want to live my life with you. I want a passel of children with you. I was just thinking, when we get to Fort Hall, I ought to go to California. Get my fill of gold and come back. Should be only a few months."

While he waited with a hopeful expression, I allowed my emotions to calm. It was for the best. In fact, this was a good thing. By the time he reached Oregon, I'd be home, my home.

"By all means, go," I said more sharply than I had intended.

He was disappointed by my tone. Maybe he wanted me to plead with him not to go. Not going to happen. I forced myself to say, "Don't worry. I'll be waiting in Oregon for you." I wouldn't, but it was what he wanted to hear.

A couple days later toward sundown, several people were spooked by a horse and rider that stood on a high bluff a half mile off just watching us. Might be Indians, someone said. We were pretty close to Shoshone country. I knew it was Beckwourth. But why was he not coming in?

When I told Julia who it was, she nodded. Anxiously, she had been watching the horizon every day for his return and now moved her great heft out fifty yards toward the bluff as if she intended to go all the way to it. That's when he turned his horse and rode down toward us. As he got closer everyone could see that, indeed, it was the mountain man.

And he was alone.

When Julia realized this, her hand went to her throat and her shoulders visibly sagged. Up until that moment, she probably held out hope that she'd get Seneca back, too. He dismounted and walked up to her. I could tell by his expression, one of abject misery, he'd rather face a thousand marauding Indians than her at this moment. Maybe that was why he hadn't come in so quickly.

"Sorry to tell you this, Mrs. Quarles, but your little girl is gone."

Julia stared at Beckwourth with a face as hard and fragile as porcelain and as white. She said nothing then. Henry wrapped his arm around her shoulders.

Beckwourth spoke slowly as if each word gave him physical pain. "I tried to pick up Brings Thunder's trail but it vanished like a fox when a wolf shows up. Maybe the man can fly. I cut the trail of a few bands though and caught up with them. At first no one knew a thing. Then I found Buffalo Horn, and he said he heard that your poor little girl done fall off of a horse and kilt herself. I am so sorry, ma'am."

Julia didn't react at first. A couple women, including Myra Langdon came up to console her.

"Is that it?" Julia asked sharply. "That's all you have? This Buffalo Horn's word?"

"He don't lie, Mrs. Quarles."

"Did this man see her fall?" she pressed. "Did he see the body?"

"Well, no, ma'am, but Buffalo Horn knows what happens in his country, and what happens to a white girl captive is going to be something known."

"But he didn't see it. Go on," Julia said. "What else?"

"Well, I still looked about trying to pick up Brings Thunder's trail just to be thorough, you see, but after a few days saw no more point in it and came here to tell you all what I learnt."

Julia sighed then stepped forward and kissed his cheek. "I thank you, Mr. Beckwourth, I owe you more than I can ever repay."

Captain Warren said to her, "We're all very sorry. You can be reassured that she is with God now. He has taken a favorite to him."

"No. She's still alive," Julia said fiercely in reply. She turned to Henry. "She's still alive."

Henry nodded, "Yes." But I could tell he didn't believe it.

Jane tugged on Julia's dress. "Mamma, she's okay. Seneca's okay. I know. And besides, she wouldn't fall off a horse."

For some reason that made everyone let loose with an abrupt tension-easing laugh. Even Julia smiled. "Yes, honey, you are right. She would never fall off a horse."

That seemed to sway everyone to Julia's more hopeful conclusion.

Beckwourth also solved the mystery of the missing Tom Fitzpatrick. He had been mauled by a grizzly bear somewhere in the Bighorns, and near death, made his way to the Arapaho with whom he had good relations. They were nursing him back to health. I was glad to hear he had survived.

That night Henry promised us all, the Quarles that is, that he would not give up the search for Seneca. The plan was to go on to Oregon, start their farm, and then come back to Fort Laramie to search for her among the Indians, to offer a reward to anyone who could find her. This sounded like a good plan on that night, but I knew it would never work out. I knew in my heart, if Seneca really were alive, she was Sioux now and would never be found.

Chapter 43

We pressed on for Oregon. Like so many others with the loss of a child, it was Julia's lot to persevere. She had taken a hard blow and would never be quite the same, but to everyone else, she seemed to be bearing up. Yet, I saw indications that this peculiar situation, Seneca caught between life and death like Schrodinger's cat, was taking its toll on her. Her long silences, vacant stares, and deep sighs, these made it clear to me that a controlling melancholy was settling in her bones. I determined to keep a close eye on her.

In the evenings, Myra and several women came to our wagons to visit and support Julia as she had done for them in past days. She played along and made as if their cheery talk was working. Even Lottie Whelan came to ask for help with recipes, basic ones like biscuits, cake and cornbread. The girl had never paid much attention to cooking before, as hard as her mother had tried to teach her, and Julia was glad to help, even sporting a smile or two at the girl's odd combination of ineptness and determination.

"You'll get the hang of it," Julia said.

Lottie shook her head. "I can burn water, Mrs. Quarles. Lordy, ma'am, Eddie was using my biscuits with his slingshot to try and kill him a rabbit."

"Call me Julia, Lottie. None of this Mrs. Quarles or ma'am stuff."

"All right, ma'am."

After several days, Julia seemed to be pulling out of her melancholia when something happened that shoved her clean off the cliff. It was a mishap while crossing another river. We had crossed so many, at least a thousand it seemed since Missouri. Late in the afternoon, we came to the river crossing about four days away from Fort Bridger. A river just twenty yards in width. That was all. Not very deep, water rising midway up the wagon wheels. Of the company's hundred wagons, our two were near the front this time. With Julia driving, the first got nearly across when the right rear wheel dipped sharply and the corner of the wagon crashed down in a hidden hole in the river bed. Water poured into the back.

Henry jumped off the second wagon and splashed forward to the foundering wagon, while several other men came to help. I was already across, but waded back in with Isaac to take hold of the oxen. After a lot of shouting, men pushing, Isaac and me pulling, and Julia standing up snapping the reins in one hand and cracking her whip in the other, we got the wagon out of the hole and up on the bank.

Once all the company made it across, Captain Warren decided to camp where we were for the night to give all of us time to dry out our belongings. For the most part, it looked like we'd gotten off lucky this day. That was till we gathered round Julia and her rocking chair to hear the latest doings of Darcy and Elizabeth Bennet, now progressed to the final chapters. I retrieved the small chest that held the books, which seemed heavy, and set it beside her. When she opened it, a look of despair crossed her face. I watched, not knowing what was wrong. She tipped the chest over and water poured out. The five books tumbling with it were waterlogged, utterly ruined.

Flopping hard into her rocker, Julia stared at nothing without speaking for a full two minutes, then Myra placed a gentle hand on her shoulder and announced to everyone, "Sorry, folks. We will pick up the readings some other time."

The next morning when the company pulled out, Julia refused to go. She didn't make a big production of it. She just sat in her rocking chair next to the ashes of the morning fire and refused to budge. Wagons passed us by, their occupants giving us concerned glances. Sam Langdon with Myra beside him halted his wagon. As I exchanged a helpless look with Caroline, he saw our oxen yoked, everything ready to go except Julia sitting in the rocker, her hands folded in her lap. Immediately, Myra sensed what was wrong and had started to climb down, but Sam stopped her.

"Morning, Henry. Julia," he said. "That wheel acting up again?"

Henry said, "It's just a bit loose. Should take me an hour or so."

"Anything I can do?"

"No, I can handle it. We'll be along."

Langdon nodded. He was something of a wheelwright, so when he glanced at the wheel he knew nothing was wrong with it.

At that moment, Captain Warren rode back to us. "What's the hold up here?"

"No, hold up," Henry replied.

Samuel said, "That wheel of Henry's needs a little more pitch, that's all. Should be 'bout an hour or so."

"We can't wait," Captain Warren said to Henry.

"Don't expect you to. We'll be along."

So, Henry sent Isaac on ahead with the company to keep herd on our livestock, and the rest of us waited the morning out by the stream. The sky was spotless blue. No rain in the offing. The land was flat and dry. The chair creaked as Julia rocked easily, her eyes sightless as a blind woman. I didn't know what to say. Books meant a lot to her, but it didn't take a genius to understand this was bigger than that, a response, maybe, to losing Seneca and to the endless hardships of the journey. And we were barely more than halfway there. The scary thing was, she was the strongest among us.

As I patted her shoulder, I thought the same probably hit every woman on the long journey at some point and in some way. And the men, too. They just acted it out differently, men on a short fuse often angry and belligerent. Women a slow fuse. There was nothing for any of them to do but to push on or perish in an endlessly barren moonscape.

Close to noon, she suddenly snapped out of it. Abruptly, she stood up and said, "What are you all doing, standing around with your hands in your pockets? Look lively, now. We have a few miles to travel today. Jane, George, get in the wagons."

Henry was not surprised at all. He knew she'd come around. Julia was the strongest woman I'd ever met, this century or the one 150 years from now, stronger even than my own mother and that was going some. Still, as we got underway, I felt my body heave an enormous sigh of relief. Without her, the Quarles would have been adrift and doomed.

And so it was that two days later, after we'd caught up with the company, Julia's water broke and her baby was ready to come. If you study history, you know the biggest killer of women in this age and all the ages before the twenti-eth century was childbirth. The main reason was the lack of hygiene. With the same dirty instruments being used again and again, many women succumbed to infection, so I insisted with Myra, who acted as the midwife, that all water be boiled, any utensils be cleaned in that water, and that Myra scrub her hands and arms clean in it with good strong lye soap.

Not only did Julia pull through, but she gave birth to a healthy boy that evening, and next day we loaded up the wagons and continued on. She expected nothing else. This was the third child born to the company on the journey. The odd habit of naming newborns after the nearest landmark, usually a river, held true. So, Black Fork Quarles—Good Lord—came into the world on August 9, 1848. Immediately, everyone, including me, called him "Blackie."

The time I had been dreading finally came. Passing Fort Hall, we made for Raft River a few miles away. It was where the Warren Company would split up, more than half now heading southwest toward California and the goldfields. The rest of us would continue along the Snake River toward trail's end at Oregon City. Daniel was among those going to California. I was sure when that happened I would never see him again.

A little before noon we reached Separation Point, a bluff near the river where wagon trains took either the northern or southern route. It was an emotional time for the entire company, time for tearful goodbyes, last hugs, and last second changes of heart. In the long journey from the States, friendships had taken root between families and individuals. And some romances. Surprisingly, I found it difficult to say goodbye to Jim Beckwourth. He was a little embarrassed by my massive hug. "I'll never be able to thank you for Jane, for what you did for me and my family," I said.

"It wasn't enough."

"It was all any man could do."

He nodded, then reflected a moment in silence. Finally, some thought brought on a gold-toothed grin. "I once thought you were evil. You're not that at all."

"Thanks," I laughed. "That's a relief."

He laughed too. I held back a tear as he rode off after the seventy wagons heading south, including those of Captain Warren and his family. Daniel was saying farewells to his family—the Langdons were going on to Oregon with us—then came over to where I stood with Jesse. When I shook hands with Jesse, he seemed disappointed. He wanted a kiss but hndshale was all I had for him.

I turned to Daniel. This was it.

My emotions were so conflicted at that moment. Anger because the bastard was not only leaving me, but his family as well to go gallivanting on this adventure. Relief because it let me off the hook from my promise to marry him. And deep, deep sorrow because I loved him and would never see him again. The bastard! I felt a terrible longing already and knew I would carry it with me forever. From his horse, Jessie sighed noisily and cleared his throat, as if five more minutes was going to matter. I glared at him. What was his problem?

"I guess it's time for me to go," Daniel said.

"You take care of yourself," I said coldly. I had no intention of kissing him either.

"It won't be that long," he said, wiping an imaginary tear off my cheek. I refused to cry.

"I'll pick those pieces of gold off the ground and come right on up to Oregon before you know it"

"You're such a romantic," I said, sarcastically.

"Libby, don't be that way," he said. My words had stung. "I want to get us a good start. This is the best way I can do it."

Romantic scenes came to mind: Elizabeth and Darcy, Romeo and Juliet. Parting is such sweet sorrow. This was nothing like those. This was my petulance versus his financial planning.

Finally, I relented and let him off the hook, throwing my arms around him. "I know. It's just that I miss you already." I could see the love in his eyes. It felt good to have someone see me that way, like nothing I'd ever known. "For Christ's sake, kiss me."

He did. It had to last forever and fell far too short of that. He squeezed the breath out of me. Not Romeo and Juliet, I thought, but it will do. That romance ended badly, anyway.

Then he was off with Jesse, California bound. I repeated to myself that this was for the best, as Julia placed her arm over my shoulders. "He'll be back," she said. "Then you can marry."

I watched them till they rode over the crest of the far hill, chasing after the wagons headed to California.

Chapter 44

Libby's diary, September 15, 1848

Hot. Fiercely hot. Temperatures above 100 most of the day. We head on to Oregon along the ever winding Snake River. I think of Daniel all the time. Two weeks ago, he left for California, and every night, he arrives in my dreams like clockwork and dominates my thoughts during the day. Missing him is too much to bear sometimes. I miss good friends Jesse Hancock and Beckwourth and Fitzpatrick and Sally, too.

We have twenty-two wagons left of the old Warren Company. With Warren himself gone, it's now the Langdon Company because Sam has been elected the new captain. Newton Rudabaugh has been elected his assistant, but Sam relies more on Henry's counsel. Pierce, who decided against going to California at the last, stood for both positions but received only three votes each time. His and Barnaby's and his remaining teamster. The two other men who worked for him have gone to California. I wish they'd taken the Pierces with them.

I feel very uneasy about the rest of the journey, especially without Beckwourth to guide us. Before heading off, he told us from here on was the worst of the journey by far. Great!

"Just follow the map I give you. You won't get lost," he said to all of us the night before he left. Then he gave a gallows laugh. "Up till now's been a Sunday promenade, folks. It sure is harder now. Laws! It is hard. Bad heat and bad cold a'fore you're done. Like nothing you done seen before." As I look out onto the barren Snake Plain, I can see that it is so.

Libby's diary, September 17
The Snake Plain is a desolate, barren expanse. Mrs. Guthrie once told me I would "rue the day." I am ruing it, Mrs. Guthrie. I am ruing it. Crossing the Snake Plain is nigh on unbearable. Walking almost every step. Riding Iris very little to spare her. Thick dust and fierce heat day after day. Little grass for the cattle and horses. Long stretches without water. The Snake River cuts through steep canyons and allows very few places for us to get down to it so we can fill our buckets. Tonight we camped beside a boiling spring. It is so hot we only have to add tea. No fire needed

Libby's diary, September 18
We are struck by the flux. Many are sick with bloody diarrhea as am I. I have never been so sick in my entire life. The wagons are halted. When everyone asks me for help, I tell them to boil water. That advice is wearing thin. The saying, seeing the elephant, can be experiencing a bad thing as well as something new and strange and good. So with the sickness all about, Henry said we are treading on the elephant's tail, meaning, I suppose, we are too close to disaster.

Julia says the sickness is due to drinking alkali water, but there's little else for us to drink. She saves our good water for Blackie—what a name for a baby—but still he is crying all the time, a regular crap machine. Aspasia, the milk cow, died from drinking the alkali water.

September 19

We are up a stump again.

Sam moved us out this morning despite so many sick, and we came to a terrible place called Bridge Creek where white water roared just below and us needing to get to the other side. A natural bridge of rock and stone spanned it, but only wide enough to allow one person at a time to cross. No wagons at all. When I first saw it an hour ago, I thought getting us and the wagons over would be impossible.

But Henry has come up with a plan. I need to stop writing now since Henry is shouting at me to get a move on. We are crossing now.

September 19

It's night. We made it. Sick and weak as we were from the flux, we unloaded all the wagons and packed everything on our backs, including babies and small children, and one by one crossed the narrow bridge. Heat came off the rocks like off a frying pan. I carried Jane, while Julia carried Blackie. You had to trust in the older children to make it on their own, and with shouted encouragements from all, they did. Then we went back for more gear.

The men drove the empty wagons, the cattle and the loose horses downriver to a less fearsome section of riverbank, one still dangerous and using chains and ropes hauled them all over. By late afternoon, the wagons were repacked and we were on our way for another ten miles.

Chapter 45

The nights were getting colder. We spent a couple days at Fort Boise, trading clothes for fish with the Indians. Unlike the Lakota, these Indians, the Coeur d'Alene, were dressed in emigrant clothing, plaid shirts, striped pants and woolen socks.

Daniel still got under my skin in so many ways. Love was hard enough. But love and anger directed at the same person was a terrible thing to deal with. After dinner the last night at the fort, I was cleaning up and spilled a can of flour onto the ground, wasting it. I let out several unladylike curses.

I was, as they say, touchy. Things set me off and Julia knew why. Later in our tent as I sat on a stool, she combed my hair and gave me advice on love, the nineteenth century way of it, "Sometimes men have a hard time seeing beyond their own selves, especially when it comes to the grand adventure."

"I know," I said derisively.

"Look at us and Oregon. You might think that's all that matters to Henry, but it is not. Some men are drawn to the grand adventure, and if you ask them why they do it, they will tell you it's for us women. That doesn't mean they are not good men. You and I have good men. Daniel shouldn't have gone off to California and left you and his ma and pa, but you point out a perfect man to me, and I'll show you one made out of wood and air. Don't give up on him just yet." She paused as she gently undid a snag in my hair.

"I won't. Thanks, Julia."

She sighed at that, and I knew why. She so desperately wanted me to call her mother or ma, but I still couldn't do it.

September 23

Tragedy struck again today. We had a hard go crossing the Snake a week or so back and leaving Fort Boise, we had to re-cross it. It was too dangerous to ford so we decided to pay the three-dollar price per wagon for the ferry, but the price for the cattle and horses was too high.

Sam Langdon and the men voted to swim the cattle and horses across to save money. That's what led to it. Several riders, including Henry, Isaac, the Pierces, Newton Rudabaugh and his daughter, Abby, took on the task. She could ride almost as well as I could. As most of us crossed on the ferry, I watched them plunge into the river to herd the animals across.

Every time you cross a river you're on edge. This time I had my heart in my throat even more so because the current was so strong. Then it happened. One of the cows drifted too far downstream and Newton Rudabaugh went after it. The animal was not worth a life. A floating bit of sagebrush frightened Rudabaugh's horse and unseated him. He grabbed at the reins, but he was swept under. Abby screamed and swam her horse after him, and she too was swept under.

Once on the far side, Henry held Isaac by the shirt to keep him from going back after Abby. She and her father had been swept too far downstream. The men followed the river trying to find a place to go in after them. Finally, Isaac saw his chance and rode into the water. Suddenly, out of nowhere, two Indians showed up paddling furiously in a canoe. They paddled past Isaac and pulled Abby out of the water, but Newton was gone. We never saw him again. He left a wife and four children.

The Blue Mountains loomed ahead, snowcapped and ponderous. As I walked beside Lottie's wagon up the Valley of the Grande Ronde, she exclaimed sternly,

"Just look at them, those big monsters. Here we are just recovering from the long go of the Snake Plains and now the mountains. Damnation, Libby, are we ever going to get to finish this journey?"

Young women didn't curse, but she was taking to it. Lottie had changed. At heart she was still as much a bitch as I was and could at times cut you to the quick, but responsibility for her siblings had made her tough and hardworking. She did not want charity from others and insisted on the Whelans making their own way.

"Maybe it will be easier when we get to Oregon City," I said.

"But probably not."

"You'll make it, Lottie. You're tough as old cowhide."

She grinned. It was true. I knew she wasn't going to quit, and neither was I. What choice did we have? Amazingly, spirits were even high. We'd left the Snake River at Farewell Bend to cut across the mountains toward the Columbia River. We all knew that the Columbia led to journey's end. A long way yet, but we could almost smell the Pacific air.

Being late September, everyone was afraid of getting caught in the mountains in a snowstorm and being trapped like the Donners. Our stores of flour and other goods were growing scarce, and the specter of those tragic people loomed heavily for all. That night in the foothills of the Blue Mountains, we sat close to the fire to keep warm and talked ghoulishly of the cannibalism of the Donners. Isaac said, "If we run out of food, I'd never eat Libby."

"Oh, how can I ever thank you," I said mockingly sweet.

"Cause she'd taste so bitter, worse than castor oil. I'd be poisoned." He guffawed. The toad. I jumped him and wrestled him to the ground, rubbing grass in his hair.

Libby's diary, October 9

Four days ago amid a steady rain, we began our climb into the clouds. We were upon the Blue Mountains. After the long haul across the plains, it was good to be travelling among trees with the fresh, wet smell of pine and fir. In the muddy ascent, the oxen suffered. Our Caesar dropped dead in his yoke. Henry and Isaac and I had a time getting him undone, and Herod put in his place. We butchered the poor beast on the spot and shared the meat with the company.

Wagons had to be lightened, which meant people left behind things they had carried all the way across the prairie. Of the things we had passed already, littered among the trees, was a porcelain bathtub, several chests of drawers, a set of china dishware, scattered and broken, and a harpsichord. Yesterday, we left an iron stove from our second wagon that should have been abandoned back in Nebraska. It was heavier than the bathtub.

So cold, overnight water freeze in the buckets. As I am writing this, Caroline and I huddle together in our blankets, shivering. Julia is telling us to get up and go hunt up firewood.

Libby's diary, Oct. 10
This morning we left Little George behind. Poor kid. No one missed him till an hour ago at the nooning when Caroline asked, "Where's George?"
Julia was beside herself, railing at Henry for losing another of her children. That hit home. He and I, along with several others, rode back along the trail till we found him about four miles back, hands in pockets, leisurely walking along where bear and mountain lion roam. When we got him back to camp, Julia scolded him, hugged him, and scolded him again. He said he'd been looking for berries, and when he came back, everyone was gone.

Towards evening, we came to an escarpment where we could see a vast treeless plain all the way west to the high Cascades. The sunset above those far mountains cast a golden hue over the land. It sent a thrill through one and all because everyone knew the Cascades were the last, great obstacle.

October 24

More than two weeks so far crossing these desolate, rolling plains south of the Columbia River, heading toward the Cascades. It's all mud and sand and swift running rivers. So many to cross. Cold, windy and rainy most of the way, as it has been today. We made fifteen miles and camped on the Columbia River. Starting a fire was difficult. Nothing to burn. Everything wet. Ate soggy bread and the last of our beef jerky for dinner. No food left. Several people sick from scurvy. I fear I am one of them. After jotting down these notes, I take to my bed.

October 25

I feel worse today. Caroline sick, too. Heavy rain all day. We came to the Deschutes, a white water monster, 150 yards wide. We found Indians waiting in abundance to pilot emigrants across. You couldn't make it otherwise. Hannibal Pierce said they were Cayuse and Nez Perce, as if he would know. He warned everyone. "Watch them Cayuse. They's them what kilt the Whitmans."

Fording was difficult, water splashing up to the tops of the wagons, but in a couple hours, the Indians got us and the live-stock across. It only cost each family a little money and some clothes. For the crossing, we traded one of Julia's old dresses and a threadbare coat, too small for Isaac, and too big for Little George. Also traded for fish.

October 26

Cold. Rained all day.

October 27
Cold. Rained all day.

October 28
Cold. Rained all day.

October 29

I didn't want to get out of bed. I am still sick, as is Caroline and several others in the company. I can't believe I have scurvy. In elementary school, studying the early explorers, Mrs. Bascomb time and again told us it was caused by a lack of vitamin C. No one here knows what that is. Citrus fruit had it and a lot of other foods. Long ago ran out of lemon extract. Unfortunately, we have nothing to eat. Only tea left.

As I write this, it is snowing. Morning chores done. Wagons packed. We have a steep climb ahead today before the snow accumulates too much. We are starting out. I must go.

Nighttime. Exhausted. Today traveled over the worst road God ever created. Steep and winding. Snow mixed with rain. Henry drove one of our wagons and Isaac the other. The rest of us walked. Three teams of oxen were yoked to each wagon to get up the slick trail. Pulling in the sucking mud, those beasts are worse off than we humans. To keep going, Henry had to drop more belongings from the wagons. Two chests of drawers, two tables.

As I plodded upward, snow and mud half way up my calves, I held Iris by the reins with Caroline and Jane aboard and drug them along. Ahead of us, Julia marched through the slop carrying Blackie in a backpack. I was exhausted, sick and so cold, my numb feet felt like falling off. It was the worst. I prayed the wagons wouldn't get stuck, because if they did, we were dead.

By late afternoon under an overcast sky, the rain and snow stopped, and we topped the crest and descended a long hill down to the Dalles where I now write this entry.

Chapter 46

At the Dalles Methodist Mission, the small company split again. Half the wagons and families went on the next day, but Henry and Sam and a few other families decided to stay over several days to let their cattle graze and people rest and get well.

From over a hundred wagons and nearly five hundred emigrants, we were down to ten wagons and no more than thirty people. The Quarles, the Langdons, the Rudabaughs, the Whelans, the Dixons—Frank Dixon, aged twenty-two and his twenty-year-old wife Clara—and the Pierces. I whispered to Caroline that the Pierces clung to us like a bad rash. Listless from illness, she managed a fair giggle before coughing. She was so thin I wanted to weep. "Dear God," I whispered so she couldn't hear, "get this journey over with before someone else dies."

On our second day at the Dalles, a cold wind blew in off the Columbia River, whipping on through the spruce forest that surrounded the mission. I couldn't tell a spruce from a palm tree, but that's what someone said the trees were. It was Halloween. I didn't even realize it till Little George asked Julia if he could dress up and go trick-or-treating. She told him not this year.

For our one meal of the day at noon, we ate fish and potatoes bartered from the missionary Indians. Fish and chips! On occasion we had butchered a cow, but Henry and all the men who owned cattle wanted to spare them. They were like our seed corn.

We met the two white families that lived among the Indians at the mission. They brought biscuits out to us in the evening, and we shared our tea with them. They were preaching families who admitted to tension if not fear in their current situation. The Whitman Massacre had occurred last year just up the road a ways. Huddling around a huge campfire, they insisted their Indians would never harm them like the Cayuse had the Whitmans. A couple Cayuse stood about the fire listening to all this, and I watched them closely for any sign of threat. No reaction at all, even though both spoke English. That night I wondered if I was going to be massacred in my sleep.

November 4

On the Columbia River in among thick forest with trees 300 hundred feet tall. Feeling much better today, as is Caroline and the others who had scurvy. Could it have been the potatoes or fish or both we got from the missionaries? So hungry, we gorged ourselves in the last five days. Three days ago, we came to this place among the tall trees where two other small emigrant companies are making large rafts to float down the river through the Cascades. We couldn't take the cattle or horses on the rafts, and so like everyone else we plan to split up and meet later. Henry, Isaac, Barnaby Pierce and Abby Rudabaugh would take the stock over the Cascade Mountains on a narrow trail and meet us many miles downriver at what people called the Big Falls.

At first, Henry wasn't going to go. We had the Rudabaugh and Whelan children, none with a man, and at the Dalles, Pierce's last teamster stole a horse and deserted us, so if Henry went with the herd, that would leave us short on men.

But Julia urged him to go and protect our property. These animals cost a lot of money. Their loss would be devastating to our future. She and I, she said, would handle things on the water. Sam Langdon said he'd look after us all like his own family, and Frank Dixon concurred. Even Hannibal Pierce promised to do his best to protect all the young ones. So a couple hours ago, we said goodbye to Henry and Isaac and Abby, and even snarky Barnaby, as they headed off with the herd into the mountains.

November 5

We took the wheels off the wagons and with the help of people from other companies, loaded all we had left onto two huge rafts, then set off on the eighty-mile passage through the treacherous and magnificent Columbia River gorge. As I write this, it is cold and damp, a drizzle falls, so I write under canvas inside one of the wagons. Water sweeps over the rafts in gushes. It's hard to concentrate on writing for fear we'll be swamped at any moment.

There are so many children, nearly twenty on the two rafts, it would be so easy for one of them to fall over the side and be lost. It scares me to death. What is a child? Abby Rudabaugh is fourteen. She's riding over the mountains right now looking after the stock with Henry and the others. Isaac is thirteen now, having had a birthday a while back. They are children, surely, but shoulder adult responsibilities. At sixteen, I am no longer thought a child by anyone.

November 7

Late afternoon. The bad weather won't let up. Rain and snow. Miserable. As we float down the river against a raw wind, the storm is worsening. With snow and sleet coming in under the canvas, stinging my face, I shield the journal as best I can and write. Mrs. Guthrie, did you know it was this bad? Keeping this journal, keeping Libby's journal, has become an obsession. I write in it every day, sometimes more than once a day. The river has turned so choppy; Sam signals the other raft that we have to pull in to shore. I need to put the pen down now and help.

Camp set up now, so I can jot down a few more notes. Even though the storm has let up, and through the narrow corridor of the high gorge a bit of sunset pokes through the clouds, Sam has decided to spend the night here instead of going back out on the river for a couple more hours.

After an hour of trying, Julia and Myra get a fire going, and we heat up some tea. Pierce—really Pierce!—shared two potatoes with everyone. The children take it all for granted, playing tag on the steep hillside. They don't know this trial of passage isn't the way life is supposed to be. Myra and Rebecca Rudabaugh, Abbey's mom, scold two of them for wandering too far into the woods. So cold I can barely write.

After writing in Libby's diary by candlelight, I came back to the fire to see if there was any tea left. Pierce was sitting there alone. A thick darkness surrounded the camp. Everyone else was huddled in one of the two shelters. Most of the children were sleeping. A few stars poked through the scudding clouds. The sound of the river rushing by was like noisy traffic on a barely remembered freeway.

I poured the tea and sat down with my hands wrapped around the cup. After a few moments, he said to me, "You done surprised me, Miss Quarles. You got this far. Maybe you will make it the whole way."

I gave a short laugh. I had surprised myself. "We're not there yet."

"I wonder what old Sally's doing right about now. I sure miss her. We were close, you know. She was like my own daughter. She was a hard worker, too."

And he meant it. Incredible. Selective memory, very selective. "You think so?"

He chuckled. "I got some good horses for her though. She was sure worth a bunch."

I looked at him, then shook my head in disgust.

"I weren't too bad to her in all honesty. It's just that, just that…" He hesitated then said, "Women. I ain't never been much good with them. Don't understand them."

I said firmly, "You don't like them. That's why."

"I don't. I surely don't." He looked at me for my reaction. He was honest at least.

"You're a misogynist."

"A miss-a-what?"

"A misogynist. It means someone who hates women."

"Now that there's a real fancy word." He laughed. "Well, ain't you the smart one. That's me I guess. A missoggy fellow." He remained silent for awhile. I finished my tea and was about to go back to the shelter when he said, "You see, women don't like me much. I don't know why. I do treat them nice."

I rolled my eyes, not caring that he saw me do it.

"You see, I travelled from place to place. Started out in Virginia. Married Barnaby's ma and moved to Tennessee. When she died, I upped and moved west again to Missouri. Never let grass grow under my feet. Only woman took to me was Sally's sister, and she not much. I married her cause Barnaby needed a ma. With Sally along, I got me two for one." He chuckled. "But old Mary died, too. I kept moving, hoping for better. Now I'm on this trail."

I didn't know what to say. Why was he telling me all this? Surely, he didn't think we were friends, everything forgotten? After another moment, he said, "Why, Miss Libby, you see, when I dream at night, living in my dreams is always better than living in the daytime. I just hate waking up sometime. So I'm on this Oregon Trail. I think things will be good for me somewhere else. Maybe somewhere else I can wake up in the morning and be glad to."

I wasn't going to feel sorry for the bastard, if that's what he wanted. "Hope it is, Mr. Pierce, because after Oregon no more west to travel, unless you're a fish."

He laughed. "I ain't no fish, that's sure." Then he nodded solemnly, as if I'd spoken some great piece of wisdom. "With Sally gone, Barnaby's all I got now. He's a good boy, ain't he?"

This was more than I could take. I wasn't close to him and I didn't want to be. I stood up, said goodnight and went to the shelter.

November 22

It took us two more weeks on this terrible river till we reached the falls, each day colder and wetter than the last, stopping on shore for long stretches because of the turbulent water and headwind. Once we passed a raft that had capsized and lay in pieces on the riverbank. We all stared at it. God knows what happened to the poor people aboard.

In a grand reunion, Henry and the others met us with the cattle a few miles before the falls. We butchered a beef that night. Better that than starving. My hands are so numb I can no longer write. Hard day tomorrow. Must try to sleep.

November 23

The hike around the falls was the hardest five miles of my life, mud, slop and snow.

November 29

We have been waiting here just past the falls for six days with hundreds of other emigrants for our turn on boats to take us down to Oregon City. We have a barge from one of the fur companies lined up this morning for after breakfast. The last leg of the journey. I can't believe it. Now, I must think more about things I dare not write. Must go. Henry and Sam are loading everyone aboard.

As I loaded onto the boat that would take the last of the old Warren Company to Oregon City and the finish of the journey, I couldn't help but wonder once again what would happen to me. Would this be the end of my cosmic adventure with Time? Finish the journey, finish the journey, the voice had told me. And so, then what? Back to the twenty-first century?

December 1
Oregon City!

Nothing happened! Not in that first week in Oregon City. I was still Libby, still in the nineteenth century. In truth, I wanted to split apart and half of me stay, the other half return. We set up outside of town while Henry and Sam investigated where each wanted to claim their 640 acres of land. One of the first things we did was get our pictures taken at a shop in the town. Photography was new and everyone wanted portraits taken. We all looked mean as sin the way we stared into the camera, but you had to. Any movement would render the object invisible. You could photograph a busy street and it would seem empty because all the people and carriages were moving. No one could hold a genuine smile for the many seconds needed to get the right exposure, so we stared frozen into the camera.

Oregon City was a thriving town of fresh lumbered buildings, brick structures, and hundreds of tents. I felt for Rebecca Rudabaugh, who rented a shed in back of a house for herself and her children. Isaac visited Abby there every day, and I went with him a couple times. He and Abby had grown close on their ride through the Cascades. Lottie Whelan and her siblings were taken in by one of the local churches. It was a massive act of kindness to take in such a large family of children.

I spent some time with her as well. She seemed happy and full of hope. From any perspective, her lot was hard, but despite the difficulties for a girl without parents or a husband, she was not worried. Lottie would do all right for herself. I had no doubts. After all, she'd just come two thousand miles through torrential rains, across arid stretches without water and food and endured. She would endure now.

Then one week after our arrival, who should come riding in on his big grey horse but Daniel. The moment he jumped down, I threw myself into his arms and asked if he was already rich. He laughed and said not quite yet. His parents and sisters swarmed about us, peppering him with questions. He explained that he had missed us all so much that, when he got to the goldfields, he just turned right and came up the coast directly here.

Mostly he missed me though. "The time has come for Libby and me to get married," he announced to everyone.

Marriage to Daniel. I could no longer duck that issue. I had not been sent back to my own time. At least not yet. So I had to confront this life in the here and now.

I realized then I was as much of Libby's time as Paula's.

"Well, let's get ourselves a preacher," I said.

Chapter 47

The Quarles and the Langdons filed claims on parcels of land next to each other far to the southwest and close to the Pacific Ocean. Daniel filed as well, and both families trekked down there in January. After we had built ourselves a nice little cabin on a creek a half mile from the Langdons, Daniel and I set off for California and the goldfields together. It was 1849.

I had three good years and two children with Daniel before he died of typhoid in the mining camp of Rough and Ready. I had a two-year-old boy, Daniel, Jr., and a little girl, Julia Myra, who we called My. I feared desperately that they too would come down with the disease, so I made sure nothing passed through their lips that wasn't cooked or boiled. I brought my knowledge to the other sick miners as well, working days without sleep to fight the illness. They called me the Angel of Rough and Ready. I just did what I could.

Finding gold was not so easy, but Daniel and I had prospered as merchants. He started a dry goods store, which I kept going after his death. It burned to the ground in a conflagration that spread and destroyed almost every building in camp. It busted me. I had to take in laundry for a time till Jesse Hancock showed up one day and proposed marriage. No courtship. He said he'd been in love with me since back in St. Jo, Missouri, all those years ago. With two children to fend for, I took no more than a second to accept. We married and headed back to Oregon, where we had my land and his joined together. It had been a long time since I thought about returning to my own time. I had five more children with him, three that survived childhood.

Periodically, Henry returned to Fort Laramie with Isaac to look for Seneca and then with Little George when he got old enough. They never found her. Little George was no longer little, but a tall young man, rather handsome, who was often besieged by the young women of the area. In 1861, at twenty-one, he went east to join the Union cause. Knowing what horror was coming, I begged him not to go, but he only laughed with the bravado of young men going to war. I expected never to see him again, yet he survived those terrible four years and came back very much changed. Bravado was no longer a part of his character. He was no longer young.

And yet, he returned to the army and took part in all the Indian Wars. When I asked him why, he merely said it was what he knew. I had to warn him. "Don't go to the Little Big Horn."

He didn't listen. He was there and again survived. He was with Reno that day and not Custer.

Isaac married Abby Rudabaugh and they had a big family. Nine children. More and more he took on the responsibility for running the Quarles family farm. Henry passed away in 1868.

He'd been weakening for several months. He never did see Seneca again, but we did. In 1881 she showed up in our valley with her two children, aged eleven and twelve. Her Lakota husband had died five years before at the Rosebud. Sponsored by missionaries, she had been looking for her white family for several months. I felt such elation that morning when one of Isaac's children had ridden over to our place to tell us she was at their home. I cried all the way there.

Dressed in white woman's dress, she was all Indian underneath, a small leathery thing, no doubt from long years living outdoors. She'd been adopted by the Sioux and treated as one of their own. Her two children stood silently, off by themselves, uncomfortable in their high collars and ties.

All of the Quarles, Langdon, and Hancock children had been told of the little girl taken by Indians, a family legend, and now here she was. One of them asked her why she had not come back sooner. That drew an awkward silence from everyone, but Seneca answered forthrightly, "I was with my people. Why would I leave?"

Her English came slowly, but she knew it well enough. She told us how she had worked in the late seventies as an interpreter. Then she added in a sad voice, "Things are changing now. The old ways are going. I think they will never come back."

Later, I was able to talk with her alone, and I asked her if she knew anything about Sally Callahan. She nodded. Sally had been killed long ago at the Washita. Saddened by the news, I remembered many good moments with her, then I became curious about something else. "Were you at the Little Big Horn?"

She beamed with pride. "The Greasy Grass? Oh, yes, I was there. That was a great day. We killed many enemy that day."

"So was George...Little George."

For a moment, she raised her eyes in what seemed a mixture of alarm and curiosity.

"He survived. He was with Reno. He's in Arizona right now chasing Apaches."

Her face hardened at that news. She really was more Indian than white, and I supposed she was entitled to hate whites. But I couldn't use hate to describe her. Calm, at peace, if rather sad, would be a better description. In fact, she talked about whites and Indians as just people, all one of the same in creation. Blaming pioneers for the destruction of her People, she told me, was like blaming a river for flooding or a cloudy sky for raining.

Jane was living several days' journey away with her husband in Vancouver, Washington. The next day Seneca set out with her children to visit her. That was a reunion I'd love to have witnessed. As it was, she stayed on there, living with her twin for a while till she married a prosperous newspaper owner with whom she had two more children.

In July of 1892, at the age of eighty, Julia died with many of her children, grandchildren and great-grandchildren around her. She was a good woman. I had started calling her mother or ma many years before. She was as much my mother as the woman I had trouble picturing after so many years. I still had that longing for my old family, but I loved my Quarles family in the same way. Julia was my mother here.

As for me, I lived with Jesse Hancock till his passing in 1905. I saw the Great War come and go. Two of my grandchildren and one great-grandchild served over there. Two of them came back. I saw the Roaring Twenties come in and became a big fan of silent movies, Mary Pickford, and movie magazines. I loved that Clara Bow, too.

In the hard winter of 1928, I began to weaken and knew my life was coming to an end. My lord, I was old. Ninety-six. In June of that year, I took to my bed for the final time. Seemed like a hundred people had squeezed into my bedroom along with that dumb doctor. People who looked familiar to me gathered around the bed.

"What are all you people doing here?" I seemed to float around the room, gazing at them from all angles. "I have too much work to do to be lying here," I told them. Then asked, "Where's Daniel? Why's he not here?"

I heard someone crying. Clammy old death was hanging around. I could see him sometimes in the room. He looked a lot like Brings Thunder, but that didn't frighten me. I'd killed him once, I could do it again. I thought about my life. Some of the memories I searched for, others came unbidden. There was Caesar, the great ox who collapsed in his yoke and gave us a time getting him out of it. The good fortune I made with Daniel in the goldfields and the years farming with Jesse. My children. My grandchildren, and more and more generations.

As I lay in my bed, someone I didn't know held a baby up for me to touch. This was a great-great-grandchild I was told. How nice.

"Where's Daniel?" I asked again. "Has Daniel come?"

Someone leaned forward to kiss me. I don't know who. I had so much work to do, I would have to get up soon. Two husbands. I'd buried two husbands. Loved both of them. Lights flickered in the room. I thought they were going out and I asked someone to light a lamp. I am dying. I know that. I am ready. I will see Daniel soon. And, yes, Jesse, too. How was that going to work?

"Mother, we're all here." I recognized my oldest living boy, Henry, speaking. He was always a smart one. He made money without even trying. Must have been seventy-five if he was a day. With a surge of strength, I grabbed the lapels of his suit. "Get your damn money out of the stock market. It's going to come down round your ears."

I thought Daniel finally had come, but I couldn't say for sure since I slept for a time. When I woke, someone must have lit a lamp because there was a bright light, like one of them movie lights, glaring at me. It was so bright I told them to put it out, but no one did. Maybe that was best. I could see only an infinite darkness surrounding it. The light drew down to a pinpoint, sputtering, flickering. Then it went out.

When I awake, I have no idea where I am. I'm lying on the ground and people who are vaguely familiar are standing over me. None of them are my children or grandchildren. Who are these people? Am I dead? Is this heaven? If so, it's not any heaven I ever imagined. Through their legs, I see the huge house and the green lawn and the pool. It finally comes to me where I am.

Oh, dear God.

Chapter 48

Two days later, on a Monday morning, I'm riding in a car to Rector Academy with my mother to begin my in-school suspension, uncomfortable in an above-the-knee skirt, the longest Paula has. I have been in shock since the moment I returned to the twenty-first century. I died, I awakened. Age ninety-six, age sixteen. To me, it's a horror. I do not want to pretend I like the idea of being sixteen again. People might think getting a second life is a wonderful miracle, but it's not. My life had been long and full, and I'm tired. As Libby, I lived through pain and triumph, tragedy and good times, love and hate. I had not wanted to become Libby, but I did. I am Libby. I died Libby. Now, I am an old woman in my mind, inside Paula's young body with another life to live. Oh, dear, dear God.

The previous Friday, after I awoke in exactly the spot I'd passed out eighty years before, my twenty-first century mother took me to a hospital, where I spent the weekend. A series of tests were done that showed nothing conclusive, as if a daguerreotype of Libby would come up on a cat scan of my head. The doctor released me Sunday night.

While I was in the hospital, mother brought Josh to see me. He was wearing the night goggles I remember giving him for his birthday so long ago. He bumped into everything but wouldn't take them off. "I can't wait till dark, Paula."

I chuckled. "Easy with those, bud. You don't want to hurt yourself." It is the only moment so far that has touched my long dormant Paula emotions.

"Are you going to die, Paula?" he asked me.

"No, sweetie, not any time soon. I'm going to be around a long time so I can pester you."

At the school, as I get out the car, mother asks me if the headaches have come back.

"I will not be getting those headaches again."

"You've been given a last chance, Paula. Behave," she warns me. "You don't have any more chances with the school or with me."

I see the worry on her face, so I smile, feeling overwhelming warmth. It can't be easy for her. That Paula was a hellion. "Don't fret. I allow I will be a perfect angel from now on."

For some reason, that doesn't reassure her. Her frown deepens and she drives away.

Inside, the school has nothing more than a trace of familiarity. After all, it has been eight decades since I've been here. As I pass down the hall, students stare at me as if I'm a circus freak. I feel like one. I'm supposed to spend my in-school suspension in Mrs. Guthrie's room, but I can't remember where it is. I'm about to ask someone when a tall, lean boy approaches me. His face seems familiar. I search for a name to go with it.

"Paula, I heard you were in the hospital," he says with genuine concern. "I hope it was nothing serious."

"Jason?"

"Yes?"

"Jason Weismann?"

He frowns. "Are you okay?"

"I'm fine, Jason. You're sweet for asking."

"Well, thanks, I guess. Just thought maybe…"

Someone shouts, "Rude Girls rock!"

I turn around and see several young people converging on me. They all talk at once about what I did at the famous assembly. Of course, I remember that. Wild Paula Masters ran naked—well sort of naked—through the auditorium. Someone betrayed her, *me* I should say, and Mrs. Guthrie turned me in. That kind of thing sticks with you. I glanced over to see what Jason thought about all this, but he was gone.

"Hey, babe, we thought you were toast," one of the boys is saying. "Way to come out on top. A little in-school suspension. You can do that easy."

He kisses me on the lips, quick and hard with a shot of tongue. I am so shocked I'm too slow to react, and the deed's done before I can shove him off. No one has kissed me like that since Mr. Hancock all those years ago.

"You're Cal, right?" I ask after a moment.

He laughs. "You bet I am."

"So freaking cool," a dark-haired girl says. This is Rachel, one of the Rude Girls. I remember them now, what we were.

"Yes, cool," I say hesitantly.

"Bramley must be going crazy," another girl says. Vanessa. Her good cheer is a front. I know why she is so nervous. She was the one who betrayed me. Not hard to figure out. I half thought it back then. But, now I know. Betrayal and hate do abide in the mind for a long time. I place a hand on her forearm. "You're such a good friend, Vanessa. What would I ever do without you?"

That makes it worse for her, as I knew it would. She blinks several times, flashes a hard glare, then forces a smile. "I feel the same way about you."

Cal puts an affectionate arm around my neck and draws me into a walk down the hall, and the others follow close behind, one big happy family. He whispers in my ear. "The prom. You worked it out with your mother, right?"

"The prom?" I sift through my brain to figure out what he's talking about. "Yes, the prom. No, sorry, I can't go."

He draws back, surprised. "What?"

"That's the spring dance, isn't it? I won't be there."

"I told you today was the deadline. I'm going with or without you."

"That's good. You attend your prom, Cal, and have a good time. Now, I have to find Mrs. Guthrie's room."

They are shocked when I walk away from them. I hear Vanessa say, "I wouldn't have believed it. Paula Masters dissing you. Hell, dissing us."

I wander about a couple more minutes then ask one of the younger students to point me to Mrs. Guthrie's classroom.

"Good morning, Mrs. Guthrie," I greet her warmly, actually glad to see her.

She gazes warily at me through her thick-rimmed glasses. "Good morning, Miss Masters. Take a seat in the back. You'll be there all day. Make sure you have work. I don't want you sitting like a rutabaga."

The week falls into a simple pattern. At home, I isolate myself in my bedroom, and at school the authorities isolate me in Guthrie's classroom. Supposedly I am working on material from all my other classes. In reality, I read from random books off her bookshelves. Most are history books but a couple novels as well. I found *Pride and Prejudice* and just had to read it again.

At home, my bedroom is plastered with posters of pop stars I don't remember, and who would probably not appeal to me now if I did. Maybe I'll get some posters of Mary Pickford and Clara Bow. Mostly, I sit at the window, staring out at the backyard but not seeing it. In fact, I see Daniel when he strode down off the hill and kissed me like he'd invented the act. I see the goldfields where we worked together, slept together, lived life together as if it would last forever. It didn't, but it was the pinnacle while it lasted.

I see Seneca at five being taken by Brings Thunder. I see my children as babes and needing me, then again when they are adults and I need them. I see the ones I put in the ground far too young, and the ones who were huddled about my bed when I, too, died. So much of my long life drifts across my view.

There's a knock on the door and mother's head pokes in. "Can I come in?" She's treating me like I'm mental, as if one wrong word will send me forever into cuckooland.

"Of course. Come in."

She comes over and sits on a footstool beside me.

I pat her hand. "You look tired."

"Paula, I'm worried about you. You're making yourself a hermit. You don't even come down for meals. Can you tell me what's wrong? I want to help you."

I smile. Can I tell her of my life as Libby Quarles Langdon Hancock? She would put me in the crazy house for sure. "I'm afraid I will have to face my own devils alone."

She closes her eyes in frustration. Then opens them again. "Look, if you don't care about me or yourself, at least think about Josh. He is very upset. He cries. He thinks you're angry with him."

This penetrates the thick layer of melancholy that surrounds my soul. "Oh, I would not want to hurt that boy. I'll speak to him. I'll do better with him, I promise."

"Paula, let me help you. I can't do anything for you if you cut me out like this."

I touch her hand again. "Please, don't fret yourself about me. There's nothing you can do."

She stands abruptly. "I'm your mother. I will fret about you and Josh till the day I die."

She leaves the room making no secret she's angry with me. As she shuts the door, it's clear to me that, hard as I try, I can't seem to leave my melancholy behind, but I feel badly for the boy, very badly. He so loves Paula. So, I go downstairs and read to him from one of his favorite books *The Hunger Games*. He sits enthralled though I know I'd read it to him before.

Then, at school on Friday, it all unravels. Everyone is excited about the prom that night at the sprawling Pacific Beachfront Hotel. Cal is taking Vanessa. All day she has smiled at me like the cat that just gobbled the parakeet. It means nothing to me. Lost in my dreams of the past, I sit in Mrs. Guthrie's classroom through a variety of subjects till sixth period Advance History class. There, the farce that is Paula Masters ends in such a painful way. All week the students have been giving their oral presentations, a big part of their semester grades, all of them nervous not knowing who is going to be called next. Their topics, a parade of well-known people and seminal events, have been presented over three days: Grant and Sherman; Lincoln and Slavery; the Battle of Gettysburg; Jay Gould and the Wall Street Barons; the Donner Party; the Oregon Trail Pioneers; and the Tragedy of the American Indian in the Path of Manifest Destiny, most of it superficial, and most of it far from the reality I knew.

So they won't have to talk so much, everyone pads their presentations with loads of photos and paintings projected onto a screen by computer. Computers and cell phones and iPads are all a mystery to me. I know once they weren't. Sitting in class, I realize I'm responsible for a presentation as well, but we are into the third day, and Mrs. Guthrie hasn't called on me. If she does, I'll just have to say I have nothing. I don't remember if Paula had anything prepared, likely not. I suppose I could talk about the Oregon Trail, but don't plan to, don't want to.

I'm listening to another round of oral presentations when a small Asian girl I can't remember comes to the front and starts her report on "The Early Migration West from the Whitmans through 1852." I pay passing attention because it deals with the time when I crossed the great prairie. Her work is actually fairly good. At least she shows some depth of understanding, presenting fairly accurately the incredible hardships along the way. Halfway through, she begins showing a series of old photos, people sitting in front of wagons, wagons crossing rivers, a woman and daughter beside a team of oxen, a man sitting horseback in front of several wagons and oxen. Almost all, I'm sure were taken after 1852 when photography was improving.

Suddenly, a picture appears on the screen that knocks the air from my lungs. It's me! Me and Daniel! It's a daguerreotype, the one we had taken right after our wedding in Oregon City. We're standing in the photographic studio with typical, frozen glares.

"Of course, like all the others, we don't know who these people are," the girl is saying. "People who faded from history generations ago. We owe them so much. They endured so much. This is an old daguerreotype, which means they were clearly part of the early pioneers going west. I wanted to show you this one because if you look closely you can see the woman has two fingers missing from her left hand, likely lost on the way west. This shows how truly difficult the journey was. She appears to be about eighteen to twenty…"

Like a sleepwalker, I tread slowly to the front of the classroom and stare at the screen. The class is shocked; two or three even laugh as if to say, good old disruptive Paula at it again. The Asian girl looks at me in alarm, then to Mrs. Guthrie, who is furious, about to explode. I barely notice them, staring at myself, my young Libby self, and at Daniel.

"She's sixteen," I say. "Her name is Libby Quarles, or it was then. That's Daniel Langdon beside her. She married him that day and became Libby Langdon. They went to the California gold rush together and lived a great life for the short time they had left together."

The Asian girl's jaw drops. I turn to her. "She lost her fingers in a blizzard before the family set out for Oregon."

"Miss Masters!" Mrs. Guthrie's voice cracks through the room like an artillery gun. She is on her feet. "This is the last straw. You have finally worn out my patience. You want to be expelled, young lady, then so be it. You will remove yourself from this room now. Go to the principal's office. I will see you there after class."

I nod, upset only because tears have welled up in the Asian girl's eyes. I have ruined her presentation. I step over to her and whisper. "I'm sorry. Don't worry, Mrs. Guthrie is fair. You deserve an A; she will give you an A."

And so, finally, I am expelled from Rector Academy.

Chapter 49

That evening when mother gets home, she upbraids me on my expulsion, but I can see her hearts not in it. She never gives up, but I think she has given up on me.

"I need to take Josh to Chuck E Cheese for a pizza party with his friends," she says and adds with a hint of sarcasm. "I know you won't mind eating alone."

"You and that boy have yourselves a good time," I say.

Shooting me a look of frustration tinged with anger, she turns away.

Later, restless and a little curious about the prom, I slip out and walk the mile or so down to the Pacific Beachfront Hotel where it is being held. I guess I'm just searching, but for what I don't know. Am I any part a teenager? Am I a woman of such advanced age that my mind has cobwebs? Who exactly am I? I doubt if I can find any answers at the hotel on a Friday night, but the curiosity factor draws me.

Wearing dark jeans and a red pullover sweater, I take a table in a small gazebo on the upper deck of the hotel's outdoor restaurant, where I have a view of both the ocean and the limousines arriving with their spectacularly dressed occupants. The students have taken over the hall and veranda on the other side of the hotel for their spring dance. Not one particle of me wants to be among them.

I think *rituals*. That's what I'm watching. Coming of age rituals. Several other patrons of the outdoor restaurant and the myriad gazebos are curious as well and certainly give the youngsters passing attention. When the waiter comes, I order a dinner of chicken curry and rice and a hot toddy: brandy with honey and lemon. The waiter cards me, and I give him one of Paula's marvelous fake IDs. I sit back to watch the veranda across the way, all the talking, laughing, dancing. Looks like they're having a good time.

An hour and a half later, after dinner, after dark, under the soft lights of the hotel, and while I'm sipping on a second toddy, a boy in a tuxedo hurries down the steps of the far veranda, strides across the beach to the gazebo deck and comes up the stairs toward me. It's Jason Weismann.

"I knew it was you over here," he says as he comes to my table. "I saw you earlier."

"Well, it's me, Jason. How are you?"

He shrugs. "Okay. Are you gone for good? Have you been expelled?"

"I'm gone for good."

"I'm sorry to hear that. I really am." He stands silent a moment then asks, "What are you doing here?"

"Eating dinner."

"You should come in. There's plenty of time to go home and change."

I shake my head. "I'm no longer a Rector Academy student, remember? Are you enjoying yourself, Jason?"

He shrugs. "Sure. It's the prom."

"Who did you ask?"

"You know Sara Gooden? She's a senior." He is nervous about something. "And a bit of a nerd like me."

"Nerds are good. Nerds will own the world."

He grins. "You got that right."

There is an awkward silence and I fill it. "Well, I'm glad you're enjoying yourself."

"To tell you the truth, I really wanted to go. I pretended like it didn't matter, but it did. What, we nerds are not supposed to have fun? It's just good to be on the inside for awhile and not always outside looking in. I'll tell you, I was sweating it all this week. Sara didn't decide to go till yesterday. It was the hardest few days of my life." He grins, wanting me to understand.

"I can imagine. I'm glad it worked out for you."

Then he falls silent and shifts from foot to foot for a minute. I know there's something else on his mind and finally I say, "Come on, out with it. Don't hem and haw. Whatever it is, you won't upset me."

"Okay. I know it's none of my business, but I'm worried about you, Paula. I've never seen anyone change so much, so fast in my life. And this isn't the first time. Two years ago, remember? But this time, it's drastic, really drastic. You are not the same person that came to school last Friday. It's like you're...I don't know...completely different."

"Nut case, huh?"

"No, no, no. I didn't mean that."

I hold up my hand to calm him down. "It's okay. I'm fine, but it's nice you are concerned."

"I know it's not an act. Some of the others are saying it is, but I know it's not."

I chuckle. "Believe me, it's not."

His face is so sincere it touches my heart. "What happened to you?" he asks.

Now that's a story I can never tell. "Cosmic forces, Jason. Cosmic forces."

Baffled, he finally nods as if he understands. Now, points made, nothing else to say, he starts to leave but suddenly turns back. "I was wondering if we could see each other this summer?"

I remember enough to know this boy is in love with me, or at least Paula. At that moment, I realize how much I need a friend. "Of course. I would like that."

"Okay. Good." With a big grin, he nods once more, then returns to his prom.

I make it home a little past midnight. We live a mile from Pacific Coast Highway, up a little canyon road with long patches of darkness. My house is surrounded by a five-foot adobe wall that would just about keep out any intruder under the age of six, but no one else. It's eerily quiet. The porch light is on but casts its light through such a thicket of vines that the front of our house is swallowed up by a shadowy gloom. Mother is so *green* she has let the vines grow wild. They are pretty, but it's like living in a tree house.

Inside, it's dark. Mother and Josh likely went to bed hours ago without even knowing I had left. As I step into the living room, I feel uneasy. I don't know what it is just yet, but ice cubes race up and down my spine. I don't flick on the lights because then Mother would know I'd slipped out without telling her.

Actually, that doesn't bother me so much, but I'd rather not have to deal with another confrontation. My heart rate rises as I feel my way along the wall.

I hear something, but see no one. My first instinct is to run, but then what about Mother and Josh? I have to make sure they are all right. I move toward the stairs and hear a soft shuffling matching my steps. In the darkness off to my left, I see a flash of movement, then it's gone.

Oh, God, I think, *I've interrupted a burglar.* That's great. After what I've been through, I get a freaking burglar now. Turn on the lights, you idiot, I tell myself, then someone touches my back and I scream. Laughter and footsteps running away. And I know who it is now. Of course. Josh. From somewhere at the edge of the room, he gives a loud, haunted-house groan.

"Who's there?" I ask, putting a tremble in my voice. "Are you a ghost?"

My eyes have adjusted to the darkness now, and I can see him just a couple yards away. He's wearing his night goggles. As he nears, I pounce and wrestle him to the floor, both of us screaming. "I got you ghost. I got you."

When I go for his belly, tickling his sides, he shrieks with delighted agony. "You're no ghost," I say, astonished. "Ghosts aren't ticklish. Who are you?"

The lights burst on and he rips off his goggles. We are on the floor, gazing up at our mother on the stairs. She glares at us with a crazed expression. "What are you two doing?"

For some reason the question strikes us as hilarious. We both erupt with laughter.

"On second thought." She doesn't finish her thought, just flicks off the light and heads back up the stairs.

Epilogue

The small museum was set back amid the trees in a park where children played on monkey bars and couples strolled on the grass. As Mrs. Guthrie pulled the rental car into the museum's parking lot, she asked herself again why she was so obsessed with finding out about Libby Quarles. Half her summer vacation had been spent on the search.

But truth be told, all her life she'd been like that, always the one who could not sit by and let questions go unanswered. And Libby Quarles was a question that had been driving her batty since Paula Masters had identified her six weeks ago. Had there even been someone of that name? Such an odd last name. At first, it only niggled at her. A couple phone calls ought to have cleared it up. A few to the Oregon Historical Society. She learned that there had indeed been someone named Libby Quarles who'd crossed the plains to Oregon, at about the time the daguerreotype Susan Chin had shown had been taken. That couldn't be a coincidence, could it? Little else was known about her. She had married a Daniel Langdon—that, too, had been true. And that did it. Now, she had to find out what she could about her. Find out if the details Paula knew were accurate, and if so, how the girl knew about them.

After calling universities and museums throughout the northwest, she finally found this little museum in the small town of Hancock, Oregon that housed a diary of Libby Quarles Langdon Hancock. Mrs. Guthrie felt tremendous excitement, as if she'd just come across the Rosetta Stone, and immediately booked a flight up to Eugene, the closest city to Hancock, rented a car, and made her way here.

Her first impression as she stepped into the museum was that it was quaint with an air of earnest dedication. Glass cases of Indian artifacts and kitchen utensils from around the 1890s filled the small lobby.

"Can I help you?" A teenage boy behind the counter asked politely.

"Yes. I'm Estelle Guthrie. I called Ms. Goodman last week about Libby Quarles."

He called on the phone and within seconds a young woman in her late twenties appeared, extending her hand. "Mrs. Guthrie, I'm Rita Goodman. So nice to meet you."

The young museum manager led her down the hall to her office. "So, you're interested in our Libby Hancock. Well, I have a lot to tell you, but first I hope you'll allow me to show you our little museum first."

Mrs. Guthrie wanted to get to the Libby material but went along with the tour politely. She was impressed. For such a small museum, it provided a remarkable glimpse into local history. Five exhibit rooms stocked with artifacts that dealt with Indians, fur traders, the town, railroads, and finally the largest room for the emigrants of the Oregon Trail who first settled the area.

Finally, she could wait no longer, "Let's talk about Libby."

Rita led her back to her office and made tea. Mrs. Guthrie sat across a small table from her and listened to the story of Libby Quarles Langdon Hancock, the journey across the country, the years in the California gold rush, the death of her first husband Daniel Langdon, and her subsequent marriage to his best friend, Jesse Hancock. Their return to Oregon and the successful farming operation here in Hancock, yes, named after him, the long years together, the children, grandchildren and great-grandchildren.

Astounding, Mrs. Guthrie thought, that Paula knew about her and this Daniel Langdon. Somehow she must have known about Susan Chin's coming presentation and done just enough research to disrupt it and the class. But why? It doesn't make sense even for her. If the girl put as much effort into her class work, she'd be valedictorian.

"Libby was a central figure in the town's early development," Rita said. "Unfortunately, she is not so well-known anymore. People move on with their lives; towns move on with theirs." She smiled. "Of course, you want to know about the diary"

"Yes."

"We have thousands of old documents in our archives. It has been gathering dust for a long time. The last person to check it out was a granddaughter of hers in 1939. When you first called, I had to search for it. I had no idea it even existed. Would you like to look at it?"

"Very much."

Settling into one of the cushioned chairs in the research room, Mrs. Guthrie spent all afternoon reading the diary. It was different from other diaries of the Oregon Trail she had read. Most were pretty straightforward, usually telling of the miles gone, the weather, the events of the day, and though Libby did that, she also noted her feelings far more than was usual in nineteenth century diaries.

As she read, Mrs. Guthrie was alarmed by the deaths along the way, not unusual for the time and journey, many due to cholera, which Libby somehow knew enough about to boil water and replace liquids. How had a simple girl of 1848 known that?

She was reading about Tom Fitzpatrick, *the* Tom Fitzpatrick, pilot of the Warren Company, when she got the shock of her life. The next passage rocked her. Everything she'd ever learned seemed to be wobbling under her feet. She read it again to make sure. At the bottom of the entry on June 24 were the words:

"Last night, a strange rider arrived and caused a stir with news of the California gold strike and a warning about possible hostile Indians ahead. This man's name is Jim Beckwourth. Incredible! Mrs. Guthrie would pee with envy."

She raced through the rest of the diary looking for her name, seeing it several more times. That was too much to comprehend. At first, she thought it must be someone else with her last name, but then the references were specific to her. How many Mrs. Guthries loved the mountain man era and Jim Beckwourth? In 1848 it wouldn't even be thought of as the mountain man era.

And how many teachers said, "you will rue the day" to students who were acting up.

Then came the entry that flipped the boundaries of time and space on its head:

January 1, 1900.

A new year, a new century. More than fifty years I've been in this life and sixteen in the other one. Sometimes I have trouble remembering things from that other life. I have become completely Libby now. There's almost nothing left of Paula Masters.

Mrs. Guthrie sat stunned for the next twenty minutes unable to comprehend it, to even read further. Finally, Rita came to fetch her at the museum's closing time.

"My goodness, what's wrong? You look like you've swallowed a cat," the young woman said.

Mrs. Guthrie was just able to mutter, "Nothing, nothing at all. I guess I'm tired. It's been a long day."

She could not tell anyone what she'd discovered. It would not be believed. She could hardly believe it herself, but there it was. This diary had not been touched in more than seventy-five years. She realized she would have to speak to Paula.

It was not till October that Mrs. Guthrie saw Paula. During the summer the girl had gone down to Guadalajara, Mexico with Jason Weismann to work in a hospital, a two-week program for teens sixteen to nineteen that Paula, breaking all the rules, had stretched into five months. Typically, she had gone on impulse, forging her mother's signature on the necessary papers. As Carolyn Masters explained it, she'd been furious that Paula had snuck away but then decided to leave her at the hospital. It was a worthy project, well monitored, and might do her some good. Mrs. Guthrie suspected that it also eased the woman's own burden of dealing with a difficult daughter.

Jason went back to start the new school year, but Paula stayed on, moving to a clinic in a mountain town a hundred miles farther to the west. What Mrs. Guthrie had found in the Oregon town of Hancock had swelled up inside her till she had to find some answers or have her entire concept of the world unravel. She had to see Paula and confront her with what she had found. She took a personal day and flew down to Guadalajara on a Thursday night and then took a bus up into the mountains the next day.

The clinic was on the crowded plaza of the small town. The square had a central fountain, park benches and trees that provided nesting for hundreds of birds. Mrs. Guthrie took a bench seat, placing her large handbag on her lap, and waited. She had not called Paula ahead of time. In fact, she was not really sure how to proceed.

After an hour Paula appeared, coming out of a magnificent church on the corner, leading at least fifty elementary school children in uniforms across the plaza toward the clinic on the opposite side. She would have to pass right by Mrs. Guthrie. She wore white shorts and a black T-shirt that Mrs. Guthrie could read as she drew nearer: *I was born intelligent but education ruined me.*

One of the boys said something and everyone laughed. Paula gave him a playful shove on the shoulder, saying something that made him giggle. As they walked past the bench, she glanced at Mrs. Guthrie but did not recognize her at first. She went on twenty yards before stopping suddenly and turning back. When she did, all fifty children stopped and looked back, too. Mrs. Guthrie now stood facing her.

Paula called over the noise of traffic, "Mrs. Guthrie?"

Hesitating only a moment, the older woman said, "I know what happened to you, Libby. I read it in your diary."

She watched the emotions play out on Paula's face from puzzlement to shock to understanding. As the girl nodded and her eyes watered, Mrs. Guthrie placed a hand over her heart in a gesture of respect and warmth, then picked her bag up off the bench and headed back toward the bus depot.

THE END

To contact Tom Reppert with any response to this work email: Repptom @hughes.net

Made in the USA
Las Vegas, NV
28 May 2022

49464694R00164